The Collected Shorter Supernatural & Weird Fiction of Algernon Blackwood Volume 6

ALGERNON BLACKWOOD

The Collected Shorter Supernatural & Weird Fiction of Algernon Blackwood Volume 6

Ten Short Stories and Two Novelettes of the Strange and Unusual Including 'The Trod', 'The Valley of the Beasts', 'Vengeance is Mine', 'Wireless Confusion', 'The Lost Valley' and 'The Willows'

Algernon Blackwood

LEONAUR

The Collected Shorter Supernatural & Weird Fiction of
Algernon Blackwood
Volume 6
Ten Short Stories and Two Novelettes of the Strange and Unusual Including 'The Trod', 'The Valley of the Beasts', 'Vengeance is Mine', 'Wireless Confusion', 'The Lost Valley' and 'The Willows'
by Algernon Blackwood

Some of the stories in this volume were originally published as by Algernon Blackwood in collaboration with an unknown contributor, Wilfred Wilson. Oakpast Limited has undertaken reasonable research on the subject, but also has been unable to fully identify this person.
Leonaur is an imprint of Oakpast Ltd

ISBN: 978-1-916535-32-9 (hardcover)
ISBN: 978-1-916535-33-6 (softcover)

http://www.leonaur.com

Publisher's Notes

The views expressed in this book are not necessarily those of the publisher.

Contents

The Little Beggar

He was on his way from his bachelor flat to the club, a man of middle age with a slight stoop, and an expression of face firm yet gentle, the blue eyes with light and courage in them, and a faint hint of melancholy—or was it resignation?—about the strong mouth. It was early in April, a slight drizzle of warm rain falling through the coming dusk; but spring was in the air, a bird sang rapturously on a pavement tree. And the man's heart wakened at the sound, for it was the lift of the year, and low in the western sky above the London roofs there was a band of tender colour.

His way led him past one of the great terminal stations that open the gates of London seawards; the birds, the coloured clouds, and the thought of a sunny coast-line worked simultaneously in his heart. These messages of spring woke music in him. The music, however, found no expression, beyond a quiet sigh, so quiet that not even a child, had he carried one in his big arms, need have noticed it. His pace quickened, his figure straightened up, he lifted his eyes and there was a new light in them. Upon the wet pavement, where the street lamps already laid their network of faint gold, he saw, perhaps a dozen yards front of him, the figure of a little boy.

The boy, for some reason, caught his attention and his interest vividly. He was dressed in Etons, the broad white collar badly rumpled, the pointed coat hitched grotesquely sidedays, while, from beneath the rather grimy straw hat, his thick light hair escaped at various angles. This general air of effort and distress was due to the fact that the little fellow was struggling with a bag packed evidently to bursting point, too big and heavy for him to manage for more than ten yards at a time. He changed it from one hand to the other, resting it in the intervals upon the ground, each effort making it rub against his leg so that the trousers were hoisted considerably above the boot. He was a pathetic figure.

'I must help him,' said the man. 'He'll never get there at this rate. He'll miss his train to the sea.' For his destination was obvious, since a pair of wooden spades was tied clumsily and insecurely to the straps of the bursting bag.

Occasionally, too, the lad, who seemed about ten years old, looked about him to right and left, questionably, anxiously, as though he expected someone—someone to help, or perhaps to meet him. His behaviour even gave the impression that he was not quite sure of his way. The man hurried to overtake him.

'I really must give the little beggar a hand,' he repeated to himself, as he went. He smiled. The fatherly, protective side of him, naturally strong, was touched—touched a little more, perhaps, than the occasion seemed to warrant. The smile broadened into a jolly laugh, as he came up against the great stuffed bag, now resting on the pavement, its owner panting beside it, still looking to right and left alternately. At which instant, exactly, the boy, hearing his step, turned round, and for the first time looked him full in the face with a pair of big blue eyes that held unabashed and happy welcome in them.

'Oh, I say, sir, it's most awfully ripping of you,' he said in a confiding voice, before the man had time to speak. 'I hunted everywhere; but I never thought of looking behind me.'

But the man, standing dumb and astonished for a few seconds beside the little fellow, missed the latter sentence altogether, for there was in the clear blue eyes an expression so trustful, so frankly affectionate almost, and in the voice music of so natural a kind, that all the tenderness in him rose; like a sudden tide, and he yearned towards the boy as though he were his little son.

Thought, born of some sudden revival of emotion, flashed back swiftly across a stretch of twelve blank years. . . and for an instant the lines of the mouth grew deeper, though in the eyes the light turned softer, brighter. . .

'It's too big for you, my boy,' he said, recovering himself with a jolly laugh; 'or, rather, you're not big enough—yet—for it—eh! Where to, now? Ah! the station, I suppose?' And he stooped to grasp the handles of the bulging bag, first poking the spades more securely in beneath the straps; but in doing so became aware that something the boy had said had given him pain. What was it? Why was it? This stray little stranger, met upon the London pavements! Yet so swift is thought that, even while he stooped and before his fingers actually touched the leather, he had found what hurt him—and smiled a little at himself.

It was the mode of address the boy made use of, contradicting faintly the affectionate expression in the eyes.

It was the word 'sir' that made him feel like a schoolmaster or a tutor; it made him feel old. It was not the word he needed, and—yes—had longed for, somehow almost expected. And there was such strange trouble in his mind and heart that, as he grasped the bag, he did not catch the boy's rejoinder to his question. But, of course, it must be the railway station; he was going to the seaside for Easter; his people would be at the ticket-office waiting for him. Bracing himself a little for the effort, he seized the leather handles and lifted the bag from the ground.

'Oh, thanks awfully, sir!' repeated the boy. He watched him with a true schoolboy grin of gratitude, as though it were great fun, yet also with a true urchin's sense that the proper thing had happened, since such jobs, of course, were for grown-up men. And this time, though he used the objectionable word again, the voice betrayed recognition of the fact that he somehow had a right to look to this particular man for help, and that this particular man only did the right and natural thing in giving help.

But the man, swaying sideways, nearly lost his balance. He had calculated automatically the probable energy necessary to lift the weight; he had put this energy forth. He received a shock as though he had been struck, for the bag had no weight at all; it was as light as a feather. It might have been of tissue-paper, a phantom bag. And the shock was mental as well as physical. His mind swayed with his body.

'By jove!' cried the boy, strutting merrily beside him, hands in his pockets. 'Thanks most awfully. This is jolly!'

The objectionable word was omitted, but the man scarcely heard the words at all. For a mist swam before his eyes, the street lamps grew blurred and distant, the drizzle thickened in the air. He still heard the wild, sweet song of the bird, still knew the west had gold upon its lips. It was the rest of the world about him that grew dim. Strange thoughts rose in a cloud. Reality and dream played games, the games of childhood, through his heart.

Memories, robed flamingly, trooped past his inner sight, radiant, swift and as of yesterday, closing his eyelids for a moment to the outer world. Rossetti came to him, singing too sweetly a hidden pain in perfect words across those twelve blank years: 'The Hour that might have been, yet might not be, which man's and woman's heart conceived and bore, yet whereof time was barren. . .' In a second's flash the entire

9

sonnet, 'Stillborn Love', passed on this inner screen 'with eyes where burning memory lights love home. . .'

Mingled with these—all in an instant of time—came practical thoughts as well. This boy! The ridiculous effort he made to carry this ridiculously light bag! The poignant tenderness, the awakened yearning! Was it a girl dressed up? The happy face, the innocent, confiding smile, the music in the voice, the dear soft blue eyes, and yet, at the same time, something that was not there—some indescribable, incalculable element that was lacking. He felt acutely this curious lack. What was it? Who was this merry youngster? He glanced down cautiously as they moved side by side. He felt shy, hopeful, marvellously tender. His heart yearned inexpressibly; the boy, looking elsewhere, did not notice the examination, did not notice, of course, that his companion caught his breath and walked uncertainly.

But the man was troubled. The face reminded him, as he gazed, of many children, of children he had loved and played with, both boys and girls, his Substitute Children, as he had always called them in his heart. . . Then, suddenly, the boy came closer and took his arm. They were close upon the station now. The sweet human perfume of a small, deeply loved, helpless and dependent little life rose past his face.

He suddenly blurted out: 'But, I say, this bag of yours—it weighs simply nothing!'

The boy laughed—a ring of true careless joy was in the sound. He looked up.

'Do you know what's in it? Shall I tell you?' He added in a whisper: 'I will, if you like.' But the man was suddenly afraid and dared not ask.

'Brown paper probably,' he evaded laughingly; 'or birds' eggs. You've been up to some wicked lark or other.'

The little chap clasped both hands upon the supporting arm. He took a quick, dancing step or two, then stopped dead, and made the man stop with him. He stood on tiptoe to reach the distant ear. His face wore a lovely smile of truth and trust and delight.

'My future,' he whispered. And the man turned into ice.

They entered the great station. The last of the daylight was shut out. They reached the ticketoffice. The crowds hurrying people surged about them. The man set down the bag. For a moment or two the boy looked quickly about him to right and left, searching, then turned his big blue eyes upon the other with his radiant smile:

'She's in the waiting-room as usual,' he said. 'I'll go and fetch her—though she ought to know you're here.' He stood on tiptoe, his hands

10

upon the other's shoulders, his face thrust close. 'Kiss me, father. I shan't be a second.'

'You little beggar!' said the man, in a voice he could not control; then, opening his big arms wide, saw only an empty space before him.

He turned and walked slowly back to his flat instead of to the club; and when he got home he read over for the thousandth time the letter—its ink a little faded during the twelve intervening years—in which she had accepted his love two short weeks before death took her.

The Occupant of the Room

He arrived late at night by the yellow *diligence*, stiff and cramped after the toilsome ascent of three slow hours. The village, a single mass of shadow, was already asleep. Only in front of the little hotel was there noise and light and bustle—for a moment. The horses, with tired, slouching gait, crossed the road and disappeared into the stable of their own accord, their harness trailing in the dust; and the lumbering *diligence* stood for the night where they had dragged it—the body of a great yellow-sided beetle with broken legs.

In spite of his physical weariness the schoolmaster revelling in the first hours of his ten-guinea holiday, felt exhilarated. For the high Alpine valley was marvellously still; stars twinkled over the torn ridges of the Dent du Midi where spectral snows gleamed against rocks that looked like ebony; and the keen air smelt of pine forests, dew-soaked pastures, and freshly sawn wood. He took it all in with a kind of bewildered delight for a few minutes, while the other three passengers gave directions about their luggage and went to their rooms. Then he turned and walked over the coarse matting into the glare of the hall, only just able to resist stopping to examine the big mountain map that hung upon the wall by the door.

And, with a sudden disagreeable shock, he came down from the ideal to the actual. For at the inn—the only inn—there was no vacant room. Even the available sofas were occupied. . . .

How stupid he had been not to write! Yet it had been impossible, he remembered, for he had come to the decision suddenly that morning in Geneva, enticed by the brilliance of the weather after a week of rain.

They talked endlessly, this gold-braided porter and the hard-faced old woman—her face was hard, he noticed—gesticulating all the time, and pointing all about the village with suggestions that he ill understood, for his French was limited and their *patois* was fearful.

13

"*There!*"—he might find a room, "or *there!* But we are, *hélas*, full—more full than we care about. Tomorrow, perhaps—if So-and-So give up their rooms——!" And then, with much shrugging of shoulders, the hard-faced old woman stared at the gold-braided porter, and the porter stared sleepily at the schoolmaster.

At length, however, by some process of hope he did not himself understand, and following directions given by the old woman that were utterly unintelligible, he went out into the street and walked towards a dark group of houses she had pointed out to him. He only knew that he meant to thunder at a door and ask for a room. He was too weary to think out details. The porter half made to go with him, but turned back at the last moment to speak with the old woman. The houses sketched themselves dimly in the general blackness. The air was cold.

The whole valley was filled with the rush and thunder of falling water. He was thinking vaguely that the dawn could not be very far away, and that he might even spend the night wandering in the woods, when there was a sharp noise behind him and he turned to see a figure hurrying after him. It was the porter—running.

And in the little hall of the inn there began again a confused three-cornered conversation, with frequent muttered colloquy and whispered asides in *patois* between the woman and the porter—the net result of which was that, " If *Monsieur* did not object—there *was* a room, after all, on the first floor—only it was in a sense 'engaged.' That is to say——"

But the schoolmaster took the room without inquiring too closely into the puzzle that had somehow provided it so suddenly. The ethics of hotel-keeping had nothing to do with him. If the woman offered him quarters it was not for him to argue with her whether the said quarters were legitimately hers to offer.

But the porter, evidently a little thrilled, accompanied the guest up to the room and supplied in a mixture of French and English details omitted by 'the landlady—and Minturn, the schoolmaster, soon shared the thrill with him, and found himself in the atmosphere of a possible tragedy.

All who know the peculiar excitement that belongs to lofty mountain valleys where dangerous climbing is a chief feature of the attractions, will understand a certain faint element of high alarm that goes with the picture. One looks up at the desolate, soaring ridges and thinks involuntarily of the men who find their pleasure for days and nights together scaling perilous summits among the clouds, and conquering inch by inch the icy peaks that for ever shake their dark terror in the sky. The atmosphere of adventure, spiced with the possible horror of a very grim order of tragedy, is inseparable from any imaginative contemplation of the scene; and the idea Minturn gleaned from the half-frightened porter lost nothing by his ignorance of the language.

This Englishwoman, the real occupant of the room, had insisted on going without a guide. She had left just before daybreak two days before—the porter had seen her start—and . . . she had not returned! The route was difficult and dangerous, yet not impossible for a skilled climber, even a solitary one. And the Englishwoman was an experienced mountaineer. Also, she was self-willed, careless of advice, bored by warnings, self-confident to a degree. Queer, moreover; for she kept entirely to herself, and sometimes remained in her room with locked doors, admitting no one, for days together; a "crank," evidently, of the first water.

This much Minturn gathered clearly enough from the porter's talk while his luggage was brought in and the room set to rights; further, too, that the search party had gone out and *might*, of course, return at any moment. In which case——. Thus, the room was empty, yet still hers. "If *Monsieur* did not object—if the risk he ran of having to turn out suddenly in the night——" It was the loquacious porter who furnished the details that made the transaction questionable; and Minturn dismissed the loquacious porter as soon as possible, and prepared to get into the hastily arranged bed and snatch all the hours of sleep he could before he was turned out.

At first, it must be admitted, he felt uncomfortable—distinctly uncomfortable. He was in someone else's room. He had really no right to be there. It was in the nature of an unwarrantable intrusion; and while he unpacked, he kept looking over his shoulder as though some one were watching him from the corners. Any moment, it seemed, he would hear a step in the passage, a knock would come at the door, the door would open, and there he would see this vigorous Englishwoman looking him up and down with anger. Worse still—he would hear her voice asking him what he was doing in her room—her bedroom. Of course, he had an adequate explanation, but still——!

Then, reflecting that he was already half undressed, the humour of it flashed for a second across his mind, and he laughed—*quietly*. And at once, after that laughter, under his breath, came the sudden sense of tragedy he had felt before. Perhaps, even while he smiled, her body

15

lay broken and cold upon those awful heights, the wind of snow playing over her hair, her glazed eyes staring sightless up to the stars. . . . It made him shudder. The sense of this woman whom he had never seen, whose name even he did not know, became extraordinarily real. Almost he could imagine that she was somewhere in the room with him, hidden, observing all he did.

He opened the door softly to put his boots outside, and when he closed it again, he turned the key. Then he finished unpacking and distributed his few things about the room. It was soon done; for, in the first place, he had only a small Gladstone and a knapsack, and secondly, the only place where he could spread his clothes was the sofa. There was no chest of drawers, and the cupboard, an unusually large and solid one, was locked. The Englishwoman's things had evidently been hastily put away in it. The only sign of her recent presence was a bunch of faded *Alpenrosen* standing in a glass jar upon the wash-hand stand. This, and a certain faint perfume, were all that remained. In spite, however, of these very slight evidences, the whole room was pervaded with a curious sense of occupancy that he found exceedingly distasteful. One moment the atmosphere seemed subtly charged with a "just left" feeling; the next it was a queer awareness of "still here" that made him turn and look hurriedly behind him.

Altogether, the room inspired him with a singular aversion, and the strength of this aversion seemed the only excuse for his tossing the faded flowers out of the window, and then hanging his mackintosh upon the cupboard door in such a way as to screen it as much as possible from view. For the sight of that big, ugly cupboard, filled with the clothing of a woman who might then be beyond any further need of covering—thus his imagination insisted on picturing it—touched in him a startled sense of the incongruous that did not stop there, but crept through his mind gradually till it merged somehow into a sense of a rather grotesque horror. At any rate, the sight of that cupboard was offensive, and he covered it almost instinctively. Then, turning out the electric light, he got into bed.

But the instant the room was dark he realised that it was more than he could stand; for, with the blackness, there came a sudden rush of cold that he found it hard to explain. And the odd thing was that, when he lit the candle beside his bed, he noticed that his hand trembled.

This, of course, was too much. His imagination was taking liberties and must be called to heel. Yet the way he called it to order was significant, and its very deliberateness betrayed a mind that has already admitted fear.

And fear, once in, is difficult to dislodge. He lay there upon his elbow in bed and carefully took note of all the objects in the room—with the intention, as it were, of taking an inventory of everything his senses perceived, then drawing a line, adding them up finally, and saying with decision, "That's all the room contains! I've counted every single thing. There is nothing more. *Now*—I may sleep in peace!"

And it was during this absurd process of enumerating the furniture of the room that the dreadful sense of distressing lassitude came over him that made it difficult even to finish counting. It came swiftly, yet with an amazing kind of violence that overwhelmed him softly and easily with a sensation of enervating weariness hard to describe. And its first effect was to banish fear. He no longer possessed enough energy to feel really afraid or nervous. The cold remained, but the alarm vanished. And into every corner of his usually vigorous personality crept the insidious poison of a *muscular* fatigue—at first—that in a few seconds, it seemed, translated itself into *spiritual* inertia. A sudden consciousness of the foolishness, the crass futility of life, of effort, of fighting—of all that makes life worth living, oozed into every fibre of his being, and left him utterly weak. A spirit of black pessimism, that was not even vigorous enough to assert itself, invaded the secret chambers of his heart. . . .

Every picture that presented itself to his mind came dressed in grey shadows; those bored and sweating horses toiling up the ascent to—nothing! that hard-faced landlady taking so much trouble to let her desire for gain conquer her sense of morality—for a few *francs!* That gold-braided porter, so talkative, fussy, energetic, and so anxious to tell all he knew! What was the use of them all? And for himself, what in the world was the good of all the labour and drudgery he went through in that preparatory school where he was junior master? What could it lead to? Wherein lay the value of so much uncertain toil, when the ultimate secrets of life were hidden and no one knew the final goal? How foolish was effort, discipline, work! How vain was pleasure! How trivial the noblest life! . . .

With a jump that nearly upset the candle Minturn challenged this weak mood. Such vicious thoughts were usually so remote from his normal character that the sudden vile invasion produced a swift reaction. Yet, only for a moment. Instantly, again, the depression descended upon him like a wave. His work—it could lead to nothing but the dreary labour of a small headmastership after all—seemed as vain and foolish as his holiday in the Alps. What an idiot he had been, to be sure, to come out with a knapsack merely to work himself into a state of exhaustion climbing over toilsome mountains that led to nowhere—resulted in nothing.

A dreariness pf the grave possessed him. Life was a ghastly fraud! Religion a childish humbug! Everything was merely a trap—a trap of death; a coloured toy that Nature used as a decoy! But a decoy for what? For nothing! There was no meaning in anything. The only *real* thing was—*DEATH*. And the happiest people were those who found it soonest.

Then why wait for it to come?

He sprang out of bed, thoroughly frightened. This was horrible. Surely mere physical fatigue could not produce a world so black, an outlook so dismal, a cowardice that struck with such sudden hopelessness at the very roots of life? For, normally, he was cheerful and strong, full of the tides of healthy living; and this appalling lassitude swept the very basis of his personality into Nothingness and the desire for death. It was like the development of a Secondary Personality.

He had read, of course, how certain persons who suffered shocks developed thereafter entirely different characteristics, memory, tastes, and so forth. It had all rather frightened him. Though scientific men vouched for it, it was hardly to be believed. Yet here was a similar thing taking place in his own consciousness. He was, beyond question, experiencing all the mental variations of—*someone else!* It was un-moral. It was awful. It was—well, after all, at the same time, it was uncommonly interesting.

And this interest he began to feel was the first sign of his returned normal self. For to feel interest is to live, and to love life.

He sprang into the middle of the room—then switched on the electric light. And the first thing that struck his eye was—the big cupboard.

"Hallo! There's that—beastly cupboard!" he exclaimed to himself, involuntarily, yet aloud. It held all the clothes, the swinging skirts and coats and summer blouses of the dead woman. For he knew now—somehow or other—that she *was* dead. . . .

At that moment, through the open windows, rushed the sound of falling water, bringing with it a vivid realisation of the desolate, snow-swept heights. He saw her—positively *saw* her!—lying where she had fallen, the frost upon her cheeks, the snow-dust eddying about her hair and eyes, her broken limbs pushing against the lumps of ice. For a moment the sense of spiritual lassitude—of the emptiness of life—vanished before this picture of broken effort—of a small human force battling pluckily, yet in vain) against the impersonal and pitiless potencies of inanimate nature—and he found himself again his normal self. Then, instantly, returned again that terrible sense of cold, nothingness, emptiness. . . .

And he found himself standing opposite the big cupboard where her clothes were. He suddenly wanted to see those clothes—things she had used and worn. Quite close he stood, almost touching it. The next second he had touched it. His knuckles struck upon the wood.

Why he knocked is hard to say. It was an instinctive movement probably. Something in his deepest self dictated it—ordered it. He knocked at the door. And the dull sound upon the wood into the stillness of that room brought—horror. Why it should have done so he found it as hard to explain to himself as why he should have felt impelled to knock. The fact remains that when he heard the faint reverberation inside the cupboard, it brought with it so vivid a realisation of the woman's presence that he stood there shivering upon the floor with a dreadful sense of anticipation; he almost expected to hear an answering knock from within—the rustling of the hanging skirts perhaps—or, worse still, to see the locked door slowly open towards him.

And from that moment, he declares that in some way or other he must have partially lost control of himself, or at least of his better judgment; for he became possessed by such an over-mastering desire to tear open that cupboard door and see the clothes within, that he tried every key in the room in the vain effort to unlock it, and then, finally, before he quite realised what he was doing—rang the bell!

But, having rung the bell for no obvious or intelligent reason at two o'clock in the morning, he then stood waiting in the middle of the floor for the servant to come, conscious for the first time that something outside his ordinary self had pushed him towards the act. It was almost like an internal voice that directed him . . . and thus, when at last steps came down the passage and he faced the cross and sleepy chambermaid, amazed at being summoned at such an hour, he found no difficulty in the matter of what he should say. For the same power that insisted he should open the cupboard door also impelled him to utter words over which he apparently had no control.

"It's not *you* I rang for!" he said with decision and impatience. "I want a man. Wake the porter and send him up to me at once—hurry!

19

I tell you, hurry——!"

And when the girl had gone, frightened at his earnestness, Minturn realised that the words surprised himself as much as they surprised her. Until they were out of his mouth, he had not known what exactly he was saying. But now he understood that some force, foreign to his own personality, was using his mind and organs. The black depression that had possessed him a few moments before was also part of it. The powerful mood of this vanished woman had somehow momentarily taken possession of him—communicated, possibly, by the atmosphere of things in the room still belonging to her. But even now, when the porter, without coat or collar, stood beside him in the room, he did not understand why he insisted, with a positive fury admitting no denial, that the key of that cupboard must be found and the door instantly opened.

The scene was a curious one. After some perplexed whispering with the chambermaid at the end of the passage, the porter managed to find and produce the key in question. Neither he nor the girl knew clearly what this excited Englishman was up to, or why he was so passionately intent upon opening the cupboard at two o'clock in the morning. They watched him with an air of wondering what was going to happen next. But something of his curious earnestness, even of his late fear, communicated itself to them, and the sound of the key grating in the lock made them both jump.

They held their breath as the creaking door swung slowly open. All heard the clatter of that other key as it fell against the wooden floor—within. The cupboard had been locked *from the inside*. But it was the scared housemaid, from her position in the corridor, who first saw—and with a wild scream fell crashing against the bannisters.

The porter made no attempt to save her. The schoolmaster and himself made a simultaneous rush towards the door, now wide open. They, too, had seen.

There were no clothes, skirts or blouses on the pegs, but they saw the body of the Englishwoman suspended in mid-air, the head bent forward. Jarred the movement of unlocking, the body swung slowly round to face them. . . . Pinned upon the inside of the door was a hotel envelope with the following words pencilled in straggling writing:

"Tired—unhappy—hopelessly depressed. . . . I cannot face life any longer. . . . All is black. I must put an end to it. . . . I meant to do it on the mountains, but was afraid. I slipped back to my room unobserved. This way is easiest and best. . ."

The Valley of the Beasts

1

As they emerged suddenly from the dense forest the Indian halted, and Grimwood, his employer, stood beside him, gazing into the beautiful wooded valley that lay spread below them in the blaze of a golden sunset. Both men leaned upon their rifles, caught by the enchantment of the unexpected scene.

"We camp here," said Tooshalli abruptly, after a careful survey. "Tomorrow we make a plan."

He spoke excellent English. The note of decision, almost of authority, in his voice was noticeable, but Grimwood set it down to the natural excitement of the moment. Every track they had followed during the last two days, but one track in particular as well, had headed straight for this remote and hidden valley, and the sport promised to be unusual.

"That's so," he replied, in the tone of one giving an order. "You can make camp ready at once." And he sat down on a fallen hemlock to take off his *moccasin* boots and grease his feet that ached from the arduous day now drawing to a close. Though under ordinary circumstances he would have pushed on for another hour or two, he was not averse to a night here, for exhaustion had come upon him during the last bit of rough going, his eye and muscles were no longer steady, and it was doubtful if he could have shot straight enough to kill. He did not mean to miss a second time.

With his Canadian friend, Iredale, the latter's half-breed, and his own Indian, Tooshalli, the party had set out three weeks ago to find the "wonderful big moose" the Indians reported were travelling in the Snow River country. They soon found that the tale was true; tracks were abundant; they saw fine animals nearly every day, but though carrying good heads, the hunters expected better still and left them alone. Pushing up the river to a chain of small lakes near its source, they then

21

separated into two parties, each with its nine-foot bark canoe, and packed in for three days after the yet bigger animals the Indians agreed would be found in the deeper woods beyond. Excitement was keen, expectation keener still. The day before they separated, Iredale shot the biggest moose of his life, and its head, bigger even than the grand Alaskan heads, hangs in his house today. Grimwood's hunting blood was fairly up. His blood was of the fiery, not to say ferocious, quality. It almost seemed he liked killing for its own sake.

Four days after the party broke into two, he came upon a gigantic track, whose measurements and length of stride keyed every nerve he possessed to its highest tension.

Tooshalli examined the tracks for some minutes with care. "It is the biggest moose in the world," he said at length, a new expression on his inscrutable red visage.

Following it all that day, they yet got no sight of the big fellow that seemed to be frequenting a little marshy dip of country, too small to be called valley, where willow and undergrowth abounded. He had not yet scented his pursuers. They were after him again at dawn. Towards the evening of the second day Grimwood caught a sudden glimpse of the monster among a thick clump of willows, and the sight of the magnificent head that easily beat all records set his heart beating like a hammer with excitement. He aimed and fired. But the moose, instead of crashing, went thundering away through the further scrub and disappeared, the sound of his plunging canter presently dying away. Grimwood had missed, even if he had wounded.

They camped, and all next day, leaving the canoe behind, they followed the huge track, but though finding signs of blood, these were not plentiful, and the shot had evidently only grazed the animal. The travelling was of the hardest. Towards evening, utterly exhausted, the spoor led them to the ridge they now stood upon, gazing down into the enchanting valley that opened at their feet. The giant moose had gone down into this valley. He would consider himself safe there. Grimwood agreed with the Indian's judgment. They would camp for the night and continue at dawn the wild hunt after "the biggest moose in the world."

Supper was over, the small fire used for cooking dying down, with Grimwood became first aware that the Indian was not behaving quite as usual. What particular detail drew his attention is hard to say. He was a slow-witted, heavy man, full-blooded, unobservant; a fact had to hurt him through his comfort, through his pleasure, before he noticed it. Yet anyone else must have observed the changed mood of the Indian long ago. Tooshalli had made the fire, fried the bacon, served the tea, and was arranging the blankets, his own and his employer's, before the latter remarked upon his—silence. Tooshalli had not uttered a word for over an hour and a half, since he had first set eyes upon the new valley, to be exact. And his employer now noticed the unaccustomed silence, because after food he liked to listen to wood talk and hunting lore.

"Tired out, aren't you?" said big Grimwood, looking into the dark face across the firelight. He resented the absence of conversation, now that he noticed it. He was over-weary himself, he felt more irritable than usual, though his temper was always vile.

"Lost your tongue, eh?" he went on with a growl, as the Indian returned his stare with solemn, expressionless face. That dark inscrutable look got on his nerves a bit. "Speak up, man!" he exclaimed sharply. "What's it all about?"

The Englishman had at last realised that there was something to "speak up" about. The discovery, in his present state, annoyed him further. Tooshalli stared gravely, but made no reply. The silence was prolonged almost into minutes. Presently the head turned sideways, as though the man listened. The other watched him very closely, anger growing in him.

But it was the way the Indian turned his head, keeping his body rigid, that gave the jerk to Grimwood's nerves, providing him with a sensation he had never known in his life before—it gave him what is generally called "the goose-flesh." It seemed to jangle his entire system, yet at the same time made him cautious. He did not like it, this combination of emotions puzzled him.

"Say something, I tell you," he repeated in a harsher tone, raising his voice. He sat up, drawing his great body closer to the fire. "Say something, damn it!"

His voice fell dead against the surrounding trees, making the silence of the forest unpleasantly noticeable. Very still the great woods stood about them; there was no wind, no stir of branches; only the crackle of a snapping twig was audible from time to time, as the night-life moved unwarily sometimes watching the humans round their little fire. The October air had a frosty touch that nipped.

The Indian did not answer. No muscle of his neck nor of his stiffened body moved. He seemed all ears.

"Well?" repeated the Englishman, lowering his voice this time in-

23

stinctively. "What d'you hear, God damn it!" The touch of odd nervousness that made his anger grow betrayed itself in his language.

Tooshalli slowly turned his head back again to its normal position, the body rigid as before.

"I hear nothing, Mr. Grimwood," he said, gazing with quiet dignity into his employer's eyes.

This was too much for the other, a man of savage temper at the best of times. He was the type of Englishman who held strong views.

"That's a lie, Tooshalli, and I won't have you lie to me. Now what was it? Tell me at once!"

"I hear nothing," repeated the other. "I only think."

"And what is it you're pleased to think?" Impatience made a nasty expression round the mouth.

"I go not," was the abrupt reply, unalterable decision in the voice.

The man's rejoinder was so unexpected that Grimwood found nothing to say at first. For a moment he did not take its meaning; his mind, always slow, was confused by impatience, also by what he considered the foolishness of the little scene. Then in a flash he understood; but he also understood the immovable obstinacy of the race he had to deal with. Tooshalli was informing him that he refused to go into the valley where the big moose had vanished. And his astonishment was so great at first that he merely sat and stared. No words came to him.

"It is——" said the Indian, but used a native term.

"What's that mean?" Grimwood found his tongue, but his quiet tone was ominous.

"Mr. Grimwood, it mean the 'Valley of the Beasts,'" was the reply in a tone quieter still.

The Englishman made a great, a genuine effort at self-control. He was dealing, he forced himself to remember, with a superstitious Indian. He knew the stubbornness of the type. If the man left him his sport was irretrievably spoilt, for he could not hunt in this wilderness alone, and even if he got the coveted head, he could never, never get it out alone. His native selfishness seconded his effort. Persuasion, if only he could keep back his rising anger, was his *rôle* to play.

"The Valley of the Beasts," he said, a smile on his lips rather than in his darkening eyes; "but that's just what we want. It's beasts we're after, isn't it?" His voice had a false cheery ring that could not have deceived a child. "But what d'you mean, anyhow—the Valley of the Beasts?" He asked it with a dull attempt at sympathy.

24

"It belong to Ishtot, Mr. Grimwood." The man looked him full in the face, no flinching in the eyes.

"My—our—big moose is there," said the other, who recognised the name of the Indian Hunting God, and understanding better, felt confident he would soon persuade his man. Tooshalli, he remembered, too, was nominally a Christian. "We'll follow him at dawn and get the biggest head the world has ever seen. You will be famous," he added, his temper better in hand again. "Your tribe will honour you. And the white hunters will pay you much money."

"He go there to save himself. I go not."

The other's anger revived with a leap at this stupid obstinacy. But, in spite of it, he noticed the odd choice of words. He began to realise that nothing now would move the man. At the same time, he also realised that violence on his part must prove worse than useless. Yet violence was natural to his "dominant" type. "That brute Grimwood" was the way most men spoke of him.

"Back at the settlement you're a Christian, remember," he tried, in his clumsy way, another line. "And disobedience means hell-fire. You know that!"

"I a Christian—at the post," was the reply, "but out here the Red God rule. Ishtot keep that valley for himself. No Indian hunt there." It was as though a granite boulder spoke.

The savage temper of the Englishman, enforced by the long difficult suppression, rose wickedly into sudden flame. He stood up, kicking his blankets aside. He strode across the dying fire to the Indian's side. Tooshalli also rose. They faced each other, two humans alone in the wilderness, watched by countless invisible forest eyes.

Tooshalli stood motionless, yet as though he expected violence from the foolish, ignorant white-face. "You go alone, Mr. Grimwood." There was no fear in him.

Grimwood choked with rage. His words came forth with difficulty, though he roared them into the silence of the forest:

"I pay you, don't I? You'll do what *I* say, not what *you* say!" His voice woke the echoes.

The Indian, arms hanging by his side, gave the old reply.

"I go not," he repeated firmly.

It stung the other into uncontrollable fury.

The beast then came uppermost; it came out. "You've said that once too often, Tooshalli!" and he struck him brutally in the face. The Indian fell, rose to his knees again, collapsed sideways beside the fire,

25

then struggled back into a sitting position. He never once took his eyes from the white man's face.

Beside himself with anger, Grimwood stood over him. "Is that enough? Will you obey me now?" he shouted.

"I go not," came the thick reply, blood streaming from his mouth. The eyes had no flinching in them. "That valley Ishtot keep. Ishtot see us now. *He see you.*" The last words he uttered with strange, almost uncanny emphasis.

Grimwood, arm raised, fist clenched, about to repeat his terrible assault, paused suddenly. His arm sank to his side. What exactly stopped him he could never say. For one thing, he feared his own anger, feared that if he let himself go, he would not stop till he had killed—committed murder. He knew his own fearful temper and stood afraid of it. Yet it was not only that. The calm firmness of the Indian, his courage under pain, and something in the fixed and burning eyes arrested him. Was it also something in the words he had used—"Ishtot see *you*"— that stung him into a queer caution midway in his violence?

He could not say. He only knew that a momentary sense of awe came over him. He became unpleasantly aware of the enveloping forest, so still, listening in a kind of impenetrable, remorseless silence. This lonely wilderness, looking silently upon what might easily prove murder, laid a faint, inexplicable chill upon his raging blood. The hand dropped slowly to his side again, the fist unclenched itself, his breath came more evenly.

"Look you here," he said, adopting without knowing it the local way of speech. "I ain't a bad man, though your going-on do make a man damned tired. I'll give you another chance." His voice was sullen, but a new note in it surprised even himself. "I'll do that. You can have the night to think it over, Tooshalli—see? Talk it over with your——"

He did not finish the sentence. Somehow the name of the Indian God refused to pass his lips. He turned away, flung himself into his blankets, and in less than ten minutes, exhausted as much by his anger as by the day's hard going, he was sound asleep.

The Indian, crouching beside the dying fire, had said nothing.

Night held the woods, the sky was thick with stars, the life of the forest went about its business quietly, with that wondrous skill which millions of years have perfected. The Indian, so close to this skill that he instinctively used and borrowed from it, was silent, alert and wise, his outline as inconspicuous as though he merged, like his four-footed teachers, into the mass of the surrounding bush.

He moved perhaps, yet nothing knew he moved. His wisdom, derived from that eternal, ancient mother who from infinite experience makes no mistakes, did not fail him. His soft tread made no sound; his breathing, as his weight, was calculated. The stars observed him, but they did not tell; the light air knew his whereabouts, yet without betrayal. . . .

The chill dawn gleamed at length between the trees, lighting the pale ashes of an extinguished fire, also of a bulky, obvious form beneath a blanket. The form moved clumsily. The cold was penetrating.

And that bulky form now moved because a dream had come to trouble it. A dark figure stole across its confused field of vision. The form started, but it did not wake. The figure spoke: "Take this," it whispered, handing a little stick, curiously carved. "It is the *totem* of great Ishtot. In the valley all memory of the White Gods will leave you. Call upon Ishtot. . . . Call on Him if you dare"; and the dark figure glided away out of the dream and out of all remembrance. . . .

2

The first thing Grimwood noticed when he woke was that Tooshalli was not there. No fire burned, no tea was ready. He felt exceedingly annoyed. He glared about him, then got up with a curse to make the fire. His mind seemed confused and troubled. At first, he only realised one thing clearly—his guide had left him in the night.

It was very cold. He lit the wood with difficulty and made his tea, and the actual world came gradually back to him. The Indian had gone; perhaps the blow, perhaps the superstitious terror, perhaps both, had driven him away. He was alone, that was the outstanding fact. For anything beyond outstanding facts, Grimwood felt little interest. Imaginative speculation was beyond his compass. Close to the brute creation, it seemed, his nature lay.

It was while packing his blankets—he did it automatically, a dull, vicious resentment in him—that his fingers struck a bit of wood that he was about to throw away when its unusual shape caught his attention suddenly. His odd dream came back then. But was it a dream? The bit of wood was undoubtedly a *totem* stick. He examined it. He paid it more attention than he meant to, wished to. Yes, it was unquestionably a *totem* stick. The dream, then, was not a dream. Tooshalli had quit, but, following with Indian faithfulness some code of his own, had left him the means of safety. He chuckled sourly, but thrust the stick inside his belt. "One never knows," he mumbled to himself.

He faced the situation squarely. He was alone in the wilderness. His capable, experienced woodsman had deserted him. The situation was serious. What should he do? A weakling would certainly retrace his steps, following the track they had made, afraid to be left alone in this vast hinterland of pathless forest. But Grimwood was of another build. Alarmed he might be, but he would not give in. He had the defects of his own qualities. The brutality of his nature argued force. He was determined and a sportsman. He would go on. And ten minutes after breakfast, having first made a *cache* of what provisions were left over, he was on his way—down across the ridge and into the mysterious valley, the Valley of the Beasts.

It looked, in the morning sunlight, entrancing. The trees closed in behind him, but he did not notice. It led him on. . . .

He followed the track of the gigantic moose he meant to kill, and the sweet, delicious sunshine helped him. The air was like wine, the seductive spoor of the great beast, with here and there a faint splash of blood on leaves or ground, lay forever just before his eyes. He found the valley, though the actual word did not occur to him, enticing; more and more he noticed the beauty, the desolate grandeur of the mighty spruce and hemlock, the splendour of the granite bluffs which in places rose above the forest and caught the sun. . . . The valley was deeper, vaster than he had imagined. He felt safe, at home in it, though, again these actual terms did not occur to him.... Here he could hide for ever and find peace. . . . He became aware of a new quality in the deep loneliness. The scenery for the first time in his life appealed to him, and the form of the appeal was curious—he felt the comfort of it.

For a man of his habit, this was odd, yet the new sensations stole over him so gently, their approach so gradual, that they were first recognised by his consciousness indirectly. They had already established themselves in him before he noticed them; and the indirectness took this form—that the passion of the chase gave place to an interest in the valley itself. The lust of the hunt, the fierce desire to find and kill, the keen wish, in a word, to see his quarry within range, to aim, to fire, to witness the natural consummation of the long expedition—these had all become measurably less, while the effect of the valley upon him had increased in strength. There was a welcome about it that he did not understand.

The change was singular, yet, oddly enough, it did not occur to him as singular; it was unnatural, yet it did not strike him so. To a dull

28

mind of his unobservant, unanalytical type, a change had to be marked and dramatic before he noticed it; something in the nature of a shock must accompany it for him to recognise it had happened. And there had been no shock. The spoor of the great moose was much cleaner, now that he caught up with the animal that made it; the blood more frequent; he had noticed the spot where it had rested, its huge body leaving a marked imprint on the soft ground; where it had reached up to eat the leaves of saplings here and there was also visible; he had come undoubtedly very near to it, and any minute now might see its great bulk within range of an easy shot. Yet his ardour had somehow lessened.

He first realised this change in himself when it suddenly occurred to him that the animal itself had grown less cautious. It must scent him easily now, since a moose, its sight being indifferent, depends chiefly for its safety upon its unusually keen sense of smell, and the wind came from behind him. This now struck him as decidedly uncommon: the moose itself was obviously careless of his close approach. It felt no fear.

It was this inexplicable alteration in the animal's behaviour that made him recognise, at last, the alteration in his own. He had followed it now for a couple of hours and had descended some eight hundred to a thousand feet; the trees were thinner and more sparsely placed; there were open, park-like places where silver birch, *sumach* and maple splashed their blazing colours; and a crystal stream, broken by many waterfalls, foamed past towards the bed of the great valley, yet another thousand feet below. By a quiet pool against some over-arching rocks, the moose had evidently paused to drink, paused at its leisure, more-over.

Grimwood, rising from a close examination of the direction the creature had taken after drinking—the hoof-marks were fresh and very distinct in the marshy ground about the pool—looked suddenly straight into the great creature's eyes. It was not twenty yards from where he stood, yet he had been standing on that spot for at least ten minutes, caught by the wonder and loneliness of the scene. The moose, therefore, had been close beside him all this time. It had been calmly drinking, undisturbed by his presence, unafraid.

The shock came now, the shock that woke his heavy nature into realisation. For some seconds, probably for minutes, he stood rooted to the ground, motionless, hardly breathing. He stared as though he saw a vision. The animal's head was lowered, but turned obliquely somewhat, so that the eyes, placed sideways in its great head, could

29

see him properly; its immense proboscis hung as though stuffed upon an English wall; he saw the fore-feet planted wide apart, the slope of the enormous shoulders dropping back towards the fine hindquarters and lean flanks. It was a magnificent bull. The horns and head justified his wildest expectations, they were superb, a record specimen, and a phrase—where had he heard it?—ran vaguely, as from far distance, through his mind: "the biggest moose in the world."

There was the extraordinary fact, however, that he did not shoot; nor feel the wish to shoot. The familiar instinct, so strong hitherto in his blood, made no sign; the desire to kill apparently had left him. To raise his rifle, aim and fire had become suddenly an absolute impossibility.

He did not move. The animal and the human stared into each other's eyes for a length of time whose interval he could not measure. Then came a soft noise close beside him: the rifle had slipped from his grasp and fallen with a thud into the mossy earth at his feet. And the moose, for the first time now, was moving. With slow, easy stride, its great weight causing a squelching sound as the feet drew out of the moist ground, it came towards him, the bulk of the shoulders giving it an appearance of swaying like a ship at sea. It reached his side, it almost touched him, the magnificent head bent low, the spread of the gigantic horns lay beneath his very eyes. He could have patted, stroked it. He saw, with a touch of pity, that blood trickled from a sore in its left shoulder, matting the thick hair. It sniffed the fallen rifle.

Then, lifting its head and shoulders again, it sniffed the air, this time with an audible sound that shook from Grimwood's mind the last possibility that he witnessed a vision or dreamed a dream. One moment it gazed into his face, its big brown eyes shining and unafraid, then turned abruptly, and swung away at a speed ever rapidly increasing across the park-like spaces till it was lost finally among the dark tangle of undergrowth beyond. And the Englishman's muscles turned to paper, his paralysis passed, his legs refused to support his weight, and he sank heavily to the ground. . . .

3

It seems he slept, slept long and heavily; he sat up, stretched himself, yawned and rubbed his eyes. The sun had moved across the sky, for the shadows, he saw, now ran from west to east, and they were long shadows. He had slept evidently for hours, and evening was drawing in. He was aware that he felt hungry. In his pouchlike pockets, he had dried meat, sugar, matches, tea, and the little billy that never left him. He would make a fire, boil some tea and eat.

But he took no steps to carry out his purpose, he felt disinclined to move, he sat thinking, thinking. . . . What was he thinking about? He did not know, he could not say exactly; it was more like fugitive pictures that passed across his mind. Who, and where, was he? This was the Valley of the Beasts, that he knew; he felt sure of nothing else. How long had he been here, and where had he come from, and why? The questions did not linger for their answers, almost as though his interest in them was merely automatic. He felt happy, peaceful, unafraid.

He looked about him, and the spell of this virgin forest came upon him like a charm; only the sound of falling water, the murmur of wind sighing among innumerable branches, broke the enveloping silence. Overhead, beyond the crests of the towering trees, a cloudless evening sky was paling into transparent orange, opal, mother of pearl. He saw buzzards soaring lazily. A scarlet *tanager* flashed by. Soon would the owls begin to call and the darkness fall like a sweet black veil and hide all detail, while the stars sparkled in their countless thousands. . . .

A glint of something that shone upon the ground caught his eye— a smooth, polished strip of rounded metal: his rifle. And he started to his feet impulsively, yet not knowing exactly what he meant to do. At the sight of the weapon, something had leaped to life in him, then faded out, died down, and was gone again.

"I'm—I'm———" he began muttering to himself, but could not finish what he was about to say. His name had disappeared completely. "I'm in the Valley of the Beasts," he repeated in place of what he sought but could not find.

This fact, that he was in the Valley of the Beasts, seemed the only positive item of knowledge that he had. About the name something known and familiar clung, though the sequence that led up to it he could not trace. Presently, nevertheless, he rose to his feet, advanced a few steps, stooped and picked up the shining metal thing, his rifle. He examined it a moment, a feeling of dread and loathing rising in him, a sensation of almost horror that made him tremble, then, with a convulsive movement that betrayed an intense reaction of some sort he could not comprehend, he flung the thing far from him into the foaming torrent. He saw the splash it made, he also saw that same instant a large grizzly bear swing heavily along the bank not a dozen yards from where he stood.

It, too, heard the splash, for it started, turned, paused a second, then changed its direction and came towards him. It came up close. Its fur brushed his body. It examined him leisurely, as the moose had done, sniffed, half rose upon its terrible hind legs, opened its mouth so that red tongue and gleaming teeth were plainly visible, then flopped back upon all fours again with a deep growling that yet had no anger in it, and swung off at a quick trot back to the bank of the torrent. He had felt its hot breath upon his face, but he had felt no fear. The monster was puzzled but not hostile. It disappeared.

"They know not——" he sought for the word "man," but could not find it. "They have never been hunted."

The words ran through his mind, if perhaps he was not entirely certain of their meaning; they rose, as it were, automatically; a familiar sound lay in them somewhere. At the same time there rose feelings in him that were equally, though in another way, familiar and quite natural, feelings he had once known intimately but long since laid aside.

What were they? What was their origin? They seemed distant as the stars, yet were actually in his body, in his blood and nerves, part and parcel of his flesh. Long, long ago. . . .Oh, how long, how long?

Thinking was difficult; feeling was what he most easily and naturally managed. He could not think for long; feeling rose up and drowned the effort quickly.

That huge and awful bear—not a nerve, not a muscle quivered in him as its acrid smell rose to his nostrils, its fur brushed down his legs. Yet he was aware that somewhere there was danger, though not here. Somewhere there was attack, hostility, wicked and calculated plans against him—as against that splendid, roaming animal that had sniffed, examined, then gone its own way, satisfied. Yes, active attack, hostility and careful, cruel plans against his safety, but—not here. Here he was safe, secure, at peace; here he was happy; here he could roam at will, no eye cast sideways into forest depths, no ear pricked high to catch sounds not explained, no nostrils quivering to scent alarm. He felt this, but he did not think it. He felt hungry, thirsty too.

Something prompted him now at last to act. His billy lay at his feet, and he picked it up; the matches—he carried them in a metal case whose screw top kept out all moisture—were in his hand. Gathering a few dry twigs, he stooped to light them, then suddenly drew back with the first touch of fear he had yet known.

Fire! What *was* fire? The idea was repugnant to him, it was impossible, he was afraid of fire. He flung the metal case after the rifle and saw it gleam in the last rays of sunset, then sink with a little splash beneath the water. Glancing down at his billy, he realised next that he could not make use of it either, nor of the dark dry dusty stuff he had meant to boil in water. He felt no repugnance, certainly no fear, in connexion with these things, only he could not handle them, he did not need them, he had forgotten, yes, "forgotten," what they meant exactly. This strange forgetfulness was increasing in him rapidly, becoming more and more complete with every minute. Yet his thirst must be quenched.

The next moment he found himself at the water's edge; he stooped to fill his billy; paused, hesitated, examined the rushing water, then abruptly moved a few feet higher up the stream, leaving the metal can behind him. His handling of it had been oddly clumsy, his gestures awkward, even unnatural. He now flung himself down with an easy, simple motion of his entire body, lowered his face to a quiet pool he had found, and drank his fill of the cool, refreshing liquid. But, though unaware of the fact, he did not drink. He lapped.

Then, crouching where he was, he ate the meat and sugar from his pockets, lapped more water, moved back a short distance again into the dry ground beneath the trees, but moved this time without rising to his feet, curled his body into a comfortable position and closed his eyes again to sleep. . . .No single question now raised its head in him. He felt contentment, satisfaction only. . . .

He stirred, shook himself, opened half an eye and saw, as he had felt already in slumber, that he was not alone. In the park-like spaces in front of him, as in the shadowed fringe of the trees at his back, there was sound and movement, the sound of stealthy feet, the movement of innumerable dark bodies. There was the pad and tread of animals, the stir of backs, of smooth and shaggy beasts, in countless numbers. Upon this host fell the light of a half-moon sailing high in a cloudless sky; the gleam of stars, sparkling in the clear night air like diamonds, shone reflected in hundreds of ever-shifting eyes, most of them but a few feet above the ground. The whole valley was alive.

He sat upon his haunches, staring, staring, but staring in wonder, not in fear, though the foremost of the great host were so near that he could have stretched an arm and touched them. It was an ever-moving, ever-shifting throng he gazed at, spell-bound, in the pale light of moon and stars, now fading slowly towards the approaching dawn. And the smell of the forest itself was not sweeter to him in that moment than the mingled perfume, raw, pungent, acrid, of this furry host of beautiful wild animals that moved like a sea, with a strange murmuring, too, like sea, as the myriad feet and bodies passed to and fro together.

Nor was the gleam of the starry, phosphorescent eyes less pleasantly friendly than those happy lamps that light home-lost wanderers to cosy rooms and safety. Through the wild army, in a word, poured to him the deep comfort of the entire valley, a comfort which held both the sweetness of invitation and the welcome of some magical home-coming.

No thoughts came to him, but feeling rose in a tide of wonder and acceptance. He was in his rightful place. His nature had come home. There was this dim, vague consciousness in him that after long, futile straying in another place where uncongenial conditions had forced him to be unnatural and therefore terrible, he had returned at last where he belonged. Here, in the Valley of the Beasts, he had found peace, security and happiness. He would be—he was at last—himself.

It was a marvellous, even a magical, scene he watched, his nerves at highest tension yet quite steady, his senses exquisitely alert, yet no uneasiness in the full, accurate reports they furnished. Strong as some deep flood-tide, yet dim, as with untold time and distance, rose over him the spell of long-forgotten memory of a state where he was content and happy, where he was natural. The outlines, as it were, of mighty, primitive pictures, flashed before him, yet were gone again before the detail was filled in.

He watched the great army of the animals, they were all about him now; he crouched upon his haunches in the centre of an ever-moving circle of wild forest life. Great timber wolves he saw pass to and fro, loping past him with long stride and graceful swing; their red tongues lolling out; they swarmed in hundreds. Behind, yet mingling freely with them, rolled the huge grizzlies, not clumsy as their uncouth bodies promised, but swiftly, lightly, easily, their half tumbling gait masking agility and speed. They gambolled, sometimes they rose and stood half upright, they were comely in their mass and power, they rolled past him so close that he could touch them. And the black bear and the brown went with them, bears beyond counting, monsters and little ones, a splendid multitude.

Beyond them, yet only a little further back, where the park-like spaces made free movement easier, rose a sea of horns and antlers like a miniature forest in the silvery moonlight. The immense tribe of deer gathered in vast throngs beneath the starlit sky. Moose and caribou, he saw, the mighty wapiti, and the smaller deer in their crowding thousands. He heard the sound of meeting horns, the tread of innumerable hoofs, the occasional pawing of the ground as the bigger creatures manoeuvred for more space about them. A wolf, he saw, was licking gently at the shoulder of a great bull-moose that had been injured. And the tide receded, advanced again, once more receded, rising and falling like a living sea whose waves were animal shapes, the inhabitants of the Valley of the Beasts.

Beneath the quiet moonlight they swayed to and fro before him. They watched him, knew him, recognised him. They made him welcome.

He was aware, moreover, of a world of smaller life that formed an under-sea, as it were, numerous under-currents rather, running in and out between the great upright legs of the larger creatures. These, though he could not see them clearly, covered the earth, he was aware, in enormous numbers, darting hither and thither, now hiding, now reappearing, too intent upon their busy purposes to pay him attention like their huger comrades, yet ever and *anon* tumbling against his back, cannoning from his sides, scampering across his legs even, then gone again with a scuttering sound of rapid little feet, and rushing back into the general host beyond. And with this smaller world also he felt at home.

How long he sat gazing, happy in himself, secure, satisfied, contented, natural, he could not say, but it was long enough for the desire to mingle with what he saw, to know closer contact, to become one with them all—long enough for this deep blind desire to assert itself, so that at length he began to move from his mossy seat towards them, to move, moreover, as they moved, and not upright on two feet.

The moon was lower now, just sinking behind a towering cedar whose ragged crest broke its light into silvery spray. The stars were a little paler too. A line of faint red was visible beyond the heights at the valley's eastern end.

He paused and looked about him, as he advanced slowly, aware that the host already made an opening in their ranks and that the bear even nosed the earth in front, as though to show the way that was easiest for him to follow. Then, suddenly, a lynx leaped past him into the low branches of a hemlock, and he lifted his head to admire its perfect poise. He saw in the same instant the arrival of the birds, the army of the eagles, hawks and buzzards, birds of prey—the awakening flight that just precedes the dawn. He saw the flocks and streaming lines, hiding the whitening stars a moment as they passed with a prodigious whirr of wings. There came the hooting of an owl from the tree immediately overhead where the lynx now crouched, but not maliciously, along its branch.

He started. He half rose to an upright position. He knew not why he did so, knew not exactly why he started. But in the attempt to find his new, and, as it now seemed, his unaccustomed balance, one hand fell against his side and came in contact with a hard straight thing that projected awkwardly from his clothing. He pulled it out, feeling it all over with his fingers. It was a little stick. He raised it nearer to his eyes, examined it in the light of dawn now growing swiftly, remembered, or half remembered what it was—and stood stock still.

"The *totem* stick," he mumbled to himself, yet audibly, finding his speech, and finding another thing—a glint of peering memory—for the first time since entering the valley.

A shock like fire ran through his body; he straightened himself, aware that a moment before he had been crawling upon his hands and knees; it seemed that something broke in his brain, lifting a veil, flinging a shutter free. And Memory peered dreadfully through the widening gap.

"I'm—I'm Grimwood," his voice uttered, though below his breath. "Tooshalli's left me. I'm alone. . . .!"

He was aware of a sudden change in the animals surrounding him. A big, grey wolf sat three feet away, glaring into his face; at its side an enormous grizzly swayed itself from one foot to the other; behind it, as if looking over its shoulder, loomed a gigantic wapiti, its horns merged in the shadows of the drooping cedar boughs. But the northern dawn was nearer, the sun already close to the horizon. He saw details with sharp distinctness now.

The great bear rose, balancing a moment on its massive hind-quarters, then took a step towards him, its front paws spread like arms. Its wicked head lolled horribly, as a huge bull-moose, lowering its horns as if about to charge, came up with a couple of long strides and joined it. A sudden excitement ran quivering over the entire host; the distant ranks moved in a new, unpleasant way; a thousand heads were lifted, ears were pricked, a forest of ugly muzzles pointed up to the wind.

And the Englishman, beside himself suddenly with a sense of ultimate terror that saw no possible escape, stiffened and stood rigid. The horror of his position petrified him. Motionless and silent he faced the awful army of his enemies, while the white light of breaking day added fresh ghastliness to the scene which was the setting for his cruel death in the Valley of the Beasts.

Above him crouched the hideous lynx, ready to spring the instant he sought safety in the tree; above it again, he was aware of a thousand talons of steel, fierce hooked beaks of iron, and the angry beating of prodigious wings.

He reeled, for the grizzly touched his body with its outstretched paw; the wolf crouched just before its deadly spring; in another second he would have been torn to pieces, crushed, devoured, when terror, operating naturally as ever, released the muscles of his throat and tongue. He shouted with what he believed was his last breath on earth. He called aloud in his frenzy. It was a prayer to whatever gods there be, it was an anguished cry for help to heaven.

"Ishtot! Great Ishtot, help me!" his voice rang out, while his hand still clutched the forgotten *totem* stick.

And the Red Heaven heard him.

Grimwood that same instant was aware of a presence that, but for his terror of the beasts, must have frightened him into sheer unconsciousness. A gigantic Red Indian stood before him. Yet, while the figure rose close in front of him, causing the birds to settle and the wild animals to crouch quietly where they stood, it rose also from a great distance, for it seemed to fill the entire valley with its influence, its power, its amazing majesty.

In some way, moreover, that he could not understand, its vast appearance included the actual valley itself with all its trees, its running streams, its open spaces and its rocky bluffs. These marked its outline, as it were, the outline of a superhuman shape. There was a mighty bow, there was a quiver of enormous arrows, there was this Indian figure to whom they belonged.

Yet the appearance, the outline, the face and figure too—these *were* the valley; and when the voice became audible, it was the valley itself that uttered the appalling words. It was the voice of trees and wind, and of running, falling water that woke the echoes in the Valley of the Beasts, as, in that same moment, the sun topped the ridge and filled the scene, the outline of the majestic figure too, with a flood of dazzling light:

"You have shed blood in this my valley. . . .*I will not save. . . .*!"

The figure melted away into the sunlit forest, merging with the new-born day. But Grimwood saw close against his face the shining teeth, hot fetid breath passed over his cheeks, a power enveloped his whole body as though a mountain crushed him. He closed his eyes.

37

He fell. A sharp, crackling sound passed through his brain, but already unconscious, he did not hear it.

★★★★★★★★★★★★

His eyes opened again, and the first thing they took in was—fire. He shrank back instinctively.

"It's all right, old man. We'll bring you round. Nothing to be frightened about." He saw the face of Iredale looking down into his own. Behind Iredale stood Tooshalli. His face was swollen. Grimwood remembered the blow. The big man began to cry.

"Painful still, is it?" Iredale said sympathetically. "Here, swallow a little more of this. It'll set you right in no time."

Grimwood gulped down the spirit. He made a violent effort to control himself, but was unable to keep the tears back. He felt no pain. It was his heart that ached, though why or wherefore, he had no idea.

"I'm all to pieces," he mumbled, ashamed yet somehow not ashamed. "My nerves are rotten. What's happened?" There was as yet no memory in him.

"You've been hugged by a bear, old man. But no bones broken. Tooshalli saved you. He fired in the nick of time—a brave shot, for he might easily have hit you instead of the brute."

"The other brute," whispered Grimwood, as the whisky worked in him and memory came slowly back.

"Where are we?" he asked presently, looking about him.

He saw a lake, canoes drawn up on the shore, two tents, and figures moving. Iredale explained matters briefly, then left him to sleep a bit. Tooshalli, it appeared, travelling without rest, had reached Iredale's camping ground twenty-four hours after leaving his employer. He found it deserted, Iredale and his Indian being on the hunt. When they returned at nightfall, he had explained his presence in his brief native fashion: "He struck me and I quit. He hunt now alone in Ishtot's Valley of the Beasts. He is dead, I think. I come to tell you."

Iredale and his guide, with Tooshalli as leader, started off then and there, but Grimwood had covered a considerable distance, though leaving an easy track to follow. It was the moose tracks and the blood that chiefly guided them. They came up with him suddenly enough—in the grip of an enormous bear.

It was Tooshalli that fired.

★★★★★★★★★★★★

The Indian lives now in easy circumstances, all his needs cared for, while Grimwood, his benefactor but no longer his employer, has giv-

38

en up hunting. He is a quiet, easy-tempered, almost gentle sort of fellow, and people wonder rather why he hasn't married. "Just the fellow to make a good father," is what they say; "so kind, good-natured and affectionate." Among his pipes, in a glass case over the mantlepiece, hangs a *totem* stick. He declares it saved his soul, but what he means by the expression he has never quite explained.

The Wolves of God

1

As the little steamer entered the bay of Kettletoft in the Orkneys the beach at Sanday appeared so low that the houses almost seemed to be standing in the water; and to the big, dark man leaning over the rail of the upper deck the sight of them came with a pang of mingled pain and pleasure. The scene, to his eyes, had not changed. The houses, the low shore, the flat treeless country beyond, the vast open sky, all looked exactly the same as when he left the island thirty years ago to work for the Hudson Bay Company in distant N. W. Canada. A lad of eighteen then, he was now a man of forty-eight, old for his years, and this was the home-coming he had so often dreamed about in the lonely wilderness of trees where he had spent his life. Yet his grim face wore an anxious rather than a tender expression. The return was perhaps not quite as he had pictured it.

Jim Peace had not done too badly, however, in the Company's service. For an islander, he would be a rich man now; he had not married, he had saved the greater part of his salary, and even in the far-away Post where he had spent so many years there had been occasional opportunities of the kind common to new, wild countries where life and law are in the making. He had not hesitated to take them.

None of the big Company Posts, it was true, had come his way, nor had he risen very high in the service; in another two years his turn would have come, yet he had left of his own accord before those two years were up. His decision, judging by the strength in the features, was not due to impulse; the move had been deliberately weighed and calculated; he had renounced his opportunity after full reflection. A man with those steady eyes, with that square jaw and determined mouth, certainly did not act without good reason.

A curious expression now flickered over his weather-hardened face as he saw again his childhood's home, and the return, so often dreamed about, actually took place at last. An uneasy light flashed for a moment in the deep-set grey eyes, but was quickly gone again, and the tanned visage recovered its accustomed look of stern composure. His keen sight took in a dark knot of figures on the landing-pier—his brother, he knew, among them. A wave of home-sickness swept over him. He longed to see his brother again, the old farm, the sweep of open country, the sand-dunes, and the breaking seas. The smell of long-forgotten days came to his nostrils with its sweet, painful pang of youthful memories.

How fine, he thought, to be back there in the old familiar fields of childhood, with sea and sand about him instead of the smother of endless woods that ran a thousand miles without a break. He was glad in particular that no trees were visible, and that rabbits scampering among the dunes were the only wild animals he need ever meet. . . .

Those thirty years in the woods, it seemed, oppressed his mind; the forests, the countless multitudes of trees, had wearied him. His nerves, perhaps, had suffered finally. Snow, frost and sun, stars, and the wind had been his companions during the long days and endless nights in his lonely Post, but chiefly—trees. Trees, trees, trees! On the whole, he had preferred them in stormy weather, though, in another way, their rigid hosts, 'mid the deep silence of still days, had been equally oppressive.

In the clear sunlight of a windless day, they assumed a waiting, listening, watching aspect that had something spectral in it, but when in motion—well, he preferred a moving animal to one that stood stock-still and stared. Wind, moreover, in a million trees, even the lightest breeze, drowned all other sounds—the howling of the wolves, for instance, in winter, or the ceaseless harsh barking of the husky dogs he so disliked.

Even on this warm September afternoon a slight shiver ran over him as the background of dead years loomed up behind the present scene. He thrust the picture back, deep down inside himself. The self-control, the strong, even violent will that the face betrayed, came into operation instantly. The background was background; it belonged to what was past, and the past was over and done with. It was dead. Jim meant it to stay dead.

The figure waving to him from the pier was his brother. He knew Tom instantly; the years had dealt easily with him in this quiet island; there was no startling, no unkindly change, and a deep emotion, though unexpressed, rose in his heart. It was good to be home again, he realised, as he sat presently in the cart, Tom holding the reins, driving slowly back to the farm at the north end of the island. Everything he found familiar, yet at the same time strange. They passed the school where he used to go as a little bare-legged boy; other boys were now learning their lessons exactly as he used to do. Through the open window he could hear the droning voice of the schoolmaster, who, though invisible, wore the face of Mr. Lovibond, his own teacher.

"Lovibond?" said Tom, in reply to his question. "Oh, he's been dead these twenty years. He went south, you know—Glasgow, I think it was, or Edinburgh. He got typhoid."

Stands of golden plover were to be seen as of old in the fields, or flashing overhead in swift flight with a whir of wings, wheeling and turning together like one huge bird. Down on the empty shore a curlew cried. Its piercing note rose clear above the noisy clamour of the gulls. The sun played softly on the quiet sea, the air was keen but pleasant, the tang of salt mixed sweetly with the clean smells of open country that he knew so well. Nothing of essentials had changed, even the low clouds beyond the heaving uplands were the clouds of childhood.

They came presently to the sand-dunes, where rabbits sat at their burrow-mouths, or ran helter-skelter across the road in front of the slow cart.

"They're safe till the colder weather comes and trapping begins," he mentioned. It all came back to him in detail.

"And they know it, too—the canny little beggars," replied Tom. "Any rabbits out where you've been?" he asked casually.

"Not to hurt you," returned his brother shortly.

Nothing seemed changed, although everything seemed different. He looked upon the old, familiar things, but with other eyes. There were, of course, changes, alterations, yet so slight, in a way so odd and curious, that they evaded him; not being of the physical order, they reported to his soul, not to his mind. But his soul, being troubled, sought to deny the changes; to admit them meant to admit a change in himself he had determined to conceal even if he could not entirely deny it.

"Same old place, Tom," came one of his rare remarks. "The years ain't done much to it." He looked into his brother's face a moment squarely. "Nor to you, either, Tom," he added, affection and tenderness just touching his voice and breaking through a natural reserve that was almost taciturnity.

His brother returned the look; and something in that instant passed between the two men, something of understanding that no words had hinted at, much less expressed. The tie was real, they loved each other, they were loyal, true, steadfast fellows. In youth they had known no secrets. The shadow that now passed and vanished left a vague trouble in both hearts.

"The forests," said Tom slowly, "have made a silent man of you, Jim. You'll miss them here, I'm thinking."

"Maybe," was the curt reply, "but I guess not."

His lips snapped to as though they were of steel and could never open again, while the tone he used made Tom realise that the subject was not one his brother cared to talk about particularly. He was surprised, therefore, when, after a pause, Jim returned to it of his own accord. He was sitting a little sideways as he spoke, taking in the scene with hungry eyes. "It's a queer thing," he observed, "to look round and see nothing but clean empty land, and not a single tree in sight. You see, it don't look natural quite."

Again, his brother was struck by the tone of voice, but this time by something else as well he could not name. Jim was excusing himself, explaining. The manner, too, arrested him. And thirty years disappeared as though they had not been, for it was thus Jim acted as a boy when there was something unpleasant, he had to say and wished to get it over. The tone, the gesture, the manner, all were there. He was edging up to something he wished to say, yet dared not utter.

"You've had enough of trees then?" Tom said sympathetically, trying to help, "and things?"

The instant the last two words were out he realised that they had been drawn from him instinctively, and that it was the anxiety of deep affection which had prompted them. He had guessed without knowing he had guessed, or rather, without intention or attempt to guess. Jim had a secret. Love's clairvoyance had discovered it, though not yet its hidden terms.

"I have———" began the other, then paused, evidently to choose his words with care. "I've had enough of trees." He was about to speak of something that his brother had unwittingly touched upon in his chance phrase, but instead of finding the words he sought, he gave a sudden start, his breath caught sharply. "What's that?" he exclaimed, jerking his body round so abruptly that Tom automatically pulled the reins. "What is it?"

"A dog barking," Tom answered, much surprised. "A farm dog

44

barking. Why? What did you think it was?" he asked, as he flicked the horse to go on again. "You made me jump," he added, with a laugh. "You're used to huskies, ain't you?"

"It sounded so—not like a dog, I mean," came the slow explanation. "It's long since I heard a sheepdog bark, I suppose it startled me."

"Oh, it's a dog all right," Tom assured him comfortingly, for his heart told him infallibly the kind of tone to use. And presently, too, he changed the subject in his blunt, honest fashion, knowing that, also, was the right and kindly thing to do. He pointed out the old farms as they drove along, his brother silent again, sitting stiff and rigid at his side. "And it's good to have you back, Jim, from those outlandish places. There are not too many of the family left now—just you and I, as a matter of fact."

"Just you and I," the other repeated gruffly, but in a sweetened tone that proved he appreciated the ready sympathy and tact. "We'll stick together, Tom, eh? Blood's thicker than water, ain't it? I've learnt that much, anyhow."

The voice had something gentle and appealing in it, something his brother heard now for the first time. An elbow nudged into his side, and Tom knew the gesture was not solely a sign of affection, but grew partly also from the comfort born of physical contact when the heart is anxious. The touch, like the last words, conveyed an appeal for help. Tom was so surprised he couldn't believe it quite.

Scared! Jim scared! The thought puzzled and afflicted him who knew his brother's character inside out, his courage, his presence of mind in danger, his resolution. Jim frightened seemed an impossibility, a contradiction in terms; he was the kind of man who did not know the meaning of fear, who shrank from nothing, whose spirits rose highest when things appeared most hopeless. It must, indeed, be an uncommon, even a terrible danger that could shake such nerves; yet Tom saw the signs and read them clearly. Explain them he could not, nor did he try. All he knew with certainty was that his brother, sitting now beside him in the cart, hid a secret terror in his heart. Sooner or later, in his own good time, he would share it with him.

He ascribed it, this simple Orkney farmer, to those thirty years of loneliness and exile in wild desolate places, without companionship, without the society of women, with only Indians, husky dogs, a few trappers or fur-dealers like himself, but none of the wholesome, natural influences that sweeten life within reach. Thirty years was a long, long time. He began planning schemes to help. Jim must see people as much as possible, and his mind ran quickly over the men and women available. In women the neighbourhood was not rich, but there were several men of the right sort who might be useful, good fellows all. There was John Rossiter, another old Hudson Bay man, who had been factor at Cartwright, Labrador, for many years, and had returned long ago to spend his last days in civilization. There was Sandy McKay, also back from a long spell of rubber-planting in Malay. . . . Tom was still busy making plans when they reached the old farm and presently sat down to their first meal together since that early breakfast thirty years ago before Jim caught the steamer that bore him off to exile—an exile that now returned him with nerves unstrung and a secret terror hidden in his heart.

"I'll ask no questions," he decided. "Jim will tell me in his own good time. And meanwhile, I'll get him to see as many folks as possible." He meant it too; yet not only for his brother's sake. Jim's terror was so vivid it had touched his own heart too.

"Ah, a man can open his lungs here and breathe!" exclaimed Jim, as the two came out after supper and stood before the house, gazing across the open country. He drew a deep breath as though to prove his assertion, exhaling with slow satisfaction again. "It's good to see a clear horizon and to know there's all that water between—between me and where I've been." He turned his face to watch the plover in the sky, then looked towards the distant shore-line where the sea was just visible in the long evening light. "There can't be too much water for me," he added, half to himself. "I guess they can't cross water—not that much water at any rate."

Tom stared, wondering uneasily what to make of it.

"At the trees again, Jim?" he said laughingly. He had overheard the last words, though spoken low, and thought it best not to ignore them altogether. To be natural was the right way, he believed, natural and cheery. To make a joke of anything unpleasant, he felt, was to make it less serious. "I've never seen a tree come across the Atlantic yet, except as a mast—dead," he added.

"I wasn't thinking of the trees just then," was the blunt reply, "but of—something else. The damned trees are nothing, though I hate the sight of 'em. Not of much account, anyway"—as though he compared them mentally with another thing. He puffed at his pipe, a moment.

"They certainly can't move," put in his brother, "nor swim either."

"Nor another thing," said Jim, his voice thick suddenly, but not with smoke, and his speech confused, though the idea in his mind was

46

certainly clear as daylight. "Things can't hide behind 'em—can they?"

"Not much cover hereabouts, I admit," laughed Tom, though the look in his brother's eyes made his laughter as short as it sounded unnatural.

"That's so," agreed the other. "But what I meant was"—he threw out his chest, looked about him with an air of intense relief, drew in another deep breath, and again exhaled with satisfaction—"if there are no trees, there's no hiding."

It was the expression on the rugged, weathered face that sent the blood in a sudden gulping rush from his brother's heart. He had seen men frightened, seen men afraid before they were actually frightened; he had also seen men stiff with terror in the face both of natural and so-called supernatural things; but never in his life before had he seen the look of unearthly dread that now turned his brother's face as white as chalk and yet put the glow of fire in two haunted burning eyes.

Across the darkening landscape the sound of distant barking had floated to them on the evening wind.

"It's only a farm-dog barking." Yet it was Jim's deep, quiet voice that said it, one hand upon his brother's arm.

"That's all," replied Tom, ashamed that he had betrayed himself, and realising with a shock of surprise that it was Jim who now played the *rôle* of comforter—a startling change in their relations. "Why, what did you think it was?"

He tried hard to speak naturally and easily, but his voice shook. So deep was the brothers' love and intimacy that they could not help but share.

Jim lowered his great head. "I thought," he whispered, his grey beard touching the other's cheek, "maybe it was the wolves"—an agony of terror made both voice and body tremble—"the Wolves of God!"

2

The interval of thirty years had been bridged easily enough; it was the secret that left the open gap neither of them cared or dared to cross. Jim's reason for hesitation lay within reach of guesswork, but Tom's silence was more complicated.

With strong, simple men, strangers to affectation or pretence, reserve is a real, almost a sacred thing. Jim offered nothing more; Tom asked no single question. In the latter's mind lay, for one thing, a singular intuitive certainty: that if he knew the truth, he would lose his

47

brother. How, why, wherefore, he had no notion; whether by death, or because, having told an awful thing, Jim would hide—physically or mentally—he knew not, nor even asked himself. No subtlety lay in Tom, the Orkney farmer. He merely felt that a knowledge of the truth involved separation which was death.

Day and night, however, that extraordinary phrase which, at its first hearing, had frozen his blood, ran on beating in his mind. With it came always the original, nameless horror that had held him motionless where he stood, his brother's bearded lips against his ear: *The Wolves of God.* In some dim way, he sometimes felt—tried to persuade himself, rather—the horror did not belong to the phrase alone, but was a sympathetic echo of what Jim felt himself. It had entered his own mind and heart. They had always shared in this same strange, intimate way. The deep brotherly tie accounted for it. Of the possible transference of thought and emotion he knew nothing, but this was what he meant perhaps.

At the same time, he fought and strove to keep it out, not because it brought uneasy and distressing feelings to him, but because he did not wish to pry, to ascertain, to discover his brother's secret as by some kind of subterfuge that seemed too near to eavesdropping almost. Also, he wished most earnestly to protect him. Meanwhile, in spite of himself, or perhaps because of himself, he watched his brother as a wild animal watches its young. Jim was the only tie he had on earth. He loved him with a brother's love, and Jim, similarly, he knew, loved him. His job was difficult. Love alone could guide him.

He gave openings, but he never questioned:

"Your letter did surprise me, Jim. I was never so delighted in my life. You had still two years to run."

"I'd had enough," was the short reply. "God, man, it was good to get home again!"

This, and the blunt talk that followed their first meeting, was all Tom had to go upon, while those eyes that refused to shut watched ceaselessly always. There was improvement, unless, which never occurred to Tom, it was self-control; there was no more talk of trees and water, the barking of the dogs passed unnoticed, no reference to the loneliness of the backwoods life passed his lips; he spent his days fishing, shooting, helping with the work of the farm, his evenings smoking over a glass—he was more than temperate—and talking over the days of long ago.

The signs of uneasiness still were there, but they were negative, far more suggestive, therefore, than if open and direct. He desired no company, for instance—an unnatural thing, thought Tom, after so many years of loneliness.

It was this and the awkward fact that he had given up two years before his time was finished, renouncing, therefore, a comfortable pension—it was these two big details that stuck with such unkind persistence in his brother's thoughts. Behind both, moreover, ran ever the strange whispered phrase. What the words meant, or whence they were derived, Tom had no possible inkling. Like the wicked refrain of some forbidden song, they haunted him day and night, even his sleep not free from them entirely. All of which, to the simple Orkney farmer, was so new an experience that he knew not how to deal with it at all. Too strong to be flustered, he was at any rate bewildered. And it was for Jim, his brother, he suffered most.

What perplexed him chiefly, however, was the attitude his brother showed towards old John Rossiter. He could almost have imagined that the two men had met and known each other out in Canada, though Rossiter showed him how impossible that was, both in point of time and of geography as well. He had brought them together within the first few days, and Jim, silent, gloomy, morose, even surly, had eyed him like an enemy. Old Rossiter, the milk of human kindness as thick in his veins as cream, had taken no offence. Grizzled veteran of the wilds, he had served his full term with the Company and now enjoyed his well-earned pension.

He was full of stories, reminiscences, adventures of every sort and kind; he knew men and values, had seen strange things that only the true wilderness delivers, and he loved nothing better than to tell them over a glass. He talked with Jim so genially and affably that little response was called for luckily, for Jim was glum and unresponsive almost to rudeness. Old Rossiter noticed nothing. What Tom noticed was, chiefly perhaps, his brother's acute uneasiness. Between his desire to help, his attachment to Rossiter, and his keen personal distress, he knew not what to do or say. The situation was becoming too much for him.

The two families, besides—Peace and Rossiter—had been neighbours for generations, had intermarried freely, and were related in various degrees. He was too fond of his brother to feel ashamed, but he was glad when the visit was over and they were out of their host's house. Jim had even declined to drink with him.

"They're good fellows on the island," said Tom on their way home, "but not specially entertaining, perhaps. We all stick together though. You can trust 'em mostly."

"I never was a talker, Tom," came the gruff reply. "You know that." And Tom, understanding more than he understood, accepted the apology and made generous allowances.

"John likes to talk," he helped him. "He appreciates a good listener."

"It's the kind of talk I'm finished with," was the rejoinder. "The Company and their goings-on don't interest me anymore. I've had enough."

Tom noticed other things as well with those affectionate eyes of his that did not want to see yet would not close. As the days drew in, for instance, Jim seemed reluctant to leave the house towards evening. Once the full light of day had passed, he kept indoors. He was eager and ready enough to shoot in the early morning, no matter at what hour he had to get up, but he refused point blank to go with his brother to the lake for an evening flight. No excuse was offered; he simply declined to go.

The gap between them thus widened and deepened, while yet in another sense it grew less formidable. Both knew, that is, that a secret lay between them for the first time in their lives, yet both knew also that at the right and proper moment it would be revealed. Jim only waited till the proper moment came. And Tom understood. His deep, simple love was equal to all emergencies. He respected his brother's reserve. The obvious desire of John Rossiter to talk and ask questions, for instance, he resisted staunchly as far as he was able. Only when he could help and protect his brother did he yield a little. The talk was brief, even monosyllabic; neither the old Hudson Bay fellow nor the Orkney farmer ran to many words:

"He ain't right with himself," offered John, taking his pipe out of his mouth and leaning forward. "That's what I don't like to see." He put a skinny hand on Tom's knee, and looked earnestly into his face as he said it.

"Jim!" replied the other. "Jim ill, you mean!" It sounded ridiculous.

"His mind is sick."

"I don't understand," Tom said, though the truth bit like rough-edged steel into the brother's heart.

"His soul, then, if you like that better."

Tom fought with himself a moment, then asked him to be more explicit.

"More'n I can say," rejoined the laconic old backwoodsman. "I don't know myself. The woods heal some men and make others sick."

"Maybe, John, maybe." Tom fought back his resentment. "You've lived, like him, in lonely places. You ought to know." His mouth shut with a snap, as though he had said too much. Loyalty to his suffering brother caught him strongly. Already his heart ached for Jim. He felt angry with Rossiter for his divination, but perceived, too, that the old fellow meant well and was trying to help him. If he lost Jim, he lost the world—his all.

A considerable pause followed, during which both men puffed their pipes with reckless energy. Both, that is, were a bit excited. Yet both had their code, a code they would not exceed for worlds.

"Jim," added Tom presently, making an effort to meet the sympathy half way, "ain't quite up to the mark, I'll admit that."

There was another long pause, while Rossiter kept his eyes on his companion steadily, though without a trace of expression in them—a habit that the woods had taught him.

"Jim," he said at length, with an obvious effort, "is skeered. And it's the soul in him that's skeered."

Tom wavered dreadfully then. He saw that old Rossiter, experienced backwoodsman and taught by the Company as he was, knew where the secret lay, if he did not yet know its exact terms. It was easy enough to put the question, yet he hesitated, because loyalty forbade.

"It's a dirty outfit somewheres," the old man mumbled to himself.

Tom sprang to his feet, "If you talk that way," he exclaimed angrily, "you're no friend of mine—or his." His anger gained upon him as he said it. "Say that again," he cried, "and I'll knock your teeth——"

He sat back, stunned a moment.

"Forgive me, John," he faltered, shamed yet still angry. "It's pain to me, it's pain. Jim," he went on, after a long breath and a pull at his glass, "Jim *is* scared, I know it." He waited a moment, hunting for the words that he could use without disloyalty. "But it's nothing he's done himself," he said, "nothing to his discredit. I know *that*."

Old Rossiter looked up, a strange light in his eyes.

"No offence," he said quietly.

"Tell me what you know," cried Tom suddenly, standing up again.

The old factor met his eye squarely, steadfastly. He laid his pipe aside.

"D'ye really want to hear?" he asked in a lowered voice. "Because, if you don't—why say so right now. I'm all for justice," he added, "and

51

always was."

"Tell me," said Tom, his heart in his mouth. "Maybe, if I knew—I might help him." The old man's words woke fear in him. He well knew his passionate, remorseless sense of justice.

"Help him," repeated the other. "For a man skeered in his soul there ain't no help. But—if you want to hear—I'll tell you."

"Tell me," cried Tom. "I *will* help him," while rising anger fought back rising fear.

John took another pull at his glass.

"Jest between you and me like."

"Between you and me," said Tom. "Get on with it."

There was a deep silence in the little room. Only the sound of the sea came in, the wind behind it.

"The Wolves," whispered old Rossiter. "The Wolves of God."

Tom sat still in his chair, as though struck in the face. He shivered. He kept silent and the silence seemed to him long and curious. His heart was throbbing, the blood in his veins played strange tricks. All he remembered was that old Rossiter had gone on talking. The voice, however, sounded far away and distant. It was all unreal, he felt, as he went homewards across the bleak, windswept upland, the sound of the sea for ever in his ears. . . .

Yes, old John Rossiter, damned be his soul, had gone on talking. He had said wild, incredible things. Damned be his soul! His teeth should be smashed for that. It was outrageous, it was cowardly, it was not true.

"Jim," he thought, "my brother, Jim!" as he ploughed his way wearily against the wind. "I'll teach him. I'll teach him to spread such wicked tales!" He referred to Rossiter. "God blast these fellows! They come home from their outlandish places and think they can say anything! I'll knock his yellow dog's teeth. . .!"

While, inside, his heart went quailing, crying for help, afraid.

He tried hard to remember exactly what old John had said. Round Garden Lake—that's where Jim was located in his lonely Post—there was a tribe of Indians. They were of unusual type. Malefactors among them—thieves, criminals, murderers—were not punished. They were merely turned out by the Tribe to die.

But how?

The Wolves of God took care of them. What were the Wolves of God?

A pack of wolves the Indians held in awe, a sacred pack, a spirit pack—God curse the man! Absurd, outlandish nonsense! Superstitious humbug! A pack of wolves that punished malefactors, killing but never eating them. "Torn but not eaten," the words came back to him, "white men as well as red. They could even cross the sea. . . ."

"He ought to be strung up for telling such wild yarns. By God—I'll teach him!"

"Jim! My brother, Jim! It's monstrous."

But the old man, in his passionate cold justice, had said a yet more terrible thing, a thing that Tom would never forget, as he never could forgive it: "You mustn't keep him here; you must send him away. We cannot have him on the island." And for that, though he could scarcely believe his ears, wondering afterwards whether he heard aright, for that, the proper answer to which was a blow in the mouth, Tom knew that his old friendship and affection had turned to bitter hatred.

"If I don't kill him, for that cursed lie, may God—and Jim—forgive me!"

3

It was a few days later that the storm caught the islands, making them tremble in their sea-born bed. The wind tearing over the treeless expanse was terrible, the lightning lit the skies. No such rain had ever been known. The building shook and trembled. It almost seemed the sea had burst her limits, and the waves poured in. Its fury and the noises that the wind made affected both the brothers, but Jim disliked the uproar most. It made him gloomy, silent, morose. It made him—Tom perceived it at once—uneasy. "Scared in his soul"—the ugly phrase came back to him.

"God save anyone who's out tonight," said Jim anxiously, as the old farm rattled about his head. Whereupon the door opened as of itself. There was no knock. It flew wide, as if the wind had burst it. Two drenched and beaten figures showed in the gap against the lurid sky—old John Rossiter and Sandy. They laid their fowling pieces down and took off their capes; they had been up at the lake for the evening flight and six birds were in the game bag. So suddenly had the storm come up that they had been caught before they could get home.

And, while Tom welcomed them, looked after their creature wants, and made them feel at home as in duty bound, no visit, he felt at the same time, could have been less opportune. Sandy did not matter—Sandy never did matter anywhere, his personality being negligible—but John Rossiter was the last man Tom wished to see just then. He hated the man; hated that sense of implacable justice that he knew was in him; with the slightest excuse he would have turned him out and sent him on to his own home, storm or no storm.

But Rossiter provided no excuse; he was all gratitude and easy politeness, more pleasant and friendly to Jim even than to his brother. Tom set out the whisky and sugar, sliced the lemon, put the kettle on, and furnished dry coats while the soaked garments hung up before the roaring fire that Orkney makes customary even when days are warm.

"It might be the equinoctials," observed Sandy, "if it wasn't late October." He shivered, for the tropics had thinned his blood.

"This ain't no ordinary storm," put in Rossiter, drying his drenched boots. "It reminds me a bit"—he jerked his head to the window that gave seawards, the rush of rain against the panes half drowning his voice—"reminds me a bit of yonder." He looked up, as though to find someone to agree with him, only one such person being in the room.

"Sure, it ain't," agreed Jim at once, but speaking slowly, "no ordinary storm." His voice was quiet as a child's. Tom, stooping over the kettle, felt something cold go trickling down his back. "It's from acrost the Atlantic too."

"All our big storms come from the sea," offered Sandy, saying just what Sandy was expected to say. His lank red hair lay matted on his forehead, making him look like an unhappy collie dog.

"There's no hospitality," Rossiter changed the talk, "like an islander's," as Tom mixed and filled the glasses. "He don't even ask 'Say when?'" He chuckled in his beard and turned to Sandy, well pleased with the compliment to his host. "Now, in Malay," he added dryly, "it's probably different, I guess."

And the two men, one from Labrador, the other from the tropics, fell to bantering one another with heavy humour, while Tom made things comfortable and Jim stood silent with his back to the fire. At each blow of the wind that shook the building, a suitable remark was made, generally by Sandy: "Did you hear that now?" "Ninety miles an hour at least." "Good thing you build solid in this country!" while Rossiter occasionally repeated that it was an "uncommon storm" and that "it reminded" him of the northern tempests he had known "out yonder."

Tom said little, one thought and one thought only in his heart—the wish that the storm would abate and his guests depart. He felt uneasy about Jim. He hated Rossiter. In the kitchen he had steadied

54

himself already with a good stiff drink, and was now half-way through a second; the feeling was in him that he would need their help before the evening was out. Jim, he noticed, had left his glass untouched. His attention, clearly, went to the wind and the outer night; he added little to the conversation.

"Hark!" cried Sandy's shrill voice. "Did you hear that? That wasn't wind, I'll swear." He sat up, looking for all the world like a dog pricking its ears to something no one else could hear.

"The sea coming over the dunes," said Rossiter. "There'll be an awful tide tonight and a terrible sea off the Swarf. Moon at the full, too." He cocked his head sideways to listen. The roaring was tremendous, waves and wind combining with a result that almost shook the ground. Rain hit the glass with incessant volleys like duck shot.

It was then that Jim spoke, having said no word for a long time.

"It's good there's no trees," he mentioned quietly. "I'm glad of that."

"There'd be fearful damage, wouldn't there?" remarked Sandy. "They might fall on the house too."

But it was the tone Jim used that made Rossiter turn stiffly in his chair, looking first at the speaker, then at his brother. Tom caught both glances and saw the hard keen glitter in the eyes. This kind of talk, he decided, had got to stop, yet how to stop it he hardly knew, for his were not subtle methods, and rudeness to his guests ran too strong against the island customs. He refilled the glasses, thinking in his blunt fashion how best to achieve his object, when Sandy helped the situation without knowing it.

"That's my first," he observed, and all burst out laughing. For Sandy's tenth glass was equally his "first," and he absorbed his liquor like a sponge, yet showed no effects of it until the moment when he would suddenly collapse and sink helpless to the ground. The glass in question, however, was only his third, the final moment still far away.

"Three in one and one in three," said Rossiter, amid the general laughter, while Sandy, grave as a judge, half emptied it at a single gulp. Good-natured, obtuse as a cart-horse, the tropics, it seemed, had first worn out his nerves, then removed them entirely from his body. "That's Malay theology, I guess," finished Rossiter. And the laugh broke out again. Whereupon, setting his glass down, Sandy offered his usual explanation that the hot lands had thinned his blood, that he felt the cold in these "arctic islands," and that alcohol was a necessity of life with him. Tom, grateful for the unexpected help, encouraged him to talk, and Sandy, accustomed to neglect as a rule, responded readily.

Having saved the situation, however, he now unwittingly led it back into the danger zone.

"A night for tales, eh?" he remarked, as the wind came howling with a burst of strangest noises against the house. "Down there in the States," he went on, "they'd say the evil spirits were out. They're a superstitious crowd, the natives. I remember once——" And he told a tale, half foolish, half interesting, of a mysterious track he had seen when following buffalo in the jungle. It ran close to the spoor of a wounded buffalo for miles, a track unlike that of any known animal, and the natives, though unable to name it, regarded it with awe. It was a good sign, a kill was certain. They said it was a spirit track.

"You got your buffalo?" asked Tom.

"Found him two miles away, lying dead. The mysterious spoor came to an end close beside the carcass. It didn't continue."

"And that reminds me——" began old Rossiter, ignoring Tom's attempt to introduce another subject. He told them of the haunted island at Eagle River, and a tale of the man who would not stay buried on another island off the coast. From that he went on to describe the strange man-beast that hides in the deep forests of Labrador, manifesting but rarely, and dangerous to men who stray too far from camp, men with a passion for wild life over-strong in their blood—the great mythical Wendigo. And while he talked, Tom noticed that Sandy used each pause as a good moment for a drink, but that Jim's glass still remained untouched.

The atmosphere of incredible things, thus, grew in the little room, much as it gathers among the shadows round a forest camp-fire when men who have seen strange places of the world give tongue about them, knowing they will not be laughed at—an atmosphere, once established, it is vain to fight against. The ingrained superstition that hides in every mother's son comes up at such times to breathe. It came up now. Sandy, closer by several glasses to the moment, Tom saw, when he would be suddenly drunk, gave birth again, a tale this time of a Scottish planter who had brutally dismissed a native servant for no other reason than that he disliked him. The man disappeared completely, but the villagers hinted that he would—soon indeed that he had—come back, though "not quite as he went."

The planter armed, knowing that vengeance might be violent. A black panther, meanwhile, was seen prowling about the bungalow. One night a noise outside his door on the veranda roused him. Just in time to see the black brute leaping over the railings into the compound, he fired, and the beast fell with a savage growl of pain. Help arrived and more shots were fired into the animal, as it lay, mortally wounded already, lashing its tail upon the grass. The lanterns, however, showed that instead of a panther, it was the servant they had shot to shreds.

Sandy told the story well, a certain odd conviction in his tone and manner, neither of them at all to the liking of his host. Uneasiness and annoyance had been growing in Tom for some time already, his inability to control the situation adding to his anger. Emotion was accumulating in him dangerously; it was directed chiefly against Rossiter, who, though saying nothing definite, somehow deliberately encouraged both talk and atmosphere. Given the conditions, it was natural enough the talk should take the turn it did take, but what made Tom more and more angry was that, if Rossiter had not been present, he could have stopped it easily enough. It was the presence of the old Hudson Bay man that prevented his taking decided action. He was afraid of Rossiter, afraid of putting his back up. That was the truth. His recognition of it made him furious.

"Tell us another, Sandy McKay," said the veteran. "There's a lot in such tales. They're found the world over—men turning into animals and the like."

And Sandy, yet nearer to his moment of collapse, but still showing no effects, obeyed willingly. He noticed nothing; the whisky was good, his tales were appreciated, and that sufficed him. He thanked Tom, who just then refilled his glass, and went on with his tale. But Tom, hatred and fury in his heart, had reached the point where he could no longer contain himself, and Rossiter's last words inflamed him. He went over, under cover of a tremendous clap of wind, to fill the old man's glass. The latter refused, covering the tumbler with his big, lean hand. Tom stood over him a moment, lowering his face. "You keep still," he whispered ferociously, but so that no one else heard it. He glared into his eyes with an intensity that held danger, and Rossiter, without answering, flung back that glare with equal, but with a calmer, anger.

The wind, meanwhile, had a trick of veering, and each time it shifted, Jim shifted his seat too. Apparently, he preferred to face the sound, rather than have his back to it.

"Your turn now for a tale," said Rossiter with purpose, when Sandy finished. He looked across at him, just as Jim, hearing the burst of wind at the walls behind him, was in the act of moving his chair again. The same moment the attack rattled the door and windows facing him. Jim, without answering, stood for a moment still as death, not knowing which way to turn.

"It's beatin' up from all sides," remarked Rossiter, "like it was goin' round the building."

There was a moment's pause, the four men listening with awe to the roar and power of the terrific wind. Tom listened too, but at the same time watched, wondering vaguely why he didn't cross the room and crash his fist into the old man's chattering mouth. Jim put out his hand and took his glass, but did not raise it to his lips. And a lull came abruptly in the storm, the wind sinking into a moment's dreadful silence. Tom and Rossiter turned their heads in the same instant and stared into each other's eyes. For Tom the instant seemed enormously prolonged. He realised the challenge in the other and that his rudeness had roused it into action. It had become a contest of wills—Justice battling against Love.

Jim's glass had now reached his lips, and the chattering of his teeth against its rim was audible.

But the lull passed quickly and the wind began again, though so gently at first, it had the sound of innumerable swift footsteps treading lightly, of countless hands fingering the doors and windows, but then suddenly with a mighty shout as it swept against the walls, rushed across the roof and descended like a battering-ram against the farther side.

"God, did you hear that?" cried Sandy. "It's trying to get in!" and having said it, he sank in a heap beside his chair, all of a sudden completely drunk. "It's wolves or panthersh," he mumbled in his stupor on the floor, "but whatsh's happened to Malay?" It was the last thing he said before unconsciousness took him, and apparently, he was insensible to the kick on the head from a heavy farmer's boot. For Jim's glass had fallen with a crash and the second kick was stopped midway. Tom stood spell-bound, unable to move or speak, as he watched his brother suddenly cross the room and open a window into the very teeth of the gale.

"Let be! Let be!" came the voice of Rossiter, an authority in it, a curious gentleness too, both of them new. He had risen, his lips were still moving, but the words that issued from them were inaudible, as the wind and rain leaped with a galloping violence into the room, smashing the glass to atoms and dashing a dozen loose objects helter-skelter on to the floor.

"I saw it!" cried Jim, in a voice that rose above the din and clamour of the elements. He turned and faced the others, but it was at Rossiter he looked. "I saw the leader." He shouted to make himself heard, although the tone was quiet. "A splash of white on his great chest. I saw them all!"

At the words, and at the expression in Jim's eyes, old Rossiter, white to the lips, dropped back into his chair as if a blow had struck him. Tom, petrified, felt his own heart stop. For through the broken window, above yet within the wind, came the sound of a wolf-pack running, howling in deep, full-throated chorus, mad for blood. It passed like a whirlwind and was gone. And, of the three men so close together, one sitting and two standing, Jim alone was in that terrible moment wholly master of himself.

Before the others could move or speak, he turned and looked full into the eyes of each in succession. His speech went back to his wilderness days:

"I done it," he said calmly. "I killed him—and I got ter go."

With a look of mystical horror on his face, he took one stride, flung the door wide, and vanished into the darkness.

So quick were both words and action, that Tom's paralysis passed only as the draught from the broken window banged the door behind him. He seemed to leap across the room, old Rossiter, tears on his cheeks and his lips mumbling foolish words, so close upon his heels that the backward blow of fury Tom aimed at his face caught him only in the neck and sent him reeling sideways to the floor instead of flat upon his back.

"Murderer! My brother's death upon you!" he shouted as he tore the door open again and plunged out into the night.

And the odd thing that happened then, the thing that touched old John Rossiter's reason, leaving him from that moment till his death a foolish man of uncertain mind and memory, happened when he and the unconscious, drink-sodden Sandy lay alone together on the stone floor of that farmhouse room.

Rossiter, dazed by the blow and his fall, but in full possession of his senses, and the anger gone out of him owing to what he had brought about, this same John Rossiter sat up and saw Sandy also sitting up and staring at him hard. And Sandy was sober as a judge, his eyes and speech both clear, even his face unflushed.

"John Rossiter," he said, "it was not God who appointed you executioner. It was the devil." And his eyes, thought Rossiter, were like the eyes of an angel.

"Sandy McKay," he stammered, his teeth chattering and breath failing him. "Sandy McKay!" It was all the words that he could find. But Sandy, already sunk back into his stupor again, was stretched drunk and incapable upon the farm-house floor, and remained in that condition till the dawn.

Jim's body lay hidden among the dunes for many months and in spite of the most careful and prolonged searching. It was another storm that laid it bare. The sand had covered it. The clothes were gone, and the flesh, torn but not eaten, was naked to the December sun and wind.

The Lost Valley

1

Mark and Stephen, twins, were remarkable even of their kind: they were not so much one soul split in twain, as two souls fashioned in precisely the same mould. Their characters were almost identical— tastes, hopes, fears, desires, everything. They even liked the same food, wore the same kind of hats, ties, suits; and, strongest link of all, of course disliked the same things too. At the age of thirty-five neither had married, for they invariably liked the same woman; and when a certain type of girl appeared upon their horizon, they talked it over frankly, agreed it was impossible to separate, and together turned their backs upon her for a change of scene before she could endanger their peace.

For their love for one another was unbounded—irresistible as a force of nature, tender beyond words— and their one keen terror was that they might one day be separated.

To look at, even for twins, they were uncommonly alike. Even their eyes were similar: that grey-green of the sea that sometimes changes to blue, and at night becomes charged with shadows. And both faces were of the same strong type with aquiline noses, stern-lipped mouths, and jaws well marked. They possessed imagination, real imagination of the winged kind, and at the same time the fine controlling will without which such a gift is apt to prove a source of weakness. Their emotions, too, were real and living: not the sort that merely tickle the surface of the heart, but the sort that plough.

Both had private means, yet both had studied medicine because it interested them, Mark specialising in diseases of eye and ear, Stephen in mental and nervous cases; and they carried on a select, even a distinguished, practice in the same house in Wimpole Street with their names, on the brass plate thus: Dr. Mark Winters, Dr. Stephen Winters.

In the summer of 1900, they went abroad together as usual for the months of July and August. It was their custom to explore successive ranges of mountains, collecting the folklore, and natural history of the region into small volumes, neatly illustrated with Stephen's photographs. And this particular year they chose the Jura, that portion of it, rather, that lies between the Lac de Joux, Baulmes and Fleurier. For, obviously, they could not exhaust a whole range in a single brief holiday. They explored it in sections, year by year. And they invariably chose for their headquarters, quiet, unfashionable places where there was less danger of meeting attractive people who might break in upon the happiness of their profound brotherly devotion—the incalculable, mystical devotion of twins.

"For abroad, you know," Mark would say, "people have an insinuating way with them that is often hard to withstand. The chilly English reserve disappears. Acquaintanceship becomes intimacy before one has time to weigh it."

"Exactly," Stephen added. "The conventions that protect one at home suddenly wear thin, don't they? And one becomes soft and open to attack—unexpected attack."

They looked up and laughed, reading each other's thoughts like trained telepathists. What each meant was the dread that one should, after all, be taken and the other left—by a woman.

"Though at our age, you know, one is almost immune," Mark observed; while Stephen smiling agreed philosophically

"Or *ought* to be."

"*Is*," quoth Mark decisively. For by common consent Mark played the role of the elder brother. His character, if anything, was a shade more practical. He was slightly more critical of life, perhaps, Stephen being ever more apt to accept without analysis, even without reflection. But Stephen had that richer heritage of dreams which comes from an imagination loved for its own sake.

2

In the peasant's chalet, where they had a sitting-room and two bedrooms, they were very comfortable. It stood on the edge of the forests that run along the slopes of Chasseront, on the side of Les Rasses farthest from Ste Croix. Marie Petavel provided them with the simple cooking they liked; and they spent their days walking, climbing, exploring, Mark collecting legend and folklore, Stephen making his natural history studies, with the little maps and surveys he drew so cleverly. Even this was only a division of labour, for each was equally interested in the occupation of the other; and they shared results in the long evenings, when expeditions brought them back in time, smoking in the rickety wooden balcony, comparing notes, shaping chapters, happy as two children. They brought the enthusiasm of boys to all they did, and they enjoyed the days apart almost as much as those they spent together. After separate expeditions each invariably returned with surprises which awakened the other's interest—even amazement.

Thus, the life of the foreign element in the hotels—unpicturesque in the daytime, noisy and overdressed at night—passed them by. The glimpses they caught as they passed these *caravansarais*, when gaieties were the order of the evening, made them value their peaceful retreat among the skirts of the forest. They brought no evening dress with them, not even "le smoking."

"The atmosphere of these huge hotels simply poisons the mountains," quoth Stephen. "All that 'haunted' feeling goes."

"Those people," agreed Mark, with scorn in his eyes, "would be far happier at Trouville or Dieppe, gambling, flirting, and the rest."

Feeling, thus, secure from that jealousy which lies so terribly close to the surface of all giant devotions where the entire life depends upon exclusive possession, the brothers regarded with indifference the signs of this gayer world about them. In that throng there was no one who could introduce an element of danger into their lives—no woman, at least, either of them could like would be found *there!*

For this thought must be emphasised, though not exaggerated. Certain incidents in the past, from which only their strength of will had made escape possible, proved the danger to be a real one. (Usually, too, it was some un-English woman: to wit, the Budapesth adventure, or the incident in London with the Greek girl who was first Mark's patient and then Stephen's.) Neither of them made definite reference to the danger, though undoubtedly it was present in their minds more or less vividly whenever they came to a new place: this singular dream that one day a woman would carry off one, and leave the other lonely. It was instinctive, probably, just as the dread of the wolf is instinctive in the deer.

The curious fact, though natural enough, was that each brother feared for the other and not for himself. Had anyone told Mark that someday he would marry, Mark would have shrugged his shoulders with a smile, and replied, "No; but I'm awfully afraid Stephen may!" And *vice versa*.

3

Then out of a clear sky the bolt fell—upon Stephen. Catching him utterly unawares it sent him fairly reeling. For Stephen even more than his brother, possessed that glorious yet fatal gift, common to poets and children, by which out of a few insignificant details the soul builds for itself a while sweet heaven to dwell in.

It was at the end of their first month, a month of unclouded happiness together. Since their exploration of the Abruzzi, two years before, they had never enjoyed anything so much. And not a soul had come to disturb their privacy. Plans were being mooted for moving their headquarters some miles farther towards the Val de Travers and the Creux du Van; only the day of departure, indeed, remained to be fixed, when Stephen, coming home from an afternoon of photography alone, saw, with bewildering and arresting suddenness—a Face. And with the effect of a blow full upon the heart it literally struck him.

How such a thing can come upon a strong man, a man of balanced mind, healthy in nerves and spirit, and in a single moment change serenity into a state of feverish and passionate desire for possession, is a mystery that lies too deep for philosophy or science to explain. It turned him dizzy with a sudden and tempestuous delight—a veritable sickness of the soul, wondrous sweet as it was deadly. Rare enough, of course, such instances may be, but that they happen is undeniable.

He was making his way home in the dusk somewhat wearily. The sun had already dipped below the horizon of France behind him. Across the open country that stretched away to the distant mountains of the Rhone Valley, the moonlight climbed with wings of ghostly radiance that fanned their way into the clefts and pinewoods of the Jura all about him. Cool airs of night stirred and whispered; lights twinkled through the openings among the trees, and all was scented like a garden.

He must have strayed considerably from the right trail—path there was none—for instead of striking the mountain road that led straight to his chalet, he suddenly emerged into a pool of electric light that shone round one of the smaller wooden hotels by the borders of the forest. He recognised it at once, because he and his brother always avoided it deliberately. Not so gay or crowded as the larger *caravansarais*, it was nevertheless full of people of the kind they did not care about. Stephen was a good half-mile out of his way.

When the mind is empty and the body tired it would seem that the system is sensitive to impressions with an acuteness impossible when these are vigorously employed. The face of this, girl, framed against the glass of the hotel verandah, rushed out towards him with a sudden invading glory, and took the most complete imaginable possession of this temporary unemployment of his spirit. Before he could think or act, accept or reject, it had lodged itself eternally at the very centre of his being. He stopped, as before an unexpected flash of lightning, caught his breath—and stared.

A little apart from the throng of "dressy" folk who sat there in the glitter of the electric light, this face of melancholy dark splendour rose close before his eyes, all soft and wondrous as though the beauty of the night—of forest, stars and moon-rise—had dropped down and focussed itself within the compass of a single human countenance. Framed within a corner pane of the big windows, peering sideways into the darkness, the vision of this girl, not twenty feet from where he stood, produced upon him a shock of the most convincing delight he had ever known. It was almost as though he saw someone who had dropped down among all these hotel people from another world.

And from another world, in a sense, she undoubtedly was; for her face held in it nothing that belonged to the European countries he knew. She was of the East. The magic of other suns swept into his soul with the vision; the pageantry of other skies flashed brilliantly and was gone. Torches flamed in recesses of his being hitherto dark.

The incongruous surroundings unquestionably deepened the contrast to her advantage, but what made this first sight of her so extraordinarily arresting was the curious chance that where she sat the glare of the electric light did not touch her. She was in shadow from the shoulders downwards. Only, as she leaned backwards against the window, the face and neck turned slightly, there fell upon her exquisite Eastern features the soft glory of the rising moon. And comely she was in Stephen's eyes as nothing in his life had hitherto seemed comely.

Apart from the vulgar throng as an exotic is apart from the weeds that choke its growth, this face seemed to swim towards him along the pathway of the slanting moonbeams. And, with it, came literally herself. Some released projection of his consciousness flew forth to meet her. The sense of nearness took his breath away with the faintness of too great happiness. She was in his arms, and his lips were buried in her scented hair. The sensation was vivid with pain and joy, as an ecstasy. And of the nature of true ecstasy, perhaps, it was: for he stood, it seemed, *outside himself.*

He remained there rivetted in the patch of moonlight at the forest edge, for perhaps a whole minute, perhaps two, before he realised what had happened. Then came a second shock, that was even more conquering than the first, for the girl, he saw, was not only gazing into his very face, she was also rising, as with an incipient gesture of recognition. As though she knew him, the little head bent itself forward gently, gracefully, and the dear eyes positively smiled.

The impetuous yearning that leaped full-fledged into his blood taught him in that instant the spiritual secret that pain and pleasure are fundamentally the same force. His attempt at self-control, made instinctively, was utterly overwhelmed. Something flashed to him from her eyes that melted the very roots of resolve; he staggered backwards, catching at the nearest tree for support, and in so doing left the patch of moonlight and stood concealed from view within the deep shadows behind.

Incredible as it must seem in these days of starved romance, this man of strength and firm character, who had hitherto known of such attacks only vicariously from the description of others, now reeled back against the trunk of a pine-tree, knowing all the sweet faintness of an overpowering love at first sight.

"For that, by God, I'd let myself waste utterly to death! To bring her an instant's happiness I'd suffer torture for a century!"

For the words, with their clumsy, concentrated passion, were out before he realised what he was saying, what he was doing; but, at once out, he knew how pitifully inadequate they were to express a tithe of what was in him like a rising storm. All words dropped away from him; the breath that came and went so quickly clothed no further speech.

With his retreat into the shadows the girl had sat down again, but she still gazed steadily at the place where he had stood. Stephen, who had lost the power of further movement, also stood and stared. The picture, meanwhile, was being traced with hot iron upon plastic deeps in his soul of which he had never before divined the existence. And, again, with the magic of this master-yearning, it seemed that he drew her out from that horde of hotel guests till she stood close before his eyes, warm, perfumed, caressing. The delicate, sharp splendour of her face, already dear beyond all else in life, flamed there within actual touch of his lips. He turned giddy with the joy, wonder and mystery of it all. The frontiers of his being melted—then extended to include her.

From the words a lover fights among to describe the face he worships one divines only a little of the picture; these dimly-coloured symbols conceal more beauty than they reveal. And of this dark, young oval face, first seen sideways in the moonlight, with drooping lids over the almond-shaped eyes, soft cloudy hair, all enwrapped with the haunting and penetrating mystery of love, Stephen never attempted to analyse the ineffable secret. He just accepted it with a plunge of utter self-abandonment. He only realised vaguely by way of detail that the little nose, without being Jewish, curved singularly down towards a chin daintily chiselled in firmness; that the mouth held in its lips the invitation of all womankind as expressed in another race, a race alien to his own—an Eastern race; and that something untamed, almost savage, in the face was corrected by the exquisite tenderness of the large dreamy, brown eyes. The mighty revolution of love spread its soft tide into every corner of his being.

Moreover, that gesture of welcome, so utterly unexpected yet so spontaneous (so natural, it seemed to him now!), the smile of recognition that had so deliciously perplexed him, he accepted in the same way. The girl had felt what he had felt, and had betrayed herself even as he had done by a sudden, uncontrollable movement of revelation and delight; and to explain it otherwise by any vulgar standard of worldly wisdom, would be to rob it of all its dear modesty, truth and wonder. She yearned to know him, even as he yearned to know her.

And all this in the little space, as men count time, of two minutes, even less.

How he was able at the moment to restrain all precipitate and impulsive action, Stephen has never properly understood. There was a fight, and it was short, painful and confused. But it ended on a note of triumphant joy—the rapture of happiness to come. . . .

With a great effort he remembers that he found the use of his feet and continued his journey homewards, passing out once more into the moonlight. The girl in the verandah followed his disappearing figure with her turning head; she craned her neck to watch till he disappeared beyond the angle of vision; she even waved her little dark hand.

"I shall be late," ran the thought sharply through Stephen's mind. It was cold; vivid with keen pain. "Mark will wonder what in the world has become of me—!"

For, with swift and terrible reaction, the meaning of it all—the possible consequences of The Face—swept over his heart and drowned it in a flood of icy water. In estimating his brotherly love, even the love of the twin, he had never conceived such a thing as this—had never reckoned with the possibility of a force that could make all else in the world seem so trivial. . . .

Mark, had he been there, with his more critical attitude to life, might have analysed something of it away. But Mark was not there. And Stephen had—*seen*.

Those mighty strings of life upon which, as upon an instrument, the heart of man lies stretched had been set powerfully a-quiver. The new vibrations poured and beat through him. Something within him swiftly disintegrated; in its place something else grew marvellously. The Face had established dominion over the secret places of his soul; thenceforward the process was automatic and inevitable.

4

Then, spectre-like and cold, the image of his brother rose before his inner vision. The profound brotherly love of the twin confronted him in the path.

He stumbled among the roots and stones, searching, for the means of self-control, but finding them with difficulty. Windows had opened everywhere in his soul; he looked out through them upon a new world, immense and gloriously coloured. Behind him in the shadows, as his vision searched and his heart sang, reared the single thought that hitherto had dominated his life: his love for Mark. It had already grown indisputably dim.

For both passions were genuine and commanding, the one built up through thirty-five years of devotion cemented by ten thousand associations and sacrifices, the other dropping out of heaven upon him with a suddenness simply appalling.

And from the very first instant he understood that both could not live. One must die to feed the other. . . .

On the staircase was the perfume of a strange tobacco, and, to his surprise and intense relief, when he entered the chalet, he found that his brother for the first time was not alone. A small, dark man stood talking earnestly with him by the open window—the window where Mark had obviously been watching with anxiety for his arrival. Before introducing him to the stranger, Mark at once gave expression to his relief.

"I was beginning to be afraid something had happened to you," he said quietly enough, but in a way that the other understood. And after a moment's pause, in which he searched Stephen's face keenly, he added, "but we didn't wait supper as you see, and old Petavel has kept yours all hot and ready for you in the kitchen."

"I—er—lost my way," Stephen said quickly, glancing from Mark to

68

the stranger, wondering vaguely who he was. "I got confused some-how in the dusk—"

Mark, remembering his manners now that his anxiety was set at rest, hastened to introduce him—a Professor in a Russian University, interested in folklore and legend, who had read their book on the Abruzzi and discovered quite by chance that they were neighbours here in the forest. He was staying in a little hotel at Les Rosses, and had ventured to come up and introduce himself. Stephen was far too occupied trying to conceal his new battling emotions to notice that Mark and the stranger seemed on quite familiar terms. He was so fear-ful lest the perturbations of his own heart should betray him that he had no power to detect anything subtle or unusual in anybody else.

"Professor Samarianz comes originally from Tiflis," Mark was ex-plaining, and has been telling me the most fascinating things about the legends and folklore of the Caucasus. We really must go there another year, Stephen. . . . Mr. Samarianz most kindly has promised me letters to helpful people. ... He tells me, too, of a charming and exquisite legend of a 'Lost Valley' that exists hereabouts, where the spirits of all who die by their own hands, or otherwise suffer violent deaths, find perpetual peace—the peace denied them by all the religions, that is. . .

Mark went on talking for some minutes while Stephen took off his knapsack and exchanged a few words with their visitor, who spoke excellent English. He was not quite sure what he said, but hoped he talked quietly and sensibly enough, in spite of the passions that waged war so terrifically in his breast. He noticed, however, that the man's face held an unusual charm, though he could not detect wherein its secret specifically lay. Presently, with excuses of hunger, he went into the kitchen for his supper, hugely relieved to find the opportunity to collect his thoughts a little; and when he returned twenty minutes later, he found that his brother was alone. Professor Samarianz had taken his leave. In the room still lingered the perfume of his peculiarly flavoured cigarettes.

Mark, after listening with half an ear to his brother's description of the day, began pouring out his new interest; he was full of the Cau-casus, and its folklore, and of the fortunate chance that had brought the stranger their way. The legend of the "Lost Valley" in the Jura, too, particularly interested him, and he spoke of his astonishment that he had hitherto come across no trace anywhere of the story.

"And fancy," he exclaimed, after a recital that lasted half-an-hour, "the man came up from one of those little hotels on the edge of the forest—that noisy one we have always been so careful to avoid. You never know where your luck hides, do you?" he added, with a laugh.

"You never do, indeed," replied Stephen quietly, now wholly master of himself, or, at least, of his voice and eyes.

And, to his secret satisfaction and delight, it was Mark who provided the excuses for staying on in the chalet, instead of moving further down the valley as they had intended. Besides, it would have been unnatural and absurd to leave without investigating so picturesque a legend as the "Lost Valley."

"We're uncommonly happy here," Mark added quietly; "why not stay on a bit?"

"Why not, indeed?" answered Stephen, trusting that the fearful inner storm instantly roused again by the prospect did not betray itself.

"You're not very keen, perhaps, old fellow?" suggested Mark gently.

"On the contrary—I am, *very*," was the reply.

"Good. Then we'll stay."

The words were spoken after a pause of some seconds. Stephen, who was down at the end of the room sorting his specimens by the lamp, looked up sharply. Mark's face, where he sat on the window-ledge in the dusk, was hardly visible. It must have been something in his voice that had shot into Stephen's heart with a flash of sudden warning.

A sensation of cold passed swiftly over him and was gone. Had he already betrayed himself? Was the subtle, almost telepathic sympathy between the twins developed to such a point that emotions could be thus transferred with the minimum of word or gesture, within the very shades of their silence even? And another thought: Was there something different in Mark to—something in him also that had changed? Or was it merely his own raging, heaving passion, though so sternly repressed, that distorted his judgment and made him imaginative?

What stood so darkly in the room—between them?

A sudden and fearful pain seared him inwardly as he realised, practically, and with cruelly acute comprehension, that one of these two loves in his heart must inevitably die to feed the other; and that it might have to be—Mark. The complete meaning of it came home to him. And at the thought all his deep love of thirty years rose in a tide within him, flooding through the gates of life, seeking to overwhelm and merge in itself all obstacles that threatened to turn it aside. Unshed tears burned behind his eyes. He ached with a degree of actual, physical pain.

70

After a moment of savage self-control he turned and crossed the room: but before he had covered half the distance that separated him from the window where his brother sat smoking, the rush of burning words—were they to have been of confession, of self-reproach, or of renewed devotion?—swept away from him, so that he wholly forgot them. In their place came the ordinary dead phrases of convention. He hardly heard them himself, though his lips uttered them.

"Come along, Mark, old chap," he said, conscious that his voice trembled, and that another face slipped imperiously in front of the one his eyes looked upon; it's time to go to bed. I'm dead tired like yourself."

"You are right," Mark replied, looking at him steadily as he turned towards the lamplight. "Besides, the night air's getting chilly—and we've been sitting in a draught, you know, all along."

For the first time in their lives the eyes of the two brothers could not quite find each other. Neither gaze hit precisely the middle of the other. It was as though a veil hung down between them and a deliberate act of focus was necessary. They looked one another straight in the face as usual, but with an effort—with momentary difficulty. The room, too, as Mark had said, was cold, and the lamp, exhausted of its oil, was beginning to smell. Both light and heat were going. It was certainly time for bed.

The brothers went out together, arm in arm, and the long shadows of the pines, thrown by the rising moon through the window, fell across the floor like arms that waved. And from the black branches outside, the wind caught up a shower of sighs and dropped them about the roofs and walls as they made their way to their bedrooms on opposite sides of the little corridor.

Four hours later, when the moon was high overhead and the room held but a single big shadow, the door opened softly and in came— Stephen. He was dressed. He crossed the floor stealthily, unfastened the windows, and let himself out upon the balcony. A minute afterwards he had disappeared into the forest beyond the strip of vegetable garden at the back of the chalet.

It was two o'clock in the morning, and no sleep had touched his eyes. For his heart burned, ached, and fought within him, and he felt the need of open spaces and the great forces of the night and mountains. No such battle had he ever known before. He remembered his brother saying years ago, with a laugh half serious, half playful, ". . . . for if ever one of us comes a cropper in love, old fellow, it will be time

71

for the other to—go!" And by "go" they both understood the ultimate meaning of the word.

Through the glades of forest, sweet-scented by the night, he made his way till he reached the spot where that Face of soft splendour had first blessed his soul with its mysterious glory. There he sat down and, with his back against the very tree that had supported him a few hours ago, he drove his thoughts forward into battle with the whole strength of his will and character behind him.

Very quietly, and with all the care, precision and steadiness of mind that he would have brought to bear upon a difficult "case" at Wimpole Street, he faced the situation and wrestled with it. The emotions during four hours' tossing upon a sleepless bed had worn themselves out a little. He was, in one sense of the word, calm, master of himself. The facts, with the huge issue that lay in their hands, he saw naked. And, as he thus saw them, he discerned how very, very far he had already travelled down the sweet path that led him towards the girl—and away from his brother.

Details about her, of course, he knew none; whether she was free even; for he only knew that he loved, and that his entire life was already breaking with the yearning to sacrifice itself for that love. That was the naked fact. The problem bludgeoned him. Could he do anything to hold back the flood still rising, to arrest its terrific flow? Could he divert its torrent, and take it, girl and all, to offer upon the altar of that other love—the devotion of the twin for its twin, the mysterious affinity that hitherto had ruled and directed all the currents of his soul?

There was no question of undoing what had already been done. Even if he never saw that face again, or heard the accents of those beloved lips; if he never was to know the magic of touch, the perfume of close thought, or the strange blessedness of telling her his burning message and hearing the murmur of her own—the fact of love was already accomplished between them. That was ineradicable. He had seen. The sensitive plate had received its undying picture.

For this was no foolish passion arising from the mere propinquity that causes so many of the world's misfit marriages. It was a profound and mystical union already accomplished, psychical in the utter sense, inevitable as the marriage of wind and fire. He almost heard his soul laugh as he thought of the revolution effected in an instant of time by the message of a single glance. What had science, or his own special department of science, to say to this tempest of force that invaded him, and swept with its beautiful terrors of wind and lightning the furthest recesses of his being? This whirlwind that so shook him, that so deliciously wounded him, that already made the thought of sacrificing his brother seem sweet—what was there to say to it, or do with it, or think of it?

Nothing, nothing, nothing! . . . He could only lie in its arms and rest, with that peace, deeper than all else in life, which the mystic knows when he is conscious that the everlasting arms are about him and that his union with the greatest force of the world is accomplished.

Yet Stephen struggled like a lion. His will rose up and opposed, itself to the whole invasion . . . and in the end his will of steel, trained as all men of character train their wills against the difficulties of life, did actually produce a certain, definite result. This result was almost a *tour de force*, perhaps, yet it seemed valid. By its aid Stephen forced himself into a position he felt intuitively was an impossible one, but in which nevertheless he determined, by a deliberate act of almost incredible volition, that he would remain fixed. He decided to conquer his obsession, and to remain true to Mark. . . .

The distant ridges of the dim blue Jura were tipped with the splendours of the coming dawn when at length he rose, chilly and exhausted, to retrace his steps to the chalet.

He realised fully the meaning of the resolve he had come to. And the knowledge of it froze something within him into a stiffness that was like the stiffness of death. The pain in his heart battling against the resolution was atrocious. He had estimated, or thought so, at least, the meaning of his sacrifice. As a matter of fact, his decision was entirely artificial, of course, and his resolve dictated by a moral code rather than by the living forces that direct life and can alone make its changes permanent. Stephen had in him the stuff of the hero; and, having said that, one has said all that language can say.

On the way home in the cool white dawn, as he crossed the open spaces of meadow where the mist rose and the dew lay like rain, he suddenly thought of her lying dead—dead, that is, as he had thus decided she was to be dead—for him. And instantly, as by a word of command, the entire light went out of the landscape and out of the world. His soul turned wintry, and all the sweetness of his life went bleak. For it was the ancient soul in him that loved, and to deny it was to deny life itself. He had pronounced upon himself a sentence of death by starvation—a lingering and prolonged death accompanied by tortures of the most exquisite description. And along this path he really believed at the moment his little human will could hold him firm.

He made his way through the dew-drenched grass with the elation caused by so vast a sacrifice singing curiously in his blood. The splendour of the mountain sunrise and all the vital freshness of the dawn was in his heart. He was upon the chalet almost before he knew it, and there on the balcony, waiting to receive him, his grey dressing-gown wrapped about his ears in the sharp air, stood—Mark!

And, somehow or other, at the sight, all this false elation passed and dropped. Stephen looked up at him, standing suddenly still there in his tracks, as he might have looked up at his executioner. The picture had restored him most abruptly, with sharpest pain, to reality again.

"Like me, you couldn't sleep, eh?" Mark called softly, so as not to waken the peasants who slept on the ground floor.

"Have you been lying awake, too?" Stephen replied.

"All night. I haven't closed an eye." Then Mark added, as his brother came up the wooden steps towards him, "I knew you were awake. I felt it. I knew, too—you had gone out."

A silence passed between them. Both had spoken quietly, naturally, neither expressing surprise.

"Yes," Stephen said slowly at length; "we always reflect each other's pai—each other's moods—" He stopped abruptly, leaving the sentence unfinished.

Their eyes met as of old. Stephen knew an instant of quite freezing terror in which he felt that his brother had divined the truth. Then Mark took his arm and led the way indoors on tiptoe.

"Look here, Stevie, old fellow," he said, with extraordinary tenderness, "there's no good saying anything, but I know perfectly well that you're unhappy about something; and so, of course, I am unhappy too." He paused, as though searching for words. Under ordinary circumstances Stephen would have caught his precise thought, but now the tumult of suppressed emotion in him clouded his divining power. He felt his arm clutched in a sudden vice. They drew closer to one another. Neither spoke. Then Mark, low and hurriedly, said—he almost mumbled it—"It's all my fault really, all my fault—dear old boy!"

Stephen turned in amazement and stared. What in the world did his brother mean? What was he talking about? Before he could find speech, however, Mark continued, speaking distinctly now, and with evidences of strong emotion in his voice—

"I'll tell you what we'll do," he exclaimed, with sudden decision;

"we'll go away; we'll leave! We've stayed here a bit too long, perhaps. Eh? What d'you say to that?"

Stephen did not notice how sharply Mark searched his face. At the thought of separation all his mighty resolution dropped like a house of cards. His entire life seemed to melt away and run in a stream of impetuous yearning towards the Face.

But he answered quietly, sustaining his purpose artificially by a force of will that seemed to break and twist his life at the source with extraordinary pain. He could not have endured the strain for more than a few seconds. His voice sounded strange and distant.

"All right; at the end of the week," he said—the faintness in him was dreadful, filling him with cold—"and that'll give us just three days to make our plans, won't it?"

Mark nodded his head. Both faces were lined and drawn like the faces of old men; only there was no one there to remark upon it—nor upon the fixed sternness that had dropped so suddenly upon their eyes and lips.

Arm in arm they entered the chalet and went to their bedrooms without another word. The sun, as they went, rose close over the tree-tops and dropped its first rays upon the spot where they had just stood.

6

They came down in dressing-gowns to a very late breakfast. They were quiet, grave and slightly preoccupied. Neither made the least reference to their meeting at sunrise. New lines had graved themselves upon their faces, identical lines it seemed, drawing the mouth down at the corners with a touch of grimness where hitherto had been merely firmness.

And the eyes of both saw new things, new distances, new terrors. Something, feared till now only as a possibility, had come close, and stood at their elbows for the first time as an actuality. Sleep, in which changes offered to the soul during the day are confirmed and ratified, had established this new element in their personal equation. They had changed— if not towards one another, then towards something else.

But Stephen saw the matter only from his own point of view. For the first time in his memory, he seemed to have lost the intuitive sympathy which enabled him to see things from his brother's point of view as well. The change, he felt positive, was in himself, not in Mark.

"He knows—he feels—something in me has altered dreadfully, but he doesn't yet understand what," his thoughts ran. "Pray to God he need never know—at least until I have utterly conquered it!"

For he still held with all the native tenacity of his strong will to the course he had so heroically chosen. The degree of self-deception his imagination brought into the contest seemed incredible when his mind looked back upon it all from the calmness of the end. But at the time he genuinely hoped, wished, intended to conquer, even *believed* that he would conquer.

Mark, he noticed, reacted in little ways that curiously betrayed his mental perturbation, and at any other time might have roused his brother's suspicions. He put sugar in Stephen's coffee, for instance; he forgot to bring him a cigarette when he went to the cupboard to get one for himself; he said and did numerous little things that were contrary to his habits, or to the habits of his twin.

In all of which, however, Stephen saw only the brotherly reaction to the change he was conscious of in himself. Nothing happened to convince him that anything in Mark had suffered revolution. With the mystical devotion peculiar to the twin, he was too keenly aware of his own falling away to imagine the falling away of the other. He, Stephen, was the guilty one, and he suffered atrociously.

Moreover, the pain of his renunciation was heightened by the sense that his ideal love for Mark had undergone a change—that he was making this fatal sacrifice, therefore, for something that perhaps no longer existed. This, however, he did not realise yet as an accomplished fact. Even if it were true, the resolution he had come to, acted by way of hypnotic suggestion to conceal it. At the same time, it added enormously to the confusion and perplexity of his mind.

That day for the brothers was practically a *dies non*. They spent what was left of the morning over many aimless and unnecessary little duties, somewhat after the way of women. Although neither referred to the decision to leave at the end of the week, both acted upon it in desultory fashion, almost as though they wished to make a point of proving to one another that it was *not* forgotten—not wholly forgotten, at any rate. They made a brave pretence of collecting various things with a view to ultimate packing. No word was spoken, however, that bore more closely upon it than occasional phrases such as, "When the time comes to go"—"when we leave "—"better put *that* out, or it will be forgotten, you know."

The sentences dropped from their mouths alternately at long intervals, the only one deceived being the utterer. It was not unlike the pretence of schoolboys, only more elaborate and infinitely more clumsy and ill-done. Stephen, at any other time, would probably have laughed aloud. Yet the curious thing was that he noticed the pretence only in his own case. Mark, he thought, was genuine, though perhaps not too eager. "He's agreed to leave, the dear old chap, because he thinks I want it, and not for himself," he said. And the idea of the small brotherly sacrifice pleased, yet pained him horribly at the same time. For it tended to rehabilitate the old love which stood in the way of the new one.

He began, however, to take less trouble to sort and find his things for packing; he wrote letters, put out photographs to print in the sun, even studied his maps for expeditions, making occasional remarks thereon aloud which Mark did not negative. Presently, he forgot altogether about packing. Mark said nothing. Mark followed his example, however.

During the afternoon both lay down and slept, meeting again for tea at five. It was rare that they found themselves in for tea. Mark today made a special little ritual of it; he made it over their own spirit-lamp—almost tenderly, looking after his brother's wants like a woman. And the little meal was hardly over when a boy in hotel livery arrived with a note—an invitation from Professor Samarianz.

"He has looked up a lot of his papers," observed Mark carelessly as he tossed the note down, "and suggests my coming in for dinner, so that he can show me everything afterwards without hurry."

"I should accept," said Stephen. "It might be valuable for us if we go to the Caucasus later."

Mark hesitated a minute or two, telling the boy to wait in the kitchen. "I think I'll go in *after* dinner instead," he decided presently. There was a trace of eagerness in his manner which Stephen, however, did not notice.

"Take your note-book and pump the old boy dry," Stephen added, with a slight laugh. "I shall go to bed early myself probably." And Mark, stuffing the note into his pocket, laughed back and consented, to the other's great relief.

It was very late when Mark returned from the visit, but his brother did not hear him come, having taken a draught to ensure sleeping. And next morning Mark was so full of the interesting information he had collected, and would continue to collect, that the question of leaving at the end of the week dropped of its own accord without further ado. Neither of the brothers made the least pretence of packing. Both wished and intended to stay on where they were.

"I shall look up Samarianz again this afternoon," Mark said casually during the morning, "and—if you've no objection—I might bring him back to supper. He's the most obliging fellow I've ever met, and crammed with information."

Stephen, signifying his agreement, took his camera, his specimen-tin and his geological hammer and went out with bread and chocolate in his knapsack for the rest of the afternoon by himself.

7

Moreover, he not only set out bravely, but for many hours held true, keeping so rigid a control over his feelings that it seemed literally to cost him blood. All the time, however, a passionate yearning most craftily attacked him, and the very memory he strove to smother rose with a persistence that ridiculed repression. Like snowflakes, whose individual weight is inappreciable but their cumulative burden irresistible, the thoughts of her gathered behind his spirit, ready at a given moment to overwhelm; and it was on the way home again in the evening that the temptation came upon him like a tidal wave that made the mere idea of resistance seem utterly absurd.

He remembered wondering with a kind of wild delight whether it could be possible for any human will to withstand such a tempest of pressure as that which took him by the shoulders and literally pushed him out of his course towards the little hotel on the edge of the forest.

It was utterly inconsistent, of course, and he made no pretence of argument or excuse. He hardly knew, indeed, what he expected to see or do; his mind, at least, framed no definite idea. But far within him that deep heart which refused to be stifled cried out for a drop of the living water that was now its very life. And, chiefly, he wanted to see.

If only he could see her once again—even from a distance—the merest glimpse! With one more sight of her that should charge his memory to the brim for life he might face the future with more courage perhaps. Ah! that *perhaps!* . . . For she was drawing him with those million invisible cords of love that persuade a man he is acting of his own volition when actually he is but obeying the inevitable forces that bind the planets and the suns.

And this time there was no hurry; there was a good hour before Mark would expect him home for supper; he could sit among the shadows of the wood, and wait.

In his pocket were the field-glasses, and he realised with a sudden secret shame that it was not by accident that they were there.

78

He stumbled, even before he got within a quarter of a mile of the place, for the idea that perhaps he would see her again made him ridiculously happy, and like a schoolboy he positively trembled, tripping over roots and misjudging the distance of his steps. It was all part of a great whirling dream in which his soul sang and shouted the first delirious nonsense that came into his head. The possibility of his eyes again meeting hers produced a sensation of triumph and exultation that only one word describes—intoxication.

As he approached the opening in the trees whence the hotel was so easily visible, he went more slowly, moving even on tiptoe. It was instinctive; for he was nearing a place made holy by his love. Picking his way almost stealthily, he found the very tree; then leaned against it while his eyes searched eagerly for a sign of her in the glass verandah. The swiftness and accuracy of sight at such a time may be cause for wonder, but it is beyond question that in less than a single second he knew that the throng of moving figures did not contain the one he sought. She was not among them.

And he was just preparing to make himself comfortable for an extended watch when a sound or movement, perhaps both, somewhere among, the trees on his right attracted his attention. There was a faint rustling; a twig snapped.

Stephen turned sharply. Under a big spruce, not half-a-dozen yards away, something moved—then rose up. At first, owing to the gloom, he took it for an animal of some kind, but the same second saw that it was a human figure. It was two human figures, standing close together. Then one moved apart from the other; he saw the outline of a man against a space of sky between the trees. And a voice spoke—a voice charged with great tenderness, yet driven by high passion——

"But it's nothing, nothing! I shall not be gone two minutes. And to save you an instant's discomfort you know that I would run the whole circle of the earth! Wait here for me!"

That was all; but the voice and figure caused Stephen's heart to stop beating as though it had been suddenly plunged into ice, for they were the voice and the figure of his brother Mark.

Quickly running down the slope towards the hotel, Mark disappeared.

The other figure, leaning against the tree, was the figure of a girl; and Stephen, even in that first instant of fearful bewilderment, understood why it was that the face of the man Samarianz had so charmed him. For this, of course, was his daughter. And then the whole thing flashed mercilessly clear upon his inner vision, and he knew that Mark, too, had been swept from his feet, and was undergoing the same fierce tortures, and fighting the same dread battle, as himself. . . .

There seemed to be no conscious act of recognition. The fire that flamed through him and set his frozen heart so fearfully beating again, hammering against his ribs, left him apparently without volition or any power of cerebral action at all. *She* stood there, not half-a-dozen yards away from where he sat all huddled upon the ground, stood there in all her beauty, her mystery, her wonder, near enough for him to have taken her almost with a single leap into his arms;—stood there, veiled a little by the shadows of the dusk—waiting for the return of—Mark!

He remembers what happened with the blurred indistinctness common to moments of overwhelming passion. For in the next few seconds, that mocked all scale of time, he lived through a series of concentrated emotions that burned his brain too vividly for precise recollection. He rose to his feet unsteadily, his hand upon the rough bark of the tree. Absurd details only seem to remain of these few moments: that a foot was "asleep" with pins and needles up to the knee, and that his slouch hat fell from his head, filling him with fury because it hid her from him for the fraction of a second. These odd details he remembers.

And then, as though the driving-power of the universe had deliberately pushed him from behind, he was advancing slowly, with short, broken steps, towards the tree where the girl stood with her back half turned against him.

He did not know her name, had never heard her voice, had never even stood close enough to "feel" her atmosphere; yet, so deeply had his love and imagination already prepared the little paths of intimacy within him, that he felt he was moving towards someone whom he had known ever since he could remember, and who belonged to him as utterly as if from the beginning of time his possession of her had been absolute. Had they shared together a whole series of previous lives, the sensation could not have been more convincing and complete.

And out of all this whirlwind and tumult two small actions, he remembers, were delivered: a confused cry that was no definite word came from his lips, and—he opened his arms to take her to his heart. Whereupon, of course, she turned with a quick start, and became for the first time aware of his near presence.

"Oh, oh! But how so softly quick you return!" she cried falteringly, looking into his eyes with a smile both of welcome and alarm. "You a little frightened me, I tell you."

It was just the voice he had known would come, with the curiously slow, dragging tone of its broken English, the words lingering against the lips as if loath to leave, the soft warmth of their sound in the throat like a caress. The next instant he held her smothered in his arms, his face buried in the scented hair about her neck.

There was an unbelievable time of forgetfulness in which touch, perfume, and a healing power that emanated from her blessed the depths of his soul with a peace that calmed all pain, stilled all tumult— a moment in which Time itself for once stopped its remorseless journey, and the very processes of life stood still to watch. Then there was a frightened cry, and she had pushed him from her. She stood there, her soft eyes puzzled and surprised, looking hard at him; panting a little, her breast heaving.

And Stephen understood then, if he had not already understood before. The gesture of recognition in the hotel verandah two days ago, and this glorious realisation of it that now seemed to have happened a century ago, shared a common origin. They were intended for another, and on both occasions the girl had taken him for his brother Mark.

And, turning sharply, almost falling with the abruptness of it all, as the girl's lips uttered that sudden cry, he saw close beside them the very person for whom they were intended. Mark had come up the slope behind them unobserved, carrying upon his arm the little red cloak he had been to fetch.

It was as though a wind of ice had struck him in the face. The revulsion of feeling with which Stephen saw the return of his brother passed rapidly into a state of numbness where all emotion whatsoever ebbed like the tides of death. He lost momentarily the power of realisation. He forgot who he was, what he was doing there. He was dazed by the fact that Mark had so completely forestalled him. His life shook and tottered upon its foundations. . . .

Then the face and figure of his brother swayed before his eyes like the branch of a tree, as an attack of passing dizziness seized him. It may have been a mere hazard that led his fingers to close, moist and clammy, upon the geological hammer at his belt. Certainly, he let it go again almost at once. . . . And, when the tide of emotion returned upon him with the dreadful momentum it had gathered during the interval, the possibility of his yielding to wild impulse and doing something mad or criminal, was obviated by the swift enactment of an exceedingly poignant little drama that made both brothers forget themselves in their desire to save the girl.

In sweetest bewilderment, like a frightened little child or animal, the girl looked from one brother to the other. Her eyes shone in the dusk. Strangely appealing her loveliness was in that moment of seeking some explanation of the double vision. She made a movement first towards Mark—turned halfway in her steps, and ran, startled, upon Stephen—then, with a sharp scream of fear, dropped in a heap to the ground midway between the two.

Her indecision of half-a-second, however, seemed to Stephen to have lasted many minutes. Had she fallen finally into the arms of his brother, he felt nothing on earth could have prevented his leaping upon him with the hands of a murderer. As it was—mercifully—the singular beauty of her little Eastern face, touched as it was by the white terror of her soul, momentarily arrested all other feeling in him. A shudder of fearful admiration passed through him as he saw her sway and fall. Thus might have dropped some soft angel from the skies. . . .

It was Mark, however, with his usual decision, who brought some possibility of focus back to his mind; and he did it with an action and a sentence so utterly unexpected, so incongruous amid this whirlwind of passion, that had he seen it on the stage or read it in a novel, he must surely have burst out laughing. For, in that very second after the dear form swayed and fell, while the eyes of the brothers met across her in one swift look that held the possibilities of the direst results, Mark, his face abruptly clearing to calmness, stooped down beside the prostrate girl, and, looking up at Stephen steadily, said in a gentle voice, but with his most deliberate professional manner—

"Stephen, old fellow, this is—*my* patient. One of us, perhaps, had better—go."

He bent down to loosen the dress at the throat and chafe the cold hands, and Stephen, uncertain exactly what he did, and trembling like a child, turned and disappeared among the thick trees in the direction of their little house. For he understood only one thing clearly in that awful moment: that he must either kill—or not see. And his will, well-nigh breaking beneath the pressure, was just able to take the latter course.

"*Go!*" it said peremptorily.

And the little word sounded through the depths of his soul like the tolling of a last bell.

8

"*This is my patient!*" The dreadful comedy of the phrase, the grim mockery of the professional manner, the contrast between the words that someone *ought* to have uttered and the words Mark actually *had* uttered—all this had the effect of restoring Stephen to some measure of sanity. No one but his brother, he felt, could have said the thing so exactly calculated to relieve the choking passion of the situation. It was an inspiration—yet horrible in its bizarre mingling of true and false.

"But it's all like a thing in a dream," he heard an inner voice murmur as he stumbled homewards without once looking back; "the kind of thing people say and do in the rooms of strange sleep-houses. We are all surely in a dream, and presently I shall wake up—!"

The voice continued talking, but he did not listen. A web of confusion began to spin itself about his thoughts, and there stole over him an odd sensation of remoteness from the actual things of life. It was surely one of those vivid, haunting dreams he sometimes had when his spirit seemed to take part in real scenes, with real people, only far, far away, and on quite another scale of time and values.

"I shall find myself in my bed at Wimpole Street!" he exclaimed. He even tried to escape from the pain closing about him like a vice—tried to escape by waking up, only to find, of course, that the effort drove him more closely to the reality of his position.

Yet the texture of a dream certainly ran through the whole thing; the outlandish proportions of dream-events showed themselves everywhere; the tiny causes and prodigious effects: the terrific power of the Face upon his soul; the uncanny semi-quenching of his love for Mark; the ridiculous way he had come upon these two in the forest, with the nightmare discovery that they had known one another for days; and then the sight of that dear, magical face dropping through the dusky forest air between the two of them.

Moreover—just when the dream ought to have ended with his sudden awakening, it had taken this abrupt and inconsequent turn, and Mark had uttered the language of—well, the impossible and rather horrible language of the nightmare world

"*This is my patient. . . .*"

Moreover, his face of ice as he said it; yet, at the same time, the wisdom, the gentleness of the decision that lay behind the words: the

83

desire to relieve an impossibly painful situation. And then—the other words, meant kindly, even meant nobly, but charged for all that with the naked cruelty of life—

"*One of us, perhaps, had better—go.*"

And he had gone—fortunately, he had gone. . . .

Yet an hour later, after lying motionless upon his bed seeking with all his power for a course of action his will could follow and his mind approve, it was no dream-voice that called softly to him through the keyhole—

"Stevie, old fellow . . . she is well . . . she is all right now. She leaves in the morning with her father . . . the first thing . . . very early. . . ."

And then, after a pause in which Stephen said nothing lest he should at the same time say all—

". . . and it is best, perhaps . . . we should not see one another . . . you and I . . . for a bit. Let us go our ways . . . till tomorrow night. Then we shall be . . . alone together again . . . you and I . . . as of old. . . ."

The voice of Mark did not tremble; but it sounded far away and unreal, almost like wind in the keyhole, thin, reedy, sighing; oddly broken and interrupted.

". . . I'm yours, Stevie, old fellow, always yours," it added far down the corridor, more like the voice of dream again than ever.

But, though he made no reply at the moment, Stephen welcomed and approved both the proposal and the spirit in which it was made; and next day, soon after sunrise, he left the chalet very quietly and went off alone into the mountains with his thoughts, and with the pain that all night long had simply been eating him alive.

9

It is impossible to know precisely what he felt all that morning in the mountains His emotions charged like wild bulls to and fro. He seemed conscious only of two master-feelings: first, that his life now belonged beyond possibility of change or control—to another; yet, secondly, that his will, tried and tempered weapon of steel that it was, held firm.

Thus, his powerful feelings flung him from one wall of his dreadful prison to another without possible means of escape. For his position involved a fundamental contradiction: the new love owned him, yet his will cried, "I love Mark; I hold true to that; in the end I shall conquer!" He refused, that is, to capitulate, or rather to acknowledge that he had capitulated. And meanwhile, even while he cried, his inmost soul listened, watched, and laughed, well content to abide the issue.

But if his feelings were in too great commotion for clear analysis, his thoughts, on the other hand, were painfully definite—some of them, at least; and, as the physical exercise lessened the assaults of emotion, these stood forth in sharp relief against the confusion of his inner world. It was now clear as the day, for instance, that Mark had been through a battle similar to his own. The chance meeting with the Professor had led to the acquaintance with his daughter. Then, swiftly and inevitably, just as it would have happened to Stephen in his place, love had accomplished its full magic. And Mark had been afraid to tell him. The twins had travelled the same path, only personal feeling having clouded their usual intuition, neither had divined the truth.

Stephen saw it now with pitiless clarity: his brother's frequent visits to the hotel, omitting to mention that the notes of invitation probably also included himself; the desire, nay, the intention to stay on; the delay in packing—and a dozen other details stood out clearly. He remembered, too, with a pang how Mark had not slept that memorable night; he recalled their enigmatical conversation on the balcony as the sun rose . . . . and all the rest of the miserable puzzle.

And, as he realised from his own torments what Mark must also have suffered—be suffering now—he was conscious of a strengthening of his will to conquer. The thought linked him fiercely again to his twin; for nothing in their lives had yet been separate, and the chain of their spiritual intimacy was of incalculably vast strength. They would win—win back to one another's side again. Mark would conquer her. He, Stephen, would also in the end conquer . . . her . . .!

But with the thought of her lying thus dead to him, and his life cold and empty without her, came the inevitable revulsion of feeling. It was the anarchy of love. The Face, the perfume, the rushing power of her melancholy dear eyes, with their singular touch of proud languor—in a word, all the amazing magic that had swept himself and Mark from their feet, tore back upon him with such an invasion of entreaty and command, that he sat down upon the very rocks where he was and buried his face in his hands, literally groaning with the pain of it. For the thought lacerated within.

To give her up was a sheer impossibility; . . . to give up his brother was equally inconceivable. The weight of thirty-five years' love and associations thus gave battle against the telling blow of a single moment. Behind the first lay all that life had built into the woof of his personality hitherto, but *beyond* the second lay the potent magic, the huge seductive invitation of what he might become in the future—with her.

The contest, in the nature of the forces engaged, was an unequal one. Yet all that morning as he wandered aimlessly over ridge and summit, and across the high Jura pastures above the forests, meeting no single human being, he fought with himself as only men with innate energy of soul know how to fight—bitterly, savagely, blindly. He did not stop to realise that he was somewhat in the position of a fly that strives to push from its appointed course the planet on which it rides through space. For the tides of life itself bore him upon their crest, and at thirty-five these tides are at the full.

Thus, gradually it was, then, as the hopelessness of the struggle became more and more apparent, that the door of the only alternative opened slightly and let him peer through. Once ajar, however, it seemed the same second wide open; he was through; and it was closed—behind him.

For a different nature the alternative might have taken a different form. As has been seen, he was too strong a man to drift merely; a definite way out that could commend itself to a man of action had to be found; and, though the raw material of heroism may have been in him, he made no claim to a martyrdom that should last as long as life itself. And this alternative dawned upon him now as the grey light of a last morning must dawn upon the condemned prisoner: given Stephen, and given this particular problem, it was the only way out.

He envisaged it thus suddenly with a kind of ultimate calmness and determination that was characteristic of the man. And in every way, it was characteristic of the man, for it involved the precise combination of courage and cowardice, weakness and strength, selfishness and sacrifice, that expressed the true resultant of all the forces at work in his soul. To him, at the moment of his rapid decision, however, it seemed that the dominant motive was the sacrifice to be offered upon the altar of his love for Mark.

The twisted notion possessed him that in this way he might atone in some measure for the waning of his brotherly devotion. His love for the girl, her possible love for him—both were to be sacrificed to obtain the happiness—the eventual happiness—of these other two. Long, long ago Mark had himself said that under such circumstances one or other of them would have to—*go*. And the decision Stephen had come to was that the one to "go" was—himself.

This day among the woods and mountains should be his last on earth. By the evening of the following day Mark should be free.

"I'll give my life for him."

His face was grey and set as he said it. He stood on the high ridge, bathed by sun and wind. He looked over the fair world of wooded vales and mountains at his feet, but his eyes, turned inwards, saw only his brother—and that sweet Eastern face—then darkness.

"He will understand— and perforce accept it—and with time, yes, with time, the new happiness shall fill his soul utterly— and hers. It is for her, too, that I give it. It *must*—under these unparalleled circumstances be right . . . !"

And although there was no single cloud in the sky, the landscape at his feet suddenly went dark and sunless from one horizon to the other.

10

Then, having come into the gloom of this terrible decision, his imaginative nature at once bounded to the opposite extreme, and a kind of exaltation possessed him. The stereotyped verdict of a coroner's jury might in this instance have been true. The prolonged stress of emotion under which he had so long been labouring had at last produced a condition of mind that could only be considered—unsound.

A cool wind swept his face as he let his tired eyes wander over the leagues of Silent forest below. The blue Jura with its myriad folded valleys lay about him like the waves of a giant sea ready to swallow up the little atom of his life within its deep heart of forgetfulness. Clear away into France he saw on the one side where, beyond the fortress of Pontarlier, white clouds sailed the horizon before a westerly wind; and, on the other, towards the white-robed Alps rising mistily through the haze of the autumn sunshine. Between these extreme distances lay all that world of a hundred intricate valleys, curiously winding, deeply wooded, little inhabited, a region of soft, confusing loveliness where a traveller might well lose himself for days together before he discovered a way out of so vast a maze.

And, as he gazed, there passed across his mind, like the dim memory of something heard in childhood, that legend of the "Lost Valley" in which the souls of the unhappy dead find the deep peace that is denied to them by all the religions—and to which hundreds, who have not yet the sad right of entry, seek to find the mournful forest gates. The memory was vivid, but swiftly engulfed by others and forgotten. They chased each other in rapid succession across his mind, as clouds at sunset pass before a high wind, merging on the horizon in a common mass.

Then, slowly, at length, he turned and made his way down the mountain-side in the direction of the French frontier for a last journey upon the sweet surface of the world he loved. In his soul was the one dominant feeling: this singular exaltation arising from the knowledge that in the long run his great sacrifice must ensure the happiness of the two beings he loved more than all else in life.

At the solitary farm where an hour later, he had his lunch of bread and cheese and milk, he learned that he had wandered many miles out of the routes with which he was more or less familiar. He had been walking faster than he knew all these hours of battle. A physical weariness came upon him that made him conscious of every muscle in his body as he realised what a long road over mountain and valley he had to retrace. But, with the heaviness of fatigue, ran still the sense of interior spiritual exaltation.

Something in him walked on air with springs of steel—something that was independent of the dragging limbs and the aching back. For the rest, his sensations seemed numb. His great Decision stood black before him, blocking the way. Thoughts and feelings forsook him as rats leave a sinking ship. The time for these was past. Two overmastering desires, however, clung fast: one, to see Mark again, and be with him; the other, to be once more—with her. These two desires left no room for others. With the former, indeed, it was almost as though Mark had called aloud to him by name.

He stood a moment where the depth of the valley he had to thread lay like a twisting shadow at his feet; it ran, soft and dim, through the slanting sunshine. From the whole surface of the woods rose a single murmur; like the whirring of voices heard in a dream, he thought. The individual purring of separate trees was merged. Peace, most ancient and profound, lay in it, and its hushed whisper soothed his spirit.

He hurried his pace a little. The cool wind that had swept his face on the heights earlier in the afternoon followed him down, urging him forwards with deliberate pressure, as though a thousand soft hands were laid upon his back. And there were spirits in the wind that day. He heard their voices; and far below he traced by the motion of the tree-tops where they coiled upwards to him through miles of forest. His way, meanwhile, dived down through dense growths of spruce and pine into a region unfamiliar.

There was an aspect of the scenery that almost suggested it was unknown—an undiscovered corner of the world. The countless signs that mark the passage of humanity were absent, or at least did not obtrude themselves upon him. Something remote from life, alien, at any rate, to the normal life he had hitherto known, began to steal gently over his burdened soul. . . .

In this way, perhaps, the effect of his dreadful Decision already showed its influence upon his mind and senses. So very soon now he would be—*going!*

The sadness of autumn lay all about him, and the loneliness of this secluded vale spoke to him of the melancholy of things that die—of vanished springs, of summers unfulfilled, of things for ever incomplete and unsatisfying. Human effort, he felt, this valley had never known. No hoofs had ever pressed the mossy turf of these forest clearings; no traffic of peasants or woodsmen won echoes from these limestone cliffs. All was hushed, lonely, deserted.

And yet? The depths to which it apparently plunged astonished him more and more. Nowhere more than a half-mile across, each turn of the shadowy trail revealed new distances below. With spots of a haunting, fairy loveliness too: for here and there, on isolated patches of lawn-like grass, stood wild lilac bushes, rounded by the wind; willows from the swampy banks of the stream waved pale hands; firs, dark and erect, guarded their eternal secrets on the heights. In one little opening, standing all by itself, he found a lime-tree; while beyond it, shining among the pines, was a group of shimmering beeches. And, although there was no wild life, there were flowers; he saw clumps of them—tall, graceful, blue flowers whose name he did not know, nodding in dream across the foaming water of the little torrent.

And his thoughts ran incessantly to Mark. Never before had he been conscious of so imperious a desire to see him, to hear his voice, to stand at his side. At moments it almost obliterated that other great desire. . . . Again, he increased his pace. And the path plunged more and more deeply into the heart of the mountains, sinking ever into deeper silence, ever into an atmosphere of deeper peace. For no sound could reach him here without first passing along great distances that were cushioned with soft wind, and padded, as it were, with a million feathery pine-tops.

A sense of peace that was beyond reach of all possible disturbance began to cover his breaking life with a garment as of softest shadows. Never before had he experienced anything approaching the wonder and completeness of it. It was a peace, still as the depths of the sea which are motionless because they *cannot* move—cannot even tremble. It was a peace unchangeable—what some have called, perhaps, the

Peace of God. . . .

"Soon the turn *must* come," he thought, yet without a trace of impatience or alarm, "and the road wind upwards again to cross the last ridge!" But he cared little enough; for this enveloping peace drowned him, hiding even the fear of death.

And still the road sank downwards into the sleep-laden atmosphere of the crowding trees, and with it his thoughts, oddly enough, sank deeper and deeper into dim recesses of his own being. As though a secret sympathy lay between the path that dived and the thoughts that plunged. Only, from time to time, the thought of his brother Mark brought him back to the surface with a violent rush. Dreadfully, in those moments, he wanted him—to feel his warm, strong hand within his own—to ask his forgiveness—perhaps, too, to grant his own . . . he hardly knew.

"But is there no end to this delicious valley?" he wondered, with something between vagueness and confusion in his mind. "Does it never stop, and the path climb again to the mountains beyond?"

Drowsily, divorced from any positive interest, the question passed through his thoughts. Underfoot the grass already grew thickly enough to muffle the sound of his footsteps. The trail even had vanished, swallowed by moss. His feet sank in.

"I wish Mark were with me now—to see and feel all this—"

He stopped short and looked keenly about him for a moment, leaving the thought incomplete, A deep sighing, instantly caught by the wind and merged in the soughing of the trees, had sounded close beside him. Was it perhaps himself that sighed—unconsciously? His heart was surely charged enough! . . .

A faint smile played over his lips—instantly frozen, however, as another sigh, more distinct than the first, and quite obviously external to himself, passed him closely in the darkening air. More like deep breathing, though, it was, than sighing. . . . It was nothing but the wind, of course. Stephen hurried on again, not surprised that he had been so easily deceived, for this valley was full of sighings and breathings—of trees and wind. It ventured upon no louder noise. Noise of any kind, indeed, seemed impossible and forbidden in this muted vale.

And so deeply had he descended now, that the sunshine, silver rather than golden, already streamed past far over his head along the ridges, and no gleam found its way to where he was. The shadows, too, no longer blue and purple, had changed to black, as though woven of some delicate substance that had definite thickness, like a veil. Across the opposite slope, one of the mountain summits in the western sky already dropped its monstrous shadow fringed with pines. The day was rapidly drawing in.

<h2 style="text-align:center">11</h2>

And here, very gradually, there began to dawn upon his over-wrought mind certain curious things. They pierced clean through the mingled gloom and exaltation that characterised his mood. And they made the skin upon his back a little to—stir and crawl.

For he now became distinctly aware that the emptiness of this lonely valley was only apparent. It is impossible to say through what sense, or combination of senses, this singular certainty was brought to him that the valley was not really as forsaken and deserted as it seemed—that, on the contrary, it was the very reverse.

It came to him suddenly—as a certainty. The valley as a matter of fact was—full. Packed, thronged and crowded it was to the very brim of its mighty wooded walls—with life. It was now borne in upon him, with an inner conviction that left no room for doubt, that on all sides living things—persons—were jostling him, rubbing elbows, watching all his movements, and only waiting till the darkness came to reveal themselves.

Moreover, with this eerie discovery came also the further knowl-edge that a vast multitude of others, again, with pallid faces and yearn-ing eyes, with arms outstretched and groping feet, were searching eve-rywhere for the way of entrance that he himself had found so easily. All about him, he felt, were people by the hundred, by the thousand, seeking with a kind of restless fever for the narrow trail that led down into the valley, longing with an intensity that beat upon his soul in a million waves, for the rest, the calm silence of the place—but most of all for its strange, deep, and unalterable peace.

He, alone of all these, had found the Entrance; he, *and one other.*

For out of this singular conviction grew another even more sin-gular; his brother Mark was also somewhere in this valley with him. Mark, too, was wandering like himself in and out among its intricate dim turns. He had said but a short time ago, "I wish Mark were here!" Mark *was* here. And it was precisely then—while he stood still a mo-ment, trying to face these overwhelming obsessions and deal with them—that the figure of a man, moving swiftly through the trees, passed him with a great gliding stride, and with averted face. Stephen started horribly, catching his breath. In an instant the man was gone again, swallowed up by the crowding pines.

With a quick movement of pursuit and a cry that should make the man turn, he sprang forward—but stopped again almost the same moment, realising that the extraordinary speed at which the man had shot past him rendered pursuit out of the question. He had been going downhill into the valley; by this time, he was already far, far ahead. But in that momentary glimpse of him he had seen enough to know. The face was turned away, and the shadows under the trees were heavy, but the figure was beyond question the figure of—his brother Mark.

It was his brother, yet not his brother. It was Mark—but Mark altered. And the alteration was in some way—awful; just as the silent speed at which he had moved—the impossible speed in so dense a forest—was likewise awful. Then, still shaking inwardly with the suddenness of it all, Stephen realised that when he called aloud, he had uttered certain definite words. And these words now came back to him—

"Mark, Mark! Don't go yet! Don't go—without me!"

Before, however, he could act, a most curious and unaccountable sensation of deadly faintness and pain came upon him, without cause, without explanation, so that he dropped backwards in momentary collapse, and but for the closeness of the tree stems would have fallen full length to the ground. From the centre of the heart it came, spreading thence throughout his whole being like a swift and dreadful fever. All the muscles of his body relaxed; icy perspiration burst forth upon his skin; the pulses of life seemed suddenly reduced to the threshold beyond which they stop. There was a thick, rushing sound in his ears and his mind went utterly blank.

These were the sensations of death by suffocation. He knew this as certainly as though another doctor stood by his side and labelled each spasm, explained each successive sinking of the vital flame. He was passing through the last throes of a dying man. And then into his mind, thus deliberately left blank, rushed at lightning speed a whole series of the pictures of his past life. Even while his breath failed, he saw his thirty-five years pictorially, successively, yet in some queer fashion *at once*, pass through the lighted chambers of his brain. In this way, it is said, they pass through the brain of a drowning man during the last seconds before death.

Childhood rose about him with its scenes, figures, voices; the Kentish lawns where he had played with Mark in stained overalls; the summer-house where they had tea, the hay-fields where they romped.

The scent of lime and walnut, of garden pinks, and roses by the tumbled rockery came back to his nostrils. . . . He heard the voices of grown-ups in the distance . . . faint barking of dogs . . . the carriage wheels upon the gravel drive . . . and then the sharp summons from the opened window—"Time to come in now! Time to come in!"

Time to come in now. It all drove before him as of yesterday on the scented winds of childhood's summer days. . . . He heard his brother's voice—dreadfully faint and far away—calling him by name in the shrill accents of the boy: "Stevie—I say, you *might* shut up . . . and play properly. . ."

And then followed the panorama of the thirty years, all the chief events drawn in steel-like lines of white and black, vivid in sunshine, alive—right down to the present moment with the portentous dark shadow of his terrible Decision closing the series like a cloud.

Yes, like a smothering black cloud that blocked the way. There was nothing visible beyond it. There, for him, life ceased

Only, as he gazed with inward-turned eyes that could not close even if they would, he saw to his amazement that the black cloud suddenly opened, and into a space of clear light there swam the vision, radiant as morning, of that dark young Eastern face—the face that held for him all the beauty in the world. The eyes instantly found his own, and smiled. Behind her, moreover, and beyond, before the moving vapours closed upon it, he saw a long *vista* of brilliance, crowded with pictures he could but half discern—as though, in spite of himself and his decision, life continued—as though, too, it *continued with her.*

And instantly, with the sight and thought of her, the consuming faintness passed; strength returned to his body with the glow of life: the pain went; the pictures vanished; the cloud was no more. In his blood the pulses of life once again beat strong, and the blackness left his soul. The smile of those beloved eyes had been charged with the invitation to live. Although his determination remained unshaken, there shone behind it the joy of this potent magic: life with her. . . .

With a strong effort, at length he recovered himself and continued on his way. More or less familiar, of course, with the psychology of vision, he dimly understood that his experiences had been in some measure subjective— within himself. To find the line of demarcation, however, was beyond him. That Mark had wandered out to fight his own battle upon the mountains, and so come into this same valley, was well within the bounds of coincidence. But the nameless and dreadful alteration discerned in that swift moment of his passing -that remained inexplicable. Only he no longer thought about it. The glory of that sweet vision had bewildered him beyond any possibility of reason or analysis.

His watch told him that the hour was past five o'clock—ten minutes past, to be exact. He still had several hours before reaching the country he was familiar with nearer home. Following the trail at an increased pace, he presently saw patches of meadow glimmering between the thinning trees, and knew that the bottom of the valley was at last in sight.

"And Mark, God bless him, is down there too—somewhere!" he exclaimed aloud. "I shall surely find him." For, strange to say, nothing could have persuaded him that his twin was not wandering among the shadows of this peaceful and haunted valley with himself, and—that he would shortly find him.

12

And a few minutes later he passed from the forest as through an open door and found himself before a farmhouse standing in a patch of bright green meadow against the mountain-side. He was in need both of food and information.

The chalet, less lumbering and picturesque than those found in the Alps, had, nevertheless, the appearance of being exceedingly ancient. It was not toy-like—as the Jura chalets sometimes are. Solidly built, its balcony and overhanging roof supported by immense beams of deeply stained wood, it stood so that the back walls merged into the mountain slope behind, and the arms of pine, spruce and fir seemed stretched out to include it among their shadows. A last ray of sunshine, dipping between two far summits overhead, touched it with pale gold, bringing out the rich beauty of the heavily-dyed beams. Though no one was visible at the moment, and no smoke rose from the shingled chimney, it had the appearance of being occupied, and Stephen approached it with the caution due to the first evidence of humanity he had come across since he entered the valley.

Under the shadow of the broad balcony roof, he noticed that the door, like that of a stable, was in two parts, and, wondering rather to find it closed, he knocked firmly upon the upper half. Under the pressure of a second knock this upper half yielded slightly, though without opening. The lower half, however, evidently barred and bolted, remained unmoved.

The third time he knocked with more force than he intended,

and the knock sounded loud and clamorous as a summons. From within, as though great spaces stretched beyond, came a murmur of voices, faint and muffled, and then almost immediately—the footsteps of some ne coming softly up to open.

But, instead of the heavy brown door opening, there came a voice. He heard it, petrified with amazement. For it was a voice he knew— hushed, soft, lingering. His heart, hammering atrociously, seemed to leave its place, and cut his breath away.

"Stephen!" it murmured, calling him by name, "what are you do- ing here so soon? And what is it that you want?"

The knowledge that only this dark door separated him from her, at first bereft him of all power of speech or movement; and the possible significance of her words escaped him. Through the sweet confusion that turned his spirit faint he only remembered, flash-like, that she and her father were indeed to have left the hotel that very morning. After that his thought stopped dead.

Then, also flash-like, swept back upon him the memory of the figure that had passed him with averted face—and, with it, the clear conviction that at this moment Mark, too, was somewhere in this very valley, even close beside him. More: Mark was in this chalet—with her.

The torrent of speech that instantly crowded to his lips was almost too thick for utterance.

"Open, open, open!" was all he heard intelligibly from the throng of words that poured out. He raised his hands to push and force; but her reply again stopped him.

"Even if I open—*you* may not enter yet," came the whisper through the door. And this time he could almost have sworn that it sounded within himself rather than without.

"I must enter," he cried. "Open to me, I say!"

"But you are trembling—"

"Open to me, O my life! Open to me!"

"But your heart—it is shaking."

"Because you—you are so near," came in passionate, stammer- ing tones; "Because you stand there beside me!" And then, before she could answer, or his will control the words, he had added: "And be- cause Mark—my brother—is in there—with you—"

"Hush, hush!" came the soft, astonishing reply. "He is in here, true; but he is not with me. And it is for my sake that he has come—for my sake and for yours. My soul, alas! has led him to the gates. . . ."

But Stephen's emotions had reached the breaking-point, and the necessity for action was upon him like a storm. He drew back a pace so as to fling himself better against the closed door, when to his utter surprise, it moved. The upper half swung slowly outwards, and he—saw.

He was aware of a vast room, with closely shuttered windows, that seemed to stretch beyond the walls into the wooded mountainside, thronged with moving figures, like forms of life gently gliding to and fro in some huge darkened tank; and there, framed against this opening—the girl herself. She stood, visible to the waist, radiant in the solitary beam of sunshine that reached the chalet, smiling down wondrously into his face with the same exquisite beauty in her eyes that he had seen before in the vision of the cloud: with, too, that supreme invitation in them—the invitation to live.

The loveliness blinded him. He could see the down upon her little dark cheeks where the sunlight kissed them; there was the cloud of hair upon her neck where his lips had lain; there, too, the dear, slight breast that not twenty-four hours ago had known the pressure of his arms. And, once again, driven forward by the love that triumphed over all obstacles, real or artificial, he advanced headlong with outstretched arms to take her.

"Katya!" he cried, never thinking how passing strange it was that he knew her name at all, much more the endearing and shortened form of it. "Katya!"

But the young girl held up her little brown hand against him with a gesture that was more strong to restrain than any number of bolted doors.

"Not here," she murmured, with her grave smile, while behind the words he caught in that darkened room the alternate hush and sighing as of a thousand sleepers. "Not here! You cannot see him now; for these are the Reception Halls of Death and here I stand in the Vestibule of the Beyond. Our way . . . your way and mine . . . lies farther yet . . . traced there since the beginning of the world . . . together. . . ."

In quaintly broken English it was spoken, but his mind remembers the singular words in their more perfect form. Even this, however, came later. At the moment he only felt the twofold wave of love surge through him with a tide of power that threatened to break him asunder: he *must* hold her to his heart; he *must* come instantly to his brother's side, meet his eyes, have speech with him. The desire to enter that great darkened room and force a path through the dimly gliding forms to his brother became irresistible, while tearing upon its heels came like a fever of joy the meaning of the words she had just uttered, and especially of that last word: "*Together!*"

Then, for an instant, all the forces in his being turned negative so that his will refused to act. The excess of feeling numbed him. A flying interval of knowledge, calm and certain, came to him. The exaltation of spirit which produced the pictures of all this spiritual clairvoyance moved a stage higher, and he realised that he witnessed an order of things pertaining to the world of eternal causes rather than of temporary effects. Someone had lifted the Veil.

With a feeling that he could only wait and let things take their extraordinary course, he stood still. For an instant, even less, he must have hidden his eyes in his hand, for when, a moment later, he again looked up, he saw that the half of the swinging door which had been open, was now closed. He stood alone upon the balcony. And the sunshine had faded entirely from the scene.

It was here, it seems, that the last vestige of self-control disappeared. He flung himself against the door; and the door met his assault like a wall of solid rock. Crying aloud alternately the names of his two loved ones, he turned, scarcely knowing what he did, and ran into the meadow. Dusk was about the chalet, drawing the encircling forests closer. Soon the true darkness would stalk down the slopes. The walls of the valley reared, it seemed, up to heaven.

Still calling, he ran about the walls, searching wildly for a way of entrance, his mind charged with bewildering fragments of what he had heard: "The Reception Halls of Death"—"The Vestibule of the Beyond"—"You cannot see him now"—"Our way lies farther—*and together!*"

And, on the far side of the chalet, by the corner that touched the trees, he suddenly stopped, feeling his gaze drawn upwards, and there, pressed close against the windowpane of an upper room, saw that someone was peering down upon him.

With a sensation of freezing terror, he realised that he was staring straight into the eyes of his brother Mark. Bent a little forward with the effort to look down, the face, pale and motionless, gazed into his own, but without the least sign of recognition. Not a feature moved: and although but a few feet separated the brothers, the face wore the dim, misty appearance of great distance. It was like the face of a man called suddenly from deep sleep—dazed, perplexed; nay, more—frightened and horribly distraught.

What Stephen read upon it, however, in that first moment of sight, was the signature of the great, eternal question men have asked since the beginning of time, yet never heard the answer. And into the heart of the twin the pain of it plunged like a sword.

"Mark!" he stammered, in that low voice the valley seemed to exact; "Mark! Is that really *you?*" Tears swam already in his eyes, and yearning in a flood choked his utterance.

And Mark, with a dreadful, steady stare that still held no touch of recognition, gazed down upon him from the closed window of that upper chamber, motionless, unblinking as an image of stone. It was almost like an imitation figure of himself—only with the effect of some added alteration. For alteration certainly there was—awful and unknown alteration—though Stephen was utterly unable to detect wherein it lay. And he remembered how the figure had passed him in the woods with averted face.

He made then, it seems, some violent sign or other, in response to which his brother at last moved—slowly opening the window. He leaned forward, stooping with lowered head and shoulders over the sill, while Stephen ran up against the wall beneath and craned up towards him. The two faces drew close; their eyes met clean and straight. Then the lips of Mark moved, and the distraught look half vanished within the borders of a little smile of puzzled and affectionate wonder.

"Stevie, old fellow," issued a tiny, far-away voice; "but where are you? I see you—so dimly?"

It was like a voice crying faintly down half-a-mile of distance. He shuddered to hear it.

"I'm here, Mark—close to you," he whispered.

"I hear your voice, I feel your presence," came the reply like a man talking in his sleep, "but I see you—as through a glass darkly. And I want to see you all clear, and close—"

"But *you!* Where are *you?*" interrupted Stephen, with anguish.

"Alone; quite alone—over here. And it's cold, oh, so cold!" The words came gently, half veiling a complaint. The wind caught them and ran round the walls towards the forest, wailing as it went.

"But how did you come, how did you come?" Stephen raised himself on tiptoe to catch the answer. But there was no answer. The face receded a little, and as it did so the wind, passing up the walls again, stirred the hair on the forehead. Stephen saw it move. He thought, too, the head moved with it, shaking slightly to and fro.

"Oh, but tell me, my dear, dear brother! Tell me—!" he cried, sweating horribly, his limbs Shaking.

Mark made a curious gesture, withdrawing at the same time a little farther into the room behind, so that he now stood upright, half in shadow by the window. The alteration in him proclaimed itself more plainly, though still without betraying its exact nature. There was something about him that was terrible. And the air that came from the open window upon Stephen was so freezing that it seemed to turn the perspiration on his face into ice.

"I do not know; I do not remember," he heard the tiny voice inside the room, ever withdrawing. "Besides—I may not speak with you—yet; it is so difficult—and it hurts."

Stephen stretched out his body, the arms scraping the wooden walls above his head, trying to climb the smooth and slippery surface.

"For the love of God!" he cried with passion, "tell me what it all means and what you are doing here—you and—and—oh, and *all three of us?*" The words rang out through the silent valley.

But the other stood there motionless again by the window, his face distraught and dazed as though the effort of speech had already been too much for him. His image had begun to fade a little. He seemed, without moving, yet to be retreating into some sort of interior distance. Presently, it seemed, he would disappear altogether.

"I don't know," came the voice at length, fainter than before, half muffled. "I have been asleep, I think. I have just waked up, and come across from somewhere else—where we were all together, you and I and—and—"

Like his brother, he was unable to speak the name. He ended the sentence a moment later in a whisper that was only just audible. "But I cannot tell you *how* I came," he said, "for I do not know the words."

Stephen, then, with a violent leap tried to reach the window-sill and pull himself up. The distance was too great, however, and he fell back upon the grass, only just keeping his feet.

"I'm coming in to you," he cried out very loud. "Wait there for me! For the love of heaven, wait till I come to you. I'll break the doors in!"

Once again Mark made that singular gesture; again, he seemed to recede a little farther into a kind of veiled perspective that caused his appearance to fade still more; and, from an incredible distance—a distance that somehow conveyed an idea of appalling height—his thin, tiny voice floated down upon his brother from the fading lips of shadow.

"Old fellow, don't you come! You are not ready—and it is too cold here. I shall wait, Stevie, I shall wait for you. Later—I mean farther from here—we shall one day all three be together. . . . Only you cannot understand now. I am here for your sake, old fellow, and for hers. She loves us both, but . . . it is . . . you . . . she loves . . . the best. . . ."

The whispering voice rose suddenly on these last words into a long high cry that the wind instantly caught away and buried far in the smothering silences of the woods. For, at the same moment, Mark had come with a swift rush back to the window, had leaned out and stretched both hands towards his brother underneath. And his face had cleared and smiled. Caught within that smile, the awful change in him had vanished.

Stephen turned and made a mad rush round the chalet to find the door he would batter in with his hands and feet and body. He searched in vain, however, for in the shadows the supporting beams of the building were indistinguishable from the stems of the trees behind; the roof sank away, blotted out by the gloom of the branches, and the darkness now wove forest, sky and mountain into a uniform black sheet against which no item was separately visible.

There was no chalet any longer. He was simply battering with bruised hands and feet upon the solid trunks of pines and spruces in his path; which he continued to do, calling ever aloud for Mark, until finally he grew dizzy with exhaustion and fell to the ground in a state of semi-consciousness.

And for the best part of half-an-hour he lay there motionless upon the moss, while the vast hands of Night drew the cloak of her softest darkness over valley and mountain, covering his small body with as much care as she covered the sky, the hemisphere, and all those leagues of velvet forest.

13

It was not long before he came to himself again—shivering with cold, for the perspiration had dried upon him where he lay. He got up and ran. The night was now fairly down, and the keen air stung his cheeks. But, with a sure instinct not to be denied, he took the direction of home.

He travelled at an extraordinary pace, considering the thickness of the trees and the darkness. How he got out of the valley he does not remember; nor how he found his way over the intervening ridges that lay between him and the country he knew. At the back of his mind crashed and tumbled the loose fragments of all he had seen and heard, forming as yet no coherent pattern. For himself, indeed, the details were of small interest. He was a man under sentence of death. His determination, in spite of everything, remained unshaken. In a few short hours he would be gone.

Yet, with the habit of the professional mind, he tried a little to sort out things. During that state of singular exaltation, for instance, he understood vaguely that his deep longings had somehow translated themselves into act and scene. For these longings were life; his decision negatived them; hence, they dramatised themselves pictorially with what vividness his imagination allowed.

They were dramatised inventions, singularly elaborate, of the emotions that burned so fiercely within. All were projections of his consciousness, maimed and incomplete, masquerading as persons before his inner vision. It began with the singular sensations of death by drowning he had experienced. From that moment the other forces at work in the problem had taken their cue and played their part more or less convincingly, according to their strength. . . .

He thought and argued a great deal as he hurried homewards through the night. But all the time he knew that it was untrue. He had no real explanation at all!

From the high ridges, cold and bleak under the stars, swept by the free wind of night, he ran almost the entire way. It was downhill. And during that violent descent of nearly an hour the details of his "going" shaped themselves. Until then he had formed no definite plans. Now he settled everything. He chose the very pool where the water coiled and bubbled as in a cauldron just where the little torrent made a turn above their house; he decided upon the very terms of the letter he would leave behind. He would put it on the kitchen table so that they should know where to find him.

He urged his pace tremendously, for the idea that his brother would have left—that he would find him gone—haunted him. It grew, doubtless, out of that singular, detailed vision that had come upon him in his great weakness in the valley. He was terrified that he would not see his brother again—that he had already gone deliberately—after her. . . .

"I *must* see Mark once more. I *must* get home before he leaves!" flashed the strong thought continually in his mind, making him run like a deer down the winding trail.

It was after ten o'clock when he reached the little clearing behind the chalet, panting with exhaustion, blinded with perspiration. There was no light visible; all the windows were dark; but presently he made out a figure moving to and fro below the balcony. It was not Mark—he saw that in a flash. It moved oddly. A sound of moaning reached him at the same time. And then he saw that it was the figure of the peasant woman who cooked for them, Marie Petavel.

And the instant he saw who it was, and heard her moaning, he knew what had happened. Mark had left a letter to explain—and gone: gone after the girl. His heart sank into death.

The woman came forward heavily through the darkness, the dew-drenched grass swishing audibly against her skirts. And the words he heard were precisely what he had expected to hear, though *patois* and excitement rendered them difficult—

"Your brother—oh, your poor brother, *Monsieur le Docteur*—he—has gone!"

And then he saw the piece of white paper glimmering in her hands as she stood quite close. He took it mechanically from her. It was the letter Mark had left behind to explain.

But before Stephen had time to read it, a man with a lantern came out of the barn that stood behind the house. It was her husband. He came slowly towards them.

"We searched for you, oh, we searched," he said in a thick voice, "my son went as far as Buttes even, and hasn't come back yet. You've been long, too long away—"

He stopped short and glanced down at his wife, telling her roughly to cease her stupid weeping. Stephen, shaking inwardly, with an icy terror in his blood, began to feel that things were not precisely as he had anticipated. Something else was the matter. The expression in the face of the peasant as the lantern's glare fell upon it came to him suddenly with the shock of a revelation.

"You have told *monsieur*—all?" the man whispered, stooping to his wife. She shook her head; and her husband led the way without another word. The interval of a few seconds seemed endless to Stephen; he was trembling all over like a man with the ague. Behind them the old woman floundered through the wet grass, moaning to herself.

"No one would have believed it could have happened—anything of that sort," the man mumbled. The lantern was unsteady in his hand. The next minute the barn, like some monstrous animal, rose against the stars, and the huge wooden doors gaped wide before them.

The peasant, uncovering his head, went first, and Stephen, following with stumbling footsteps, saw the shadows of the beams and posts shift across the boarded floor. Against the wall, whither the man led, was a small littered heap of hay, and upon this, covered by a white sheet, was stretched a human body. The peasant drew back the sheet gently with his heavy brown hand, stooping close over it so that the lantern threw its light full upon the act.

And Stephen, tumbling forward, scarcely knowing what he did, without further warning or preparation, looked down upon the face of his brother Mark. The eyes stared fixedly into—nothing; the features wore the distraught expression he had seen upon them a few hours before through the window-pane of that upper chamber.

"We found him in that deep pool just where the stream makes the quick turn above the house," the peasant whispered. "He left a bit of paper on the kitchen table to say where he would be. It was after dark when we got there. His watch had stopped, though, long before—" He muttered on unintelligibly.

Stephen looked up at the man, unable to utter a word, and the man replied to the unspoken question—

"At ten minutes past five the watch had stopped," he said. "That was when the water reached it."

By the flicker of the lantern, then, sitting beside that still figure covered with the sheet, Stephen read the letter Mark had left for him—

"Stevie, old fellow, one of us, you know, has got to—go; and it is better, I think, that it should not be you. I know all you have been through, for I have fought and suffered every step with you. I have been along the same path, loving her too much for you, and you too much for her. And I leave her to you, boy, because I am convinced, she now loves you even as she first believed she loved me. But all that evening she cried incessantly for you. More I cannot explain to you now; she will do that. And she need never know more than that I have withdrawn in your favour: she need never know *how*. Perhaps, one day, when there is no marriage or giving in marriage, we may all three be together, and happy. I have often wondered, as you know . . ."

The remainder of the sentence was scratched out and illegible.

". . . And, if it be possible, old fellow, of course *I shall wait*."

Then came more words blackened out.

". . . I am now going, within a few minutes of writing this last word to you of blessing and forgiveness (for I know you will want that, although there is nothing, nothing to *forgive!*)—going down into that Lost Valley her father told us about—the Valley hidden among these mountains we love—the Lost Valley where even the unhappy dead find peace. There I shall wait for you both.—Mark."

★★★★★★★★★★★★

Several weeks later, before he took the train eastwards, Stephen retraced his steps to the farmhouse where he had bought milk and asked for directions. Thence for some distance he followed the path he well remembered. At a point, however, the confusion of the woods grew strangely upon him. The mountains, true to the map, were not true to his recollections. The trail stopped; high, unknown ridges intervened; and no such deep and winding valley as he had travelled that afternoon for so many hours was anywhere to be found. The map, the peasants, the very configuration of the landscape even, denied its existence.

Vengeance is Mine

1

An active, vigorous man in Holy orders, yet compelled by heart trouble to resign a living in Kent before full middle age, he had found suitable work with the Red Cross in France; and it rather pleased a strain of innocent vanity in him that Rouen, whence he derived his Norman blood, should be the scene of his activities.

He was a gentle-minded soul, a man deeply read and thoughtful, but goodness perhaps his out-standing quality, believing no evil of others. He had been slow, for instance, at first to credit the German atrocities, until the evidence had compelled him to face the appalling facts. With acceptance, then, he had experienced a revulsion which other gentle minds have probably also experienced—a burning desire, namely, that the perpetrators should be fitly punished.

This primitive instinct of revenge—he called it a lust—he sternly repressed; it involved a descent to lower levels of conduct irreconcilable with the progress of the race he so passionately believed in. Revenge pertained to savage days. But though he hid away the instinct in his heart, afraid of its clamour and persistency, it revived from time to time, as fresh horrors made it bleed anew. It remained alive, unsatisfied; while, with its analysis, his mind strove unconsciously. That an intellectual nation should deliberately include frightfulness as a chief item in its creed perplexed him horribly; it seemed to him conscious spiritual evil openly affirmed.

Some genuine worship of Odin, Wotan, Moloch lay still embedded in the German outlook, and beneath the veneer of their pretentious culture. He often wondered, too, what effect the recognition of these horrors must have upon gentle minds in other men, and especially upon imaginative minds. How did they deal with the fact that this appalling thing existed in human nature in the twentieth century? Its survival, indeed, caused his belief in civilisation as a whole to waver.

Was progress, his pet ideal and cherished faith, after all a mockery? Had human nature not advanced. . .?

His work in the great hospitals and convalescent camps beyond the town was tiring; he found little time for recreation, much less for rest; a light dinner and bed by ten o'clock was the usual way of spending his evenings. He had no social intercourse, for everyone else was as busy as himself. The enforced solitude, not quite wholesome, was unavoidable. He found no outlet for his thoughts. First-hand acquaintance with suffering, physical and mental, was no new thing to him, but this close familiarity, day by day, with maimed and broken humanity preyed considerably on his mind, while the fortitude and cheerfulness shown by the victims deepened the impression of respectful, yearning wonder made upon him. They were so young, so fine and careless, these lads whom the German lust for power had robbed of limbs, and eyes, of mind, of life itself. The sense of horror grew in him with cumulative but unrelieved effect.

With the lengthening of the days in February, and especially when March saw the welcome change to summer time, the natural desire for open air asserted itself. Instead of retiring early to his dingy bedroom, he would stroll out after dinner through the ancient streets. When the air was not too chilly, he would prolong these outings, starting at sunset and coming home beneath the bright mysterious stars. He knew at length every turn and winding of the old-world alleys, every gable, every tower and spire, from the *Vieux Marché*, where Joan of Arc was burnt, to the busy quays, thronged now with soldiers from half a dozen countries.

He wandered on past grey gateways of crumbling stone that marked the former banks of the old tidal river. An English Army, five centuries ago, had camped here among reeds and swamps, besieging the Norman capital, where now they brought in supplies of men and material upon modern docks, a mighty invasion of a very different kind. Imaginative reflection was his constant mood.

But it was the haunted streets that touched him most, stirring some chord his ancestry had planted in him. The forest of spires thronged the air with strange stone flowers, silvered by moonlight as though white fire streamed from branch and petal; the old church towers soared; the cathedral touched the stars. After dark the modern note, paramount in the daylight, seemed hushed; with sunset it underwent a definite night-change. Although the darkened streets kept alive in him the menace of fire and death, the crowding soldiers, dipped to the face in shadow, seemed somehow negligible; the leaning roofs and gables hid them in a purple sea of mist that blurred their modern garb, steel weapons, and the like. Shadows themselves, they entered the being of the town; their feet moved silently; there was a hush and murmur; the brooding buildings absorbed them easily.

Ancient and modern, that is, unable successfully to mingle, let fall grotesque, incongruous shadows on his thoughts. The spirit of medieval days stole over him, exercising its inevitable sway upon a temperament already predisposed to welcome it. Witchcraft and wonder, pagan superstition and speculation, combined with an ancestral tendency to weave a spell, half of acceptance, half of shrinking, about his imaginative soul in which poetry and logic seemed otherwise fairly balanced. Too weary for critical judgment to discern clear outlines, his mind, during these magical twilight walks, became the playground of opposing forces, some power of dreaming, it seems, too easily in the ascendant. The soul of ancient Rouen, stealing beside his footsteps in the dusk, put forth a shadowy hand and touched him.

This shadowy spell he denied as far as in him lay, though the resistance offered by reason to instinct lacked true driving power. The dice were loaded otherwise in such a soul. His own blood harked back unconsciously to the days when men were tortured, broken on the wheel, walled up alive, and burnt for small offences. This shadowy hand stirred faint ancestral memories in him, part instinct, part desire. The next step, by which he saw a similar attitude flowering full blown in the German frightfulness, was too easily made to be rejected. The German horrors made him believe that this ignorant cruelty of olden days threatened the world now in a modern, organised shape that proved its survival in the human heart. Shuddering, he fought against the natural desire for adequate punishment, but forgot that repressed emotions sooner or later must assert themselves. Essentially irrepressible, they may force an outlet in distorted fashion. He hardly recognized, perhaps, their actual claim, yet it was audible occasionally. For, owing to his loneliness, the natural outlet, in talk and intercourse, was denied.

Then, with the softer winds, he yearned for country air. The sweet spring days had come; morning and evening were divine; above the town the orchards were in bloom. Birds blew their tiny bugles on the hills. The midday sun began to burn.

It was the time of the final violence, when the German hordes flung like driven cattle against the Western line where free men fought for liberty. Fate hovered dreadfully in the balance that spring of 1918; Amiens was threatened, and if Amiens fell, Rouen must be evacuated. The town, already full, became now over-full. On his way home one evening he passed the station, crowded with homeless new arrivals. "Got the wind up, it seems, in Amiens!" cried a cheery voice, as an officer he knew went by him hurriedly. And as he heard it the mood of the spring became of a sudden uppermost. He reached a decision. The German horror came abruptly closer. This further overcrowding of the narrow streets was more than he could face.

It was a small, personal decision merely, but he *must* get out among woods and fields, among flowers and wholesome, growing things, taste simple, innocent life again. The following evening he would pack his haversack with food and tramp the four miles to the great *Forêt Verte*— delicious name!—and spend the night with trees and stars, breathing his full of sweetness, calm and peace. He was too accustomed to the thunder of the guns to be disturbed by it. The song of a thrush, the whistle of a blackbird, would easily drown that. He made his plan accordingly.

The next two nights, however, a warm soft rain was falling; only on the third evening could he put his little plan into execution. Anticipatory enjoyment, meanwhile, lightened his heart; he did his daily work more competently, the spell of the ancient city weakened somewhat. The shadowy hand withdrew.

2

Meanwhile, a curious adventure intervened.

His good and simple heart, disciplined these many years in the way a man should walk, received upon its imaginative side, a stimulus that, in his case, amounted to a shock. That a strange and comely woman should make eyes at him disturbed his equilibrium considerably; that he should enjoy the attack, though without at first responding openly—even without full comprehension of its meaning—disturbed it even more. It was, moreover, no ordinary attack.

He saw her first the night after his decision when, in a mood of disappointment due to the rain, he came down to his lonely dinner. The room, he saw, was crowded with new arrivals, from Amiens, doubtless, where they had "the wind up." The wealthier civilians had fled for safety to Rouen. These interested and, in a measure, stimulated him. He looked at them sympathetically, wondering what dear home-life they had so hurriedly relinquished at the near thunder of the enemy guns, and, in so doing, he noticed, sitting alone at a small table just in front of his own—yet with her back to him—a woman.

She drew his attention instantly. The first glance told him that she was young and well-to-do; the second, that she was unusual. What precisely made her unusual he could not say, although he at once began to study her intently. Dignity, atmosphere, personality, he perceived beyond all question. She sat there with an air. The becoming little hat with its challenging feather slightly tilted, the set of the shoulders, the neat waist and slender outline; possibly, too, the hair about the neck, and the faint perfume that was wafted towards him as the serving girl swept past, combined in the persuasion. Yet he felt it as more than a persuasion. She attracted him with a subtle vehemence he had never felt before. The instant he set eyes upon her his blood ran faster. The thought rose passionately in him, almost the words that phrased it: "I wish I knew her."

This sudden flash of response his whole being certainly gave—to the back of an unknown woman. It was both vehement and instinctive. He lay stress upon its instinctive character; he was aware of it before reason told him why. That it was "in response" he also noted, for although he had not seen her face and she assuredly had made no sign, he felt that attraction which involves also invitation. So vehement, moreover, was this response in him that he felt shy and ashamed the same instant, for it almost seemed he had expressed his thought in audible words. He flushed, and the flush ran through his body; he was conscious of heated blood as in a youth of twenty-five, and when a man past forty knows this touch of fever he may also know, though he may not recognise it, that the danger signal which means possible abandon has been lit.

Moreover, as though to prove his instinct justified, it was at this very instant that the woman turned and stared at him deliberately. She looked into his eyes, and he looked into hers. He knew a moment's keen distress, a sharpest possible discomfort, that after all he *had* expressed his desire audibly. Yet, though he blushed, he did not lower his eyes. The embarrassment passed instantly, replaced by a thrill of strangest pleasure and satisfaction. He knew a tinge of inexplicable dismay as well. He felt for a second helpless before what seemed a challenge in her eyes. The eyes were too compelling. They mastered him.

In order to meet his gaze, she had to make a full turn in her chair, for her table was placed directly in front of his own. She did so without concealment. It was no mere attempt to see what lay behind by making a half-turn and pretending to look elsewhere; no corner of the eye business; but a full, straight, direct, significant stare. She looked into his soul as though she called him, he looked into hers as though he answered. Sitting there like a statue, motionless, without a bow, without a smile, he returned her intense regard unflinchingly and yet unwillingly. He made no sign.

He shivered again. . . . It was perhaps ten seconds before she turned away with an air as if she had delivered her message and received his answer, but in those ten seconds a series of singular ideas crowded his mind, leaving an impression that ten years could never efface. The face and eyes produced a kind of intoxication in him. There was almost recognition, as though she said: "Ah, there you are! I was waiting; you'll have to come, of course. You must!" And just before she turned away, she smiled.

He felt confused and helpless.

The face he described as unusual; familiar, too, as with the atmosphere of some long forgotten dream, and if beauty perhaps was absent, character and individuality were supreme. Implacable resolution was stamped upon the features, which yet were sweet and womanly, stirring an emotion in him that he could not name and certainly did not recognize. The eyes, slanting a little upwards, were full of fire, the mouth voluptuous but very firm, the chin and jaw most delicately modelled, yet with a masculine strength that told of inflexible resolve. The resolution, as a whole, was the most relentless he had ever seen upon a human countenance. It dominated him. "How vain to resist the will," he thought, "that lies behind!" He was conscious of enslavement; she conveyed a message that he must obey, admitting compliance with her unknown purpose.

That some extraordinary wordless exchange was registered thus between them seemed very clear; and it was just at this moment, as if to signify her satisfaction, that she smiled. At his feeling of willing compliance with some purpose in her mind, the smile appeared. It was faint, so faint indeed that the eyes betrayed it rather than the mouth and lips; but it was there; he saw it and he thrilled again to this added touch of wonder and enchantment.

Yet, strangest of all, he maintains that with the smile there fluttered over the resolute face a sudden arresting tenderness, as though some wild flower lit a granite surface with its melting loveliness. He was aware in the clear strong eyes of unshed tears, of sympathy, of self-sacrifice he called maternal, of clinging love. It was this tenderness, as of a soft and gracious mother, and this implacable resolution, as of a stern, relentless man, that left upon his receptive soul the strange impression of sweetness yet of domination.

The brief ten seconds were over. She turned away as deliberately as she had turned to look. He found himself trembling with confused emotions he could not disentangle, could not even name; for, with the subtle intoxication of compliance in his soul lay also a vigorous protest that included refusal, even a violent refusal given with horror This unknown woman, without actual speech or definite gesture, had lit a flame in him that linked on far away and out of sight with the magic of the ancient city's medieval spell. Both, he decided, were undesirable, both to be resisted.

He was quite decided about this. She pertained to forgotten yet unburied things, her modern aspect a mere disguise, a disguise that some deep unsatisfied instinct in him pierced with ease.

He found himself equally decided, too, upon another thing which, in spite of his momentary confusion, stood out clearly: the magic of the city, the enchantment of the woman, both attacked a constitutional weakness in his blood, a line of least resistance. It wore no physical aspect, breathed no hint of ordinary romance; the mere male and female, moral or immoral touch was wholly absent; yet passion lurked there, tumultuous if hidden, and a tract of consciousness, long untravelled, was lit by sudden ominous flares. His character, his temperament, his calling in life as a former clergyman and now a Red Cross worker, being what they were, he stood on the brink of an adventure not dangerous alone but containing a challenge of fundamental kind that involved his very soul.

No further thrill, however, awaited him immediately. He left his table before she did, having intercepted no slightest hint of desired acquaintanceship or intercourse. He, naturally, made no advances; she, equally, made no smallest sign. Her face remained hidden, he caught no flash of eyes, no gesture, no hint of possible invitation. He went upstairs to his dingy room, and in due course fell asleep.

The next day he saw her not, her place in the dining-room was empty; but in the late evening of the following day, as the soft spring sunshine found him prepared for his postponed expedition, he met her suddenly on the stairs. He was going down with haversack and in walking kit to an early dinner, when he saw her coming up; she was perhaps a dozen steps below him; they must meet. A wave of confused, embarrassed pleasure swept him. He realised that this was no chance meeting. She meant to speak to him.

Violent attraction and an equally violent repulsion seized him. There was no escape, nor, had escape been possible, would he have attempted it. He went down four steps, she mounted four towards him; then he took one and she took one. They met. For a moment they stood level, while he shrank against the wall to let her pass. He had the feeling that but for the support of that wall he must have lost his balance and fallen into her, for the sunlight from the landing window caught her face and lit it, and she was younger, he saw, than he had thought, and far more comely. Her atmosphere enveloped him, the sense of attraction and repulsion became intense. She moved past him with the slightest possible bow of recognition; then, having passed, she turned.

She stood a little higher than himself, a step at most, and she thus looked down at him. Her eyes blazed into his. She smiled, and he was aware again of the domination and the sweetness. The perfume of her near presence drowned him; his head swam. "We count upon you," she said in a low firm voice, as though giving a command; "I know . . . we may. We do." And, before he knew what he was saying, trembling a little between deep pleasure and a contrary impulse that sought to choke the utterance, he heard his own voice answering. "You can count upon me. . . ." And she was already half-way up the next flight of stairs ere he could move a muscle, or attempt to thread a meaning into the singular exchange.

Yet meaning, he well knew, there was.

She was gone; her footsteps overhead had died away. He stood there trembling like a boy of twenty, yet also like a man of forty in whom fires, long dreaded, now blazed sullenly. She had opened the furnace door, the draught rushed through. He felt again the old unwelcome spell; he saw the twisted streets 'mid leaning gables and shadowy towers of a day forgotten; he heard the ominous murmurs of a crowd that thirsted for wheel and scaffold and fire; and, aware of vengeance, sweet and terrible, aware, too, that he welcomed it, his heart was troubled and afraid.

In a brief second the impression came and went; following it swiftly, the sweetness of the woman swept him: he forgot his shrinking in a rush of wild delicious pleasure. The intoxication in him deepened. She had recognized him! She had bowed and even smiled; she had spoken, assuming familiarity, intimacy, including him in her secret purposes! It was this sweet intimacy cleverly injected, that overcame the repulsion he acknowledged, winning complete obedience to the unknown meaning of her words. This meaning, for the moment, lay in darkness; yet it was a portion of his own self, he felt, that concealed it of set purpose. He kept it hid, he looked deliberately another way; for, if he faced it with full recognition, he knew that he must resist it to the death. He allowed himself to ask vague questions—then let her dominating spell confuse the answers so that he did not hear them. The challenge to his soul, that is, he evaded.

What is commonly called sex lay only slightly in his troubled emotions; her purpose had nothing that kept step with chance acquaintanceship. There lay meaning, indeed, in her smile and voice, but these were no hand-maids to a vulgar intrigue in a foreign hotel. Her will breathed cleaner air; her purpose aimed at some graver, mightier climax than the mere subjection of an elderly victim like himself. That will, that purpose, he felt certain, were implacable as death, the resolve in those bold eyes was not a common one. For, in some strange way, he divined the strong maternity in her; the maternal instinct was deeply, even predominantly, involved; he felt positive that a divine tenderness, deeply outraged, was a chief ingredient too. In some way, then, she needed him, yet not she alone, for the pronoun "we" was used, and there were others with her; in some way, equally, a part of him was already her and their accomplice, an unresisting slave, a willing co-conspirator.

He knew one other thing, and it was this that he kept concealed so carefully from himself. His recognition of it was sub-conscious possibly, but for that very reason true: her purpose was consistent with the satisfaction at last of a deep instinct in him that clamoured to know gratification. It was for these odd, mingled reasons that he stood trembling when she left him on the stairs, and finally went down to his hurried meal with a heart that knew wonder, anticipation, and delight, but also dread.

3

The table in front of him remained unoccupied; his dinner finished, he went out hastily.

As he passed through the crowded streets, his chief desire was to be quickly free of the old muffled buildings and airless alleys with their clinging atmosphere of other days. He longed for the sweet taste of the heights, the smells of the forest whither he was bound. This *Forêt Verte*, he knew, rolled for leagues towards the north, empty of houses as of human beings; it was the home of deer and birds and rabbits, of wild boar too. There would be spring flowers among the brushwood, anemones, celandine, oxslip, daffodils. The vapours of the town oppressed him, the warm and heavy moisture stifled; he wanted space and the sight of clean simple things that would stimulate his mind with lighter thoughts.

He soon passed the Rampe, skirted the ugly villas of modern Bihorel and, rising now with every step, entered the *Route Neuve*. He went unduly fast; he was already above the Cathedral spire; below him the Seine meandered round the chalky hills, laden with warbarges, and across a dip, still pink in the afterglow, rose the blunt Down of Bonsecours with its anti-aircraft batteries. Poetry and violent fact crashed everywhere; he longed to top the hill and leave these unhappy reminders of death behind him. In front the sweet woods already beckoned through the twilight. He hastened. Yet while he deliberately fixed his imagination on promised peace and beauty, an undercurrent ran sullenly in his mind, busy with quite other thoughts.

The unknown woman and her singular words, the following mystery of the ancient city, the soft beating wonder of the two together, these worked their incalculable magic persistently about him. Repression merely added to their power. His mind was a prey to some shadowy, remote anxiety that, intangible, invisible, yet knocked with ghostly fingers upon some door of ancient memory. . . . He watched the moon rise above the eastern ridge, in the west the afterglow of sunset still hung red. But these did not hold his attention as they normally must have done. Attention seemed elsewhere. The undercurrent bore him down a siding, into a backwater, as it were, that clamoured for discharge.

He thought suddenly, then, of weather, what he called "German weather"—that combination of natural conditions which so oddly favoured the enemy always. It had often occurred to him as strange; on sea and land, mist, rain and wind, the fog and drying sun worked ever on *their* side. The coincidence was odd, to say the least. And now this glimpse of rising moon and sunset sky reminded him unpleasantly of the subject. Legends of pagan weather-gods passed through his mind like hurrying shadows.

These shadows multiplied, changed form, vanished and returned. They came and went with incoherence, a straggling stream, rushing from one point to another, manoeuvring for position, but all unled, unguided by his will. The physical exercise filled his brain with blood, and thought danced undirected, picture upon picture driving by, so that soon he slipped from German weather and pagan gods to the witchcraft of past centuries, of its alleged association with the natural powers of the elements, and thus, eventually, to his cherished beliefs that humanity had advanced.

Such remnants of primitive days were grotesque superstition, of course. But had humanity advanced? Had the individual progressed after all? Civilization, was it not the merest artificial growth? And the old perplexity rushed through his mind again—the German barbarity and blood-lust, the savagery, the undoubted sadic impulses, the frightfulness taught with cool calculation by their highest minds, approved by their professors, endorsed by their clergy, applauded by their women even—all the unwelcome, undesired thoughts came flocking back upon him, escorted by the trooping shadows. They lay, these questions, still unsolved within him; it was the undercurrent, flowing more swiftly now, that bore them to the surface. It had acquired momentum; it was leading somewhere.

They were a thoughtful, intellectual race, these Germans; their music, literature, philosophy, their science—how reconcile the opposing qualities? He had read that their herd-instinct was unusually developed, though betraying the characteristics of a low wild savage type—the lupine. It might be true. Fear and danger wakened this collective instinct into terrific activity, making them blind and humourless; they fought best, like wolves, in contact; they howled and whined and boasted loudly all together to inspire terror; their Hymn of Hate was but an elaboration of the wolf's fierce bark, giving them herd-courage; and a savage discipline was necessary to their lupine type.

These reflections thronged his mind as the blood coursed in his veins with the rapid climbing; yet one and all, the beauty of the evening, the magic of the hidden town, the thoughts of German horror, German weather, German gods, all these, even the odd detail that they revived a pagan practice by hammering nails into effigies and idols—all led finally to one blazing centre that nothing could dislodge nor anything conceal; a woman's voice and eyes. To these he knew quite well, was due the undesired intensification of the very mood, the very emotions, the very thoughts he had come out on purpose to escape.

"It is the night of the vernal equinox," occurred to him suddenly, sharp as a whispered voice beside him. He had no notion whence the idea was born. It had no particular meaning, so far as he remembered.

"It had *then* . . ." said the voice imperiously, rising, it seemed, directly out of the undercurrent in his soul.

It startled him. He increased his pace. He walked very quickly, whistling softly as he went.

The dusk had fallen when at length he topped the long, slow hill, and left the last of the atrocious straggling villas well behind him. The ancient city lay far below in murky haze and smoke, but tinged now with the silver of the growing moon.

4

He stood now on the open plateau. He was on the heights at last.

The night air met him freshly in the face, so that he forgot the fatigue of the long climb uphill, taken too fast somewhat for his years. He drew a deep draught into his lungs and stepped out briskly.

Far in the upper sky light flaky clouds raced through the reddened air, but the wind kept to these higher strata, and the world about him lay very still. Few lights showed in the farms and cottages, for this was the direct route of the Gothas, and nothing that could help the German hawks to find the river was visible.

His mind cleared pleasantly; this keen sweet air held no mystery; he put his best foot foremost, whistling still, but a little more loudly than before. Among the orchards he saw the daisies glimmer. Also, he heard the guns, a thudding concussion in the direction of the coveted Amiens, where, some sixty miles as the crow flies, they roared their terror into the calm evening skies. He cursed the sound, in the town below it was not audible. Thought jumped then to the men who fired them, and so to the prisoners who worked on the roads outside the hospitals and camps he visited daily. He passed them every morning and night, and the N.C.O. invariably saluted his Red Cross uniform, a salute he returned, when he could not avoid it, with embarrassment.

One man in particular stood out clearly in this memory; he had exchanged glances with him, noted the expression of his face, the number of his gang printed on coat and trousers—"82." The fellow had somehow managed to establish a relationship; he would look up and smile or frown; if the news, from his point of view, was good, he smiled; if it was bad, he scowled; once, insolently enough—when the Germans had taken Albert, Péronne, Bapaume—he grinned.

Something about the sullen, close-cropped face, typically Prussian, made the other shudder. It was the visage of an animal, neither evil nor malignant, even good-natured sometimes when it smiled, yet of an animal that could be fierce with the lust of happiness, ferocious with delight. The sullen savagery of a human wolf lay in it somewhere. He pictured its owner impervious to shame, to normal human instinct as civilized people know these. Doubtless he read his own feelings into it. He could imagine the man doing anything and everything, regarding chivalry and sporting instinct as proof of fear or weakness. He could picture this member of the wolf-pack killing a woman or a child, mutilating, cutting off little hands even, with the conscientious conviction that it was right and sensible to destroy *any* individual of an enemy tribe. It was, to him, an atrocious and inhuman face.

It now cropped up with unpleasant vividness, as he listened to the distant guns and thought of Amiens with its back against the wall, its inhabitants flying——

Ah! Amiens. . . ! He again saw the woman staring into his obedient eyes across the narrow space between the tables. He smelt the delicious perfume of her dress and person on the stairs. He heard her commanding voice, her very words: "We count on you. . . . I know we can . . . we do." And her background was of twisted streets, dark alley-ways and leaning gables. . . .

He hurried, whistling loudly an air that he invented suddenly, using his stick like a golf club at every loose stone his feet encountered, making as much noise as possible. He told himself he was a parson and a Red Cross worker. He looked up and saw that the stars were out. The pace made him warm, and he shifted his haversack to the other shoulder. The moon, he observed, now cast his shadow for a long distance on the sandy road.

After another mile, while the air grew sharper and twilight surrendered finally to the moon, the road began to curve and dip, the cottages lay farther out in the dim fields, the farms and barns occurred at longer intervals. A dog barked now and again; he saw cows lying down for the night beneath shadowy fruit-trees. And then the scent in the air changed slightly, and a darkening of the near horizon warned him that the forest had come close.

This was an event. Its influence breathed already a new perfume; the shadows from its myriad trees stole out and touched him. Ten minutes later he reached its actual frontier cutting across the plateau like a line of sentries at attention. He slowed down a little. Here, within sight and touch of his long-desired objective, he hesitated. It stretched, he knew from the map, for many leagues to the north, uninhabited, lonely, the home of peace and silence; there were flowers there, and cool sweet spaces where the moonlight fell. Yet here, within scent and touch of it, he slowed down a moment to draw breath. A forest on the map is one thing; visible before the eyes when night has fallen, it is another. It is real.

The wind, not noticeable hitherto, now murmured towards him from the serried trees that seemed to manufacture darkness out of nothing. This murmur hummed about him. It enveloped him. Piercing it, another sound that was not the guns just reached him, but so distant that he hardly noticed it. He looked back. Dusk suddenly merged in night. He stopped.

"How practical the French are," he said to himself—aloud—as he looked at the road running straight as a ruled line into the heart of the trees. "They waste no energy, no space, no time. Admirable!"

It pierced the forest like a lance, tapering to a faint point in the misty distance. The trees ate its undeviating straightness as though they would smother it from sight, as though its rigid outline marred their mystery. He admired the practical makers of the road, yet sided, too, with the poetry of the trees. He stood there staring, waiting, dawdling. . . . About him, save for this murmur of the wind, was silence. Nothing living stirred. The world lay extraordinarily still. That other distant sound had died away.

He lit his pipe, glad that the match blew out and the damp tobacco needed several matches before the pipe drew properly. His *puttees* hurt him a little, he stooped to loosen them. His haversack swung round in front as he straightened up again, he shifted it laboriously to the other shoulder. A tiny stone in his right boot caused irritation. Its removal took a considerable time, for he had to sit down, and a log was not at once forthcoming. Moreover, the laces gave him trouble, and his fingers had grown thick with heat and the knots were difficult to tie. . . .

"There!" He said it aloud, standing up again. "Now at last, I'm ready!" Then added a mild imprecation, for his pipe had gone out while he stooped over the recalcitrant boot, and it had to be lighted once again. "Ah!" he gasped finally with a sigh as, facing the forest for the third time, he shuffled his tunic straight, altered his haversack once more, changed his stick from the right hand to the left—and faced the foolish truth without further pretence.

He mopped his forehead carefully, as though at the same time trying to mop away from his mind a faint anxiety, a very faint uneasiness, that gathered there. Was someone standing near him? Had somebody come close? He listened intently. It was the blood singing in his ears, of course, that curious distant noise. For, truth to tell, the loneliness bit just below the surface of what he found enjoyable. It seemed to him that somebody was coming, someone he could not see, so that he looked back over his shoulder once again, glanced quickly right and left, then peered down the long opening cut through the woods in front—when there came suddenly a roar and a blaze of dazzling light from behind, so instantaneously that he barely had time to obey the instinct of self-preservation and step aside. He actually leapt. Pressed against the hedge, he saw a motorcar rush past him like a whirlwind, flooding the sandy road with fire; a second followed it; and, to his complete amazement, then, a third.

They were powerful, private cars, so-called. This struck him instantly. Two other things he noticed, as they dived down the throat of the long white road—they showed no tail-lights. This made him wonder. And, secondly, the drivers, clearly seen, were women. They were not even in uniform—which made him wonder even more. The occupants, too, were women. He caught the outline of toque and feather—or was it flowers?—against the closed windows in the moonlight as the procession rushed past him.

He felt bewildered and astonished. Private motors were rare, and military regulations exceedingly strict; the danger of spies dressed in French uniform was constant; cars armed with machine guns, he knew, patrolled the countryside in all directions. Shaken and alarmed, he thought of favoured persons fleeing stealthily by night, of treachery, disguise and swift surprise; he thought of various things as he stood peering down the road for ten minutes after all sight and sound of the cars had died away. But no solution of the mystery occurred to him. Down the white throat the motors vanished. His pipe had gone out; he lit it, and puffed furiously.

His thoughts, at any rate, took temporarily a new direction now. The road was not as lonely as he had imagined. A natural reaction set in at once, and this proof of practical, modern life banished the shadows from his mind effectually. He started off once more, oblivious of his former hesitation. He even felt a trifle shamed and foolish, pretending that the vanished mood had not existed. The tobacco had been damp. His boot had really hurt him.

Yet bewilderment and surprise stayed with him. The swiftness of the incident was disconcerting; the cars arrived and vanished with such extraordinary rapidity; their noisy irruption into this peaceful spot seemed incongruous; they roared, blazed, rushed and disappeared; silence resumed its former sway.

But the silence persisted, whereas the noise was gone.

This touch of the incongruous remained with him as he now went ever deeper into the heart of the quiet forest. This odd incongruity of dreams remained.

5

The keen air stole from the woods, cooling his body and his mind; anemones gleamed faintly among the brushwood, lit by the pallid moonlight. There were beauty, calm and silence, the slow breathing of the earth beneath the comforting sweet stars. War, in this haunt of ancient peace, seemed an incredible anachronism. His thoughts turned to gentle happy hopes of a day when the lion and the lamb would yet lie down together, and a little child would lead them without fear. His soul dwelt with peaceful longings and calm desires.

He walked on steadily, until the inflexible straightness of the endless road began to afflict him, and he longed for a turning to the right or left. He looked eagerly about him for a woodland path. Time mattered little; he could wait for the sunrise and walk home "beneath the young grey dawn"; he had food and matches, he could light a fire, and sleep—— No!—after all, he would not light a fire, perhaps; he might be accused of signalling to hostile aircraft, or a *garde forestière* might catch him. He would not bother with a fire. The night was warm, he could enjoy himself and pass the time quite happily without artificial heat; probably he would need no sleep at all. . . . And just then he noticed an opening on his right, where a seductive pathway led in among the trees. The moon, now higher in the sky, lit this woodland trail enticingly; it seemed the very opening he had looked for, and with a thrill of pleasure he at once turned down it, leaving the ugly road behind him with relief.

The sound of his footsteps hushed instantly on the leaves and moss; the silence became noticeable; an unusual stillness followed; it seemed that something in his mind was also hushed. His feet moved stealthily, as though anxious to conceal his presence from surprise. His steps dragged purposely; their rustling through the thick dead leaves, perhaps, was pleasant to him. He was not sure.

The path opened presently into a clearing where the moonlight made a pool of silver, the surrounding brushwood fell away; and in the centre a gigantic outline rose. It was, he saw, a beech tree that dwarfed the surrounding forest by its grandeur. Its bulk loomed very splendid against the sky, a faint rustle just audible in its myriad tiny leaves.

Dipped in the moonlight, it had such majesty of proportion, such symmetry, that he stopped in admiration. It was, he saw, a multiple tree, five stems springing with attempted spirals out of an enormous trunk; it was immense; it had a presence, the space framed it to perfection.

The clearing, evidently, was a favourite resting place for summer picknickers, a playground, probably, for city children on holiday afternoons; woodcutters, too, had been here recently, for he noticed piled brushwood ready to be carted. It indicated admirably, he felt, the limits of his night expedition. Here he would rest awhile, eat his late supper, sleep perhaps round a small—— No! again—a fire he need *not* make; a spark might easily set the woods ablaze, it was against both forest and military regulations. This idea of a fire, otherwise so natural, was distasteful, even repugnant, to him. He wondered a little why it recurred. He noticed this time, moreover, something unpleasant connected with the suggestion of a fire, something that made him shrink; almost a ghostly dread lay hidden in it.

This startled him. A dozen excellent reasons, supplied by his brain, warned him that a fire was unwise; but the true reason, supplied by another part of him, concealed itself with care, as though afraid that reason might detect its nature and fix the label on. Disliking this reminder of his earlier mood, he moved forward into the clearing, swinging his stick aggressively and whistling. He approached the tree, where a dozen thick roots dipped into the earth. Admiring, looking up and down, he paced slowly round its prodigious girth, then stood absolutely still. His heart stopped abruptly, his blood became congealed. He saw something that filled him with a sudden emptiness of terror. On this western side the shadow lay very black; it was between the thick limbs, half stem, half root, where the dark hollows gave easy hiding-places, that he was positive he detected movement. A portion of the trunk had moved.

He stood stock still and stared—not three feet from the trunk—when there came a second movement. Concealed in the shadows there crouched a living form. The movement defined itself immediately. Half reclining, half standing, a living being pressed itself close against the tree, yet fitting so neatly into the wide scooped hollows, that it was scarcely distinguishable from its ebony background. But for the chance movement he must have passed it undetected. Equally, his outstretched fingers might have touched it. The blood rushed from his heart, as he saw this second movement.

Detaching itself from the obscure background, the figure rose and stood before him. It swayed a little, then stepped out into the patch of moonlight on his left. Three feet lay between them. The figure then bent over. A pallid face with burning eyes thrust forward and peered straight into his own.

The human being was a woman. The same instant he recognized the eyes that had stared him out of countenance in the dining-room two nights ago. He was petrified. She stared him out of countenance now.

And, as she did so, the undercurrent he had tried to ignore so long swept to the surface in a tumultuous flood, obliterating his normal self. Something elaborately built up in his soul by years of artificial training collapsed like a house of cards, and he knew himself undone.

"They've got me. . . !" flashed dreadfully through his mind. It was, again, like a message delivered in a dream where the significance of acts performed and language uttered, concealed at the moment, is revealed much later only.

"After all—they've got me. . . !"

6

The dialogue that followed seemed strange to him only when looking back upon it. The element of surprise again was negligible if not wholly absent, but the incongruity of dreams, almost of nightmare, became more marked. Though the affair was unlikely, it was far from incredible. So completely were this man and woman involved in some purpose common to them both that their talk, their meeting, their instinctive sympathy at the time seemed natural. The same stream bore them irresistibly towards the same far sea. Only, as yet, this common purpose remained concealed. Nor could he define the violent emotions that troubled him. Their exact description was in him, but so deep that he could not draw it up. Moonlight lay upon his thought, merging clear outlines.

Divided against himself, the cleavage left no authoritative self in control; his desire to take an immediate decision resulted in a confused struggle, where shame and pleasure, attraction and revulsion mingled painfully. Incongruous details tumbled helter-skelter about his mind: for no obvious reason, he remembered again his Red Cross uniform, his former holy calling, his nationality too; he was a servant of mercy, a teacher of the love of God; he was an English gentleman. Against which rose other details, as in opposition, holding just beyond the reach of words, yet rising, he recognized well enough, from the bed-rock of the human animal, whereon a few centuries have imposed the thin crust of refinement men call civilization. He was aware of joy and loathing.

In the first few seconds he knew the clash of a dreadful fundamental struggle, while the spell of this woman's strange enchantment poured over him, seeking the reconciliation he himself could not achieve. Yet the reconciliation *she* sought meant victory or defeat; no compromise lay in it. Something imperious emanating from her already dominated the warring elements towards a coherent whole. He stood before her, quivering with emotions he dared not name. Her great womanhood he recognised, acknowledging obedience to her undisclosed intentions. And this idea of coming surrender terrified him. Whence came, too, that queenly touch about her that made him feel he should have sunk upon his knees?

The conflict resulted in a curious compromise. He raised his hand; he saluted; he found very ordinary words.

"You passed me only a short time ago," he stammered, "in the motors. There were others with you——"

"Knowing that you would find us and come after. We count on your presence and your willing help." Her voice was firm as with unalterable conviction. It was persuasive too. He nodded, as though acquiescence seemed the only course.

"We need your sympathy; we must have your power too."

He bowed again. "My power!" Something exulted in him. But he murmured only. It was natural, he felt; he gave consent without a question.

Strange words he both understood and did not understand. Her voice, low and silvery, was that of a gentle, cultured woman, but command rang through it with a clang of metal, terrible behind the sweetness. She moved a little closer, standing erect before him in the moonlight, her figure borrowing something of the great tree's majesty behind her. It was incongruous, this gentle and yet sinister air she wore. Whence came, in this calm peaceful spot, the suggestion of a wild and savage background to her? Why were there tumult and oppression in his heart, pain, horror, tenderness and mercy, mixed beyond disentanglement? Why did he think already, but helplessly, of escape, yet at the same time burn to stay? Whence came again, too, a certain queenly touch he felt in her?

"The gods have brought you," broke across his turmoil in a half whisper whose breath almost touched his face. "You belong to us."

The deeps rose in him. Seduced by the sweetness and the power, the warring divisions in his being drew together. His under-self more and more obtained the mastery she willed. Then something in the French she used flickered across his mind with a faint reminder of normal things again.

"Belgian———" he began, and then stopped short, as her instant rejoinder broke in upon his halting speech and petrified him. In her voice sang that triumphant tenderness that only the feminine powers of the Universe may compass: it seemed the sky sang with her, the mating birds, wild flowers, the south wind and the running streams. All these, even the silver birches, lent their fluid, feminine undertones to the two pregnant words with which she interrupted him and completed his own unfinished sentence:

"——— and mother."

With the dreadful calm of an absolute assurance, she stood and watched him.

His understanding already showed signs of clearing. She stretched her hands out with a passionate appeal, a yearning gesture, the eloquence of which should explain all that remained unspoken. He saw their grace and symmetry, exquisite in the moonlight, then watched them fold together in an attitude of prayer. Beautiful mother hands they were; hands made to smooth the pillows of the world, to comfort, bless, caress, hands that little children everywhere must lean upon and love-perfect symbol of protective, self-forgetful motherhood.

This tenderness he noted; he noted next—the strength. In the folded hands he divined the expression of another great world-power, fulfilling the implacable resolution of the mouth and eyes. He was aware of relentless purpose, more—of merciless revenge, as by a protective motherhood outraged beyond endurance. Moreover, the gesture held appeal; these hands, so close that their actual perfume reached him, sought his own in help. The power in himself as man, as male, as father—this was required of him in the fulfilment of the unknown purpose to which this woman summoned him. His understanding cleared still more.

The couple faced one another, staring fixedly beneath the giant beech that overarched them. In the dark of his eyes, he knew, lay growing terror. He shivered, and the shiver passed down his spine, making his whole body tremble. There stirred in him an excitement he loathed, yet welcomed, as the primitive male in him, answering the summons, reared up with instinctive, dreadful glee to shatter the bars that civilization had so confidently set upon its freedom. A primal emotion of his under-being, ancient lust that had too long gone hungry and unfed, leaped towards some possible satisfaction. It was incredible; it was, of course, a dream.

But judgment wavered; increasing terror ate his will away. Violence and sweetness, relief and degradation, fought in his soul, as he trembled before a power that now slowly mastered him. This glee and loathing formed their ghastly partnership. He could have strangled the woman where she stood. Equally, he could have knelt and kissed her feet.

The vehemence of the conflict paralysed him.

"A mother's hands . . ." he murmured at length, the words escaping like bubbles that rose to the surface of a seething cauldron and then burst.

And the woman smiled as though she read his mind and saw his little trembling. The smile crept down from the eyes towards the mouth; he saw her lips part slightly; he saw her teeth.

But her reply once more transfixed him. Two syllables she uttered in a voice of iron:

"Louvain."

★★★★★★★★★★★★

The sound acted upon him like a Word of Power in some Eastern fairy tale. It knit the present to a past that he now recognized could never die. Humanity had *not* advanced. The hidden source of his secret joy began to glow. For this woman focused in him passions that life had hitherto denied, pretending they were atrophied, and the primitive male, the naked savage rose up, with glee in its lustful eyes and blood upon its lips. Acquired civilization, a pitiful mockery, split through its thin veneer and fled.

"Belgian . . . Louvain . . . Mother . . ." he whispered, yet astonished at the volume of sound that now left his mouth. His voice had a sudden fullness. It seemed a cave-man roared the words.

She touched his hand, and he knew a sudden intensification of life within him; immense energy poured through his veins; a mediæval spirit used his eyes; great pagan instincts strained and urged against his heart, against his very muscles. He longed for action.

And he cried aloud: "I am with you, with you to the end!"

Her spell had vivified beyond all possible resistance that primitive consciousness which is ever the bed-rock of the human animal.

A racial memory, inset against the forest scenery, flashed suddenly through the depths laid bare. Below a sinking moon dark figures flew in streaming lines and groups; tormented cries went down the wind; he saw torn, blasted trees that swayed and rocked; there was a leaping fire, a gleaming knife, an altar. He saw a sacrifice.

It flashed away and vanished. In its place the woman stood, with shining eyes fixed on his face, one arm outstretched, one hand upon his flesh. She shifted slightly, and her cloak swung open. He saw clinging skins wound closely about her figure; leaves, flowers and trailing green hung from her shoulders, fluttering down the lines of her triumphant physical beauty. There was a perfume of wild roses, incense, ivy bloom, whose subtle intoxication drowned his senses. He saw a sparkling girdle round the waist, a knife thrust through it tight against the hip. And his secret joy, the glee, the pleasure of some unlawful and unholy lust leaped through his blood towards the abandonment of satisfaction.

The moon revealed a glimpse, no more. An instant he saw her thus, half savage and half sweet, symbol of primitive justice entering the present through the door of vanished centuries.

The cloak swung back again, the outstretched hand withdrew, but from a world he knew had altered.

Today sank out of sight. The moon shone pale with terror and delight on Yesterday.

7

Across this altered world a faint new sound now reached his ears, as though a human wail of anguished terror trembled and changed into the cry of some captured helpless animal. He thought of a wolf apart from the comfort of its pack, savage yet abject. The despair of a last appeal was in the sound. It floated past, it died away. The woman moved closer suddenly.

"All is prepared," she said, in the same low, silvery voice; "we must not tarry. The equinox is come, the tide of power flows. The sacrifice is here; we hold him fast. We only awaited you." Her shining eyes were raised to his. "Your soul is with us now?" she whispered.

"My soul is with you."

"And midnight," she continued, "is at hand. We use, of course, their methods. Henceforth the gods—their old-world gods—shall work on our side. They demand a sacrifice, and justice has provided one."

His understanding cleared still more then; the last veil of confusion was drawing from his mind. The old, old names went thundering through his consciousness—Odin, Wotan, Moloch—accessible ever to

126

invocation and worship of the rightful kind. It seemed as natural as though he read in his pulpit the prayer for rain, or gave out the hymn for those at sea. That was merely an empty form, whereas this was real. Sea, storm and earthquake, all natural activities, lay under the direction of those elemental powers called the gods. Names changed, the principle remained.

"Their weather shall be ours," he cried, with sudden passion, as a memory of unhallowed usages he had thought erased from life burned in him; while, stranger still, resentment stirred—revolt—against the system, against the very deity he had worshipped hitherto. For these had never once interfered to help the cause of right; their feebleness was now laid bare before his eyes. And a two-fold lust rose in him. "Vengeance is ours!" he cried in a louder voice, through which this sudden loathing of the cross poured hatred. "Vengeance and justice! Now bind the victim! Bring on the sacrifice!"

"He is already bound." And as the woman moved a little, the curious erection behind her caught his eye—the piled brushwood he had imagined was the work of woodmen, picnickers, or playing children. He realised its true meaning.

It now delighted and appalled him. Awe deepened in him, a wind of ice passed over him. Civilization made one more fluttering effort. He gasped, he shivered; he tried to speak. But no words came. A thin cry, as of a frightened child, escaped him.

"It is the only way," the woman whispered softly. "We steal from them the power of their own deities." Her head flung back with a marvellous gesture of grace and power; she stood before him a figure of perfect womanhood, gentle and tender, yet at the same time alive and cruel with the passions of an ignorant and savage past. Her folded hands were clasped, her face turned heavenwards. "I am a mother," she added, with amazing passion, her eyes glistening in the moonlight with unshed tears. "We all"—she glanced towards the forest, her voice rising to a wild and poignant cry—"all, all of us are mothers!"

It was then the final clearing of his understanding happened, and he realised his own part in what would follow. Yet before the realisation he felt himself not merely ineffective, but powerless. The struggling forces in him were so evenly matched that paralysis of the will resulted. His dry lips contrived merely a few words of confused and feeble protest.

"Me!" he faltered. "My help——?"

"Justice," she answered; and though softly uttered, it was as though the medieval towers clanged their bells. That secret, ghastly joy again rose in him; admiration, wonder, desire followed instantly. A fugitive memory of Joan of Arc flashed by, as with armoured wings, upon the moonlight. Some power similarly heroic, some purpose similarly inflexible, emanated from this woman, the savour of whose physical enchantment, whose very breath, rose to his brain like incense. Again, he shuddered. The spasm of secret pleasure shocked him. He sighed. He felt alert, yet stunned.

Her words went down the wind between them:

"You are so weak, you English," he heard her terrible whisper, "so nobly forgiving, so fine, yet so forgetful. You refuse the weapon *they* place within your hands." Her face thrust closer, the great eyes blazed upon him. "If we would save the children"—the voice rose and fell like wind—"we must worship where they worship, we must sacrifice to their savage deities . . ."

The stream of her words flowed over him with this nightmare magic that seemed natural, without surprise. He listened, he trembled, and again he sighed. Yet in his blood there was sudden roaring.

". . .Louvain . . .the hands of little children . . .we have the proof," he heard, oddly intermingled with another set of words that clamoured vainly in his brain for utterance; "the diary in his own handwriting, his gloating pleasure . . .the little, innocent hands . . ."

"Justice is mine!" rang through some fading region of his now fainting soul, but found no audible utterance.

". . .Mist, rain and wind . . .the gods of German Weather . . .We all . . .are mothers . . ."

"I will repay," came forth in actual words, yet so low he hardly heard the sound. But the woman heard.

"*We!*" she cried fiercely, "*we* will repay!" . . .

"God!" The voice seemed torn from his throat. "Oh God—*my* God!"

"*Our* gods," she said steadily in that tone of iron, "are near. The sacrifice is ready. And *you*—servant of mercy, priest of a younger deity, and English—you bring the power that makes it effectual. The circuit is complete."

It was perhaps the tears in her appealing eyes, perhaps it was her words, her voice, the wonder of her presence; all combined possibly in the spell that finally then struck down his will as with a single blow that paralysed his last resistance. The monstrous, half-legendary spirit of a primitive day recaptured him completely; he yielded to the spell of this tender, cruel woman, mother and avenging angel, whom horror and suffering had flung back upon the practices of uncivilized centuries. A common desire, a common lust and purpose, degraded both of them. They understood one another. Dropping back into a gulf of savage worship that set up idols in the place of God, they prayed to Odin and his awful crew . . .

It was again the touch of her hand that galvanised him. She raised him; he had been kneeling in slavish wonder and admiration at her feet. He leaped to do the bidding, however terrible, of this woman who was priestess, queen indeed, of a long-forgotten orgy.

"Vengeance at last!" he cried, in an exultant voice that no longer frightened him. "Now light the fire! Bring on the sacrifice!"

There was a rustling among the nearer branches, the forest stirred; the leaves of last year brushed against advancing feet. Yet before he could turn to see, before even the last words had wholly left his lips, the woman, whose hand still touched his fingers, suddenly tossed her cloak aside, and flinging her bare arms about his neck, drew him with impetuous passion towards her face and kissed him, as with delighted fury of exultant passion, full upon the mouth. Her body, in its clinging skins, pressed close against his own; her heat poured into him. She held him fiercely, savagely, and her burning kiss consumed his modern soul away with the fire of a primal day.

"The gods have given you to us," she cried, releasing him. "Your soul is ours!"

She turned—they turned together—to look for one upon whose last hour the moon now shed her horrid silver.

8

This silvery moonlight fell upon the scene.

Incongruously he remembered the flowers that soon would know the cuckoo's call; the soft mysterious stars shone down; the woods lay silent underneath the sky.

An amazing fantasy of dream shot here and there. "I am a man, an Englishman, a *padre*!" ran twisting through his mind, as though *she* whispered them to emphasise the ghastly contrast of reality. A memory of his own Kentish village with its Sunday school fled past, his dream of the Lion and the Lamb close after it. He saw children playing on the green . . . He saw their happy little hands . . .

Justice, punishment, revenge—he could not disentangle them. No longer did he wish to. The tide of violence was at his lips, quenching an ancient thirst. He drank. It seemed he could drink forever. These tender pictures only sweetened horror. That kiss had burned his modern soul away.

The woman waved her hand; there swept from the underbrush a score of figures dressed like herself in skins, with leaves and flowers entwined among their flying hair. He was surrounded in a moment. Upon each face he noted the same tenderness and terrible resolve that their commander wore. They pressed about him, dancing with enchanting grace, yet with full-blooded abandon, across the chequered light and shadow. It was the brimming energy of their movements that swept him off his feet, waking the desire for fierce rhythmical expression.

His own muscles leaped and ached; for this energy, it seemed, poured into him from the tossing arms and legs, the shimmering bodies whence hair and skins flung loose, setting the very air awhirl. It flowed over into inanimate objects even, so that the trees waved their branches although no wind stirred—hair, skins and hands, rushing leaves and flying fingers touched his face, his neck, his arms and shoulders, catching him away into this orgy of an ancient, sacrificial ritual.

Faces with shining eyes peered into his, then sped away; grew in a cloud upon the moonlight; sank back in shadow; reappeared, touched him, whispered, vanished. Silvery limbs gleamed everywhere. Chanting rose in a wave, to fall away again into forest rustlings; there were smiles that flashed, then fainted into moonlight, red lips and gleaming teeth that shone, then faded out. The secret glade, picked from the heart of the forest by the moon, became a torrent of tumultuous life, a whirlpool of passionate emotions Time had not killed.

But it was the eyes that mastered him, for in their yearning, mating so incongruously with the savage grace—in the eyes shone ever tears. He was aware of gentle women, of womanhood, of accumulated feminine power that nothing could withstand, but of feminine power in majesty, its essential protective tenderness roused, as by tribal instinct, into a collective fury of implacable revenge. He was, above all, aware of motherhood—of mothers. And the man, the male, the father in him rose like a storm to meet it.

From the torrent of voices certain sentences emerged; sometimes chanted, sometimes driven into his whirling mind as though big whispers thrust them down his ears. "You are with us to the end," he caught. "We have the proof. And punishment is ours!"

It merged in wind, others took its place:

"We hold him fast. The old gods wait and listen."

The body of rushing whispers flowed like a storm-wind past.

A lovely face, fluttering close against his own, paused an instant, and starry eyes gazed into his with a passion of gratitude, dimming a moment their stern fury with a mother's tenderness: "For the little ones . . . it is necessary, it is the only way . . . Our own children . . ." The face went out in a gust of blackness, as the chorus rose with a new note of awe and reverence, and a score of throats uttered in unison a single cry: "The raven! The White Horses! His signs! Great Odin hears!"

He saw the great dark bird flap slowly across the clearing, and melt against the shadow of the giant beech; he heard its hoarse, croaking note; the crowds of heads bowed low before its passage. The White Horses he did not see; only a sound as of considerable masses of air regularly displaced was audible far overhead. But the veiled light, as though great thunder-clouds had risen, he saw distinctly. The sky above the clearing where he stood, panting and dishevelled, was blocked by a mass that owned unusual outline. These clouds now topped the forest, hiding the moon and stars. The flowers went out like nightlights blown. The wind rose slowly, then with sudden violence. There was a roaring in the tree-tops. The branches tossed and shook.

"The White Horses!" cried the voices, in a frenzy of adoration. "He is here!"

It came swiftly, this collective mass; it was both apt and terrible. There was an immense footstep. It was there.

Then panic seized him, he felt an answering tumult in himself, the Past surged through him like a sea at flood. Some inner sight, peering across the wreckage of Today, perceived an outline that in its size dwarfed mountains, a pair of monstrous shoulders, a face that rolled through a full quarter of the heavens. Above the ruin of civilization, now fulfilled in the microcosm of his own being, the menacing shadow of a forgotten deity peered down upon the earth, yet upon one detail of it chiefly—the human group that had been wildly dancing, but that now chanted in solemn conclave about a forest altar.

For some minutes a dead silence reigned; the pouring winds left emptiness in which no leaf stirred; there was a hush, a stillness that could be felt. The kneeling figures stretched forth a level sea of arms towards the altar; from the lowered heads the hair hung down in torrents, against which the naked flesh shone white; the skins upon the rows of backs gleamed yellow. The obscurity deepened overhead.

It was the time of adoration. He knelt as well, arms similarly outstretched, while the lust of vengeance burned within him.

Then came, across the stillness, the stirring of big wings, a rustling as the great bird settled in the higher branches of the beech. The ominous note broke through the silence; and with one accord the shining backs were straightened. The company rose, swayed, parting into groups and lines. Two score voices resumed the solemn chant. The throng of pallid faces passed to and fro like great fire-flies that shone and vanished. He, too, heard his own voice in unison, while his feet, as with instinctive knowledge, trod the same measure that the others trod.

Out of this tumult and clearly audible above the chorus and the rustling feet rang out suddenly, in a sweetly fluting tone, the leader's voice:

"The Fire! But first the hands!"

A rush of figures set instantly towards a thicket where the underbrush stood densest. Skins, trailing flowers, bare waving arms and tossing hair swept past on a burst of perfume. It was as though the trees themselves sped by. And the torrent of voices shook the very air in answer:

"The Fire! But first—the hands!"

Across this roaring volume pierced then, once again, that wailing sound which seemed both human and non-human—the anguished cry as of some lonely wolf in metamorphosis, apart from the collective safety of the pack, abjectly terrified, feeling the teeth of the final trap, and knowing the helpless feet within the steel. There was a crash of rending boughs and tearing branches. There was a tumult in the thicket, though of brief duration—then silence.

He stood watching, listening, overmastered by a diabolical sensation of expectancy he knew to be atrocious.

Turning in the direction of the cry, his straining eyes seemed filled with blood; in his temples the pulses throbbed and hammered audibly. The next second he stiffened into a stone-like rigidity, as a figure, struggling violently yet half collapsed, was borne hurriedly past by a score of eager arms that swept it towards the beech tree, and then proceeded to fasten it in an upright position against the trunk. It was a man bound tight with thongs, adorned with leaves and flowers and trailing green. The face was hidden, for the head sagged forward on the breast, but he saw the arms forced flat against the giant trunk, held helpless beyond all possible escape; he saw the knife, poised and aimed by slender, graceful fingers above the victim's wrists laid bare; he saw the—hands.

"An eye for an eye," he heard, "a tooth for a tooth!" It rose in awful chorus. Yet this time, although the words roared close about him, they seemed farther away, as if wind brought them through the crowding trees from far off.

"Light the fire! Prepare the sacrifice!" came on a following wind; and, while strange distance held the voices as before, a new faint sound now audible was very close. There was a crackling. Some ten feet beyond the tree a column of thick smoke rose in the air; he was aware of heat not meant for modern purposes; of yellow light that was not the light of stars.

The figure writhed, and the face swung suddenly sideways. Glaring with panic hopelessness past the judge and past the hanging knife, the eyes found his own. There was a pause of perhaps five seconds, but in these five seconds centuries rolled by. The priest of Today looked down into the well of time. For five hundred years he gazed into those twin eyeballs, glazed with the abject terror of a last appeal. They recognised one another.

The centuries dragged appallingly. The drama of civilisation, in a sluggish stream, went slowly by, halting, meandering, losing itself, then reappearing. Sharpest pains, as of a thousand knives, accompanied its dreadful, endless lethargy. Its million hesitations made him suffer a million deaths of agony. Terror, despair and anger, all futile and without effect upon its progress, destroyed a thousand times his soul, which yet some hope—a towering, indestructible hope—a thousand times renewed. This despair and hope alternately broke his being, ever to fashion it anew. His torture seemed not of this world. Yet hope survived. The sluggish stream moved onward, forward. . . .

There came an instant of sharpest, dislocating torture. The yellow light grew slightly brighter. He saw the eyelids flicker.

It was at this moment he realised abruptly that he stood alone, apart from the others, unnoticed apparently, perhaps forgotten; his feet held steady; his voice no longer sang. And at this discovery a quivering shock ran through his being, as though the will were suddenly loosened into a new activity, yet an activity that halted between two terrifying alternatives.

It was as though the flicker of those eyelids loosed a spring.

Two instincts, clashing in his being, fought furiously for the mastery. One, ancient as this sacrifice, savage as the legendary figure brooding in the heavens above him, battled fiercely with another, acquired more recently in human evolution, that had not yet crystallized into permanence. He saw a child, playing in a Kentish orchard with toys and flowers the little innocent hands made living ... he saw a lowly manger, figures kneeling round it, and one star shining overhead in piercing and prophetic beauty.

Thought was impossible; he saw these symbols only, as the two contrary instincts, alternately hidden and revealed, fought for permanent possession of his soul. Each strove to dominate him; it seemed that violent blows were struck that wounded physically; he was bruised, he ached, he gasped for breath; his body swayed, held upright only, it seemed, by the awful appeal in the fixed and staring eyes.

The challenge had come at last to final action; the conqueror, he well knew, would remain an integral portion of his character, his soul.

It was the old, old battle, waged eternally in every human heart, in every tribe, in every race, in every period, the essential principle indeed, behind the great world-war. In the stress and confusion of the fight, as the eyes of the victim, savage in victory, abject in defeat—the appealing eyes of that animal face against the tree stared with their awful blaze into his own, this flashed clearly over him. It was the battle between might and right, between love and hate, forgiveness and vengeance, Christ and the Devil. He heard the menacing thunder of "an eye for an eye, a tooth for a tooth," then above its angry volume rose suddenly another small silvery voice that pierced with sweetness:— "Vengeance is mine, I will repay . . ." sang through him as with unimaginable hope.

Something became incandescent in him then. He realised a singular merging of powers in absolute opposition to each other. It was as though they harmonized. Yet it was through this small, silvery voice the apparent magic came. The words, of course, were his own in memory, but they rose from his modern soul, now reawakening . . . He started painfully. He noted again that he stood apart, alone, perhaps forgotten of the others. The woman, leading a dancing throng about the blazing brushwood, was far from him. Her mind, too sure of his compliance, had momentarily left him. The chain was weakened. The circuit knew a break.

But this sudden realisation was not of spontaneous origin. His heart had not produced it of its own accord. The unholy tumult of the orgy held him too slavishly in its awful sway for the tiny point of his modern soul to have pierced it thus unaided. The light flashed to him from an outside, natural source of simple loveliness—the singing of a bird. From the distance, faint and exquisite, there had reached him the silvery notes of a happy thrush, awake in the night, and telling its joy over and over again to itself. The innocent beauty of its song came through the forest and fell into his soul . . . The eyes, he became aware, had shifted, focusing now upon an object nearer to them. The knife was moving. There was a convulsive wriggle of the body, the head dropped loosely forward, no cry was audible. But, at the same moment, the inner battle ceased and an unexpected climax came.

Did the soul of the bully faint with fear? Did the spirit leave him at the actual touch of earthly vengeance? The watcher never knew. In that appalling moment when the knife was about to begin the mission that the fire would complete, the roar of inner battle ended abruptly, and that small silvery voice drew the words of invincible power from his reawakening soul. "Ye do it also unto me. . ." pealed o'er the forest.

He reeled. He acted instantaneously. Yet before he had dashed the knife from the hand of the executioner, scattered the pile of blazing wood, plunged through the astonished worshippers with a violence of strength that amazed even himself; before he had torn the thongs apart and loosened the fainting victim from the tree; before he had uttered a single word or cry, though it seemed to him he roared with a voice of thousands—he witnessed a sight that came surely from the Heaven of his earliest childhood days, from that Heaven whose God is love and whose forgiveness was taught him at his mother's knee.

With superhuman rapidity it passed before him and was gone. Yet it was no earthly figure that emerged from the forest, ran with this incredible swiftness past the startled throng, and reached the tree. He saw the shape; the same instant it was there; wrapped in light, as though a flame from the sacrificial fire flashed past him over the ground. It was of an incandescent brightness, yet brightest of all were the little outstretched hands. These were of purest gold, of a brilliance incredibly shining.

It was no earthly child that stretched forth these arms of generous forgiveness and took the bewildered prisoner by the hand just as the knife descended and touched the helpless wrists. The thongs were already loosened, and the victim, fallen to his knees, looked wildly this way and that for a way of possible escape, when the shining hands were laid upon his own. The murderer rose. Another instant and the throng must have been upon him, tearing him limb from limb. But the radiant little face looked down into his own; she raised him to his feet; with superhuman swiftness she led him through the infuriated concourse as though he had become invisible, guiding him safely past the furies into the cover of the trees. Close before his eyes, this happened; he saw the waft of golden brilliance, he heard the final gulp of it, as wind took the dazzling of its fiery appearance into space. They were gone . . .

9

He stood watching the disappearing motor-cars, wondering uneasily who the occupants were and what their business, whither and why did they hurry so swiftly through the night? He was still trying to light his pipe, but the damp tobacco would not burn.

The air stole out of the forest, cooling his body and his mind; he saw the anemones gleam; there was only peace and calm about him, the earth lay waiting for the sweet, mysterious stars. The moon was higher; he looked up; a late bird sang. Three strips of cloud, spaced far apart, were the footsteps of the South Wind, as she flew to bring more birds from Africa. His thoughts turned to gentle, happy hopes of a day when the lion and the lamb should lie down together, and a little child should lead them. War, in this haunt of ancient peace, seemed an incredible anachronism.

He did not go farther; he did not enter the forest; he turned back along the quiet road he had come, ate his food on a farmer's gate, and over a pipe sat dreaming of his sure belief that humanity had advanced. He went home to his hotel soon after midnight. He slept well, and next day walked back the four miles from the hospitals, instead of using the car. Another hospital searcher walked with him. They discussed the news.

"The weather's better anyhow," said his companion. "In our favour at last!"

"That's something," he agreed, as they passed a gang of prisoners and crossed the road to avoid saluting.

"Been another escape, I hear," the other mentioned. "He won't get far. How on earth do they manage it? The M.O. had a yarn that he was helped by a motor-car. I wonder what they'll do to him."

"Oh, nothing much. Bread and water and extra work, I suppose?"

The other laughed. "I'm not so sure," he said lightly. "Humanity hasn't advanced very much in that kind of thing."

A fugitive memory flashed for an instant through the other's brain as he listened. He had an odd feeling for a second that he had heard this conversation before somewhere. A ghostly sense of familiarity brushed his mind, then vanished. At dinner that night the table in front of him was unoccupied. He did not, however, notice that it was unoccupied.

The Trod

Young Norman was being whirled in one of the newest stream-lined expresses towards the north. He leaned back in his first-class Smoker and lit a cigarette. On the rack in front of him was his gun-case with the pair of guns he never willingly allowed out of his sight, his magazine with over a thousand cartridges beside it, and the rest of his luggage, he knew, was safely in the van. He was looking forward to a really good week's shooting at Greystones, one of the best moors in England.

He realised that he was uncommonly lucky to have been invited at all. Yet a question mark lay in him. Why precisely, he wondered, had he been asked? For one thing, he knew his host, Sir Hiram Digby, very slightly. He had met him once or twice at various shoots in Norfolk, and while he had acquitted himself well when standing near him, he could not honestly think this was the reason for the invitation. There had been too many good shots present, and far better shots, for him to have been specially picked out. There was another reason, he was certain. His thoughts, as he puffed his cigarette reflectively, turned easily enough in another direction—towards Diana Travers, Sir Hiram Digby's niece.

The wish, he remembered, is often father to the thought, yet he clung to it obstinately, and with lingering enjoyment. It was Diana Travers who had suggested his name; it well might be, it probably was, and the more he thought it over, the more positive he felt. It explained the invitation, at any rate.

A curious thrill of excitement and delight ran through him as memory went backwards and played about her. A curious being, he saw quite unlike the usual run of girls, but curious, in the way that he himself perhaps was curious, for he was just old enough to have dis-covered that he was curious, standing apart somehow from the young men of his age and station. Well born, rich, sporting and all the rest, he yet did not quite belong to his time in certain ways. He could drink, revel, go wild, enjoy himself with his companions, but up to a point only—when he withdrew unsatisfied.

There were "other things" that claimed him with some terrible inner power; and the two could not mix. These other things he could not quite explain even to himself, but to his boon companions—never. Were they things of the spirit? He could not say. Wild, pagan things belonging to an older day? He knew not. They were of unspeakable loveliness and power, drawing him away from ordinary modern life— *that* he knew. He could not define them to himself, much less speak of them to others.

And then he met Diana Travers and knew, though he did not dare put his discovery into actual words, that she felt something similar.

He came across her first at a dance in town, he remembered, remembering also how bored he had been until the casual introduction, and after it, how happy, enchanted, satisfied. It was assuredly not that he had fallen suddenly in love, nor that she was wildly beautiful—a tall, fair girl with a radiant, yet not lovely face, soft voice, graceful movements—for there were thousands, Norman knew, who excelled her in all these qualities.

No, it was not the usual love attack, the mating fever, the herd-instinct that she might be his girl, but the old conviction, rather, that there lay concealed in her the same nameless, mysterious longings that lay also in himself—the terrible and lovely power that drew him from his human kind towards unknown "other things."

As they stood together on the balcony, where they had escaped from the heat and clamour of the ballroom, he acknowledged to himself, yet without utterance, this overpowering, strange conviction that their fates were in some way linked together. He could not explain it at the time, he could not explain it now—while he thought it over in the railway carriage, and his conscious mind rejected it as imagination. Yet it remained.

Their talk, indeed, had been ordinary enough, nor was he conscious of the slightest desire to flirt or make love; it was just that, as the saying is, they "clicked and that each felt delightfully easy in the other's company, happy and at home. It was almost, he reflected, as though they shared some rather wonderful deep secret that had no need of words, a secret that lay, indeed, beyond the reach of words altogether.

They had met several times since, and on each occasion, he had been aware of the same feeling; and once when he ran across her by chance in the park, they walked together for over an hour and she had talked more freely. Talked suddenly about herself, moreover, openly and naturally, as though she knew he would understand. In the open air, it struck him, she was more spontaneous than in the artificial surroundings of walls and furniture. It was not so much that she said anything significant, but rather the voice and manner and gestures that she used.

She had been admitting how she disliked London and all its works, loathing especially the Season with its glittering routine of so-called gaiety, adding that she always longed to get back to Marston, Sir Hiram's place in Essex. "There are the marshes," she said, with quiet enthusiasm, "and the sea, and I go with my uncle duck-flighting in the twilight, or in the dawn when the sun comes up like a red ball out of the sea, and the mist over the marshes drifts away . . . and things, you know, may happen. . . ."

He had been watching her movements with admiration as she spoke, thinking the name of huntress was well chosen, and now there was a note of strange passion in her voice that he heard for the first time. Her whole being, moreover, conveyed the sense that he would understand some emotional yearning in her that her actual words omitted.

He stopped and stared at her.

"That's to be alive," she added with a laugh that made her eyes shine. "The wind and the rain blowing in your face and the ducks streaming by. You feel yourself part of nature. Gates open, as it were. It was how we were meant to live. I'm sure."

Such phrases from any other girl must have made him feel shy and embarrassed, from her they were merely natural and true. He had not taken her up, however, beyond confessing that he agreed with her, and the conversation had passed on to other things. Yet the reason he had not become enthusiastic or taken up the little clue she offered, was because his inmost heart knew what she meant.

Her confession, not striking in itself, concealed while it revealed, a whole region of significant, mysterious "other things" best left alone in words. "You and I think alike," was what she had really said, "You and I share this strange, unearthly longing, only for God's sake, don't let us talk about it . . . !"

"A queer girl, anyhow," he now smiled to himself, as the train rushed northwards, and then asked himself what exactly he knew about her? Very little, practically nothing, beyond that, both parents

141

being dead, she lived with her elderly bachelor uncle and was doing the London Season. "A thoroughbred anyhow," he told, himself, "lovely as a nymph into the bargain . . ." and his thoughts went dreaming rather foolishly. Then suddenly, as he lit another cigarette, a much more definite thought emerged. It gave him something of a start, for it sprang up abruptly out of his mood of reverie in the way that a true judgment sometimes leaps to recognition in the state between sleeping and waking.

"She knows. Knows about these other lovely and mysterious things that have always haunted me. She has—yes, experienced them. She can explain them to me. She wants to share them with me. , . ."

Norman sat up with a jerk, as though something had scared him. He had been dreaming, these ideas were the phantasmagoria of a dream. Yet his heart, he noticed, was beating rather rapidly, as though a deep inner excitement had touched him in his condition of half-dream.

He looked up at his gun-cases and cartridges in the rack, then shaded his eyes and gazed out of the window. The train was doing at least sixty. The character of the country it rushed through was changing. The hedges of the midlands had gone, and stone walls were beginning to take their place. The country was getting wilder, lonelier, less inhabited. He drew unconsciously a deep breath of satisfaction. He must actually have slept for a considerable time, he realised, for his watch told him that in a few minutes he would reach the junction where he had to change.

Bracendale, the local station for Greystones, he remembered, was on a little branch line that wandered away among the hills. And some fifteen minutes later he found himself, luggage and all, in the creaky, grunting train that would land him at Bracendale towards five o'clock. The dusk had fallen when, with great effort apparently, the struggling engine deposited him with his precious guns and cartridges on the deserted platform amid swirling mists a damp wind prepared for his reception. To his considerable relief a car was there to carry him the remaining ten miles to the Lodge, and he was soon comfortably installed among its luxurious rugs for the drive across the hills.

He settled back comfortably to enjoy the keen mountain air.

After leaving the station, the car followed a road up a narrow valley for a time; a small beck fell tumbling from the hills on the left, where occasionally dark plantations of fir trooped down to the side of the road; but what struck him chiefly was the air of desolation and loneliness that hung over all the countryside. The landscape seemed to him wilder and less inhabited even than the Scottish Highlands. Not a house, not a croft, was to be seen. A sense of desertion, due partly to the dusk no doubt, hung brooding over everything, as though human influence was not welcomed here, perhaps not possible. Bleak and inhospitable it looked certainly, though for himself this loneliness held a thrill of wild beauty that appealed to him,

A few black-faced sheep strung occasionally across the road, and once they passed a bearded shepherd harrying downhill with his dog. They vanished into the mist like wraiths. It seemed impossible to Norman that the country could be so desolate and uninhabited when he knew that only a few score miles away lay the large manufacturing towns of Lancashire. The car, meanwhile, was steadily climbing up the valley and presently they came to more open country and passed a few scattered farmhouses with an occasional field of oats besides them.

Norman asked the chauffeur if many people lived hereabouts, and the man was clearly delighted to be spoken to.

"No, sir," he said, "it's a right desolate spot at the best of times, and I'm glad enough," he added, "when it's time for us to go back south again." It has been a wonderful season for the grouse, and there was every promise of a record year.

Norman noticed an odd thing about the farmhouses they passed, for many of them, if not all, had a large cross carved over the lintel of the doors, and even some of the gates leading from the road into the fields had a smaller cross cut into the top bar. The car's flash-light picked them out. It reminded him of the shrines and crosses scattered over the countryside in Catholic countries abroad, but seemed a little incongruous in England. He asked the chauffeur if most of the people hereabout were Catholics, and the man's answer, given with emphasis, touched his curiosity.

"Oh, no, I don't think so," was the reply. "In fact, sir, if you ask me, the people round here are about as heathen as you could find in any Christian country."

Norman drew his attention to the crosses everywhere, asking him how he accounted for them if the inhabitants were heathen, and the man hesitated a moment before replying, as though, glad to talk otherwise, the subject was not wholly to his liking.

"Well, sir," he said at length, watching the road carefully in front of him, "they don't tell *me* much about what they think, counting me for a foreigner like, as I come from the south. But they're a rum lot to my way of thinking. What I'm told," he added after a further pause, "is that they carve these crosses to protect themselves."

"Protect themselves! "exclaimed Norman a little startled. "Protect themselves from—what?"

"Ah, there, sir," said the man after hesitating again, "that's more than I can say. I've heard of a haunted house before now, but never a haunted countryside. Yet that's what they believe, I take it. It's all haunted, sir—everywhere. It's the devil of a job to get any of them to turn out after dark, as I know well, and even in the daytime they won't stir far without a crucifix hung round their neck. Even the men won't."

The car had put on speed while he spoke and Norman had to ask him to ease up a bit; the man, he felt sure, was prey to a touch of superstitious fear as they raced along the darkening road, yet glad enough to talk, provided he was not laughed at. After his last burst of speech, he had drawn a deep breath, as though glad to have got it off his chest.

"What you tell me is most interesting," Norman commented invitingly. "I've come across that sort of thing abroad, but never yet in England. There's something in it, you know," he added persuasively, "if we only knew what. I wish I knew the reason, for I'm sure it's a mistake just to laugh it all away." He lit a cigarette, handing one also to his companion, and making him slow down while they lighted them. "You're an observant fellow, I see," he went on, "and I'll be bound you've come across some queer things. I wish I had your opportunity. It interests me very much."

"You're right, sir," the chauffeur agreed, as they drove on again, "and it can't be laughed away, not *all* of it. There's something about the whole place 'ere that ain't right, as you might say. It 'got' me a bit when I first came 'ere some years ago, but now I'm kind of used to it."

"I don't think I should ever get *quite* used to it," said Norman, "till I'd got to the bottom of it. Do tell me anything you've noticed. I'd like to know—and I'll keep it to myself."

Feeling sure the man had interesting things to tell and having now won his confidence, he begged him to drive more slowly; he was afraid they would reach the house before there had been time to tell more, possibly even some personal experiences.

"There's a funny sort of road, or track rather, you may be seeing out shooting," the chauffeur went on eagerly enough, yet half nervously. It leads across the moor, and no man or woman will set foot on it to save their lives, not even in the daytime, let alone at night."

Norman said eagerly that he would like to see it, asking its whereabouts, but of course the directions only puzzled him.

"You'll be seeing it, sir, one of these days out shooting and if you watch the natives, you'll find I'm telling you right."

"What's wrong with it? "Norman asked. "Haunted—eh?"

"That's it, sir," the man admitted, after a longish pause. "But a queer kind of 'aunting. They do say it's just too lovely to look at—and keep your senses."

It was the other's turn to hesitate, for something in him trembled.

Now, young Norman was aware of two things very clearly: first, that it wasn't "quite the thing" to pump his host's *employé* in this way; second, that what the man told him held an extraordinary almost alarming interest for him. All folk-lore interested him intensely, legends and local superstitions included. Was this, perhaps a "fairy-ridden" stretch of country, he asked himself? Yet he was not in Ireland, where it would have been natural, but in stolid, matter-of-fact England. The chauffeur was obviously an observant, commonplace southerner, and yet he had become impressed, even a little scared, by what he had noticed. That lay beyond question: the man was relieved to talk to someone who would not laugh at him, while at the same time he was obviously a bit frightened.

A third question rose in his mind as well: this talk of haunted country, of bogies, fairies and the rest, fantastic though it was, perhaps, stirred a queer, yet delicious feeling in him—in his heart, doubtless— that his host's niece, Diana, had a link with it somewhere. The origin of a deep intuition is hardly discoverable. He made no attempt to probe it. This was Diana's country, she must know all the chauffeur hinted, and more besides. There must be something in the atmosphere that attracted her. She had been instrumental in making her uncle invite him. She wanted him to come, she wanted him to taste and share things, "other things," that to her were vital.

These thoughts flashed across him with an elaboration of detail impossible to describe. That the wish was, again, father to the thoughts, doubtless operated, yet the conviction persistently remained and the intuitive flash provided, apparently, inspiration, so that he plied the chauffeur with further questions that produced valuable results. He referred even to the Little People, the Fairies, without exciting contempt or laughter—with the result that the man gave him finally a somewhat dangerous confidence. Solemnly warning his passenger that

"Sir Hiram mustn't hear of it" or he'd lose his job, the man described a remarkable incident that had happened, so to speak, under his own eyes. Sir Hiram's sister was lost on the moors some years ago and was never found . . . and the local talk and belief had it that she had been "carried off."Yet not carried off against her will: she had wanted to go.

"Would that be Mrs. Travers?" Norman asked.

"That's who it was, sir, exactly, seeing as 'ow you know the family. And it was the strangest disappearance that ever came *my* way," He gave a slight shudder and, if not quite to his listener's surprise, suddenly crossed himself.

Diana's mother!

A pause followed the extraordinary story, and then, for once, Norman used words first spoken (to Horatio) to a man who had never heard them before and received them with appropriate satisfaction.

"Yes, sir," he went on, "and now he's got her up here for the first time since it happened years ago—in the very country where her mother was taken—and I'm told his idea is that he 'opes it will put her right—"

"Put her right?"

"I should say—cure her, sir. She's supposed to have the same—the same—" he fumbled for a word—"unbalance as wot her mother had." A strange rush of hope and terror swept across Norman's heart and mind, but he made a great effort and denied them both, so that his companion little guessed this raging storm. Changing the subject as best he could, controlling his voice with difficulty so as to make it sound normal, he asked casually:

"Do other people—I mean, *have* other people disappeared here?"

"They do say so, sir," was the reply. "I've heard many a tale, though I couldn't say as I proved anything. Natives, according to the talk, 'ave disappeared, nor no trace of them ever found. Children mostly. But the people round here won't speak of it and it's difficult to find out, as they never go to the police and keep it dark among themselves—"

"Couldn't they have fallen into potholes, or something like that? "Norman interrupted, to which the man replied that there was only one pothole in the whole district and the danger spot most carefully fenced round. "It's the place itself, sir," he added finally with conviction, as though he could tell of a first-hand personal experience if he dared, "it's the whole country that's so strange."

Norman risked the direct question.

"And what you've seen yourself, with your own eyes," he asked, "did it—sort of frighten you? I mean, you observe so carefully that anything you reported would be valuable."

"Well, sir," came the reply after a little hesitation, "I can't say 'frightened' exactly, though—if you ask me—I didn't like it. It made me feel queer all over, and I ain't a religious man—"

"Do tell me," Norman pressed, feeling the house was now not far away and time was short. "I shall keep it to myself—and I shall believe you. I've had odd experiences myself."

The man needed no urging, however: he seemed glad to tell his tale.

"It's not really very much," he said lowering his voice. "It was like this, you see, sir. The garage and my rooms lie down at an old farmhouse about a quarter-mile from the Lodge, and from my bedroom window I can see across the moor quite a way. It takes in that trail I was speaking of before, and along that track exactly I sometimes saw lights moving in a sort of wavering line. A bit faint, they were, and sort of dancing about and going out and coming on again, and at first, I took them for marsh lights—I've seen marsh lights down at our marshes at home—marsh gas we call it. That's what I thought at first, but I know better now."

"You never went out to examine them closer?"

"No, sir, I did *not*," came the emphatic reply.

"Or asked any of the natives what they thought?"

The chauffeur gave a curious little laugh; it was a half shy, half embarrassed laugh. Yes, he had once got a native who was willing to say something, but it was only with difficulty that Norman persuaded him to repeat it.

"Well, sir, what he told me"—again that embarrassed little laugh—"the words *he* used were 'It was the Gay People changing their hunting grounds.' That's what *he* said and crossed himself as he said it. They always changed their grounds at what he called the equinox."

"The Gay People . . . the equinox. . . ."

The odd phrases were not new to Norman, but he heard them now as though for the first time, they had meaning. The equinox, the solstice, he knew naturally what the words meant, but the "Gay People" belonged to some inner phantasmagoria of his own he had hitherto thought of only imaginatively. It pertained, that is, to some private "imaginative creed" he believed in when he had been reading Yeats, James Stephens A.E., or when he was trying to write poetry of his own.

Now, side by side with this burly chauffeur from the sceptical South, he came up against it—bang. And he admitted frankly to himself, it gave him a half-incredible thrill of wonder, delight and passion.

"The Gay People," he repeated, half to himself, half to the driver. "The fellow called them *that?*"

"That's wot he called them," repeated the matter-of-fact chauffeur. "And they were passing," he added, almost defiantly, as though he expected to be called a liar and deserved it, "passing in a stream of dancing lights along the Trod."

"The Trod," murmured Norman under his breath.

"The Trod," repeated the man in a whisper, "that track I spoke of—" and the car swerved, as though the touch on the wheel was unsteady for a second, though it instantly recovered itself as they swung into the drive.

The Lodge flew past, carrying a cross, Norman noticed, like all the other buildings; and a few minutes later the grey stone shooting-box, small and unpretentious, came in sight, Diana herself was on the step to welcome him, to his great delight.

"What a picture," he thought, as he saw her in her tweeds, her retriever beside her, the hall lamp blazing on her golden hair, one hand shading her eyes. Radiant, intoxicating, delicious, unearthly—he could not find the words—and he knew in that sudden instant that he loved her far beyond all that language could express. The dark background of the grey stone building, with the dim, mysterious moors behind, was exactly right. She stood there, framed in the wonder of two worlds—his girl!

Yet her reception chilled him to the bone. Excited, bubbling over, as he was, his words of pleasure ready to tumble about each other, his heart primed with fairy tales and wonder, she had nothing to say except that—tea was waiting, and that she hoped he had had a good journey. Response to his own inner convulsions there was none: she was polite, genial, cordial even, but beyond that—nothing. They exchanged commonplaces and she mentioned that the grouse were plentiful, that her uncle had got some of the best "guns" in England—which pleased his vanity for a moment—and that she hoped he would enjoy himself.

His leaden reaction left him speechless. He felt convicted of boyish, idiotic fantasy.

"I asked particularly for you to come," she admitted frankly, as they crossed the hall. "I had an idea somehow you'd like to be here."

He thanked her, but betrayed nothing of his first delight now chilled and rendered voiceless.

"It's your sort of country," she added, turning towards him with a swish of her skirts. "At least, I think it is."

"If *you* like it," he returned quietly, "I certainly shall like it too."

She stopped a moment and looked hard at him. "But of course, I like it," she said with conviction. "And it's much lovelier than those Essex marshes."

Remembering her first description of those Essex marshes, he thought of a hundred answers, but before the right one came to him, he found himself in the drawing-room chatting to his hostess. Lady Digby. The rest of the house-party were still out on the moor.

"Diana will show you the garden before the darkness comes," Lady Digby suggested presently. "It's quite a pretty view."

The "pretty view" thrilled Norman with its wild beauty, for the moor beyond stretched right down to the sea at Saltbeck, and in the other direction the hills ran away, fold upon fold, into a dim blue distance. The Lodge and its garden seemed an oasis in a wilderness of primeval loveliness, unkempt and wild as when God first made it. He was aware of its intense, seductive loveliness that appealed to all the strange, unearthly side of him, but at the same time he felt the powerful, enticing human seductiveness of the girl who was showing him round. And the two conflicted violently in his soul.

The conflict left him puzzled, distraught, stupid, since first one, then the other, took the upper hand. What saved him from a sudden tumultuous confession of his imagined passion, probably, was the girl's calm, almost cold, indifference. Obviously without response, she felt nothing of the tumult that possessed him.

Exchanging commonplaces, they admired the "pretty view" together, then turned back in due course to the house. "I catch their voices," remarked Diana. "Let's go in and hear all about it and how many birds they got." And it was on the door of the French window that she suddenly amazed—and, truth to tell—almost frightened him.

"Dick," she said using his first name, to his utter bewilderment and delight, and grasping his hand tightly in both of her own, "I may need your help." She spoke with a fiery intensity. Her eyes went blazing suddenly. "It was here, you know, that mother—went. And I think— I'm certain of it—they're *after me, too*. And I don't know which is right—to go or to stay. All this"—she swept her arm to include the house, the chattering room, the garden—"is such rubbish—cheap, nasty, worthless. The other is so satisfying—its eternal loveliness, and yet—" her voice dropped to a whisper—"*soulless*, without hope or future. You may help me." Her eyes turned upon him with a sudden amazing fire. "That's why I asked you here."

She kissed him on the eyes—an impersonal, passionless kiss, and the next minute they were in the room, crowded, with the "guns "from a large shooting brake which had just arrived.

★★★★★★★★★★★★★★

How Norman staggered in among the noisy throng and played his part as a fellow guest, he never understood. He managed it somehow, while in his heart sang the wild music of the Irish Fairy's enticing whisper: "I kiss you and the world begins to fade." A queer feeling came to him that he was going lost to life as he knew it, that Diana with her sweet passionless kiss had sealed his fate, that the known world must fade and die because she knew the way to another, lovelier region where nothing could ever pass or die because it was literally everlasting—the state of evolution belonging to fairyland, the land of the deathless Gay People. . . .

Sir Hiram welcomed him cordially, then introduced him to the others, upon which followed the usual description by the "guns" of the day's sport. They drank their whiskies and sodas, in due course they went up to dress for dinner, but after dinner there was no carousing, for their host bundled them all off to an early bed. The next day they were going to shoot the best beat on the moor and clear eyes and steady hands were important. The two drives for which Greystones was celebrated were to be taken—Telegraph Hill and Silvermine—both well known wherever shooting men congregated so that anticipation and excitement were understandable.

An early bed was a small price to pay and Norman, keen and eager as any of them, was glad enough to get to his room when the others trooped upstairs. To be included as a crack shot among all these famous guns was, naturally, a great event to him. He longed to justify himself.

Yet his heart was heavy and dissatisfied, a strange uneasiness gnawed at him despite all his efforts to think only of the morrow's thrill. For Diana had not come down to dinner, nor had he set eyes on her the whole evening. His polite enquiry about her was met by his host's cheery laugh: "Oh, she's all right, Norman, thank 'ee; she keeps to herself a bit when a shoot's on. Shooting, you see, ain't her line exactly, but she may come out with us tomorrow." He brushed her tastes aside.

"Try and persuade her, if you can. The air'll do her good."

Once in his room, his thoughts and emotions tried in vain to sort themselves out satisfactorily: there was a strange confusion in his mind, an uneasy sense of excitement that was half delight, half fearful anticipation, yet anticipation of he knew not exactly what. That sudden use of his familiar first name, the extraordinary kiss, establishing an unprepared intimacy, deep if passionless, had left him the entire evening in a state of hungry expectancy with nerves on edge. If only she had made an appearance at dinner, if only he could have had a further word with her! He wondered how he would ever get to sleep with this inner turmoil in his brain, and if he slept badly, he would shoot badly.

It was this reflection about shooting badly that convinced him abruptly that his sudden "love" was not of the ordinary accepted kind; had he been humanly "in love," no consideration of that sort could have entered his head for a moment. His queer uneasiness, half mixed with delight as it was, increased. The tie was surely of another sort.

Turning out the electric light, he looked from his window across the moor, wondering if he might see the strange lights the chauffeur had told him about. He saw only the dim carpet of the rolling moorland fading into darkness where a moon hid behind fleecy, drifting clouds. A soft, sweet, fragrant air went past him; there was a murmur of falling water. It was intoxicating; he drew in a deep delicious breath. For a second he imagined a golden-haired Diana, with flying hair and flaming eyes pursuing her lost mother midway between the silvery clouds and shadowy moor . . . then turned back into his room and flooded it with light . . . in which instant he saw something concrete lying on his pillow—a scrap of paper—no, an envelope. He tore it open.

Always wear this when you go out. I wear one too. They cannot come up with you unless you wish, if you wear it. Mother . . . .

The word "mother," full of imaginative suggestion, was crossed out; the signature was "Diana." With a faint musical tinkle, a little silver crucifix slipped from the pencilled note and fell to the floor.

As Norman stood beside the bed with the note in his hand, and before he stooped to recover the crucifix, there fell upon him with an amazing certainty the eerie conviction that all this had happened before. As a rule, this odd sensation is too fleeting to be retained for analysis; yet he held it now for several seconds without effort. Startled,

151

he saw quite clearly that it was not passing in ordinary time, but somewhere outside ordinary time as he knew it. It has happened "before" because it was happening "always." He had caught it in the act.

For a flashing instant he understood; the crucifix symbolised security among known conditions, and if he held to it, he would be protected, mentally and spiritually, against a terrific draw into unknown conditions. It meant no more than that—a support to the mind.

That antagonistic "draw" of terrific power, involved the nameless, secret yearnings of his fundamental nature. Diana, aware of this inner conflict, shared the terror and the joy. Her mother, whence she derived the opportunity, had yielded—and had disappeared from life as humans know it. Diana herself was now tempted and afraid. She asked his help. Both he and she together, in some condition outside ordinary time, had met this conflict many times already. He had experienced all this before—the incident of the crucifix, its appeal for help, the delight, the joy, the fear involved.

And even as he realised all this, the strange, eerie sensation vanished and was gone, as though it never had been. It became unseizable, lost beyond recapture. It left him with a sensation of loss, of cold, of isolation, a realisation of homelessness, yet of intense attraction towards a world unrealised.

He stooped, picked up the small silver crucifix, re-read the pencilled note letter by letter, kissed the paper that her hand had touched, then sat down on the bed and smiled with a sudden gush of human relief and happiness. The eerie sensation had gone its way beyond recovery. That Diana had thought about him was all that mattered. This little superstition about wearing the crucifix was sweet and touching, and of course he would wear the thing against his heart. And see that she came out tomorrow with him too! His relief was sincere.

Now he could sleep. And tomorrow he might not shoot too badly. But before he climbed into bed, he looked in his diary to find out when the equinox was due, and found to his astonishment that it was on the 23rd of September, and that tonight was the 21st! The discovery gave him something of a turn, but he soon fell asleep with the letter against his cheek and the little silver crucifix hung round his neck.

★★★★★★★★★★★★

He woke next morning when he was called to find the sun streaming into his room, promising perfect shooting weather. In broad daylight the normal reactions followed as they usually do; the incidents of the day before now seemed slightly ridiculous—his talk with Diana, the crucifix, the chauffeur's fairy-tales above all. He had stumbled upon a nest of hysterical delusions, born of a mysterious disappearance many years ago. It was natural, he thought, as he shaved himself, that his host disliked all reference to the subject and its aftermath. For all that, as he went down to breakfast, he felt secretly comforted that he had hung the little silver crucifix round his neck. No one, at any rate, he reflected, could see it.

He had done full justice to the well-stocked sideboard and was just finishing his coffee when Diana came into the empty room, and his mind, now charged with the prosaic prospects of the coming shoot, acknowledged a shock. Fact and imagination clashed. The girl was white and drawn. Before he could rise to greet her, she came straight across to the chair beside him.

"Dick," she began at once, "have you got it on?"

He produced the crucifix after a moment's fumbling.

"Of course, I have," he said. "You asked me to wear it." Remembering the hesitation in his bedroom, he felt rather foolish. He felt foolish, anyhow, wearing a superstitious crucifix on a day's shooting.

Her next words dispelled the feeling of incongruity.

"I was out early," she said in a tense, low voice, "and I heard mother's voice calling me on the moor. It was unmistakeable. Close in my ear, then far away. I was with the dog and the dog heard it too and ran for shelter. His hair was up."

"What did you hear?" Norman asked gently, taking her hand.

"My pet name—'Dis,'" she told him, "the name only mother used."

"What words did you hear? "he asked, trembling in spite of himself.

"Quite distinctly—in that distant muffled voice—I heard her call: 'Come to me, Dis, oh, come to me quickly!'"

For a moment Norman made no answer. He felt her hand trembling in his. Then he turned and looked straight into her eyes.

"Did you *want* to go?" he asked.

There was a pause before she replied. "Dick," she said, "when I heard that voice, *nothing else in the world seemed to matter*—!" at which moment her uncle's figure, bursting in through the door, shouted that the cars were ready and waiting, and the conversation came to an abrupt end.

This abrupt interruption at the moment of deepest interest left Norman, as may be imagined, excusably and dreadfully disturbed. A word from his host on this particular shooting party was, of course, a

153

command. He dared not keep these great "guns" waiting. Diana, too, shot out as though a bullet had hit her. But her last words went on ringing in his ears, in his heart as well: "Nothing else in the world seemed to matter." He understood in his deepest being what she meant. There was a "call" away from human things, a call into some unimaginable state of bliss no words described, and she had heard it, heard it in her *mother's* voice—the strongest tie humanity knows. Her mother, having left the world, sent back a message.

Norman, trembling unaccountably, hurried to fetch his gun and join the car, and Diana, obeying the orders of her uncle, was shoved into the Ford with her retriever. She had just time to whisper to him "Keep off the Trod—don't put a foot on it," and the two cars whisked off and separated them.

The "shoot" took place, nevertheless, ordinarily, so far as Norman was concerned, for the hunter's passion was too strong in him to be smothered. If his mind was mystical, his body was primitive. He was by nature a hunter before the Lord. The imaginative, mystical view of life, as with peasants and woodsmen, lay deep below. The first birds put an end to all reflection. He was soon too busy to bother about anything else but firing as fast as he could and changing his guns swiftly and smoothly. Breaking through this practical excitement, none the less, flashed swift, haunting thoughts and fancies—Diana's face and voice and eyes, her mother's supernatural call, his own secret yearnings, and, above all, her warning about the Trod. Both sides of his mixed' nature operated furiously. Apparently, he shot well, but how he managed it, heaven only knew.

The drive in due course was over and the pick-up completed. Sir Hiram came over and asked if he would mind taking the outside butt at the next drive.

"You see," he explained courteously, "I always ask the youngest of the party to take the outside, as it's a devil of a walk for the old 'uns. Probably," he added, "you'll get more shooting than anyone, as the birds slip away over yonder butt down a little gully. So, you'll find it worth the extra swot!"

Norman and his loader set off on their long tramp, while the rest of the guns made their way down to the road where the cars would carry them as far as the track allowed. After nearly a mile's detour Norman was puzzled by his loader striking across the heather instead of following the obvious path. He himself, naturally, kept to the smooth track. He had not gone ten yards along the track before the loader's startled voice shouted at him:

"For the love, of God, sir, come off! You're walking on the Trod!"

"It's a good path," cried Norman. What's wrong with it?"

The man eyed him a moment. "It's the Trod, sir," he said gravely, as though that were enough. "We don't walk on it—not at this time o' year especially." He crossed himself. "Come off it, sir, into the heather."

The two men stood facing one another for a minute.

"If you don't believe me, sir, just watch them sheep," said the man in a voice full of excitement and emotion. "You'll see they won't put foot on it. Nor any other animal either."

Norman watched a band of black-faced sheep move hesitatingly down the moorland slope. He was impatient to get on, half angry. For the moment he had forgotten all about Diana's warning. Fuming and annoyed, he watched. To his amazement, the little band of black-faced sheep, on reaching the obvious path, jumped clear over it. They jumped the Trod. Not one of them would touch it. It was an astonishing sight. Each animal leapt across, as though the Trod might burn or injure them. They went their way across the rough heather and disappeared from sight.

Norman, remembering the warning uncomfortably, paused and lit a cigarette.

"That's odd," he said. "It's the easiest way."

"Maybe," replied the loader. "But the easiest way may not be the best—or safest."

"The safest?"

"I've got children of me own," said the loader.

It was a significant statement. It made Norman reflect a moment.

"Safest," he repeated, remembering all he had heard, yet longing eagerly to hear more. "You mean, children especially are in danger? Young folks—eh?—is that it?" A moment later, he added, "I can quite believe it, you' know, it's a queer bit of country—to my way of thinking."

The understanding sympathy won the man's confidence, as it was meant to do.

"And it's equinox time, isn't it?" Norman ventured further.

The man responded quickly enough, finding a "gun" who wouldn't laugh at him. As with the chauffeur, he was evidently relieved to give some kind of utterance to fears and superstitions he was at heart ashamed of and yet believed in.

"I don't mind for myself, sir," he broke out, obviously glad to talk, "for I'm leaving these parts as soon as the grouse shooting's over, but I've two little 'uns up here just now, and I want to keep 'em. Too many young 'uns get lost on the moor for my liking. I'm sending 'em tomorrow down to my aunt at Crossways—"

"Good for you," put in Norman. "It's the equinox just now, isn't it? And that's the dangerous time, they say."

The loader eyed him cautiously a moment, weighing perhaps his value as a recipient of private fears, beliefs, fancies and the rest, yet deciding finally that Norman was worthy of his confidences.

"That's what my father always said," he agreed.

"Your father? It's always wise to listen to what a father tells," the other suggested. "No doubt he'd seen something—worth seeing."

A silence fell between them. Norman felt he had been, perhaps, too eager to draw the man out; yet the loader was reflecting merely. There was something he yearned to tell.

"Worth seeing," the man repeated, "well—that's as may be. But not of this world, and wonderful, it certainly was. It put ice into his bones, that's all I can swear to. And he wasn't the sort to be fooled easy, let me tell you. It was on his dying bed he told me—and a man doesn't lie with death in his eyes."

That Norman was standing idly on this important shoot was sufficient proof of his tremendous interest, and the man beyond question was aware of it.

"In daylight," Norman asked quietly, assuming the truth of what he hoped to hear.

"It was just at nightfall," the other said, "and he was coming from a sick friend at a farm beyond the Garage. The doctor had frightened him, I take it, so it was a bit late when he started for home across the moor and, without realising that it was equinox time, he found himself on the Trod before he knew it. And, to his terror, the whole place was lit up, and he saw a column of figures moving down it towards him. They was all bright and lovely, he described 'em, gay and terrible, laughing and singing and crying, and jewels shining in their hair, and—worst of all—he swears he saw young children who had gone lost on the moor years before, and a girl he had loved these twenty years back, no older than when he saw her last, and as gay and happy and laughing as though the passing years was nothing—"

"They called to him? "asked Norman, strangely moved. "They asked him to join them?"

"The girl did," replied the man. "The girl, he said, with no years to her back, drew him something terrible. 'Come with us,' he swears she sang to him, 'come with us and be happy and young forever,' and, if my father hadn't clutched hold of his crucifix in time—my God—he would have gone—"

The loader stopped, embarrassed lest he had told too much.

"If he'd gone, he'd have lost his soul," put in Norman, guided by a horrible intuition of his own.

"That's what they say, sir," agreed the man, obviously relieved.

Simultaneously, they hurried on, Sir Hiram's practical world breaking in upon this strange interlude. A big shoot was in progress. They must not be late at their appointed place.

"And where does the Trod start?" Norman asked presently, and the man described the little cave of the Black Waters whence the beck, dark with the peat, ran thence towards the sea across the bleak moors. The scenery provided an admirable setting for the "fairy-tale" he had just listened to; yet his thoughts, as they ploughed forward through the heather, went back to the lovely, fascinating tale, to the superstitious dream of the "Gay People" changing their hunting grounds along that unholy Trod when the equinox flamed with unearthly blazing, when the human young, unsatisfied with earthly pleasures, might be invited to join another ageless evolution that, if it knew no hope, shared at least an unstained, eternal, happy present. Diana's temptation, her mother's incredible disappearance, his own heart-shearing yearnings in the balance to boot, took strange shape as practical possibilities.

The cumulative effect of all he had heard, from chauffeur, loader, and from the girl herself, began, it may be, to operate, since the human mind, especially the imaginative human mind, is ever open to attack along the line of least resistance.

He stumbled on, holding his gun firmly, as though a modem weapon of destruction helped to steady his feet, to say nothing of his mind, now full of seething dreams. They reached the appointed butt. And hardly had they settled themselves in it than the first birds began to come, and all conversation was impossible. This was the celebrated "Silvermine Drive," and Norman had never in his life seen so many grouse as he now saw. His guns got too hot to hold, yet still the grouse poured over. . . .

The Drive finished in due course, and after a hurried lunch came the equally famous Telegraph Hill Drive, where there were even more birds than before, and when this came to an end Norman found that his shoulder was sore from the recoil and that he had developed a slight gun-headache, so that he was glad enough to climb into the car that took him back to the Lodge and tea. The excitement, naturally had been great, the nervous hope that he had shot well enough to justify his inclusion in the great shoot had also played upon his vitality. He found himself exhausted, and after tea he was relieved to slip up to his bedroom for a quiet hour or two.

Lying comfortably on his sofa with a cigarette, thinking over the fire and fury of the recent hours, his thoughts turned gradually aside to other things. The hunter, it seemed, withdrew; the dreamer, never wholly submerged, re-appeared. His mind reviewed the tales he had heard from the chauffeur and the loader, while the story of Diana's mother, the strange words of the girl herself, took possession of his thoughts. Too weary to be critical, he remembered them. His own natural leaning enforced their possible truth, while fatigue made analysis too difficult to bother about, so that imagination cast its spell of glamour undefied. . . . He burned to know the truth. In the end he made up his mind to creep out the following night and watch the Trod. It would be the night of the equinox. That ought to settle things one way or the other—proof or disproof. Only he must examine it in the daylight first.

It was disturbing at dinner to find that the girl was absent, had in fact, according to Sir Hiram, gone away for a day or so to see an old schoolfriend in a neighbouring town. She would be back, however, for the final shoot, he added, an explanation which Norman interpreted to mean that her uncle had deliberately sent her out of danger. He felt positive he was right. Sir Hiram might scorn such "rubbishy tales," but he was taking no chances. It was at the equinox that his sister had mysteriously disappeared. The girl was best elsewhere. Nor could all the pleasant compliments about Norman's good shooting on the two Drives conceal his host's genuine uneasiness. Diana was "best elsewhere."

Norman fell asleep with the firm determination that he must explore the Trod next day in good light, making sure of his landmarks and then creep out at night when the household was quiet, and see what happened.

There was no shooting next day. His task was easy. Keepers and dogs went out to pick up any birds that had been left from the previous day. After breakfast he slipped off across the waste of heather and soon found it—a deep smooth groove running through occasional hollows where no water lay, nor any faintest track of man or beast upon its soft, black peaty surface. Obviously, it was a track through the deep heather no one—neither man nor animal—used. He again noted the landmarks carefully, and felt sure he could find it again in the darkness . . . and, in due course, the day passed along its normal course, the "guns" after dinner discussed the next day's beat, and all turned in early in pleasurable anticipation of the shoot to come.

Norman went up to bed with a beating heart, for his plan to slip out of the sleeping house later and explore the moorland with its "haunted Trod," was not exactly what a host expected of a guest. The absence of Diana, moreover, deliberately planned, added to his deep uneasiness. Her sudden disappearance to visit "an old schoolfriend" was not convincing. Nor had she even left a line of explanation. It came to him that others besides the chauffeur and the loader took these fantastic fairy-tales seriously. His thoughts flew buzzing like bees outside a beehive. . . .

★★★★★★★★★★★★

From his window he looked out upon the night. The moon, in her second quarter, shone brightly at moments, then became hidden behind fleecy clouds. Higher up, evidently, a raging wind was driving, but below over the moorland a deathly stillness reigned. This stillness touched his nerves, and the dogs, howling in their kennels, added to a sense of superstitious uneasiness in his blood. The deep stillness seemed to hide a busy activity behind the silence. Something was stirring in the night, something out on the moor.

He turned back from the window and saw the lighted room, its cosy comfort, its well-lit luxury, its delicious bed waiting for weary limbs. He hesitated. The two sides of his nature clashed . . . but in the end the strange absence of Diana, her words, her abrupt sensational kiss, her odd silence . . . the quixotic feeling that he *might* help—these finally decided him.

Changing quickly into his shooting clothes, and making sure that the lights in all the bedroom windows he could see were out, he crept down in stockinged feet to the front door, carrying a pair of tennis shoes in his hand. The front door was unlocked, opening without noise, so that he slipped quietly across the gravel drive on to the grass, and thence, having now put on his shoes, on to the moor beyond.

The house faded behind him, patches of silvery moonlight shone through thin racing clouds, the taste of the night air was intoxicating. How could he ever have hesitated? The wonder and mystery of the wild country side, haunted or otherwise, caught him by the throat.

As he climbed the railings leading from the cultivated garden to the moor, there came a faint odd whispering sound behind him, so that he paused and listened for a moment. Was it wind or footsteps? It was neither—merely the flap of his open coat trailing across the fence. Ban! his nerves were jumpy. He laughed—almost laughed aloud, such was the exhilaration in him—and moved on quickly through the weird half lights. And for some reason his spirits rose, his blood went racing; here was an adventure the other side of his nature delighted in, yet this "other side" now took ominously the upper hand.

How primitive, after all, these "shooting parties" were! For men of brains and character, the best that England could produce, to spend all this time and money, hunting as the cave-men hunted! The fox, the deer, the bird—earlier men needed these for food, yet thousands of years later the finest males of the twentieth century—sportsmen all— spent millions on superior weapons, which gave the hunted animal no chance, to bring them down. Not to be a "sportsman" was to be an inferior Englishman. . . ! The "sportsman" was the flower of the race. It struck him, not for the first time, as a grim, a cheap, ideal. Was there no other climax of chivalric achievement more desirable?

This flashed across his mind as a hundred times before, while yet he himself, admittedly, was a "sportsman "born. Against it, at the same time, rose some strange glamour of eternal, deathless things that took no account of killing, things that caught his soul away in ecstasy. Fairy tales, of course, were fairy tales, yet they enshrined the undying truths of life and human nature within their golden "nonsense," catching at the skirts of radiant wonder whispering ageless secrets of the soul, giving hints of ineffable glories that lay outside the normal scales of space and 'time as accepted by the reasoning mind. And this attitude now rose upon him like a wild ungovernable wind of spring, fragrant, delicious, intoxicating. Fairies, the Little People, the "Gay People" happy dwellers in some non-human state. . .

Diana's mother had disappeared, yearning with secret, surreptitious calls for her daughter to come and join her. The girl herself acknowledged the call and was afraid, while yet her practical, hard-boiled uncle took particular trouble to keep her out of the way. Even for him, typical "sportsman," the time of the equinox was dangerous. These reflections, tumbling about his mind and heart, flooded Norman's being, while his yearning and desire for the girl came over him like a flame.

The moor, meanwhile, easy enough to walk on in the daytime, seemed unexpectedly difficult at night, the heather longer, the ground very uneven. He was always putting his legs into little hollows that he could not see, and he was relieved when at last he could make out the loom of the Garage which was one of his landmarks. He knew that he had not much further to go before he reached the Trod,

The turmoil in his mind had been such that he had paid little attention to the occasional slight sounds he heard as though somebody were at his heels, but now, on reaching the Trod, he became uneasily convinced that someone was not far behind him. So certain, indeed, was he of someone else that he let himself down silently into the deep heather and waited.

He listened intently, breathing very softly. The same instant he knew that he was right. Those sounds were not imagination. Footsteps were at his heels. The swish through the heather of a moving body was unmistakeable. He caught distinct footsteps then. The footsteps came to a pause quite near to where he crouched. At which moment exactly, the clouds raced past the moon, letting down a clear space of silvery light, so that he saw the "follower" brilliantly defined.

It was Diana.

"I knew it," he said half aloud, "I was sure of it long ago," while his heart, faced with a yearning hope and fear, both half-fulfilled, yet gave no leap of relief or pleasure. A shiver ran up and down his spine. Crouching there deep among the heather on the edge of the Trod, he knew more of terror than of happiness. It was all too clear for misunderstanding. She had been drawn irresistibly on the night of the equinox to the danger zone where her mother had so mysteriously "disappeared."

"I'm here," he added with a great effort in the same low whisper. "You asked my help. I'm here to meet you . . . dear . . . ."

The words, even if he actually uttered them died on his lips. The girl, he saw, stood still a moment, gazing in a dazed way, as though puzzled by something that obstructed her passage. Like a sleep walker, she stared about her, beautiful as a dream, yet only half conscious of her surroundings. Her eyes shone in the moonlight, her hands were half outstretched, yet not towards himself.

"Diana," he heard himself crying, "can you see me? Do you see who I am? Don't you recognise me? I've come to help—to save—you!"

It was plain she neither heard nor saw him standing there in front of her. She was aware of an obstructing presence, no more than that. Her glazed, shining eyes looked far beyond him—along the Trod. And

161

a terror clutched him that, unless he quickly did the right thing, she would be lost to him for ever.

He sprang to his feet and went towards her, but with the extraordinary sensation that he at once came up against some intervening wall of resistance that made normal movement difficult. It was almost like forcing his way through moving water or a drift of wind, and it was with an effort that he reached her side and stood now close against her.

"Diana! "he cried, "Dis—Dis," using the name her mother used. "Can't you see who I am? Don't you know me? I've come to save you—" and he stretched his hands towards her.

There was no response; she made no sign.

"I've come to lead you back—to lead you home—for God's sake, answer me, look into my eyes!"

She turned her head in his direction, as though to look into his face, but her eyes went past him towards the moonlit moor beyond. He noticed only, while she stared with those unseeing eyes, that her left hand fumbled weakly at a tiny crucifix that hung on a thin silver chain about her neck. He put out his hand and seized her by the arm, but the instant he touched her he found himself suddenly powerless to move. There came this strange arrest. And at the same instant, the whole Trod became startlingly lit up with a kind of unearthly radiance, and a strange greenish light shone upon the track right across the moor beyond where they stood. A deep terror for himself as well .as for her rose over him simultaneously. It came to him, with a shock of ice, that his own soul as well as hers, lay in sudden danger.

His eyes turned irresistibly towards the Trod, so strangely shining in the night. Though his hand still touched the girl, his mind was caught away in phantasmal possibilities. For two passions seized and fought within him: the fierce desire to possess her in the world of men and women, or to go with her headlong, recklessly, and share some ineffable ecstasy of happiness beyond the familial world where ordinary time and space held sway. Her own nature already held the key and knew the danger. . . . His whole being rocked.

The two incompatible passions gored the very heart in him. In a flash he realised his alternative—the dreary desolation of human progress with its grinding future, the joy and glory of a soulless happiness that reason denied and yet the heart welcomed as an ultimate truth. These two!

Yet of what value and meaning could she ever be to him as wife and mother if she were now drawn away—away to where her mother now eternally passed her golden, time-less life? How could he face this daily exile of her soul, this hourly isolation, this rape of her normal being his earthly nature held so dear and precious? While—should he save her, keeping her safe against the *human* hearth—how should he hold her to him, he himself tainted with the golden poison . . .?

Norman saw both sides with remorseless clarity in that swift instant while the Trod took on its shining radiance. His reasoning mind, he knew, had sunk away; his heart, wildly beating, was uppermost. With a supreme effort he kept his touch upon Diana's arm. His fingers clutched at the rough tweed of her sleeve. His entire being seemed rapt in some incredible ecstasy. He stood, he stared, he wondered, lost in an ineffable dream of beauty. One link only with the normal he held to like a vice—his touch upon her rough tweed sleeve, and. in his fading memory, the picture of a crucifix her weakening fingers weakly fumbled.

Figures were now moving fast and furious along the Trod; he could see them approaching from the distance. It was an inspiring, an intoxicating vision, and yet quite credible, with no foolish phantasmagoria of any childish sort. He saw everything as plainly as though he watched a parade in Whitehall, or a procession at some southern Battle of Flowers. Yet lovely, happy, radiant—and irresistibly enticing. As the figures came nearer, the light increased, so that it was obvious *they* emanated light of their own against the dark moorland. Nor were the individual figures particularly striking, least of all sensational. They seemed "natural," yet natural only because they were true and justified.

In the lead, as they drew nearer, Norman saw a tall dark man riding a white horse, close behind him a fair shining woman in a green dress, her long, golden hair falling to her waist. On her head he saw a circlet of gold in which was set a red stone that shone and glowed like burning flame. Beside her was another woman, dark and beautiful, with white stones sparkling in her hair as diamonds or crystals sparkle. It was a gorgeous and a radiant sight. Their faces shone with the ecstasy of youth. In some indescribable way they all spread happiness and joy about them, their eyes blazing with a peace and beneficence he had never seen in any human eyes.

These passed, and more and more poured by, some riding, some walking, young and old and children, men with hunting spears and unstrung bows, the youthful figures with harps and lyres, and one and all making friendly gestures of invitation to come and join them, as they flowed past silently. Silently, yes, silently, without a sound of foot-steps or of rustling heather, silently along the illuminated Trod, and yet, silent though their passing was, there came to him an impression of singing, laughter, even an air of dancing.

Such figures, he realised, could not move without rhythm, rhythm of sound and gesture, for it was as essential to them as breathing. Happy, radiant, gay they were, free for ever from the grinding effort and struggle of the world's strenuous evolutionary battles—free, if soulless. The "Gay People" as the natives called them. And the sight wrenched at the deepest roots of his own mixed being. To go with them and share their soulless bliss forever . . . or to stay and face the grim battle of Humanity's terrific—noble, yes—but almost hopeless, evolution?

That he was torn in two seemed an understatement. The pain seared and burned him in his very vitals. Diana, the girl, drew him as with some power of the stars themselves, and his hand still felt the tweed of her cloth beneath his fingers. His mind and heart, his nerves, his straining muscles, seemed fused in a fury of contradictions and acceptances. The glorious procession flowed streaming by, as though the stars had touched the common moorland earth, dripping their lavish gold in quiet glory—when suddenly Diana wrenched herself away and ran headlong towards them.

A golden-haired woman, he saw, had stepped out of the actual Trod, and had come to a halt directly in front of where he stood. Radiant and wonderful, she stood for a moment poised.

"Dis . . . Dis . . ." he heard in tones like music. "Come . . . come to me. Come and join us! The way is always open. There are no regrets . . .!"

The girl was half way to her mother before he could break the awful spell that held him motionless. But the rough cloth of her sleeve held clutched between his fingers, and with it the broken chain that caught her little crucifix. The silver cross swung and dangled a moment, then dropped among the heather.

It was as he stooped frantically to recover it that Fate played that strange, unusual card she keeps in reserve for moments when the world seems lost; for, as he fell, his own chain and crucifix, to which he had not once given a thought, flicked up and caught him on the lip. Thinking it was a broken edge of torn heather that stung him into pain, he dashed it aside—only to find it was the foolish metal symbol Diana had made him promise to wear, in his own safety. It was the sharp stab of pain, not the superstitious mental reaction, that roused immediate action in him.

In a second he was on his feet again, and a second later he had overtaken the striding girl and had both arms possessingly round her figure. An instant afterwards his lips were on her own, her head and shoulders torn backwards against his breast.

"Dis!" he cried wildly, "we must stay here together! You belong to me! I hold you tight—forever . . . here!"

What else he cried he hardly knows. He felt her weight sink back into his arms. It seems he carried her. He felt her convulsive weeping sobs against his heart. Her arms clung tightly round him.

In the distance he saw the line of moving figures die fading off into the enveloping moorland, dipping down into the curving dimness. Clouds raced back across the moon. There was no sound, the wind lay still, no tumbling beck was audible, the peewits slept.

Putting his own coat about her, he carried her home . . . and in due course he married her; he married Diana, he married Dis as well, a queer, lovely girl, but a girl without a soul, almost without a mind—a girl as commonplace as the radiant nonentity pictured with shining teeth on the cover of a popular magazine—a standardised creature whose essence had "gone elsewhere."

The Singular Death of Morton

Dusk was melting into darkness as the two men slowly made their way through the dense forest of spruce and fir that clothed the flanks of the mountain. They were weary with the long climb, for neither was in his first youth, and the July day had been a hot one. Their little inn lay further in the valley among the orchards that separated the forest from the vineyards.

Neither of them talked much. The big man led the way, carrying the knapsack, and his companion, older, shorter, evidently the more fatigued of the two, followed with small footsteps.

From time to time he stumbled among the loose rocks. An exceptionally observant mind would possibly have divined that his stumbling was not entirely due to fatigue, but to an absorption of spirit that made him careless how he walked.

'All right behind?' the big man would call from time to time, half glancing back.

'Eh? What?' the other would reply, startled out of a reverie.

'Pace too fast?'

'Not a bit. I'm coming.' And once he added: 'You might hurry on and see to supper, if you feel like it. I shan't be long behind you.'

But his big friend did not adopt the suggestion. He kept the same distance between them. He called out the same question at intervals, Once or twice he stopped and looked back too.

In this way they came at length to the skirts of the wood. A deep hush covered all the valley; the limestone ridges they had climbed gleamed down white and ghostly upon them from the fading sky. Midway in its journeys, the evening wind dropped suddenly to watch the beauty of the moonlight—to hold the branches still so that the light might slip between and weave its silver pattern on the moss below.

And, as they stood a moment to take it in, a step sounded behind them on the soft pine-needles, and the older man, still a little in the rear, turned with a start as though he had been suddenly called by name.

'There's that girl—again!' he said, and his voice expressed a curious mingling of pleasure, surprise and—apprehension.

Into a patch of moonlight passed the figure of a young girl, looked at them as though about to stop yet thinking better of it, smiled softly, and moved on out of sight into the surrounding darkness. The moon just caught her eyes and teeth, so that they shone; the rest of her body stood in shadow; the effect was striking—almost as though head and shoulders hung alone in mid-air, watching them with this shining smile, then fading away.

'Come on, for heaven's sake,' the big man cried. There was impatience in his manner, not unkindness. The other lingered a moment, peering closely into the gloom where the girl had vanished. His friend repeated his injunction, and a moment later the two had emerged upon the high road with the village lights in sight beyond, and the forest left behind them like a vast mantle that held the night within its folds.

For some minutes neither of them spoke; then the big man waited for his friend to draw up alongside.

'About all this valley of the Jura,' he said presently, 'there seems to me something—rather weird.' He shifted the knapsack vigorously on his back. It was a gesture of unconscious protest.

'Something uncanny,' he added, as he set a good pace.

'But extraordinarily beautiful—'

'It attracts you more than it does me, I think,' was the short reply.

'The picturesque superstitions still survive here,' observed the older man. 'They touch the imagination in spite of oneself.'

A pause followed during which the other tried to increase the pace. The subject evidently made him impatient for some reason.

'Perhaps,' he said presently. 'Though I think myself it's due to the curious loneliness of the place. I mean, we're in the middle of tourist-Europe here, yet so utterly remote. It's such a neglected little corner of the world. The contradiction bewilders. Then, being so near the frontier, too, with the clock changing an hour a mile from the village, makes one think of time as unreal and imaginary.' He laughed. He produced several other reasons as well. His friend admitted their value, and agreed half-heartedly. He still turned occasionally to look back. The mountain ridge where they had climbed was clearly visible in the moonlight.

'Odd,' he said, 'but I don't see that farmhouse where we got the milk anywhere. It ought to be easily visible from here.'

'Hardly—in this light. It was a queer place rather, I thought,' he added. He did not deny the curiously suggestive atmosphere of the region, he merely wanted to find satisfactory explanations. 'A case in point, I mean. I didn't like it quite—that farmhouse—yet I'm hanged if I know why. It made me feel uncomfortable. That girl appeared so suddenly, although the place seemed deserted. And her silence was so odd. Why in the world couldn't she answer a single question? I'm glad I didn't take the milk. I spat it out. I'd like to know where she got it from, for there was no sign of a cow or a goat to be seen anywhere!'

'I swallowed mine—in spite of the taste,' said the other, half smiling at his companion's sudden volubility.

Very abruptly, then, the big man turned and faced his friend. Was it merely an effect of the moonlight, or had his skin really turned pale beneath the sunburn?

'I say, old man,' he said, his face grave and serious, 'What do you think she was? What made her seem like that, and why the devil do you think she followed us?'

'I think,' was the slow reply, 'it was me she was following.'

The words, and particularly the tone of conviction in which they were spoken, clearly were displeasing to the big man, who already regretted having spoken so frankly what was in his mind. With a companion so imaginative, so impressionable, so nervous, it had been foolish and unwise. He led the way home at a pace that made the other arrive five minutes in his rear, panting, limping and perspiring as if he had been running.

'I'm rather for going on into Switzerland tomorrow, or the next day,' he ventured that night in the darkness of their two-bedded room. I think we've had enough of this place. Eh? What do you think?'

But there was no answer from the bed across the room, for its occupant was sound asleep and snoring.

'Dead tired, I suppose!' he muttered to himself, and then turned over to follow his friend's example. But for a long time, sleep refused him. Queer, unwelcome thoughts and feelings kept him awake—of a kind he rarely knew, and thoroughly disliked. It was rubbish, yet it made him uncomfortable so that his nerves tingled. He tossed about in the bed. 'I'm overtired,' he persuaded himself, 'that's all.'

The strange feelings that kept him thus awake were not easy to analyse, perhaps, but their origin was beyond all question: they grouped themselves about the picture of that deserted, tumble-down chalet on the mountain ridge where they had stopped for refreshment a few hours before. It was a farmhouse, dilapidated and dirty, and the name stood in big black letters against a blue background on the wall above the door: 'La Chenille.' Yet not a living soul was to be seen anywhere about it; the doors were fastened, windows shuttered; chimneys smokeless; dirt, neglect and decay everywhere in evidence.

Then, suddenly, as they had turned to go, after much vain shouting and knocking at the door, a face appeared for an instant at a window, the shutter of which was half open. His friend saw it first, and called aloud. The face nodded in reply, and presently a young girl came round the corner of the house, apparently by a back door, and stood staring at them both from a little distance.

And from that very instant, so far as he could remember, these queer feelings had entered his heart—fear, distrust, misgiving. The thought of it now, as he lay in bed in the darkness, made his hair rise. There was something about that girl that struck cold into the soul. Yet she was a mere slip of a thing, very pretty, seductive even, with a certain serpent-like fascination about her eyes and movements; and although she only replied to their questions as to refreshment with a smile, uttering no single word, she managed to convey the impression that she was a managing little person who might make herself very disagreeable if she chose. In spite of her undeniable charm there was about her an atmosphere of something sinister. He himself did most of the questioning, but it was his older friend who had the benefit of her smile. Her eyes hardly ever left his face, and once she had slipped quite close to him and touched his arm.

The strange part of it now seemed to him that he could not remember in the least how she was dressed, or what was the colouring of her eyes and hair. It was almost as though he had felt, rather than seen, her presence.

The milk—she produced a jug and two wooden bowls after a brief disappearance round the corner of the house—was—well, it tasted so odd that he had been unable to swallow it, and had spat it out. His friend, on the other hand, savage with thirst, had drunk his bowl to the last drop too quickly to taste it even, and, while he drank, had kept his eyes fixed on those of the girl, who stood close in front of him.

And from that moment his friend had somehow changed. On the way down he said things that were unusual, talking chiefly about the

'Chenille', and the girl, and the delicious, delicate flavour of the milk, yet all phrased in such a way that it sounded singular, unfamiliar, un-pleasant even.

Now that he tried to recall the sentences the actual words evaded him; but the memory of the uneasiness and apprehension they caused him to feel remained. And night ever italicizes such memories!

Then, to cap it all, the girl had followed them. It was wholly fool-ish and absurd to feel the things he did feel; yet there the feelings were, and what was the good of arguing? That girl frightened him; the change in his friend was in some way or other a danger signal. More than this he could not tell. An explanation might come later, but for the present his chief desire was to get away from the place and to get his friend away, too.

And on this thought sleep overtook him—heavily.

The windows were wide open; outside was a garden with a rather high enclosing wall, and at the far end a gate that was kept locked because it led into private fields and so, by a back way, to the cemetery and the little church. When it was open the guests of the inn made use of it and got lost in the network of fields and vines, for there was no proper route that way to the road or the mountains. They usually ended up prematurely in the cemetery, and got back to the village by passing through the church, which was always open; or by knocking at the kitchen doors of the other houses and explaining their position. Hence the gate was locked now to save trouble.

After several hours of hot, unrefreshing sleep the big man turned in his bed and woke. He tried to stretch, but couldn't; then sat up panting with a sense of suffocation. And by the faint starlight of the summer night, he saw next that his friend was up and moving about the room.

Remembering that sometimes he walked in his sleep, he called to him gently:

'Morton, old chap,' he said in a low voice, with a touch of author-ity in it, 'go back to bed!

You've walked enough for one day!'

And the figure, obeying as sleepwalkers often will, passed across the room and disappeared among the shadows over his bed. The other plunged and burrowed himself into a comfortable position again for sleep, but the heat of the room, the shortness of the bed, and this tire-some interruption of his slumbers made it difficult to lose conscious-ness. He forced his eyes to keep shut, and his body to cease from fidg-eting, but there was something nibbling at his mind like a spirit mouse that never permitted him to cross the frontier into actual oblivion. He slept with one eye open, as the saying is. Odours of hay and flowers and baked ground stole in through the open window; with them, too, came from time-to-time sounds—little sounds that disturbed him without being ever loud enough to claim definite attention.

Perhaps, after all, he did lose consciousness for a moment—when, suddenly, a thought came with a sharp rush into his mind and galvanized him once more into utter wakefulness. It amazed him that he had not grasped it before. It was this: the figure he had seen was not the figure of his friend.

Alarm gripped him at once before he could think or argue, and a cold perspiration broke out all over his body. He fumbled for matches, couldn't find them; then, remembering there was electric light, he scraped the wall with his fingers—and turned on the little white switch. In the sudden glare that filled the room he saw instantly that his friend's bed was no longer occupied. And his mind, then acting instinctively, without process of conscious reasoning, flew like a flash to their walk of the day—to the tumble-down. 'Chenille,' the glass of milk, the odd behaviour of his friend, and—to the girl.

At the same second, he noticed that the odour in the room which hitherto he had taken to be the composite odour of fields, flowers and night, was really something else: it was the odour of freshly turned earth. Immediately on the top of this discovery came another. Those slight sounds he had heard outside the window were not ordinary night-sounds, the murmur of wind and insects: they were footsteps moving softly, stealthily down the little paths of crushed granite.

He was dressed in wonderful short order, noticing as he did so that his friend's night-garments lay upon the bed, and that he, too, had therefore dressed; further—that the door had been unlocked and stood half an inch ajar. There was now no question that he had slept again:

Between the present and the moment when he had seen the figure there had been a considerable interval. A couple of minutes later he had made his way cautiously downstairs and was standing on the garden path in the moonlight. And as he stood there, his mind filled with the stories the proprietor had told a few days before of the superstitions that still lived in the popular imagination and haunted this little, remote pine-clad valley.

The thought of that girl sickened him. The odour of newly-turned earth remained in his nostrils and made his gorge rise. Utterly and vigorously, he rejected the monstrous fictions he had heard, yet for all that, could not prevent their touching his imagination as he stood there in the early hours of the morning, alone with night and silence. The spell was undeniable; only a mind without sensibility could have ignored it.

He searched the little garden from end to end. Empty! Opposite the high gate he stopped, peering through the iron bars, wet with dew to his hands. Far across the intervening fields he fancied something moved. A second later he was sure of it. Something down there to the right beyond the trees was astir. It was in the cemetery.

And this definite discovery sent a shudder of terror and disgust through him from head to foot.

He framed the name of his friend with his lips, yet the sound did not come forth. Some deeper instinct warned him to hold it back. Instead, after incredible efforts, he climbed that iron gate and dropped down into the soaking grass upon the other side. Then, taking advantage of all the cover he could find, he ran, swiftly and stealthily, towards the cemetery. On the way, without quite knowing why he did so, he picked up a heavy stick; and a moment later he stood beside the low wall that separated the fields from the churchyard—stood and stared.

There, beside the tombstones, with their hideous metal wreaths and crowns of faded flowers, he made out the figure of his friend; he was stooping, crouched down upon the ground; behind him rose a couple of bushy yew trees, against the dark of which his form was easily visible. He was not alone; in front of him, bending close over him it seemed, was another figure—a slight, shadowy, slim figure.

This time the big man found his voice and called aloud:

'Morton, Morton!' he cried. 'What, in the name of heaven, are you doing? What's the matter?'

And the instant his deep voice broke the stillness of the night with its clamour, the little figure, half hiding his friend, turned about and faced him. He saw a white face with shining eyes and teeth as the form rose; the moonlight painted it with its own strange pallor; it was weird, unreal, horrible; and across the mouth, downwards from the lips to the chin, ran a deep stain of crimson.

The next moment the figure slid with a queer, gliding motion towards the trees, and disappeared among the yews and tombstones in the direction of the church. The heavy stick, hurled whirling after it, fell harmlessly halfway, knocking a metal cross from its perch upon an upright grave; and the man who had thrown it raced full speed towards the huddled-up figure of his friend, hardly noticing the thin, wailing cry that rose trembling through the night air from the vanished form. Nor did he notice more particularly that several of the graves, newly made, showed signs of recent disturbance, and that the odour of turned earth he had noticed in the room grew stronger. All his attention was concentrated upon the figure at his feet.

'Morton, man, get up! Wake for God's sake! You've been walking in—'

Then the words died upon his lips. The unnatural attitude of his friend's shoulders, and the way the head dropped back to show the neck, struck him like a blow in the face. There was no sign of movement. He lifted the body up and carried it, all limp and unresisting, by ways he never remembered afterwards, back to the inn.

It was all a dreadful nightmare—a nightmare that carried over its ghastly horror into waking life. He knew that the proprietor and his wife moved busily to and fro about the bed, and that in due course the village doctor was upon the scene, and that he was giving a muddled and feverish description of all he knew, telling how his friend was a confirmed sleep-walker and all the rest.

But he did not realise the truth until he saw the face of the doctor as he straightened up from the long examination.

'Will you wake him?' he heard himself asking, 'or let him sleep it out till morning?' And the doctor's expression, even before the reply came to confirm it, told him the truth. 'Ah, *monsieur*, your friend will not ever wake again, I fear! It is the heart, you see; *hélas*, it is sudden failure of the heart!' The final scenes in the little tragedy which thus brought his holiday to so abrupt and terrible a close need no description, being in no way essential to this strange story. There were one or two curious details, however, that came to light afterwards.

One was, that for some weeks before there had been signs of disturbance among newly-made graves in the cemetery, which the authorities had been trying to trace to the nightly wanderings of the village madman—in vain; and another, that the morning after the death a trail of blood had been found across the church floor, as though someone had passed through from the back entrance to the front. A special service was held that very week to cleanse the holy building from the evil of that stain; for the villagers, deep in their superstitions, declared that nothing human had left that trail; nothing could have made those marks but a vampire disturbed at midnight in its awful occupation among the dead.

Apart from such idle rumours, however, the bereaved carried with him to this day certain other remarkable details which cannot be so easily dismissed. For he had a brief conversation with the doctor, it appears, that impressed him profoundly. And the doctor, an intelligent man, prosaic as granite into the bargain, had questioned him rather closely as to the recent life and habits of his dead friend. The account of their climb to the 'Chenille' he heard with an amazement he could not conceal.

'But no such chalet exists,' he said. 'There is no 'Chenille''. A long time ago, fifty years or more, there was such a place, but it was destroyed by the authorities on account of the evil reputation of the people who lived there. They burnt it. Nothing remains today but a few bits of broken wall and foundation.'

'Evil reputation—?'

The doctor shrugged his shoulders 'Travellers, even peasants, disappeared,' he said. 'An old woman lived there with her daughter, and poisoned milk was supposed to be used. But the neighbourhood accused them of worse than ordinary murder—'

'In what way?'

'Said the girl was a vampire,' answered the doctor shortly.

And, after a moment's hesitation, he added, turning his face away as he spoke:

'It was a curious thing, though, that tiny hole in your friend's throat, small as a pinprick, yet so deep. And the heart—did I tell you?—was almost completely drained of blood.'

The Second Generation

Sometimes, in a moment of sharp experience, comes that vivid flash of insight that makes a platitude suddenly seem a revelation—its full content is abruptly realised. "Ten years is a long time, yes," he thought, as he walked up the drive to the great Kensington house where she still lived.

Ten years—long enough, at any rate, for her to have married and for her husband to have died. More than that he had not heard, in the outlandish places where life had cast him in the interval. He wondered whether there had been any children. All manner of thoughts and questions, confused a little, passed across his mind. He was well-to-do now, though probably his entire capital did not amount to her income for a single year. He glanced at the huge, forbidding mansion. Yet that pride was false which had made of poverty an insuperable obstacle. He saw it now. He had learned values in his long exile.

But he was still ridiculously timid. This confusion of thought, of mental images rather, was due to a kind of fear, since worship ever is akin to awe. He was as nervous as a boy going up for a *viva voce;* and with the excitement was also that unconquerable sinking—that horrid shrinking sensation that excessive shyness brings. Why in the world had he come? Why had he telegraphed the very day after his arrival in England? Why had he not sent a tentative, tactful letter, feeling his way a little?

Very slowly he walked up the drive, feeling that if a reasonable chance of escape presented itself, he would almost take it. But all the windows stared so hard at him that retreat was really impossible now and though no faces were visible behind the curtains, all had seen him, possibly she herself—his heart beat absurdly at the extravagant suggestion. Yet it was odd—he felt so certain of being seen, and that someone watched him. He reached the wide stone steps that were clean as marble, and shrank from the mark his boots must make upon their spotlessness.

In desperation, then, before he could change his mind, he touched the bell. But he did not hear it ring—mercifully; that irrevocable sound must have paralyzed him altogether. If no one came to answer, he might still leave a card in the letter-box and slip away. Oh, how utterly he despised himself for such a thought! A man of thirty with such a chicken heart was not fit to protect a child, much less a woman. And he recalled with a little stab of pain that the man she married had been noted for his courage, his determined action, his inflexible firmness in various public situations, head and shoulders above lesser men. What presumption on his own part ever to dream! . . . He remembered, too, with no apparent reason in particular, that this man had a grown-up son already, by a former marriage.

And still no one came to open that huge, contemptuous door with its so menacing, so hostile air. His back was to it, as he carelessly twirled his umbrella, but he felt its sneering expression behind him while it looked him up and down. It seemed to push him away. The entire mansion focused its message through that stern portal: Little timid men are not welcomed here.

How well he remembered the house! How often in years gone by had he not stood and waited just like this, trembling with delight and anticipation, yet terrified lest the bell should be answered and the great door actually swung wide! Then, as now, he would have run, had he dared. He was still afraid—his worship was so deep. But in all these years of exile in wild places, farming, mining, working for the position he had at last attained, her face and the memory of her gracious presence had been his comfort and support, his only consolation, though never his actual joy. There was so little foundation for it all, yet her smile and the words she had spoken to him from time to time in friendly conversation had clung, inspired, kept him going—for he knew them all by heart. And more than once in foolish optimistic moods, he had imagined, greatly daring, that she possibly had meant more. . . .

He touched the bell a second time—with the point of his umbrella. He meant to go in, carelessly as it were, saying as lightly as might be, "Oh, I'm back in England again—if you haven't quite forgotten my existence—I could not forego the pleasure of saying 'How-do-you-do?' and hearing that you are well . . . ," and the rest; then presently bow himself easily out—into the old loneliness again. But he would at least have seen her; he would have heard her voice, and looked into her gentle, amber eyes; he would have touched her hand. She might even ask him to come in another day and see her! He had rehearsed it all a hundred times, as certain feeble temperaments do rehearse such scenes.

And he came rather well out of that rehearsal, though always with an aching heart, the old great yearnings unfulfilled. All the way across the Atlantic he had thought about it, though with lessening confidence as the time drew near. The very night of his arrival in London he wrote, then, tearing up the letter (after sleeping over it), he had telegraphed next morning, asking if she would be in. He signed his surname—such a very common name, alas! but surely, she would know—and her reply, "Please call 4:30," struck him as rather oddly worded. Yet here he was.

There was a rattle of the big door knob, that aggressive, hostile knob that thrust out at him insolently like a fist of bronze. He started, angry with himself for doing so. But the door did not open. He became suddenly conscious of the wilds he had lived in for so long; his clothes were hardly fashionable; his voice probably had a twang in it, and he used tricks of speech that must betray the rough life so recently left. What would she think of him, now? He looked much older, too. And how brusque it was to have telegraphed like that! He felt awkward, gauche, tongue-tied, hot and cold by turns. The sentences, so carefully rehearsed, fled beyond recovery.

Good heavens—the door was open! It had been open for some minutes. It moved noiselessly on big hinges. He acted automatically; he heard himself asking if her ladyship was at home, though his voice was nearly inaudible. The next moment he was standing in the great, dim hall, so poignantly familiar, and the remembered perfume almost made him sway. He did not hear the door close, but he knew. He was caught. The butler betrayed an instant's surprise—or was it overwrought imagination again?—when he gave his name. It seemed to him—though only later did he grasp the significance of that curious intuition—that the man had expected another caller instead. The man took his card respectfully and disappeared. These flunkeys were so marvellously trained. He was too long accustomed to straight question and straight answer, but here, in the Old Country, privacy was jealously guarded with such careful ritual.

And almost immediately the butler returned, still expressionless, and showed him into the large drawing-room on the ground floor that he knew so well. Tea was on the table—tea for one. He felt puzzled. "If you will have tea first, sir, her ladyship will see you afterwards," was what he heard.

And though his breath came thickly, he asked the question that forced itself out. Before he knew what he was saying he asked it, "Is she ill?"

"Oh, no, her ladyship is quite well, thank you, sir. If you will have tea first, sir, her ladyship will see you afterwards."

The horrid formula was repeated, word for word. He sank into an armchair and mechanically poured out his own tea. What he felt he did not exactly know.

It seemed so unusual, so utterly unexpected, so unnecessary, too. Was it a special attention, or was it merely casual? That it could mean anything else did not occur to him. How was she busy, occupied—not here to give him tea? He could not understand it. It seemed such a farce having tea alone like this—it was like waiting for an audience, it was like a doctor's or a dentist's room. He felt bewildered, ill at ease, cheap. . . . But after ten years in primitive lands perhaps London usages had changed in some extraordinary manner.

He recalled his first amazement at the motor-omnibuses, taxicabs, and electric tubes. All were new. London was otherwise than when he left it. Piccadilly and the Marble Arch themselves had altered. And, with his reflection, a shade more confidence stole in. She knew that he was there and presently she would come in and speak with him, explaining everything by the mere fact of her delicious presence. He was ready for the ordeal, he would see her—and drop out again. It was worth all manner of pain, even of mortification. He was in her house, drinking her tea, sitting in a chair she used herself perhaps.

Only he would never dare to say a word or make a sign that might betray his changeless secret. He still felt the boyish worshipper, worshipping in dumbness from a distance, one of a group of many others like himself. Their dreams had faded, his had continued, that was the difference. Memories tore and raced and poured upon him. How sweet and gentle she had always been to him! He used to wonder sometimes. . . . Once, he remembered, he had rehearsed a declaration, but while rehearsing the big man had come in and captured her, though he had only read the definite news long after by chance in an Arizona paper.

He gulped his tea down. His heart alternately leaped and stood still. A sort of numbness held him most of that dreadful interval, and no clear thought came at all. Every ten seconds his head turned towards the door that rattled, seemed to move, yet never opened. But any moment now it must open, and he would be in her very presence, breathing the same air with her. He would see her, charge himself with her beauty once more to the brim, and then go out again into the wilderness—the wilderness of life—without her, and not for a mere ten years but for always. She was so utterly beyond his reach. He felt like a backwoodsman, he was a backwoodsman.

For one thing only was he duly prepared, though he thought about it little enough—she would, of course, have changed. The photograph he owned, cut from an illustrated paper, was not true now. It might even be a little shock perhaps. He must remember that. Ten years cannot pass over a woman without—

Before he knew it the door was open, and she was advancing quietly towards him across the thick carpet that deadened sound. With both hands outstretched she came, and with the sweetest welcoming smile upon her parted lips he had seen in any human face. Her eyes were soft with joy. His whole heart leaped within him; for the instant he saw her it all flashed clear as sunlight—that she knew and understood. She had always known, had always understood. Speech came easily to him in a flood, had he needed it, but he did not need it. It was all so adorably easy, simple, natural, and true. He just took her hands—those welcoming, outstretched hands—in both of his own, and led her to the nearest sofa. He was not even surprised at himself. Inevitably, out of depths of truth, this meeting came about. And he uttered a little foolish commonplace, because he feared the huge revulsion that his sudden glory brought, and loved to taste it slowly:

"So, you live here still?"

"Here, and here," she answered softly, touching his heart, and then her own. "I am attached to this house, too, because you used to come and see me here, and because it was here, I waited so long for you, and still wait. I shall never leave it—unless you change. You see, we live together here."

He said nothing. He leaned forward to take and hold her. The abrupt knowledge of it all somehow did not seem abrupt—it was as though he had known it always; and the complete disclosure did not seem disclosure either—rather as though she told him something he had inexplicably left unrealised, yet not forgotten. He felt absolutely master of himself, yet, in a curious sense, outside of himself at the same time. His arms were already open—when she gently held her hands up to prevent. He heard a faint sound outside the door.

"But you are free," he cried, his great passion breaking out and flooding him, yet most oddly well controlled, "and I—"

She interrupted him in the softest, quietest whisper he had ever heard:

"You are not free, as I am free—not yet."

The sound outside came suddenly closer. It was a step. There was a faint click on the handle of the door. In a flash, then, came the dreadful shock that overwhelmed him—the abrupt realisation of the truth that was somehow horrible—that Time, all these years, had left no mark upon her and that she had not changed. Her face was as young as when he saw her last.

With it there came cold and darkness into the great room. He shivered with cold, but an alien, unaccountable cold. Some great shadow dropped upon the entire earth, and though but a second could have passed before the handle actually turned, and the other person entered, it seemed to him like several minutes. He heard her saying this amazing thing that was question, answer, and forgiveness all in one—this, at least, he divined before the ghastly interruption came—"But, George—if you had only spoken—!"

With ice in his blood, he heard the butler saying that her ladyship would be "pleased" to see him if he had finished his tea and would be "so good as to bring the papers and documents upstairs with him." He had just sufficient control of certain muscles to stand upright and murmur that he would come. He rose from a sofa that held no one but himself. All at once he staggered. He really did not know exactly what happened, or how he managed to stammer out the medley of excuses and semi-explanations that battered their way through his brain and issued somehow in definite words from his lips.

Somehow or other he accomplished it. The sudden attack, the faintness, the collapse!. . . He vaguely remembered afterwards—with amazement too—the suavity of the butler as he suggested telephoning for a doctor, and that he just managed to forbid it, refusing the offered glass of brandy as well, remembered contriving to stumble into the taxicab and give his hotel address with a final explanation that he would call another day and "bring the papers." It was quite clear that his telegram had been attributed to someone else, someone "with papers"—perhaps a solicitor or architect. His name was such an ordinary one, there were so many Smiths. It was also clear that she whom he had come to see and had seen, no longer lived here in the flesh. . . .

And just as he left the hall he had the vision—mere fleeting glimpse it was—of a tall, slim, girlish figure on the stairs asking if anything was wrong, and realised vaguely through his atrocious pain that she was, of course, the wife of the son who had inherited. . . .

Wireless Confusion

"Goodnight, Uncle," whispered the child, as she climbed on to his knee and gave him a resounding kiss. "It's time for me to disappop into bed—at least, so mother says."

"Disappop, then," he replied, returning her kiss, "although I doubt."

He hesitated. He remembered the word was her father's invention, descriptive of the way rabbits pop into their holes and disappear, and the way *good* children should leave the room the instant bed-time was announced. The father—his twin brother—seemed to enter the room and stand beside them. "Then give me another kiss, and disappop!" he said quickly. The child obeyed the first part of his injunction, but had not obeyed the second when the queer thing happened.

She had not left his knee; he was still holding her at the full stretch of both arms; he was staring into her laughing eyes, when she suddenly went far away into an extraordinary distance. She retired. Minute, tiny, but still in perfect proportion and clear as before, she was withdrawn in space till she was small as a doll. He saw his own hands holding her, and they too were minute. Down this long corridor of space, as it were, he saw her diminutive figure.

"Uncle!" she cried, yet her voice was loud as before, "but what a funny face! You're pretending you've seen a ghost"—and she was gone from his knee and from the room, the door closing quietly behind her. He saw her cross the floor, a tiny figure. Then, just as she reached the door, she became of normal size again, as if she crossed a line.

He felt dizzy. The loud voice close to his ear issuing from a diminutive figure half a mile away had a distressing effect upon him. He knew a curious qualm as he sat there in the dark. He heard the wind walking round the house, trying the doors and windows. He was troubled by a memory he could not seize.

Yet the emotion instantly resolved itself into one of personal anxiety: something had gone wrong with his eyes. Sight, his most precious possession as an artist, was of course affected. He was conscious of a little trembling in him, as he at once began trying his sight at various objects—his hands, the high ceiling, the trees dim in the twilight on the lawn outside. He opened a book and read half a dozen lines, at changing distances; finally, he stared carefully at the second hand of his watch. "Right as a trivet!" he exclaimed aloud. He emitted a long sigh; he was immensely relieved. "Nothing wrong with my eyes."

He thought about the actual occurrence a great deal—he felt as puzzled as any other normal person must have felt. While he held the child actually in his arms, gripping her with both hands, he had seen her suddenly half a mile away. "Half a mile!" he repeated under his breath, "why it was even more, it was easily a mile." It had been exactly as though he suddenly looked at her down the wrong end of a powerful telescope. It had really happened; he could not explain it; there was no more to be said.

This was the first time it happened to him.

At the theatre, a week later, when the phenomenon was repeated, the stage he was watching fixedly at the moment went far away, as though he saw it from a long way off. The distance, so far as he could judge, was the same as before, about a mile. It was an Eastern scene, realistically costumed and produced, that without an instant's warning withdrew. The entire stage went with it, although he did not actually see it go. He did not see movement, that is.

It was suddenly remote, while yet the actors' voices, the orchestra, the general hubbub retained their normal volume. He experienced again the distressing dizziness; he closed his eyes, covering them with his hand, then rubbing the eyeballs slightly; and when he looked up the next minute, the world was as it should be, as it had been, at any rate. Unwilling to experience a repetition of the thing in a public place, however, and fortunately being alone, he left the theatre at the end of the act.

Twice this happened to him, once with an individual, his brother's child, and once with a landscape, an Eastern stage scene. Both occurrences were within the week, during which time he had been considering a visit to the oculist, though without putting his decision into execution. He was the kind of man that dreaded doctors, dentists, oculists, always postponing, always finding reasons for delay. He found reasons now, the chief among them being an unwelcome one—that it was perhaps a brain specialist, rather than an oculist, he ought to consult. This particular notion hung unpleasantly about his mind, when, the day after the theatre visit, the thing recurred, but with a startling difference.

While idly watching a blue-bottle fly that climbed the window-pane with remorseless industry, only to slip down again at the very instant when escape into the open air was within its reach, the fly grew abruptly into gigantic proportions, became blurred and indistinct as it did so, covered the entire pane with its furry, dark, ugly mass, and frightened him so that he stepped back with a cry and nearly lost his balance altogether. He collapsed into a chair. He listened with closed eyes. The metallic buzzing was audible, a small, exasperating sound, ordinarily unable to stir any emotion beyond a mild annoyance. Yet it was terrible; that so huge an insect should make so faint a sound seemed to him terrible.

At length he cautiously opened his eyes. The fly was of normal size once more. He hastily flicked it out of the window.

An hour later he was talking with the famous oculist in Harley Street … about the advisability of starting reading-glasses. He found it difficult to relate the rest. A curious shyness restrained him.

"Your optic nerves might belong to a man of twenty," was the verdict. "Both are perfect. But at your age it is wise to save the sight as much as possible. There is a slight astigmatism...." And a prescription for the glasses was written out. It was only when paying the fee, and as a means of drawing attention from the awkward moment, that his story found expression. It seemed to come out in spite of himself. He made light of it even then, telling it without conviction. It seemed foolish suddenly as he told it.

"How very odd," observed the oculist vaguely, "dear me, yes, curious indeed. But that's nothing. H'm, h'm!" Either it was no concern of his, or he deemed it negligible. . . . His only other confidant was a friend of psychological tendencies who was interested and eager to explain. It is on the instant plausible explanation of anything and everything that the reputation of such folk depends; this one was true to type: "A spontaneous invention, my dear fellow—a pictorial rendering of your thought. You are a painter, aren't you? Well, this is merely a rendering in picture-form of"—he paused for effect, the other hung upon his words—"of the odd expression 'disappop.'"

"Ah!" exclaimed the painter.

"You see everything pictorially, of course, don't you?"

"Yes—as a rule."

"There you have it. Your painter's psychology saw the child 'disap-

187

popping.' That's all."

"And the fly?" but the fly was easily explained, since it was merely the process reversed. "Once a process has established itself in your mind, you see, it may act in either direction. When a madman says 'I'm afraid Smith will do me an injury,' it means, 'I will do an injury to Smith,'" And he repeated with finality, "That's it."

The explanations were not very satisfactory, the illustration even tactless, but then the problem had not been stated quite fully. Neither to the oculist nor to the other had *all* the facts been given. The same shyness had been a restraining influence in both cases; a detail had been omitted, and this detail was that he connected the occurrences somehow with his brother whom the war had taken.

The phenomenon made one more appearance—the last—before its character, its field of action rather, altered. He was reading a book when the print became now large, now small; it blurred, grew remote and tiny, then so huge that a single word, a letter even, filled the whole page. He felt as if someone were playing optical tricks with the mechanism of his eyes, trying first one, then another focus.

More curious still, the meaning of the words themselves became uncertain; he did not understand them anymore; the sentences lost their meaning, as though he read a strange language, or a language little known. The flash came then—someone was using his eyes—someone else was looking through them.

No, it was not his brother. The idea was preposterous in any case. Yet he shivered again, as when he heard the walking wind, for an uncanny conviction came over him that it was someone who did not understand eyes but was manipulating their mechanism experimentally. With the conviction came also this: that, while not his brother, it was someone connected with his brother.

Here, moreover, was an explanation of sorts, for if the supernatural existed—he had never troubled his head about it—he could accept this odd business as a manifestation, and leave it at that. He did so, and his mind was eased. This was his attitude: "The supernatural *may* exist. Why not? We cannot know. But we can watch." His eyes and brain, at any rate, were proved in good condition.

He watched. No change of focus, no magnifying or diminishing, came again. For some weeks he noticed nothing unusual of any kind, except that his mind often filled now with Eastern pictures. Their sudden irruption caught his attention, but no more than that; they were sometimes blurred and sometimes vivid; he had never been in the East; he attributed them to his constant thinking of his brother, missing in Mesopotamia these six months. Photographs in magazines and newspapers explained the rest.

Yet the persistence of the pictures puzzled him: tents beneath hot cloudless skies, palms, a stretch of desert, dry watercourses, camels, a mosque, a minaret—typical snatches of this kind flashed into his mind with a sense of faint familiarity often. He knew, again, the return of a fugitive memory he could not seize. . . . He kept a note of the dates, all of them subsequent to the day he read his brother's fate in the official Roll of Honour: "Believed missing; now killed." Only when the original phenomenon returned, but in its altered form, did he stop the practice. The change then affected his life too fundamentally to trouble about mere dates and pictures.

For the phenomenon, shifting its field of action, abruptly became mental, and the singular change of focus took place now in his mind. Events magnified or contracted themselves out of all relation with their intrinsic values, sense of proportion went hopelessly astray. Love, hate and fear experienced sudden intensification, or abrupt dwindling into nothing; the familiar everyday emotions, commonplace daily acts, suffered exaggerated enlargement, or reduction into insignificance, that threatened the stability of his personality.

Fortunately, as stated, they were of brief duration; to examine them in detail were to touch the painful absurdities of incipient mania almost; that a lost collar stud could block his exasperated mind for hours, filling an entire day with emotion, while a deep affection of long standing could ebb towards complete collapse suddenly without apparent cause. . .!

It was the unexpected suddenness of Turkey's spectacular defeat that closed the painful symptoms. The Armistice saw them go. He knew a quick relief he was unable to explain. The telegram that his brother was alive and safe came *after* his recovery of mental balance. It was a shock. But the phenomena had ceased before the shock.

It was in the light of his brother's story that he reviewed the puzzling phenomena described. The story was not more curious than many another, perhaps, yet the details were queer enough. That a wounded Turk to whom he gave water should have remembered gratitude was likely enough, for all travellers know that these men are kindly gentlemen at times; but that this Mohammedan peasant should have been later a member of a prisoner's escort and have provided the means of escape and concealment—weeks in a dry watercourse

189

and months in a hut outside the town—seemed an incredible stroke of good fortune. "He brought me food and water three times a week. I had no money to give him, so I gave him my Zeiss glasses. I taught him a bit of English too. But he liked the glasses best. He was never tired of playing with 'em—making big and little, as he called it. He learned precious little English. . . ."

"My pair, weren't they?" interrupted his brother. "My old climbing glasses."

"Your present to me when I went out, yes. So really you helped me to save my life. I told the old Turk that. I was always thinking about you."

"And the Turk?"

"No doubt. . . . Through *my* mind, that is. At any rate, he asked a lot of questions about you. I showed him your photo. He died, poor chap—at least they told me so. Probably they shot him."

The Willows

1

After leaving Vienna, and long before you come to Budapest, the Danube enters a region of singular loneliness and desolation, where its waters spread away on all sides regardless of a main channel, and the country becomes a swamp for miles upon miles, covered by a vast sea of low willow-bushes. On the big maps this deserted area is painted in a fluffy blue, growing fainter in colour as it leaves the banks, and across it may be seen in large straggling letters the word *Sümpfe*, meaning marshes.

In high flood this great acreage of sand, shingle-beds, and willow-grown islands is almost topped by the water, but in normal seasons the bushes bend and rustle in the free winds, showing their silver leaves to the sunshine in an ever-moving plain of bewildering beauty. These willows never attain to the dignity of trees; they have no rigid trunks; they remain humble bushes, with rounded tops and soft outline, swaying on slender stems that answer to the least pressure of the wind; supple as grasses, and so continually shifting that they somehow give the impression that the entire plain is moving and alive. For the wind sends waves rising and falling over the whole surface, waves of leaves instead of waves of water, green swells like the sea, too, until the branches turn and lift, and then silvery white as their underside turns to the sun.

Happy to slip beyond the control of the stern banks, the Danube here wanders about at will among the intricate network of channels intersecting the islands everywhere with broad avenues down which the waters pour with a shouting sound; making whirlpools, eddies, and foaming rapids; tearing at the sandy banks; carrying away masses of shore and willow-clumps; and forming new islands innumerably which shift daily in size and shape and possess at best an impermanent life, since the flood-time obliterates their very existence.

Properly speaking, this fascinating part of the river's life begins soon after leaving Pressburg, and we, in our Canadian canoe, with gipsy tent and frying-pan on board, reached it on the crest of a rising flood about mid-July. That very same morning, when the sky was reddening before sunrise, we had slipped swiftly through still-sleeping Vienna, leaving it a couple of hours later a mere patch of smoke against the blue hills of the Wienerwald on the horizon; we had breakfasted below Fischeramend under a grove of birch trees roaring in the wind; and had then swept on the tearing current past Orth, Hainburg, Petronell (the old Roman Carnuntum of Marcus Aurelius), and so under the frowning heights of Theben on a spur of the Carpathians, where the March steals in quietly from the left and the frontier is crossed between Austria and Hungary.

Racing along at twelve kilometres an hour soon took us well into Hungary, and the muddy waters—sure sign of flood—sent us aground on many a shingle-bed, and twisted us like a cork in many a sudden belching whirlpool before the towers of Pressburg (Hungarian, Poszony) showed against the sky; and then the canoe, leaping like a spirited horse, flew at top speed under the grey walls, negotiated safely the sunken chain of the Fliegende Brücke ferry, turned the corner sharply to the left, and plunged on yellow foam into the wilderness of islands, sandbanks, and swamp-land beyond—the land of the willows.

The change came suddenly, as when a series of bioscope pictures snaps down on the streets of a town and shifts without warning into the scenery of lake and forest. We entered the land of desolation on wings, and in less than half an hour there was neither boat nor fishing-hut nor red roof, nor any single sign of human habitation and civilisation within sight. The sense of remoteness from the world of humankind, the utter isolation, the fascination of this singular world of willows, winds, and waters, instantly laid its spell upon us both, so that we allowed laughingly to one another that we ought by rights to have held some special kind of passport to admit us, and that we had, somewhat audaciously, come without asking leave into a separate little kingdom of wonder and magic—a kingdom that was reserved for the use of others who had a right to it, with everywhere unwritten warnings to trespassers for those who had the imagination to discover them.

Though still early in the afternoon, the ceaseless buffetings of a most tempestuous wind made us feel weary, and we at once began casting about for a suitable camping-ground for the night. But the bewildering character of the islands made landing difficult; the swirling flood carried us in shore and then swept us out again; the willow branches tore our hands as we seized them to stop the canoe, and we pulled many a yard of sandy bank into the water before at length we shot with a great sideways blow from the wind into a backwater and managed to beach the bows in a cloud of spray. Then we lay panting and laughing after our exertions on the hot yellow sand, sheltered from the wind, and in the full blaze of a scorching sun, a cloudless blue sky above, and an immense army of dancing, shouting willow bushes, closing in from all sides, shining with spray and clapping their thousand little hands as though to applaud the success of our efforts.

"What a river!" I said to my companion, thinking of all the way we had travelled from the source in the Black Forest, and how he had often been obliged to wade and push in the upper shallows at the beginning of June.

"Won't stand much nonsense now, will it?" he said, pulling the canoe a little farther into safety up the sand, and then composing himself for a nap.

I lay by his side, happy and peaceful in the bath of the elements—water, wind, sand, and the great fire of the sun—thinking of the long journey that lay behind us, and of the great stretch before us to the Black Sea, and how lucky I was to have such a delightful and charming traveling companion as my friend, the Swede.

We had made many similar journeys together, but the Danube, more than any other river I knew, impressed us from the very beginning with its *aliveness*. From its tiny bubbling entry into the world among the pinewood gardens of Donaueschingen, until this moment when it began to play the great river-game of losing itself among the deserted swamps, unobserved, unrestrained, it had seemed to us like following the grown of some living creature. Sleepy at first, but later developing violent desires as it became conscious of its deep soul, it rolled, like some huge fluid being, through all the countries we had passed, holding our little craft on its mighty shoulders, playing roughly with us sometimes, yet always friendly and well-meaning, till at length we had come inevitably to regard it as a Great Personage.

How, indeed, could it be otherwise, since it told us so much of its secret life? At night we heard it singing to the moon as we lay in our tent, uttering that odd sibilant note peculiar to itself and said to be caused by the rapid tearing of the pebbles along its bed, so great is its hurrying speed. We knew, too, the voice of its gurgling whirlpools, suddenly bubbling up on a surface previously quite calm; the roar of its shallows and swift rapids; its constant steady thundering below all mere surface sounds; and that ceaseless tearing of its icy waters at the banks. How it stood up and shouted when the rains fell flat upon its face!

And how its laughter roared out when the wind blew upstream and tried to stop its growing speed! We knew all its sounds and voices, its tumblings and foamings, its unnecessary splashing against the bridges; that self-conscious chatter when there were hills to look on; the affected dignity of its speech when it passed through the little towns, far too important to laugh; and all these faint, sweet whisperings when the sun caught it fairly in some slow curve and poured down upon it till the steam rose.

It was full of tricks, too, in its early life before the great world knew it. There were places in the upper reaches among the Swabian forests, when yet the first whispers of its destiny had not reached it, where it elected to disappear through holes in the ground, to appear again on the other side of the porous limestone hills and start a new river with another name; leaving, too, so little water in its own bed that we had to climb out and wade and push the canoe through miles of shallows.

And a chief pleasure, in those early days of its irresponsible youth, was to lie low, like Brer Fox, just before the little turbulent tributaries came to join it from the Alps, and to refuse to acknowledge them when in, but to run for miles side by side, the dividing line well marked, the very levels different, the Danube utterly declining to recognize the newcomer. Below Passau, however, it gave up this particular trick, for there the Inn comes in with a thundering power impossible to ignore, and so pushes and incommodes the parent river that there is hardly room for them in the long twisting gorge that follows, and the Danube is shoved this way and that against the cliffs, and forced to hurry itself with great waves and much dashing to and fro in order to get through in time.

And during the fight our canoe slipped down from its shoulder to its breast, and had the time of its life among the struggling waves. But the Inn taught the old river a lesson, and after Passau it no longer pretended to ignore new arrivals.

This was many days back, of course, and since then we had come to know other aspects of the great creature, and across the Bavarian wheat plain of Straubing she wandered so slowly under the blazing June sun that we could well imagine only the surface inches were

194

water, while below, there moved, concealed as by a silken mantle, a whole army of Undines, passing silently and unseen down to the sea, and very leisurely too, lest they be discovered.

Much, too, we forgave her because of her friendliness to the birds and animals that haunted the shores. Cormorants lined the banks in lonely places in rows like short black palings; grey crows crowded the shingle-beds; storks stood fishing in the vistas of shallower water that opened up between the islands, and hawks, swans, and marsh birds of all sorts filled the air with glinting wings and singing, petulant cries.

It was impossible to feel annoyed with the river's vagaries after seeing a deer leap with a splash into the water at sunrise and swim past the bows of the canoe; and often we saw fawns peering at us from the underbrush, or looked straight into the brown eyes of a stag as we charged full tilt round a corner and entered another reach of the river. Foxes, too, everywhere haunted the banks, tripping daintily among the driftwood and disappearing so suddenly that it was impossible to see how they managed it.

But now, after leaving Pressburg, everything changed a little, and the Danube became more serious. It ceased trifling. It was half-way to the Black Sea, within seeming distance almost of other, stranger countries where no tricks would be permitted or understood. It became suddenly grown-up, and claimed our respect and even our awe. It broke out into three arms, for one thing, that only met again a hundred kilometres farther down, and for a canoe there were no indications which one was intended to be followed.

"If you take a side channel," said the Hungarian officer we met in the Pressburg shop while buying provisions, "you may find yourselves, when the flood subsides, forty miles from anywhere, high and dry, and you may easily starve. There are no people, no farms, no fishermen. I warn you not to continue. The river, too, is still rising, and this wind will increase."

The rising river did not alarm us in the least, but the matter of being left high and dry by a sudden subsidence of the waters might be serious, and we had consequently laid in an extra stock of provisions. For the rest, the officer's prophecy held true, and the wind, blowing down a perfectly clear sky, increased steadily till it reached the dignity of a westerly gale.

It was earlier than usual when we camped, for the sun was a good hour or two from the horizon, and leaving my friend still asleep on the hot sand, I wandered about in desultory examination of our hotel.

The island, I found, was less than an acre in extent, a mere sandy bank standing some two or three feet above the level of the river. The far end, pointing into the sunset, was covered with flying spray which the tremendous wind drove off the crests of the broken waves. It was triangular in shape, with the apex upstream.

I stood there for several minutes, watching the impetuous crimson flood bearing down with a shouting roar, dashing in waves against the bank as though to sweep it bodily away, and then swirling by in two foaming streams on either side. The ground seemed to shake with the shock and rush, while the furious movement of the willow bushes as the wind poured over them increased the curious illusion that the island itself actually moved. Above, for a mile or two, I could see the great river descending upon me; it was like looking up the slope of a sliding hill, white with foam, and leaping up everywhere to show itself to the sun.

The rest of the island was too thickly grown with willows to make walking pleasant, but I made the tour, nevertheless. From the lower end the light, of course, changed, and the river looked dark and angry. Only the backs of the flying waves were visible, streaked with foam, and pushed forcibly by the great puffs of wind that fell upon them from behind.

For a short mile it was visible, pouring in and out among the islands, and then disappearing with a huge sweep into the willows, which closed about it like a herd of monstrous antediluvian creatures crowding down to drink. They made me think of gigantic sponge-like growths that sucked the river up into themselves. They caused it to vanish from sight. They herded there together in such overpowering numbers.

Altogether it was an impressive scene, with its utter loneliness, its bizarre suggestion; and as I gazed, long and curiously, a singular emotion began to stir somewhere in the depths of me. Midway in my delight of the wild beauty, there crept, unbidden and unexplained, a curious feeling of disquietude, almost of alarm.

A rising river, perhaps, always suggests something of the ominous; many of the little islands I saw before me would probably have been swept away by the morning; this resistless, thundering flood of water touched the sense of awe. Yet I was aware that my uneasiness lay deeper far than the emotions of awe and wonder. It was not that I felt. Nor had it directly to do with the power of the driving wind—this shouting hurricane that might almost carry up a few acres of willows into the air and scatter them like so much chaff over the landscape. The wind was simply enjoying itself, for nothing rose out of the flat landscape to stop it, and I was conscious of sharing its great game with a kind of pleasurable excitement.

Yet this novel emotion had nothing to do with the wind. Indeed, so vague was the sense of distress I experienced, that it was impossible to trace it to its source and deal with it accordingly, though I was aware somehow that it had to do with my realisation of our utter insignificance before this unrestrained power of the elements about me. The huge-grown river had something to do with it too—a vague, unpleasant idea that we had somehow trifled with these great elemental forces in whose power we lay helpless every hour of the day and night. For here, indeed, they were gigantically at play together, and the sight appealed to the imagination.

But my emotion, so far as I could understand it, seemed to attach itself more particularly to the willow bushes, to these acres and acres of willows, crowding, so thickly growing there, swarming everywhere the eye could reach, pressing upon the river as though to suffocate it, standing in dense array mile after mile beneath the sky, watching, waiting, listening. And, apart quite from the elements, the willows connected themselves subtly with my malaise, attacking the mind insidiously somehow by reason of their vast numbers, and contriving in some way or other to represent to the imagination a new and mighty power, a power, moreover, not altogether friendly to us.

Great revelations of nature, of course, never fail to impress in one way or another, and I was no stranger to moods of the kind. Mountains overawe and oceans terrify, while the mystery of great forests exercises a spell peculiarly its own. But all these, at one point or another, somewhere link on intimately with human life and human experience. They stir comprehensible, even if alarming, emotions. They tend on the whole to exalt.

With this multitude of willows, however, it was something far different, I felt. Some essence emanated from them that besieged the heart. A sense of awe awakened, true, but of awe touched somewhere by a vague terror. Their serried ranks, growing everywhere darker about me as the shadows deepened, moving furiously yet softly in the wind, woke in me the curious and unwelcome suggestion that we had trespassed here upon the borders of an alien world, a world where we were intruders, a world where we were not wanted or invited to remain—where we ran grave risks perhaps!

The feeling, however, though it refused to yield its meaning entirely to analysis, did not at the time trouble me by passing into menace. Yet it never left me quite, even during the very practical business of putting up the tent in a hurricane of wind and building a fire for the stew-pot. It remained, just enough to bother and perplex, and to rob a most delightful camping-ground of a good portion of its charm. To my companion, however, I said nothing, for he was a man I considered devoid of imagination. In the first place, I could never have explained to him what I meant, and in the second, he would have laughed stupidly at me if I had.

There was a slight depression in the centre of the island, and here we pitched the tent. The surrounding willows broke the wind a bit.

"A poor camp," observed the imperturbable Swede when at last the tent stood upright, "no stones and precious little firewood. I'm for moving on early tomorrow—eh? This sand won't hold anything."

But the experience of a collapsing tent at midnight had taught us many devices, and we made the cosy gipsy house as safe as possible, and then set about collecting a store of wood to last till bedtime. Willow bushes drop no branches, and driftwood was our only source of supply. We hunted the shores pretty thoroughly. Everywhere the banks were crumbling as the rising flood tore at them and carried away great portions with a splash and a gurgle.

"The island's much smaller than when we landed," said the accurate Swede. "It won't last long at this rate. We'd better drag the canoe close to the tent, and be ready to start at a moment's notice. I shall sleep in my clothes."

He was a little distance off, climbing along the bank, and I heard his rather jolly laugh as he spoke.

"By Jove!" I heard him call, a moment later, and turned to see what had caused his exclamation. But for the moment he was hidden by the willows, and I could not find him.

"What in the world's this?" I heard him cry again, and this time his voice had become serious.

I ran up quickly and joined him on the bank. He was looking over the river, pointing at something in the water.

"Good heavens, it's a man's body!" he cried excitedly. "Look!"

A black thing, turning over and over in the foaming waves, swept rapidly past. It kept disappearing and coming up to the surface again. It was about twenty feet from the shore, and just as it was opposite to where we stood it lurched round and looked straight at us. We saw its eyes reflecting the sunset, and gleaming an odd yellow as the body turned over. Then it gave a swift, gulping plunge, and dived out of sight in a flash.

"An otter, by gad!" we exclaimed in the same breath, laughing.

It *was* an otter, alive, and out on the hunt; yet it had looked exactly like the body of a drowned man turning helplessly in the current. Far below it came to the surface once again, and we saw its black skin, wet and shining in the sunlight.

Then, too, just as we turned back, our arms full of driftwood, another thing happened to recall us to the river bank. This time it really was a man, and what was more, a man in a boat. Now a small boat on the Danube was an unusual sight at any time, but here in this deserted region, and at flood time, it was so unexpected as to constitute a real event. We stood and stared.

Whether it was due to the slanting sunlight, or the refraction from the wonderfully illumined water, I cannot say, but, whatever the cause, I found it difficult to focus my sight properly upon the flying apparition. It seemed, however, to be a man standing upright in a sort of flat-bottomed boat, steering with a long oar, and being carried down the opposite shore at a tremendous pace.

He apparently was looking across in our direction, but the distance was too great and the light too uncertain for us to make out very plainly what he was about. It seemed to me that he was gesticulating and making signs at us. His voice came across the water to us shouting something furiously, but the wind drowned it so that no single word was audible. There was something curious about the whole appearance—man, boat, signs, voice—that made an impression on me out of all proportion to its cause.

"He's crossing himself!" I cried. "Look, he's making the sign of the Cross!"

"I believe you're right," the Swede said, shading his eyes with his hand and watching the man out of sight. He seemed to be gone in a moment, melting away down there into the sea of willows where the sun caught them in the bend of the river and turned them into a great crimson wall of beauty. Mist, too, had begun to ruse, so that the air was hazy.

"But what in the world is he doing at nightfall on this flooded river?" I said, half to myself. "Where is he going at such a time, and what did he mean by his signs and shouting? D'you think he wished to warn us about something?"

"He saw our smoke, and thought we were spirits probably," laughed my companion. "These Hungarians believe in all sorts of rubbish; you remember the shopwoman at Pressburg warning us that no one ever landed here because it belonged to some sort of beings outside man's world! I suppose they believe in fairies and elementals, possibly demons, too. That peasant in the boat saw people on the islands for the first time in his life," he added, after a slight pause, "and it scared him, that's all."

The Swede's tone of voice was not convincing, and his manner lacked something that was usually there. I noted the change instantly while he talked, though without being able to label it precisely.

"If they had enough imagination," I laughed loudly—I remember trying to make as much noise as I could—"they might well people a place like this with the old gods of antiquity. The Romans must have haunted all this region more or less with their shrines and sacred groves and elemental deities."

The subject dropped and we returned to our stew-pot, for my friend was not given to imaginative conversation as a rule. Moreover, just then I remember feeling distinctly glad that he was not imaginative; his stolid, practical nature suddenly seemed to me welcome and comforting.

It was an admirable temperament, I felt; he could steer down rapids like a Red Indian, shoot dangerous bridges and whirlpools better than any white man I ever saw in a canoe. He was a grand fellow for an adventurous trip, a tower of strength when untoward things happened. I looked at his strong face and light curly hair as he staggered along under his pile of driftwood (twice the size of mine!), and I experienced a feeling of relief. Yes, I was distinctly glad just then that the Swede was—what he was, and that he never made remarks that suggested more than they said.

"The river's still rising, though," he added, as if following out some thoughts of his own, and dropping his load with a gasp. "This island will be under water in two days if it goes on."

"I *wish* the wind would go down," I said. "I don't care a fig for the river."

The flood, indeed, had no terrors for us; we could get off at ten minutes' notice, and the more water the better we liked it. It meant an increasing current and the obliteration of the treacherous shingle-beds that so often threatened to tear the bottom out of our canoe.

Contrary to our expectations, the wind did not go down with the sun. It seemed to increase with the darkness, howling overhead and shaking the willows round us like straws. Curious sounds accompanied it sometimes, like the explosion of heavy guns, and it fell upon the water and the island in great flat blows of immense power. It made me think of the sounds a planet must make, could we only hear it, driving along through space.

But the sky kept wholly clear of clouds, and soon after supper the full moon rose up in the east and covered the river and the plain of shouting willows with a light like the day.

We lay on the sandy patch beside the fire, smoking, listening to the noises of the night round us, and talking happily of the journey we had already made, and of our plans ahead. The map lay spread in the door of the tent, but the high wind made it hard to study, and presently we lowered the curtain and extinguished the lantern. The firelight was enough to smoke and see each other's faces by, and the sparks flew about overhead like fireworks. A few yards beyond, the river gurgled and hissed, and from time to time a heavy splash announced the falling away of further portions of the bank.

Our talk, I noticed, had to do with the faraway scenes and incidents of our first camps in the Black Forest, or of other subjects altogether remote from the present setting, for neither of us spoke of the actual moment more than was necessary—almost as though we had agreed tacitly to avoid discussion of the camp and its incidents. Neither the otter nor the boatman, for instance, received the honour of a single mention, though ordinarily these would have furnished discussion for the greater part of the evening. They were, of course, distinct events in such a place.

The scarcity of wood made it a business to keep the fire going, for the wind, that drove the smoke in our faces wherever we sat, helped at the same time to make a forced draught. We took it in turn to make some foraging expeditions into the darkness, and the quantity the Swede brought back always made me feel that he took an absurdly long time finding it; for the fact was I did not care much about being left alone, and yet it always seemed to be my turn to grub about among the bushes or scramble along the slippery banks in the moonlight. The long day's battle with wind and water—such wind and such water!—had tired us both, and an early bed was the obvious program.

Yet neither of us made the move for the tent. We lay there, tending the fire, talking in desultory fashion, peering about us into the dense willow bushes, and listening to the thunder of wind and river. The loneliness of the place had entered our very bones, and silence seemed natural, for after a bit the sound of our voices became a trifle unreal and forced; whispering would have been the fitting mode of communication, I felt, and the human voice, always rather absurd amid the roar of the elements, now carried with it something almost illegitimate. It was like talking out loud in church, or in some place where it was not lawful, perhaps not quite *safe*, to be overheard.

The eeriness of this lonely island, set among a million willows, swept by a hurricane, and surrounded by hurrying deep waters, touched us both, I fancy. Untrodden by man, almost unknown to man, it lay there beneath the moon, remote from human influence, on the frontier of another world, an alien world, a world tenanted by willows only and the souls of willows. And we, in our rashness, had dared to invade it, even to make use of it! Something more than the power of its mystery stirred in me as I lay on the sand, feet to fire, and peered up through the leaves at the stars. For the last time I rose to get firewood.

"When this has burnt up," I said firmly, "I shall turn in," and my companion watched me lazily as I moved off into the surrounding shadows.

For an unimaginative man I thought he seemed unusually receptive that night, unusually open to suggestion of things other than sensory. He too was touched by the beauty and loneliness of the place. I was not altogether pleased, I remember, to recognize this slight change in him, and instead of immediately collecting sticks, I made my way to the far point of the island where the moonlight on plain and river could be seen to better advantage. The desire to be alone had come suddenly upon me; my former dread returned in force; there was a vague feeling in me I wished to face and probe to the bottom.

When I reached the point of sand jutting out among the waves, the spell of the place descended upon me with a positive shock. No mere "scenery" could have produced such an effect. There was something more here, something to alarm.

I gazed across the waste of wild waters; I watched the whispering willows; I heard the ceaseless beating of the tireless wind; and, one and all, each in its own way, stirred in me this sensation of a strange distress. But the *willows* especially; for ever they went on chattering and talking among themselves, laughing a little, shrilly crying out, sometimes sighing—but what it was they made so much to-do about belonged to the secret life of the great plain they inhabited. And it was utterly alien to the world I knew, or to that of the wild yet kindly elements.

They made me think of a host of beings from another plane of life, another evolution altogether, perhaps, all discussing a mystery known only to themselves. I watched them moving busily together, oddly shaking their big bushy heads, twirling their myriad leaves even when there was no wind. They moved of their own will as though alive, and they touched, by some incalculable method, my own keen sense of the *horrible*.

There they stood in the moonlight, like a vast army surrounding our camp, shaking their innumerable silver spears defiantly, formed all ready for an attack.

The psychology of places, for some imaginations at least, is very vivid; for the wanderer, especially, camps have their "note" either of welcome or rejection. At first it may not always be apparent, because the busy preparations of tent and cooking prevent, but with the first pause—after supper usually—it comes and announces itself. And the note of this willow-camp now became unmistakably plain to me; we were interlopers, trespassers; we were not welcomed. The sense of un-familiarity grew upon me as I stood there watching. We touched the frontier of a region where our presence was resented. For a night's lodging we might perhaps be tolerated; but for a prolonged and in-quisitive stay—No! by all the gods of the trees and wilderness, no! We were the first human influences upon this island, and we were not wanted. *The willows were against us.*

Strange thoughts like these, bizarre fancies, borne I know not whence, found lodgement in my mind as I stood listening. What, I thought, if, after all, these crouching willows proved to be alive; if suddenly they should rise up, like a swarm of living creatures, mar-shalled by the gods whose territory we had invaded, sweep towards us off the vast swamps, booming overhead in the night—and then *settle down!* As I looked it was so easy to imagine they actually moved, crept nearer, retreated a little, huddled together in masses, hostile, waiting for the great wind that should finally start them a-running. I could have sworn their aspect changed a little, and their ranks deepened and pressed more closely together.

The melancholy shrill cry of a night-bird sounded overhead, and suddenly I nearly lost my balance as the piece of bank I stood upon fell with a great splash into the river, undermined by the flood. I stepped back just in time, and went on hunting for firewood again, half laughing at the odd fancies that crowded so thickly into my mind and cast their spell upon me. I recalled the Swede's remark about moving on next day, and I was just thinking that I fully agreed with him, when I turned with a start and saw the subject of my thoughts standing immediately in front of me. He was quite close. The roar of the elements had covered his approach.

"You've been gone so long," he shouted above the wind, "I thought something must have happened to you."

But there was that in his tone, and a certain look in his face as well, that conveyed to me more than his usual words, and in a flash, I understood the real reason for his coming. It was because the spell of the place had entered his soul too, and he did not like being alone.

"River still rising," he cried, pointing to the flood in the moon-light, "and the wind's simply awful."

He always said the same things, but it was the cry for companion-ship that gave the real importance to his words.

"Lucky," I cried back, "our tent's in the hollow. I think it'll hold all right." I added something about the difficulty of finding wood, in order to explain my absence, but the wind caught my words and flung them across the river, so that he did not hear, but just looked at me through the branches, nodding his head.

"Lucky if we get away without disaster!" he shouted, or words to that effect; and I remember feeling half angry with him for putting the thought into words, for it was exactly what I felt myself. There was disaster impending somewhere, and the sense of presentiment lay unpleasantly upon me.

We went back to the fire and made a final blaze, poking it up with our feet. We took a last look round. But for the wind the heat would have been unpleasant. I put this thought into words, and I remember my friend's reply struck me oddly: that he would rather have the heat, the ordinary July weather, than this "diabolical wind."

Everything was snug for the night; the canoe lying turned over beside the tent, with both yellow paddles beneath her; the provision sack hanging from a willow-stem, and the washed-up dishes removed to a safe distance from the fire, all ready for the morning meal.

We smothered the embers of the fire with sand, and then turned in. The flap of the tent door was up, and I saw the branches and the stars and the white moonlight. The shaking willows and the heavy buffetings of the wind against our taut little house were the last things I remembered as sleep came down and covered all with its soft and delicious forgetfulness.

Suddenly I found myself lying awake, peering from my sandy mattress through the door of the tent. I looked at my watch pinned against the canvas, and saw by the bright moonlight that it was past twelve o'clock—the threshold of a new day—and I had therefore slept a couple of hours. The Swede was asleep still beside me; the wind howled as before; something plucked at my heart and made me feel afraid. There was a sense of disturbance in my immediate neighbourhood.

I sat up quickly and looked out. The trees were swaying violently to and fro as the gusts smote them, but our little bit of green canvas lay snugly safe in the hollow, for the wind passed over it without meeting enough resistance to make it vicious. The feeling of disquietude did not pass, however, and I crawled quietly out of the tent to see if our belongings were safe. I moved carefully so as not to waken my companion. A curious excitement was on me.

I was half-way out, kneeling on all fours, when my eye first took in that the tops of the bushes opposite, with their moving tracery of leaves, made shapes against the sky. I sat back on my haunches and stared. It was incredible, surely, but there, opposite and slightly above me, were shapes of some indeterminate sort among the willows, and as the branches swayed in the wind, they seemed to group themselves about these shapes, forming a series of monstrous outlines that shifted rapidly beneath the moon. Close, about fifty feet in front of me, I saw these things.

My first instinct was to waken my companion, that he too might see them, but something made me hesitate—the sudden realisation, probably, that I should not welcome corroboration; and meanwhile I crouched there staring in amazement with smarting eyes. I was wide awake. I remember saying to myself that I was not dreaming.

They first became properly visible, these huge figures, just within the tops of the bushes—immense, bronze-coloured, moving, and wholly independent of the swaying of the branches. I saw them plainly and noted, now I came to examine them more calmly, that they were very much larger than human, and indeed that something in their appearance proclaimed them to be *not human* at all. Certainly, they were not merely the moving tracery of the branches against the moonlight.

They shifted independently. They rose upwards in a continuous stream from earth to sky, vanishing utterly as soon as they reached the dark of the sky. They were interlaced one with another, making a great column, and I saw their limbs and huge bodies melting in and out of each other, forming this serpentine line that bent and swayed and twisted spirally with the contortions of the wind-tossed trees. They were nude, fluid shapes, passing up the bushes, *within* the leaves almost—rising up in a living column into the heavens. Their faces I never could see. Unceasingly they poured upwards, swaying in great bending curves, with a hue of dull bronze upon their skins.

I stared, trying to force every atom of vision from my eyes. For a long time, I thought they *must* every moment disappear and resolve themselves into the movements of the branches and prove to be an optical illusion. I searched everywhere for a proof of reality, when all the while I understood quite well that the standard of reality had changed. For the longer I looked the more certain I became that these figures were real and living, though perhaps not according to the standards that the camera and the biologist would insist upon.

Far from feeling fear, I was possessed with a sense of awe and wonder such as I have never known. I seemed to be gazing at the personified elemental forces of this haunted and primeval region. Our intrusion had stirred the powers of the place into activity. It was we who were the cause of the disturbance, and my brain filled to bursting with stories and legends of the spirits and deities of places that have been acknowledged and worshipped by men in all ages of the world's history.

But, before I could arrive at any possible explanation, something impelled me to go farther out, and I crept forward on the sand and stood upright. I felt the ground still warm under my bare feet; the wind tore at my hair and face; and the sound of the river burst upon my ears with a sudden roar. These things, I knew, were real, and proved that my senses were acting normally. Yet the figures still rose from earth to heaven, silent, majestically, in a great spiral of grace and strength that overwhelmed me at length with a genuine deep emotion of worship. I felt that I must fall down and worship—absolutely worship.

Perhaps in another minute I might have done so, when a gust of wind swept against me with such force that it blew me sideways, and I nearly stumbled and fell. It seemed to shake the dream violently out of me. At least it gave me another point of view somehow. The figures still remained, still ascended into heaven from the heart of the night, but my reason at last began to assert itself. It must be a subjective experience, I argued—none the less real for that, but still subjective. The moonlight and the branches combined to work out these pictures upon the mirror of my imagination, and for some reason I projected them outwards and made them appear objective. I knew this must be the case, of course. I took courage, and began to move forward across the open patches of sand. By Jove, though, was it all hallucination? Was it merely subjective? Did not my reason argue in the old futile way from the little standard of the known?

I only know that great column of figures ascended darkly into the sky for what seemed a very long period of time, and with a very complete measure of reality as most men are accustomed to gauge reality. Then suddenly they were gone!

And, once they were gone and the immediate wonder of their great presence had passed, fear came down upon me with a cold rush. The esoteric meaning of this lonely and haunted region suddenly flamed up within me, and I began to tremble dreadfully. I took a quick look round—a look of horror that came near to panic—calculating vainly ways of escape; and then, realising how helpless I was to achieve anything really effective, I crept back silently into the tent and lay down again upon my sandy mattress, first lowering the door-curtain to shut out the sight of the willows in the moonlight, and then burying my head as deeply as possible beneath the blankets to deaden the sound of the terrifying wind.

3

As though further to convince me that I had not been dreaming, I remember that it was a long time before I fell again into a troubled and restless sleep; and even then only the upper crust of me slept, and underneath there was something that never quite lost consciousness, but lay alert and on the watch.

But this second time I jumped up with a genuine start of terror. It was neither the wind nor the river that woke me, but the slow approach of something that caused the sleeping portion of me to grow smaller and smaller till at last it vanished altogether, and I found myself sitting bolt upright—listening.

Outside there was a sound of multitudinous little patterings. They had been coming, I was aware, for a long time, and in my sleep they had first become audible. I sat there nervously wide awake as though I had not slept at all. It seemed to me that my breathing came with difficulty, and that there was a great weight upon the surface of my body. In spite of the hot night, I felt clammy with cold and shivered. Something surely was pressing steadily against the sides of the tent and weighing down upon it from above. Was it the body of the wind? Was this the pattering rain, the dripping of the leaves? The spray blown from the river by the wind and gathering in big drops? I thought quickly of a dozen things.

Then suddenly the explanation leaped into my mind: a bough from the poplar, the only large tree on the island, had fallen with the wind. Still half caught by the other branches, it would fall with the next gust and crush us, and meanwhile its leaves brushed and tapped upon the tight canvas surface of the tent. I raised a loose flap and rushed out, calling to the Swede to follow.

But when I got out and stood upright, I saw that the tent was free. There was no hanging bough; there was no rain or spray; nothing approached.

A cold, grey light filtered down through the bushes and lay on the faintly gleaming sand. Stars still crowded the sky directly overhead, and the wind howled magnificently, but the fire no longer gave out any glow, and I saw the east reddening in streaks through the trees. Several hours must have passed since I stood there before watching the ascending figures, and the memory of it now came back to me horribly, like an evil dream. Oh, how tired it made me feel, that ceaseless raging wind! Yet, though the deep lassitude of a sleepless night was on me, my nerves were tingling with the activity of an equally tireless apprehension, and all idea of repose was out of the question. The river I saw had risen further. Its thunder filled the air, and a fine spray made itself felt through my thin sleeping shirt.

Yet nowhere did I discover the slightest evidence of anything to cause alarm. This deep, prolonged disturbance in my heart remained wholly unaccounted for.

My companion had not stirred when I called him, and there was no need to waken him now. I looked about me carefully, noting everything; the turned-over canoe; the yellow paddles—two of them, I'm certain; the provision sack and the extra lantern hanging together from the tree; and, crowding everywhere about me, enveloping all, the willows, those endless, shaking willows. A bird uttered its morning cry, and a string of duck passed with whirring flight overhead in the twilight. The sand whirled, dry and stinging, about my bare feet in the wind.

I walked round the tent and then went out a little way into the bush, so that I could see across the river to the farther landscape, and the same profound yet indefinable emotion of distress seized upon me again as I saw the interminable sea of bushes stretching to the horizon, looking ghostly and unreal in the wan light of dawn. I walked softly here and there, still puzzling over that odd sound of infinite pattering, and of that pressure upon the tent that had wakened me. It *must* have been the wind, I reflected—the wind bearing upon the loose, hot sand, driving the dry particles smartly against the taut canvas—the wind dropping heavily upon our fragile roof.

Yet all the time my nervousness and malaise increased appreciably.

I crossed over to the farther shore and noted how the coast-line had altered in the night, and what masses of sand the river had torn away. I dipped my hands and feet into the cool current, and bathed my forehead. Already there was a glow of sunrise in the sky and the exquisite freshness of coming day. On my way back I passed purposely beneath the very bushes where I had seen the column of figures rising into the air, and midway among the clumps I suddenly found myself overtaken by a sense of vast terror. From the shadows a large figure went swiftly by. Someone passed me, as sure as ever man did . . .

It was a great staggering blow from the wind that helped me forward again, and once out in the more open space, the sense of terror diminished strangely. The winds were about and walking, I remember saying to myself, for the winds often move like great presences under the trees. And altogether the fear that hovered about me was such an unknown and immense kind of fear, so unlike anything I had ever felt before, that it woke a sense of awe and wonder in me that did much to counteract its worst effects; and when I reached a high point in the middle of the island from which I could see the wide stretch of river, crimson in the sunrise, the whole magical beauty of it all was so overpowering that a sort of wild yearning woke in me and almost brought a cry up into the throat.

But this cry found no expression, for as my eyes wandered from the plain beyond to the island round me and noted our little tent half hidden among the willows, a dreadful discovery leaped out at me, compared to which my terror of the walking winds seemed as nothing at all.

For a change, I thought, had somehow come about in the arrangement of the landscape. It was not that my point of vantage gave me a different view, but that an alteration had apparently been effected in the relation of the tent to the willows, and of the willows to the tent. Surely the bushes now crowded much closer—unnecessarily, unpleasantly close. *They had moved nearer.*

Creeping with silent feet over the shifting sands, drawing imperceptibly nearer by soft, unhurried movements, the willows had come closer during the night. But had the wind moved them, or had they moved of themselves? I recalled the sound of infinite small patterings and the pressure upon the tent and upon my own heart that caused me to wake in terror. I swayed for a moment in the wind like a tree, finding it hard to keep my upright position on the sandy hillock. There was a suggestion here of personal agency, of deliberate intention, of aggressive hostility, and it terrified me into a sort of rigidity.

Then the reaction followed quickly. The idea was so bizarre, so absurd, that I felt inclined to laugh. But the laughter came no more readily than the cry, for the knowledge that my mind was so receptive to such dangerous imaginings brought the additional terror that it was through our minds and not through our physical bodies that the attack would come, and was coming.

The wind buffeted me about, and, very quickly it seemed, the sun came up over the horizon, for it was after four o'clock, and I must have stood on that little pinnacle of sand longer than I knew, afraid to come down to close quarters with the willows. I returned quietly, creepily, to the tent, first taking another exhaustive look round and—yes, I confess it—making a few measurements. I paced out on the warm sand the distances between the willows and the tent, making a note of the shortest distance particularly.

I crawled stealthily into my blankets. My companion, to all appearances, still slept soundly, and I was glad that this was so. Provided my experiences were not corroborated, I could find strength somehow to deny them, perhaps. With the daylight I could persuade myself that it was all a subjective hallucination, a fantasy of the night, a projection of the excited imagination.

Nothing further came in to disturb me, and I fell asleep almost at once, utterly exhausted, yet still in dread of hearing again that weird sound of multitudinous pattering, or of feeling the pressure upon my heart that had made it difficult to breathe.

4

The sun was high in the heavens when my companion woke me from a heavy sleep and announced that the porridge was cooked and there was just time to bathe. The grateful smell of frizzling bacon entered the tent door.

"River still rising," he said, "and several islands out in midstream have disappeared altogether. Our own island's much smaller."

"Any wood left?" I asked sleepily.

"The wood and the island will finish tomorrow in a dead heat," he laughed, "but there's enough to last us till then."

I plunged in from the point of the island, which had indeed altered a lot in size and shape during the night, and was swept down in a moment to the landing-place opposite the tent. The water was icy, and the banks flew by like the country from an express train. Bathing under such conditions was an exhilarating operation, and the terror of the night seemed cleansed out of me by a process of evaporation in the brain. The sun was blazing hot; not a cloud showed itself anywhere; the wind, however, had not abated one little jot.

Quite suddenly then the implied meaning of the Swede's words flashed across me, showing that he no longer wished to leave post-haste, and had changed his mind. "Enough to last till tomorrow"—he assumed we should stay on the island another night. It struck me as odd. The night before he was so positive the other way. How had the change come about?

Great crumblings of the banks occurred at breakfast, with heavy splashings and clouds of spray which the wind brought into our frying-pan, and my fellow-traveller talked incessantly about the difficulty the Vienna-Pesth steamers must have to find the channel in flood. But the state of his mind interested and impressed me far more than the state of the river or the difficulties of the steamers. He had changed somehow since the evening before. His manner was different—a trifle excited, a trifle shy, with a sort of suspicion about his voice and gestures. I hardly know how to describe it now in cold blood, but at the time I remember being quite certain of one thing—that he had become frightened?

He ate very little breakfast, and for once omitted to smoke his pipe. He had the map spread open beside him, and kept studying its markings.

"We'd better get off sharp in an hour," I said presently, feeling for an opening that must bring him indirectly to a partial confession at any rate. And his answer puzzled me uncomfortably: "Rather! If they'll let us."

"Who'll let us? The elements?" I asked quickly, with affected indifference.

"The powers of this awful place, whoever they are," he replied, keeping his eyes on the map. "The gods are here, if they are anywhere at all in the world."

211

"The elements are always the true immortals," I replied, laughing as naturally as I could manage, yet knowing quite well that my face reflected my true feelings when he looked up gravely at me and spoke across the smoke:

"We shall be fortunate if we get away without further disaster."

This was exactly what I had dreaded, and I screwed myself up to the point of the direct question. It was like agreeing to allow the dentist to extract the tooth; it *had* to come anyhow in the long run, and the rest was all pretence.

"Further disaster! Why, what's happened?"

"For one thing—the steering paddle's gone," he said quietly.

"The steering paddle gone!" I repeated, greatly excited, for this was our rudder, and the Danube in flood without a rudder was suicide. "But what—"

"And there's a tear in the bottom of the canoe," he added, with a genuine little tremor in his voice.

I continued staring at him, able only to repeat the words in his face somewhat foolishly. There, in the heat of the sun, and on this burning sand, I was aware of a freezing atmosphere descending round us. I got up to follow him, for he merely nodded his head gravely and led the way towards the tent a few yards on the other side of the fireplace. The canoe still lay there as I had last seen her in the night, ribs uppermost, the paddles, or rather, *the* paddle, on the sand beside her.

"There's only one," he said, stooping to pick it up. "And here's the rent in the base-board."

It was on the tip of my tongue to tell him that I had clearly noticed *two* paddles a few hours before, but a second impulse made me think better of it, and I said nothing. I approached to see.

There was a long, finely made tear in the bottom of the canoe where a little slither of wood had been neatly taken clean out; it looked as if the tooth of a sharp rock or snag had eaten down her length, and investigation showed that the hole went through. Had we launched out in her without observing it we must inevitably have foundered. At first the water would have made the wood swell so as to close the hole, but once out in midstream the water must have poured in, and the canoe, never more than two inches above the surface, would have filled and sunk very rapidly.

"There, you see an attempt to prepare a victim for the sacrifice," I heard him saying, more to himself than to me, "two victims rather," he added as he bent over and ran his fingers along the slit.

I began to whistle—a thing I always do unconsciously when utterly nonplussed—and purposely paid no attention to his words. I was determined to consider them foolish.

"It wasn't there last night," he said presently, straightening up from his examination and looking anywhere but at me.

"We must have scratched her in landing, of course," I stopped whistling to say. "The stones are very sharp."

I stopped abruptly, for at that moment he turned round and met my eye squarely. I knew just as well as he did how impossible my explanation was. There were no stones, to begin with.

"And then there's this to explain too," he added quietly, handing me the paddle and pointing to the blade.

A new and curious emotion spread freezingly over me as I took and examined it. The blade was scraped down all over, beautifully scraped, as though someone had sand-papered it with care, making it so thin that the first vigorous stroke must have snapped it off at the elbow.

"One of us walked in his sleep and did this thing," I said feebly, "or—or it has been filed by the constant stream of sand particles blown against it by the wind, perhaps."

"Ah," said the Swede, turning away, laughing a little, "you can explain everything."

"The same wind that caught the steering paddle and flung it so near the bank that it fell in with the next lump that crumbled," I called out after him, absolutely determined to find an explanation for everything he showed me.

"I see," he shouted back, turning his head to look at me before disappearing among the willow bushes.

Once alone with these perplexing evidences of personal agency, I think my first thoughts took the form of "One of us must have done this thing, and it certainly was not I." But my second thought decided how impossible it was to suppose, under all the circumstances, that either of us had done it. That my companion, the trusted friend of a dozen similar expeditions, could have knowingly had a hand in it, was a suggestion not to be entertained for a moment. Equally absurd seemed the explanation that this imperturbable and densely practical nature had suddenly become insane and was busied with insane purposes.

Yet the fact remained that what disturbed me most, and kept my fear actively alive even in this blaze of sunshine and wild beauty, was the clear certainty that some curious alteration had come about in *his* mind—that he was nervous, timid, suspicious, aware of goings on he did not speak about, watching a series of secret and hitherto unmentionable events—waiting, in a word, for a climax that he expected, and, I thought, expected very soon. This grew up in my mind intuitively—I hardly knew how.

I made a hurried examination of the tent and its surroundings, but the measurements of the night remained the same. There were deep hollows formed in the sand I now noticed for the first time, basin-shaped and of various depths and sizes, varying from that of a tea-cup to a large bowl. The wind, no doubt, was responsible for these miniature craters, just as it was for lifting the paddle and tossing it towards the water. The rent in the canoe was the only thing that seemed quite inexplicable; and, after all, it *was* conceivable that a sharp point had caught it when we landed.

The examination I made of the shore did not assist this theory, but all the same I clung to it with that diminishing portion of my intelligence which I called my "reason." An explanation of some kind was an absolute necessity, just as some working explanation of the universe is necessary—however absurd—to the happiness of every individual who seeks to do his duty in the world and face the problems of life. The simile seemed to me at the time an exact parallel.

I at once set the pitch melting, and presently the Swede joined me at the work, though under the best conditions in the world the canoe could not be safe for traveling till the following day. I drew his attention casually to the hollows in the sand.

"Yes," he said, "I know. They're all over the island. But *you* can explain them, no doubt!"

"Wind, of course," I answered without hesitation. "Have you never watched those little whirlwinds in the street that twist and twirl everything into a circle? This sand's loose enough to yield, that's all."

He made no reply, and we worked on in silence for a bit. I watched him surreptitiously all the time, and I had an idea he was watching me. He seemed, too, to be always listening attentively to something I could not hear, or perhaps for something that he expected to hear, for he kept turning about and staring into the bushes, and up into the sky, and out across the water where it was visible through the openings among the willows. Sometimes he even put his hand to his ear and held it there for several minutes. He said nothing to me, however, about it, and I asked no questions. And meanwhile, as he mended that torn canoe with the skill and address of a Red Indian, I was glad to notice his absorption in the work, for there was a vague dread in my heart that he would speak of the changed aspect of the willows. And, if he had noticed *that*, my imagination could no longer be held a sufficient explanation of it.

At length, after a long pause, he began to talk.

"Queer thing," he added in a hurried sort of voice, as though he wanted to say something and get it over. "Queer thing. I mean, about that otter last night."

I had expected something so totally different that he caught me with surprise, and I looked up sharply.

"Shows how lonely this place is. Otters are awfully shy things—"

"I don't mean that, of course," he interrupted. "I mean—do you think—did you think it really was an otter?"

"What else, in the name of Heaven, what else?"

"You know, I saw it before you did, and at first it seemed—so *much* bigger than an otter."

"The sunset as you looked upstream magnified it, or something," I replied.

He looked at me absently a moment, as though his mind were busy with other thoughts.

"It had such extraordinary yellow eyes," he went on half to himself.

"That was the sun too," I laughed, a trifle boisterously. "I suppose you'll wonder next if that fellow in the boat—"

I suddenly decided not to finish the sentence. He was in the act again of listening, turning his head to the wind, and something in the expression of his face made me halt. The subject dropped, and we went on with our caulking. Apparently, he had not noticed my unfinished sentence. Five minutes later, however, he looked at me across the canoe, the smoking pitch in his hand, his face exceedingly grave.

"I *did* rather wonder, if you want to know," he said slowly, "what that thing in the boat was. I remember thinking at the time it was not a man. The whole business seemed to rise quite suddenly out of the water."

I laughed again boisterously in his face, but this time there was impatience, and a strain of anger too, in my feeling.

"Look here now," I cried, "this place is quite queer enough without going out of our way to imagine things! That boat was an ordinary boat, and the man in it was an ordinary man, and they were both going down-stream as fast as they could lick. And that otter was an otter, so don't let's play the fool about it!"

He looked steadily at me with the same grave expression. He was not in the least annoyed. I took courage from his silence.

"And, for Heaven's sake," I went on, "don't keep pretending you hear things, because it only gives me the jumps, and there's nothing to hear but the river and this cursed old thundering wind."

"You *fool!*" he answered in a low, shocked voice, "you utter fool. That's just the way all victims talk. As if you didn't understand just as well as I do!" he sneered with scorn in his voice, and a sort of resignation. "The best thing you can do is to keep quiet and try to hold your mind as firm as possible. This feeble attempt at self-deception only makes the truth harder when you're forced to meet it."

My little effort was over, and I found nothing more to say, for I knew quite well his words were true, and that *I* was the fool, not *he*. Up to a certain stage in the adventure he kept ahead of me easily, and I think I felt annoyed to be out of it, to be thus proved less psychic, less sensitive than himself to these extraordinary happenings, and half ignorant all the time of what was going on under my very nose. *He knew* from the very beginning, apparently. But at the moment I wholly missed the point of his words about the necessity of there being a victim, and that we ourselves were destined to satisfy the want. I dropped all pretence thenceforward, but thenceforward likewise my fear increased steadily to the climax.

"But you're quite right about one thing," he added, before the subject passed, "and that is that we're wiser not to talk about it, or even to think about it, because what one *thinks* finds expression in words, and what one *says*, happens."

That afternoon, while the canoe dried and hardened, we spent trying to fish, testing the leak, collecting wood, and watching the enormous flood of rising water. Masses of driftwood swept near our shores sometimes, and we fished for them with long willow branches. The island grew perceptibly smaller as the banks were torn away with great gulps and splashes. The weather kept brilliantly fine till about four o'clock, and then for the first time for three days the wind showed signs of abating. Clouds began to gather in the south-west, spreading thence slowly over the sky.

This lessening of the wind came as a great relief, for the incessant roaring, banging, and thundering had irritated our nerves. Yet the silence that came about five o'clock with its sudden cessation was in a manner quite as oppressive. The booming of the river had everything in its own way then; it filled the air with deep murmurs, more musical than the wind noises, but infinitely more monotonous. The wind held many notes, rising, falling always beating out some sort of great elemental tune; whereas the river's song lay between three notes at most—dull pedal notes, that held a lugubrious quality foreign to the wind, and somehow seemed to me, in my then nervous state, to sound wonderfully well the music of doom.

It was extraordinary, too, how the withdrawal suddenly of bright sunlight took everything out of the landscape that made for cheerfulness; and since this particular landscape had already managed to convey the suggestion of something sinister, the change of course was all the more unwelcome and noticeable. For me, I know, the darkening outlook became distinctly more alarming, and I found myself more than once calculating how soon after sunset the full moon would get up in the east, and whether the gathering clouds would greatly interfere with her lighting of the little island.

With this general hush of the wind—though it still indulged in occasional brief gusts—the river seemed to me to grow blacker, the willows to stand more densely together. The latter, too, kept up a sort of independent movement of their own, rustling among themselves when no wind stirred, and shaking oddly from the roots upwards. When common objects in this way become charged with the suggestion of horror, they stimulate the imagination far more than things of unusual appearance; and these bushes, crowding huddled about us, assumed for me in the darkness a bizarre *grotesquerie* of appearance that lent to them somehow the aspect of purposeful and living creatures.

Their very ordinariness, I felt, masked what was malignant and hostile to us. The forces of the region drew nearer with the coming of night. They were focusing upon our island, and more particularly upon ourselves. For thus, somehow, in the terms of the imagination, did my really indescribable sensations in this extraordinary place present themselves.

I had slept a good deal in the early afternoon, and had thus recovered somewhat from the exhaustion of a disturbed night, but this only served apparently to render me more susceptible than before to the obsessing spell of the haunting. I fought against it, laughing at my feelings as absurd and childish, with very obvious physiological explanations, yet, in spite of every effort, they gained in strength upon me so that I dreaded the night as a child lost in a forest must dread the approach of darkness.

The canoe we had carefully covered with a waterproof sheet during the day, and the one remaining paddle had been securely tied by the Swede to the base of a tree, lest the wind should rob us of that too. From five o'clock onwards I busied myself with the stew-pot and preparations for dinner, it being my turn to cook that night. We had potatoes, onions, bits of bacon fat to add flavour, and a general thick residue from former stews at the bottom of the pot; with black bread broken up into it the result was most excellent, and it was followed by a stew of plums with sugar and a brew of strong tea with dried milk. A good pile of wood lay close at hand, and the absence of wind made my duties easy.

My companion sat lazily watching me, dividing his attentions between cleaning his pipe and giving useless advice—an admitted privilege of the off-duty man. He had been very quiet all the afternoon, engaged in re-caulking the canoe, strengthening the tent ropes, and fishing for driftwood while I slept. No more talk about undesirable things had passed between us, and I think his only remarks had to do with the gradual destruction of the island, which he declared was not fully a third smaller than when we first landed.

The pot had just begun to bubble when I heard his voice calling to me from the bank, where he had wandered away without my noticing. I ran up.

"Come and listen," he said, "and see what you make of it." He held his hand cupwise to his ear, as so often before.

"*Now* do you hear anything?" he asked, watching me curiously.

We stood there, listening attentively together. At first, I heard only the deep note of the water and the hissings rising from its turbulent surface. The willows, for once, were motionless and silent. Then a sound began to reach my ears faintly, a peculiar sound—something like the humming of a distant gong. It seemed to come across to us in the darkness from the waste of swamps and willows opposite. It was repeated at regular intervals, but it was certainly neither the sound of a bell nor the hooting of a distant steamer. I can liken it to nothing so much as to the sound of an immense gong, suspended far up in the sky, repeating incessantly its muffled metallic note, soft and musical, as it was repeatedly struck. My heart quickened as I listened.

"I've heard it all day," said my companion. "While you slept this afternoon, it came all round the island. I hunted it down, but could never get near enough to see—to localise it correctly. Sometimes it was overhead, and sometimes it seemed under the water. Once or

218

twice, too, I could have sworn it was not outside at all, but *within myself*—you know—the way a sound in the fourth dimension is supposed to come."

I was too much puzzled to pay much attention to his words. I listened carefully, striving to associate it with any known familiar sound I could think of, but without success. It changed in the direction, too, coming nearer, and then sinking utterly away into remote distance. I cannot say that it was ominous in quality, because to me it seemed distinctly musical, yet I must admit it set going a distressing feeling that made me wish I had never heard it.

"The wind blowing in those sand-funnels," I said determined to find an explanation, "or the bushes rubbing together after the storm perhaps."

"It comes off the whole swamp," my friend answered. "It comes from everywhere at once." He ignored my explanations. "It comes from the willow bushes somehow—"

"But now the wind has dropped," I objected. "The willows can hardly make a noise by themselves, can they?"

His answer frightened me, first because I had dreaded it, and secondly, because I knew intuitively it was true.

"It is *because* the wind has dropped, we now hear it. It was drowned before. It is the cry, I believe, of the—"

I dashed back to my fire, warned by the sound of bubbling that the stew was in danger, but determined at the same time to escape further conversation. I was resolute, if possible, to avoid the exchanging of views. I dreaded, too, that he would begin about the gods, or the elemental forces, or something else disquieting, and I wanted to keep myself well in hand for what might happen later. There was another night to be faced before we escaped from this distressing place, and there was no knowing yet what it might bring forth.

"Come and cut up bread for the pot," I called to him, vigorously stirring the appetising mixture. That stew-pot held sanity for us both, and the thought made me laugh.

He came over slowly and took the provision sack from the tree, fumbling in its mysterious depths, and then emptying the entire contents upon the ground-sheet at his feet.

"Hurry up!" I cried; "it's boiling."

The Swede burst out into a roar of laughter that startled me. It was forced laughter, not artificial exactly, but mirthless.

"There's nothing here!" he shouted, holding his sides.

219

"Bread, I mean."

"It's gone. There is no bread. They've taken it!"

I dropped the long spoon and ran up. Everything the sack had contained lay upon the ground-sheet, but there was no loaf.

The whole dead weight of my growing fear fell upon me and shook me. Then I burst out laughing too. It was the only thing to do: and the sound of my laughter also made me understand his. The stain of psychical pressure caused it—this explosion of unnatural laughter in both of us; it was an effort of repressed forces to seek relief; it was a temporary safety-valve. And with both of us it ceased quite suddenly.

"How criminally stupid of me!" I cried, still determined to be consistent and find an explanation. "I clean forgot to buy a loaf at Pressburg. That chattering woman put everything out of my head, and I must have left it lying on the counter or—"

"The oatmeal, too, is much less than it was this morning," the Swede interrupted.

Why in the world need he draw attention to it? I thought angrily.

"There's enough for tomorrow," I said, stirring vigorously, "and we can get lots more at Komorn or Gran. In twenty-four hours, we shall be miles from here."

"I hope so—to God," he muttered, putting the things back into the sack, "unless we're claimed first as victims for the sacrifice," he added with a foolish laugh. He dragged the sack into the tent, for safety's sake, I suppose, and I heard him mumbling to himself, but so indistinctly that it seemed quite natural for me to ignore his words.

Our meal was beyond question a gloomy one, and we ate it almost in silence, avoiding one another's eyes, and keeping the fire bright. Then we washed up and prepared for the night, and, once smoking, our minds unoccupied with any definite duties, the apprehension I had felt all day long became more and more acute. It was not then active fear, I think, but the very vagueness of its origin distressed me far more that if I had been able to ticket and face it squarely. The curious sound I have likened to the note of a gong became now almost incessant, and filled the stillness of the night with a faint, continuous ringing rather than a series of distinct notes.

At one time it was behind and at another time in front of us. Sometimes I fancied it came from the bushes on our left, and then again from the clumps on our right. More often it hovered directly overhead like the whirring of wings. It was really everywhere at once, behind, in front, at our sides and over our heads, completely surrounding us. The sound really defies description. But nothing within my knowledge is like that ceaseless muffled humming rising off the deserted world of swamps and willows.

We sat smoking in comparative silence, the strain growing every minute greater. The worst feature of the situation seemed to me that we did not know what to expect, and could therefore make no sort of preparation by way of defence. We could anticipate nothing. My explanations made in the sunshine, moreover, now came to haunt me with their foolish and wholly unsatisfactory nature, and it was more and more clear to us that some kind of plain talk with my companion was inevitable, whether I liked it or not. After all, we had to spend the night together, and to sleep in the same tent side by side. I saw that I could not get along much longer without the support of his mind, and for that, of course, plain talk was imperative. As long as possible, however, I postponed this little climax, and tried to ignore or laugh at the occasional sentences he flung into the emptiness.

Some of these sentences, moreover, were confoundedly disquieting to me, coming as they did to corroborate much that I felt myself; corroboration, too—which made it so much more convincing—from a totally different point of view. He composed such curious sentences, and hurled them at me in such an inconsequential sort of way, as though his main line of thought was secret to himself, and these fragments were mere bits he found it impossible to digest. He got rid of them by uttering them. Speech relieved him. It was like being sick.

"There are things about us, I'm sure, that make for disorder, disintegration, destruction, our destruction," he said once, while the fire blazed between us. "We've strayed out of a safe line somewhere."

And, another time, when the gong sounds had come nearer, ringing much louder than before, and directly over our heads, he said as though talking to himself:

"I don't think a gramophone would show any record of that. The sound doesn't come to me by the ears at all. The vibrations reach me in another manner altogether, and seem to be within me, which is precisely how a fourth dimensional sound might be supposed to make itself heard."

I purposely made no reply to this, but I sat up a little closer to the fire and peered about me into the darkness. The clouds were massed all over the sky, and no trace of moonlight came through. Very still, too, everything was, so that the river and the frogs had things all their own way.

"It has that about it," he went on, "which is utterly out of common experience. It is *unknown*. Only one thing describes it really; it is a non-human sound; I mean a sound outside humanity."

Having rid himself of this indigestible morsel, he lay quiet for a time, but he had so admirably expressed my own feeling that it was a relief to have the thought out, and to have confined it by the limitation of words from dangerous wandering to and fro in the mind.

The solitude of that Danube camping-place, can I ever forget it? The feeling of being utterly alone on an empty planet! My thoughts ran incessantly upon cities and the haunts of men. I would have given my soul, as the saying is, for the "feel" of those Bavarian villages we had passed through by the score; for the normal, human commonplaces; peasants drinking beer, tables beneath the trees, hot sunshine, and a ruined castle on the rocks behind the red-roofed church. Even the tourists would have been welcome.

Yet what I felt of dread was no ordinary ghostly fear. It was infinitely greater, stranger, and seemed to arise from some dim ancestral sense of terror more profoundly disturbing than anything I had known or dreamed of. We had "strayed," as the Swede put it, into some region or some set of conditions where the risks were great, yet unintelligible to us; where the frontiers of some unknown world lay close about us. It was a spot held by the dwellers in some outer space, a sort of peep-hole whence they could spy upon the earth, themselves unseen, a point where the veil between had worn a little thin. As the final result of too long a sojourn here, we should be carried over the border and deprived of what we called "our lives," yet by mental, not physical, processes. In that sense, as he said, we should be the victims of our adventure—a sacrifice.

It took us in different fashion, each according to the measure of his sensitiveness and powers of resistance. I translated it vaguely into a personification of the mightily disturbed elements, investing them with the horror of a deliberate and malefic purpose, resentful of our audacious intrusion into their breeding-place; whereas my friend threw it into the unoriginal form at first of a trespass on some ancient shrine, some place where the old gods still held sway, where the emotional forces of former worshippers still clung, and the ancestral portion of him yielded to the old pagan spell.

At any rate, here was a place unpolluted by men, kept clean by the winds from coarsening human influences, a place where spiritual agencies were within reach and aggressive. Never, before or since, have

I been so attacked by indescribable suggestions of a "beyond region," of another scheme of life, another revolution not parallel to the human. And in the end our minds would succumb under the weight of the awful spell, and we should be drawn across the frontier into *their* world.

Small things testified to the amazing influence of the place, and now in the silence round the fire they allowed themselves to be noted by the mind. The very atmosphere had proved itself a magnifying medium to distort every indication: the otter rolling in the current, the hurrying boatman making signs, the shifting willows, one and all had been robbed of its natural character, and revealed in something of its other aspect—as it existed across the border to that other region. And this changed aspect I felt was now not merely to me, but to the race. The whole experience whose verge we touched was unknown to humanity at all. It was a new order of experience, and in the true sense of the word *unearthly*.

"It's the deliberate, calculating purpose that reduces one's courage to zero," the Swede said suddenly, as if he had been actually following my thoughts. "Otherwise, imagination might count for much. But the paddle, the canoe, the lessening food—"

"Haven't I explained all that once?" I interrupted viciously.

"You have," he answered dryly; "you have indeed."

He made other remarks too, as usual, about what he called the "plain determination to provide a victim"; but, having now arranged my thoughts better, I recognized that this was simply the cry of his frightened soul against the knowledge that he was being attacked in a vital part, and that he would be somehow taken or destroyed. The situation called for a courage and calmness of reasoning that neither of us could compass, and I have never before been so clearly conscious of two persons in me—the one that explained everything, and the other that laughed at such foolish explanations, yet was horribly afraid.

Meanwhile, in the pitchy night the fire died down and the wood pile grew small. Neither of us moved to replenish the stock, and the darkness consequently came up very close to our faces. A few feet beyond the circle of firelight it was inky black. Occasionally a stray puff of wind set the willows shivering about us, but apart from this not very welcome sound a deep and depressing silence reigned, broken only by the gurgling of the river and the humming in the air overhead.

We both missed, I think, the shouting company of the winds.

At length, at a moment when a stray puff prolonged itself as though the wind were about to rise again, I reached the point for me of saturation, the point where it was absolutely necessary to find relief in plain speech, or else to betray myself by some hysterical extravagance that must have been far worse in its effect upon both of us. I kicked the fire into a blaze, and turned to my companion abruptly. He looked up with a start.

"I can't disguise it any longer," I said; "I don't like this place, and the darkness, and the noises, and the awful feelings I get. There's something here that beats me utterly. I'm in a blue funk, and that's the plain truth. If the other shore was—different, I swear I'd be inclined to swim for it!"

The Swede's face turned very white beneath the deep tan of sun and wind. He stared straight at me and answered quietly, but his voice betrayed his huge excitement by its unnatural calmness. For the moment, at any rate, he was the strong man of the two. He was more phlegmatic, for one thing.

"It's not a physical condition we can escape from by running away," he replied, in the tone of a doctor diagnosing some grave disease; "we must sit tight and wait. There are forces close here that could kill a herd of elephants in a second as easily as you or I could squash a fly. Our only chance is to keep perfectly still. Our insignificance perhaps may save us."

I put a dozen questions into my expression of face, but found no words. It was precisely like listening to an accurate description of a disease whose symptoms had puzzled me.

"I mean that so far, although aware of our disturbing presence, they have not *found* us—not 'located' us, as the Americans say," he went on. "They're blundering about like men hunting for a leak of gas. The paddle and canoe and provisions prove that. I think they *feel* us, but cannot actually see us. We must keep our minds quiet—it's our minds they feel. We must control our thoughts, or it's all up with us."

"Death, you mean?" I stammered, icy with the horror of his suggestion.

"Worse—by far," he said. "Death, according to one's belief, means either annihilation or release from the limitations of the senses, but it involves no change of character. *You* don't suddenly alter just because the body's gone. But this means a radical alteration, a complete change, a horrible loss of oneself by substitution—far worse than death, and not even annihilation. We happen to have camped in a spot where their region touches ours, where the veil between has worn thin"—

horrors! he was using my very own phrase, my actual words—"so that they are aware of our being in their neighbourhood."

"But *who* are aware?" I asked.

I forgot the shaking of the willows in the windless calm, the humming overhead, everything except that I was waiting for an answer that I dreaded more than I can possibly explain.

He lowered his voice at once to reply, leaning forward a little over the fire, an indefinable change in his face that made me avoid his eyes and look down upon the ground.

"All my life," he said, "I have been strangely, vividly conscious of another region—not far removed from our own world in one sense, yet wholly different in kind—where great things go on unceasingly, where immense and terrible personalities hurry by, intent on vast purposes compared to which earthly affairs, the rise and fall of nations, the destinies of empires, the fate of armies and continents, are all as dust in the balance; vast purposes, I mean, that deal directly with the soul, and not indirectly with more expressions of the soul—"

"I suggest just now—" I began, seeking to stop him, feeling as though I was face to face with a madman. But he instantly overbore me with his torrent that *had* to come.

"You think," he said, "it is the spirit of the elements, and I thought perhaps it was the old gods. But I tell you now it is—*neither*. These would be comprehensible entities, for they have relations with men, depending upon them for worship or sacrifice, whereas these beings who are now about us have absolutely nothing to do with mankind, and it is mere chance that their space happens just at this spot to touch our own."

The mere conception, which his words somehow made so convincing, as I listened to them there in the dark stillness of that lonely island, set me shaking a little all over. I found it impossible to control my movements.

"And what do you propose?" I began again.

"A sacrifice, a victim, might save us by distracting them until we could get away," he went on, "just as the wolves stop to devour the dogs and give the sleigh another start. But—I see no chance of any other victim now."

I stared blankly at him. The gleam in his eye was dreadful. Presently he continued.

"It's the willows, of course. The willows mask the others, but the others are feeling about for us. If we let our minds betray our fear, we're lost, lost utterly." He looked at me with an expression so calm, so determined, so sincere, that I no longer had any doubts as to his sanity. He was as sane as any man ever was. "If we can hold out through the night," he added, "we may get off in the daylight unnoticed, or rather, *undiscovered.*"

"But you really think a sacrifice would——"

That gong-like humming came down very close over our heads as I spoke, but it was my friend's scared face that really stopped my mouth.

"Hush!" he whispered, holding up his hand. "Do not mention them more than you can help. Do not refer to them *by name.* To name is to reveal; it is the inevitable clue, and our only hope lies in ignoring them, in order that they may ignore us."

"Even in thought?" He was extraordinarily agitated.

"Especially in thought. Our thoughts make spirals in their world. We must keep them *out of our minds* at all costs if possible."

I raked the fire together to prevent the darkness having everything its own way. I never longed for the sun as I longed for it then in the awful blackness of that summer night.

"Were you awake all last night?" he went on suddenly.

"I slept badly a little after dawn," I replied evasively, trying to follow his instructions, which I knew instinctively were true, "but the wind, of course——"

"I know. But the wind won't account for all the noises."

"Then you heard it too?"

"The multiplying countless little footsteps I heard," he said, adding, after a moment's hesitation, "and that other sound——"

"You mean above the tent, and the pressing down upon us of something tremendous, gigantic?"

He nodded significantly.

"It was like the beginning of a sort of inner suffocation?" I said.

"Partly, yes. It seemed to me that the weight of the atmosphere had been altered—had increased enormously, so that we should have been crushed."

"And *that,*" I went on, determined to have it all out, pointing upwards where the gong-like note hummed ceaselessly, rising and falling like wind. "What do you make of that?"

"It's *their* sound," he whispered gravely. "It's the sound of their world, the humming in their region. The division here is so thin that it leaks through somehow. But, if you listen carefully, you'll find it's not above so much as around us. It's in the willows. It's the willows themselves humming, because here the willows have been made symbols of the forces that are against us."

I could not follow exactly what he meant by this, yet the thought and idea in my mind were beyond question the thought and idea in his. I realised what he realised, only with less power of analysis than his. It was on the tip of my tongue to tell him at last about my hallucination of the ascending figures and the moving bushes, when he suddenly thrust his face again close into mine across the firelight and began to speak in a very earnest whisper. He amazed me by his calmness and pluck, his apparent control of the situation. This man I had for years deemed unimaginative, stolid!

"Now listen," he said. "The only thing for us to do is to go on as though nothing had happened, follow our usual habits, go to bed, and so forth; pretend we feel nothing and notice nothing. It is a question wholly of the mind, and the less we think about them the better our chance of escape. Above all, don't *think*, for what you think happens!"

"All right," I managed to reply, simply breathless with his words and the strangeness of it all; "all right, I'll try, but tell me one more thing first. Tell me what you make of those hollows in the ground all about us, those sand-funnels?"

"No!" he cried, forgetting to whisper in his excitement. "I dare not, simply dare not, put the thought into words. If you have not guessed I am glad. Don't try to. *They* have put it into my mind; try your hardest to prevent their putting it into yours."

He sank his voice again to a whisper before he finished, and I did not press him to explain. There was already just about as much horror in me as I could hold. The conversation came to an end, and we smoked our pipes busily in silence.

Then something happened, something unimportant apparently, as the way is when the nerves are in a very great state of tension, and this small thing for a brief space gave me an entirely different point of view. I chanced to look down at my sandshoe—the sort we used for the canoe—and something to do with the hole at the toe suddenly recalled to me the London shop where I had bought them, the difficulty the man had in fitting me, and other details of the uninteresting but practical operation.

At once, in its train, followed a wholesome view of the modern sceptical world I was accustomed to move in at home. I thought of roast beef, and ale, motorcars, policemen, brass bands, and a dozen other things that proclaimed the soul of ordinariness or utility. The effect was immediate and astonishing even to myself. Psychologically, I suppose, it was simply a sudden and violent reaction after the strain of living in an atmosphere of things that to the normal consciousness must seem impossible and incredible. But, whatever the cause, it momentarily lifted the spell from my heart, and left me for the short space of a minute feeling free and utterly unafraid. I looked up at my friend opposite.

"You damned old pagan!" I cried, laughing aloud in his face. "You imaginative idiot! You superstitious idolater! You—"

I stopped in the middle, seized anew by the old horror. I tried to smother the sound of my voice as something sacrilegious. The Swede, of course, heard it too—the strange cry overhead in the darkness—and that sudden drop in the air as though something had come nearer.

He had turned ashen white under the tan. He stood bolt upright in front of the fire, stiff as a rod, staring at me.

"After that," he said in a sort of helpless, frantic way, "we must go! We can't stay now; we must strike camp this very instant and go on—down the river."

He was talking, I saw, quite wildly, his words dictated by abject terror—the terror he had resisted so long, but which had caught him at last.

"In the dark?" I exclaimed, shaking with fear after my hysterical outburst, but still realising our position better than he did. "Sheer madness! The river's in flood, and we've only got a single paddle. Besides, we only go deeper into their country! There's nothing ahead for fifty miles but willows, willows, willows!"

He sat down again in a state of semi-collapse. The positions, by one of those kaleidoscopic changes nature loves, were suddenly reversed, and the control of our forces passed over into my hands. His mind at last had reached the point where it was beginning to weaken.

"What on earth possessed you to do such a thing?" he whispered with the awe of genuine terror in his voice and face.

I crossed round to his side of the fire. I took both his hands in mine, kneeling down beside him and looking straight into his frightened eyes.

"We'll make one more blaze," I said firmly, "and then turn in for the night. At sunrise we'll be off full speed for Komorn. Now, pull yourself together a bit, and remember your own advice about *not thinking fear!*"

He said no more, and I saw that he would agree and obey. In some measure, too, it was a sort of relief to get up and make an excursion into the darkness for more wood. We kept close together, almost touching, groping among the bushes and along the bank. The humming overhead never ceased, but seemed to me to grow louder as we increased our distance from the fire. It was shivery work!

We were grubbing away in the middle of a thickish clump of willows where some driftwood from a former flood had caught high among the branches, when my body was seized in a grip that made me half drop upon the sand. It was the Swede. He had fallen against me, and was clutching me for support. I heard his breath coming and going in short gasps.

"Look! By my soul!" he whispered, and for the first time in my experience I knew what it was to hear tears of terror in a human voice. He was pointing to the fire, some fifty feet away. I followed the direction of his finger, and I swear my heart missed a beat.

There, in front of the dim glow, *something was moving.*

I saw it through a veil that hung before my eyes like the gauze drop-curtain used at the back of a theatre—hazily a little. It was neither a human figure nor an animal. To me it gave the strange impression of being as large as several animals grouped together, like horses, two or three, moving slowly. The Swede, too, got a similar result, though expressing it differently, for he thought it was shaped and sized like a clump of willow bushes, rounded at the top, and moving all over upon its surface—"coiling upon itself like smoke," he said afterwards.

"I watched it settle downwards through the bushes," he sobbed at me. "Look, by God! It's coming this way! Oh, oh!"—he gave a kind of whistling cry. "*They've found us.*"

I gave one terrified glance, which just enabled me to see that the shadowy form was swinging towards us through the bushes, and then I collapsed backwards with a crash into the branches. These failed, of course, to support my weight, so that with the Swede on top of me we fell in a struggling heap upon the sand. I really hardly knew what was happening. I was conscious only of a sort of enveloping sensation of icy fear that plucked the nerves out of their fleshly covering, twisted them this way and that, and replaced them quivering. My eyes were tightly shut; something in my throat choked me; a feeling that my consciousness was expanding, extending out into space, swiftly gave way to another feeling that I was losing it altogether, and about to die.

An acute spasm of pain passed through me, and I was aware that the Swede had hold of me in such a way that he hurt me abominably. It was the way he caught at me in falling.

But it was the pain, he declared afterwards, that saved me; it caused me to *forget them* and think of something else at the very instant when they were about to find me. It concealed my mind from them at the moment of discovery, yet just in time to evade their terrible seizing of me. He himself, he says, actually swooned at the same moment, and that was what saved him.

I only know that at a later date, how long or short is impossible to say, I found myself scrambling up out of the slippery network of willow branches, and saw my companion standing in front of me holding out a hand to assist me. I stared at him in a dazed way, rubbing the arm he had twisted for me. Nothing came to me to say, somehow.

"I lost consciousness for a moment or two," I heard him say. "That's what saved me. It made me stop thinking about them."

"You nearly broke my arm in two," I said, uttering my only connected thought at the moment. A numbness came over me.

"That's what saved *you!*" he replied. "Between us, we've managed to set them off on a false tack somewhere. The humming has ceased. It's gone—for the moment at any rate!"

A wave of hysterical laughter seized me again, and this time spread to my friend too—great healing gusts of shaking laughter that brought a tremendous sense of relief in their train. We made our way back to the fire and put the wood on so that it blazed at once. Then we saw that the tent had fallen over and lay in a tangled heap upon the ground.

We picked it up, and during the process tripped more than once and caught our feet in sand.

"It's those sand-funnels," exclaimed the Swede, when the tent was up again and the firelight lit up the ground for several yards about us. "And look at the size of them!"

All round the tent and about the fireplace where we had seen the moving shadows there were deep funnel-shaped hollows in the sand, exactly similar to the ones we had already found over the island, only far bigger and deeper, beautifully formed, and wide enough in some instances to admit the whole of my foot and leg.

Neither of us said a word. We both knew that sleep was the safest thing we could do, and to bed we went accordingly without further delay, having first thrown sand on the fire and taken the provision sack and the paddle inside the tent with us. The canoe, too, we propped in such a way at the end of the tent that our feet touched it, and the least motion would disturb and wake us.

In case of emergency, too, we again went to bed in our clothes, ready for a sudden start.

<h1 style="text-align:center">5</h1>

It was my firm intention to lie awake all night and watch, but the exhaustion of nerves and body decreed otherwise, and sleep after a while came over me with a welcome blanket of oblivion. The fact that my companion also slept quickened its approach. At first, he fidgeted and constantly sat up, asking me if I "heard this" or "heard that." He tossed about on his cork mattress, and said the tent was moving and the river had risen over the point of the island, but each time I went out to look I returned with the report that all was well, and finally he grew calmer and lay still. Then at length his breathing became regular and I heard unmistakable sounds of snoring—the first and only time in my life when snoring has been a welcome and calming influence.

This, I remember, was the last thought in my mind before dozing off.

A difficulty in breathing woke me, and I found the blanket over my face. But something else besides the blanket was pressing upon me, and my first thought was that my companion had rolled off his mattress on to my own in his sleep. I called to him and sat up, and at the same moment it came to me that the tent was *surrounded*. That sound of multitudinous soft pattering was again audible outside, filling the night with horror.

I called again to him, louder than before. He did not answer, but I missed the sound of his snoring, and also noticed that the flap of the tent was down. This was the unpardonable sin. I crawled out in the darkness to hook it back securely, and it was then for the first time I realised positively that the Swede was not here. He had gone.

I dashed out in a mad run, seized by a dreadful agitation, and the moment I was out I plunged into a sort of torrent of humming that surrounded me completely and came out of every quarter of the heavens at once. It was that same familiar humming—gone mad! A swarm of great invisible bees might have been about me in the air. The sound seemed to thicken the very atmosphere, and I felt that my lungs worked with difficulty.

But my friend was in danger, and I could not hesitate.

The dawn was just about to break, and a faint whitish light spread upwards over the clouds from a thin strip of clear horizon. No wind stirred. I could just make out the bushes and river beyond, and the pale sandy patches. In my excitement I ran frantically to and fro about the island, calling him by name, shouting at the top of my voice the first words that came into my head. But the willows smothered my voice, and the humming muffled it, so that the sound only travelled a few feet round me. I plunged among the bushes, tripping headlong, tumbling over roots, and scraping my face as I tore this way and that among the preventing branches.

Then, quite unexpectedly, I came out upon the island's point and saw a dark figure outlined between the water and the sky. It was the Swede. And already he had one foot in the river! A moment more and he would have taken the plunge.

I threw myself upon him, flinging my arms about his waist and dragging him shorewards with all my strength. Of course, he struggled furiously, making a noise all the time just like that cursed humming, and using the most outlandish phrases in his anger about "going *inside* to Them," and "taking the way of the water and the wind," and God only knows what more besides, that I tried in vain to recall afterwards, but which turned me sick with horror and amazement as I listened. But in the end I managed to get him into the comparative safety of the tent, and flung him breathless and cursing upon the mattress where I held him until the fit had passed.

I think the suddenness with which it all went and he grew calm, coinciding as it did with the equally abrupt cessation of the humming and pattering outside—I think this was almost the strangest part of the whole business perhaps. For he had just opened his eyes and turned his tired face up to me so that the dawn threw a pale light upon it through the doorway, and said, for all the world just like a frightened child:

"My life, old man—it's my life I owe you. But it's all over now anyhow. They've found a victim in our place!"

Then he dropped back upon his blankets and went to sleep literally under my eyes. He simply collapsed, and began to snore again as healthily as though nothing had happened and he had never tried to offer his own life as a sacrifice by drowning. And when the sunlight woke him three hours later—hours of ceaseless vigil for me—it became so clear to me that he remembered absolutely nothing of what he had attempted to do, that I deemed it wise to hold my peace and ask no dangerous questions.

He woke naturally and easily, as I have said, when the sun was already high in a windless hot sky, and he at once got up and set about the preparation of the fire for breakfast. I followed him anxiously at bathing, but he did not attempt to plunge in, merely dipping his head and making some remark about the extra coldness of the water.

"River's falling at last," he said, "and I'm glad of it."

"The humming has stopped too," I said.

He looked up at me quietly with his normal expression. Evidently, he remembered everything except his own attempt at suicide.

"Everything has stopped," he said, "because—"

He hesitated. But I knew some reference to that remark he had made just before he fainted was in his mind, and I was determined to know it.

"Because 'They've found another victim'?" I said, forcing a little laugh.

"Exactly," he answered, "exactly! I feel as positive of it as though—as though—I feel quite safe again, I mean," he finished.

He began to look curiously about him. The sunlight lay in hot patches on the sand. There was no wind. The willows were motionless. He slowly rose to feet.

"Come," he said; "I think if we look, we shall find it."

He started off on a run, and I followed him. He kept to the banks, poking with a stick among the sandy bays and caves and little backwaters, myself always close on his heels.

"Ah!" he exclaimed presently, "ah!"

The tone of his voice somehow brought back to me a vivid sense of the horror of the last twenty-four hours, and I hurried up to join him. He was pointing with his stick at a large black object that lay half in the water and half on the sand. It appeared to be caught by some twisted willow roots so that the river could not sweep it away. A few hours before the spot must have been under water.

"See," he said quietly, "the victim that made our escape possible!"

And when I peered across his shoulder, I saw that his stick rested on the body of a man. He turned it over. It was the corpse of a peasant, and the face was hidden in the sand. Clearly the man had been drowned, but a few hours before, and his body must have been swept down upon our island somewhere about the hour of the dawn—*at the very time the fit had passed.*

"We must give it a decent burial, you know."

"I suppose so," I replied. I shuddered a little in spite of myself, for there was something about the appearance of that poor drowned man that turned me cold.

The Swede glanced up sharply at me, an undecipherable expression on his face, and began clambering down the bank. I followed him more leisurely. The current, I noticed, had torn away much of the clothing from the body, so that the neck and part of the chest lay bare.

Halfway down the bank my companion suddenly stopped and held up his hand in warning; but either my foot slipped, or I had gained too much momentum to bring myself quickly to a halt, for I bumped into him and sent him forward with a sort of leap to save himself. We tumbled together on to the hard sand so that our feet splashed into the water. And, before anything could be done, we had collided a little heavily against the corpse.

The Swede uttered a sharp cry. And I sprang back as if I had been shot.

At the moment we touched the body there rose from its surface the loud sound of humming—the sound of several hummings—which passed with a vast commotion as of winged things in the air about us and disappeared upwards into the sky, growing fainter and fainter till they finally ceased in the distance. It was exactly as though we had disturbed some living yet invisible creatures at work.

My companion clutched me, and I think I clutched him, but before either of us had time properly to recover from the unexpected shock, we saw that a movement of the current was turning the corpse round so that it became released from the grip of the willow roots. A moment later it had turned completely over, the dead face uppermost, staring at the sky. It lay on the edge of the main stream. In another moment it would be swept away.

The Swede started to save it, shouting again something I did not catch about a "proper burial"—and then abruptly dropped upon his knees on the sand and covered his eyes with his hands. I was beside him in an instant.

I saw what he had seen.

For just as the body swung round to the current the face and the exposed chest turned full towards us, and showed plainly how the skin and flesh were indented with small hollows, beautifully formed, and exactly similar in shape and kind to the sand-funnels that we had found all over the island.

"Their mark!" I heard my companion mutter under his breath. "Their awful mark!"

And when I turned my eyes again from his ghastly face to the river, the current had done its work, and the body had been swept away into mid-stream and was already beyond our reach and almost out of sight, turning over and over on the waves like an otter.

Initiation

A few years ago, on a Black Sea steamer heading for the Caucasus, I fell into conversation with an American. He mentioned that he was on his way to the Baku oilfields, and I replied that I was going up into the mountains. He looked at me questioningly a moment. "Your first trip?" he asked with interest. I said it was. A conversation followed; it was continued the next day, and renewed the following day, until we parted company at Batoum. I don't know why he talked so freely to me in particular. Normally, he was a taciturn, silent man. We had been fellow travellers from Marseilles, but after Constantinople we had the boat pretty much to ourselves. What struck me about him was his vehement, almost passionate, love of natural beauty—in seas and woods and sky, but above all in mountains. It was like a religion in him. His taciturn manner hid deep poetic feeling.

And he told me it had not always been so with him. A kind of friendship sprang up between us. He was a New York business man—buying and selling exchange between banks—but was English born. He had gone out thirty years before, and become naturalised. His talk was exceedingly "American," slangy, and almost Western. He said he had roughed it in the West for a year or two first. But what he chiefly talked about was mountains. He said it was in the mountains an unusual experience had come to him that had opened his eyes to many things, but principally to the beauty that was now everything to him, and to the—insignificance of death.

He knew the Caucasus well where I was going. I think that was why he was interested in me and my journey. "Up there," he said, "you'll feel things—and maybe find out things you never knew before."

"What kind of things?" I asked.

"Why, for one," he replied with emotion and enthusiasm in his voice, "that living and dying ain't either of them of much account.

237

That if you know Beauty, I mean, and Beauty is in your life, you live on in it and with it for others—even when you're dead."

The conversation that followed is too long to give here, but it led to his telling me the experience in his own life that had opened his eyes to the truth of what he said. "Beauty is imperishable," he declared, "and if you live with it, why, you're imperishable too!"

The story, as he told it verbally in his curious language, remains vividly in my memory. But he had written it down, too, he said. And he gave me the written account, with the remark that I was free to hand it on to others if I "felt that way." He called it "Initiation." It runs as follows.

1

In my own family this happened, for Arthur was my nephew. And a remote Alpine valley was the place. It didn't seem to me in the least suitable for such occurrences, except that it was Catholic, and the "Church," I understand—at least, scholars who ought to know have told me so—has subtle Pagan origins incorporated unwittingly in its observations of certain Saints' Days, as well as in certain ceremonials. All this kind of thing is Dutch to me, a form of poetry or superstition, for I am interested chiefly in the buying and selling of exchange, with an office in New York City, just off Wall Street, and only come to Europe now occasionally for a holiday.

I like to see the dear old musty cities, and go to the Opera, and take a motor run through Shakespeare's country or round the Lakes, get in touch again with London and Paris at the Ritz Hotels—and then back again to the greatest city on earth, where for years now I've been making a good thing out of it. Repton and Cambridge, long since forgotten, had their uses. They were all right enough at the time. But I'm now "on the make," with a good fat partnership, and have left all that truck behind me.

My half-brother, however—he was my senior and got the cream of the family wholesale chemical works—has stuck to the trade in the Old Country, and is making probably as much as I am. He approved my taking the chance that offered, and is only sore now because his son, Arthur, is on the stupid side. He agreed that finance suited my temperament far better than drugs and chemicals, though he warned me that all American finance was speculative and therefore dangerous. "Arthur is getting on," he said in his last letter, "and will someday take the director's place you would be in now had you cared to stay. But he's a plodder, rather."

That meant, I knew, that Arthur was a fool. Business, at any rate, was not suited to his temperament. Five years ago, when I came home with a month's holiday to be used in working up connections in English banking circles, I saw the boy. He was fifteen years of age at the time, a delicate youth, with an artist's dreams in his big blue eyes, if my memory goes for anything, but with a tangle of yellow hair and features of classical beauty that would have made half the young girls of my New York set in love with him, and a choice of heiresses at his disposal when he wanted them.

I have a clear recollection of my nephew then. He struck me as having grit and character, but as being wrongly placed. He had his grandfather's tastes. He ought to have been, like him, a great scholar, a poet, an editor of marvellous old writings in new editions. I couldn't get much out of the boy, except that he "liked the chemical business fairly," and meant to please his father by "knowing it thoroughly" so as to qualify later for his directorship. But I have never forgotten the evening when I caught him in the hall, staring up at his grandfather's picture, with a kind of light about his face, and the big blue eyes all rapt and tender (almost as if he had been crying) and replying, when I asked him what was up: "*That* was worth living for. He brought Beauty back into the world!"

"Yes," I said, "I guess that's right enough. He did. But there was no money in it to speak of."

The boy looked at me and smiled. He twigged somehow or other that deep down in me, somewhere below the money-making instinct, a poet, but a dumb poet, lay in hiding. "You know what I mean," he said. "It's in you too."

The picture was a copy—my father had it made—of the presentation portrait given to Baliol, and "the grandfather" was celebrated in his day for the translations he made of Anacreon and Sappho, of Homer, too, if I remember rightly, as well as for a number of classical studies and essays that he wrote. A lot of stuff like that he did, and made a name at it too. His *Lives of the Gods* went into six editions. They said—the big critics of his day—that he was "a poet who wrote no poetry, yet lived it passionately in the spirit of old-world, classical Beauty," and I know he was a wonderful fellow in his way and made the dons and schoolmasters all sit up. We're proud of him all right.

After twenty-five years of successful "exchange" in New York City, I confess I am unable to appreciate all that, feeling more in touch with the commercial and financial spirit of the age, progress, development and the rest. But, still, I'm not ashamed of the classical old boy, who seems to have been a good deal of a Pagan, judging by the records we have kept. However, Arthur peering up at that picture in the dusk, his eyes half moist with emotion, and his voice gone positively shaky, is a thing I never have forgotten. He stimulated my curiosity uncommonly. It stirred something deep down in me that I hardly cared to acknowledge on Wall Street—something burning.

And the next time I saw him was in the summer of 1910, when I came to Europe for a two months' look around—my wife at Newport with the children—and hearing that he was in Switzerland, learning a bit of French to help him in the business, I made a point of dropping in upon him just to see how he was shaping generally and what new kinks his mind had taken on. There was something in Arthur I never could quite forget. Whenever his face came into my mind I began to think. A kind of longing came over me—a desire for Beauty, I guess, it was. It made me dream.

I found him at an English tutor's—a lively old dog, with a fondness for the cheap native wines, and a financial interest in the tourist development of the village. The boys learnt French in the mornings, possibly, but for the rest of the day were free to amuse themselves exactly as they pleased and without a trace of supervision—provided the parents footed the bills without demur.

This suited everybody all round; and as long as the boys came home with an accent and a vocabulary, all was well. For myself, having learned in New York to attend strictly to my own business—exchange between different countries with a profit—I did not deem it necessary to exchange letters and opinions with my brother—with no chance of profit anywhere. But I got to know Arthur, and had a queer experience of my own into the bargain. Oh, there was profit in it for me. I'm drawing big dividends to this day on the investment.

I put up at the best hotel in the village, a one-horse show, differing from the other inns only in the prices charged for a lot of cheap decoration in the dining-room, and went up to surprise my nephew with a call the first thing after dinner. The tutor's house stood some way back from the narrow street, among fields where there were more flowers than grass, and backed by a forest of fine old timber that stretched up several thousand feet to the snow. The snow at least was visible, peeping out far overhead just where the dark line of forest stopped; but in reality, I suppose, that was an effect of foreshortening, and whole valleys and pastures intervened between the trees and the snow-fields.

The sunset, long since out of the valley, still shone on those white ridges, where the peaks stuck up like the teeth of a gigantic saw. I guess it meant five or six hours' good climbing to get up to them—and nothing to do when you got there. Switzerland, anyway, seemed a poor country, with its little bit of watch-making, sour wines, and every square yard hanging upstairs at an angle of 60 degrees used for hay. Picture postcards, chocolate and cheap tourists kept it going apparently, but I dare say it was all right enough to learn French in—and cheap as Hoboken to live in!

Arthur was out; I just left a card and wrote on it that I would be very pleased if he cared to step down to take luncheon with me at my hotel next day. Having nothing better to do, I strolled homewards by way of the forest.

Now what came over me in that bit of dark pine forest is more than I can quite explain, but I think it must have been due to the height—the village was 4,000 feet above sea-level—and the effect of the rarefied air upon my circulation. The nearest thing to it in my experience is rye whisky, the queer touch of wildness, of self-confidence, a kind of whooping rapture and the reckless sensation of being a tin god of sorts that comes from a lot of alcohol—a memory, please understand, of years before, when I thought it a grand thing to own the earth and paint the old town red. I seemed to walk on air, and there was a smell about those trees that made me suddenly—well, that took my mind clean out of its accustomed rut. It was just too lovely and wonderful for me to describe it.

I had got well into the forest and lost my way a bit. The smell of an old-world garden wasn't in it. It smelt to me as if someone had just that minute turned out the earth all fresh and new. There was moss and tannin, a hint of burning, something between smoke and incense, say, and a fine clean odour of pitch-pine bark when the sun gets on it after rain—and a flavour of the sea thrown in for luck. That was the first I noticed, for I had never smelt anything half so good since my camping days on the coast of Maine. And I stood still to enjoy it. I threw away my cigar for fear of mixing things and spoiling it. "If that could be bottled," I said to myself, "it'd sell for two dollars a pint in every city in the Union!"

And it was just then, while standing and breathing it in, that I got the queer feeling of someone watching me. I kept quite still. Someone was moving near me. The sweat went trickling down my back. A kind of childhood thrill got hold of me.

It was very dark. I was not afraid exactly, but I was a stranger in these parts and knew nothing about the habits of the mountain peasants. There might be tough customers lurking around after dark on the chance of striking some guy of a tourist with money in his pockets. Yet, somehow, that wasn't the kind of feeling that came to me at all, for, though I had a pocket Browning at my hip, the notion of getting at it did not even occur to me. The sensation was new—a kind of lifting, exciting sensation that made my heart swell out with exhilaration. There was happiness in it. A cloud that *weighed* seemed to roll off my mind, same as that light-hearted mood when the office door is locked and I'm off on a two months' holiday—with gaiety and irresponsibility at the back of it. It was invigorating. I felt youth sweep over me.

I stood there, wondering what on earth was coming on me, and half expecting that any moment someone would come out of the darkness and show himself; and as I held my breath and made no movement at all the queer sensation grew stronger. I believe I even resisted a temptation to kick up my heels and dance, to let out a flying shout as a man with liquor in him does. Instead of this, however, I just kept dead still. The wood was black as ink all round me, too black to see the tree-trunks separately, except far below where the village lights came up twinkling between them, and the only way I kept the path was by the soft feel of the pine-needles that were thicker than a Brussels carpet. But nothing happened, and no one stirred. The idea that I was being watched remained, only there was no sound anywhere except the roar of falling water that filled the entire valley. Yet some one was very close to me in the darkness.

I can't say how long I might have stood there, but I guess it was the best part of ten minutes, and I remember it struck me that I had run up against a pocket of extra-rarefied air that had a lot of oxygen in it—oxygen or something similar—and that was the cause of my elation. The idea was nonsense, I have no doubt; but for the moment it half explained the thing to me. I realised it was all *natural* enough, at any rate—and so moved on. It took a longish time to reach the edge of the wood, and a footpath led me—oh, it was quite a walk, I tell you—into the village street again. I was both glad and sorry to get there. I kept myself busy thinking the whole thing over again. What caught me all of a heap was that million-dollar sense of beauty, youth, and happiness. Never in my born days had I felt anything to touch it. And it hadn't cost a cent!

Well, I was sitting there enjoying my smoke and trying to puzzle it all out, and the hall was pretty full of people smoking and talking and reading papers, and so forth, when all of a sudden, I looked up and caught my breath with such a jerk that I actually bit my tongue. There was grandfather in front of my chair! I looked into his eyes. I saw him as clear and solid as the porter standing behind his desk across the lounge, and it gave me a touch of cold all down the back that I needn't forget unless I want to. He was looking into my face, and he had a cap in his hand, and he was speaking to me. It was my grandfather's picture come to life, only much thinner and younger and a kind of light in his eyes like fire.

"I beg your pardon, but you *are*—Uncle Jim, aren't you?"

And then, with another jump of my nerves, I understood.

"You, Arthur! Well, I'm jiggered. So it is. Take a chair, boy. I'm right glad you found me. Shake! Sit down." And I shook his hand and pushed a chair up for him. I was never so surprised in my life. The last time I set eyes on him he was a boy. Now he was a young man, and the very image of his ancestor.

He sat down, fingering his cap. He wouldn't have a drink and he wouldn't smoke. "All right," I said, "let's talk then. I've lots to tell you and I've lots to hear. How are you, boy?"

He didn't answer at first. He eyed me up and down. He hesitated. He was as handsome as a young Greek god.

"I say, Uncle Jim," he began presently, "it *was* you—just now—in the wood—wasn't it?" It made me start, that question put so quietly.

"I *have* just come through that wood up there," I answered, pointing in the direction as well as I could remember, "if that's what you mean. But why? *You* weren't there, were you?" It gave me a queer sort of feeling to hear him say it. What in the name of heaven did he mean?

He sat back in his chair with a sigh of relief.

"Oh, that's all right then," he said, "if it *was* you. Did you see," he asked suddenly; "did you see—anything?"

"Not a thing," I told him honestly. "It was far too dark." I laughed. I fancied I twigged his meaning. But I was not the sort of uncle to come prying on him. Life must be dull enough, I remembered, in this mountain village.

But he didn't understand my laugh. He didn't mean what I meant.

And there came a pause between us. I discovered that we were talking different lingoes. I leaned over towards him.

"Look here, Arthur," I said in a lower voice, "what is it, and what do you mean? I'm all right, you know, and you needn't be afraid of telling me. What d'you mean by—did I see anything?"

We looked each other squarely in the eye. He saw he could trust me, and I saw—well, a whole lot of things, perhaps, but I felt chiefly that he liked me and would tell me things later, all in his own good time. I liked him all the better for that too.

"I only meant," he answered slowly, "whether you really *saw*—anything?"

"No," I said straight, "I didn't see a thing, but, by the gods, I *felt* something."

He started. I started too. An astonishing big look came swimming over his fair, handsome face. His eyes seemed all lit up. He looked as if he'd just made a cool million in wheat or cotton.

"I knew—you were that sort," he whispered. "Though I hardly remembered what you looked like."

"Then what on earth was it?" I asked.

His reply staggered me a bit. "It was just that," he said—"the Earth!"

And then, just when things were getting interesting and promising a dividend, he shut up like a clam. He wouldn't say another word. He asked after my family and business, my health, what kind of crossing I'd had, and all the rest of the common stock. It fairly bowled me over. And I couldn't change him either.

I suppose in America we get pretty free and easy, and don't quite understand reserve. But this young man of half my age kept me in my place as easily as I might have kept a nervous customer quiet in my own office. He just refused to take me on. He was polite and cool and distant as you please, and when I got pressing sometimes, he simply pretended he didn't understand. I could no more get him back again to the subject of the wood than a customer could have gotten me to tell him about the prospects of exchange being cheap or dear—when I didn't know myself but wouldn't let him see I didn't know. He was charming, he was delightful, enthusiastic and even affectionate; downright glad to see me, too, and to chin with me—but I couldn't draw him worth a cent. And in the end, I gave up trying.

And the moment I gave up trying he let down a little—but only a very little.

"You'll stay here some time, Uncle Jim, won't you?"

"That's my idea," I said, "if I can see you, and you can show me round some."

He laughed with pleasure. "Oh, rather. I've got lots of time. After three in the afternoon, I'm free till—any time you like. There's a lot to see," he added.

"Come along tomorrow then," I said. "If you can't take lunch, perhaps you can come just afterwards. You'll find me waiting for you—right here."

"I'll come at three," he replied, and we said goodnight.

2

He turned up sharp at three, and I liked his punctuality. I saw him come swinging down the dusty road; tall, deep-chested, his broad shoulders a trifle high, and his head set proudly. He looked like a young chap in training, a thoroughbred, every inch of him. At the same time there was a touch of something a little too refined and delicate for a man, I thought. That was the poetic, scholarly vein in him, I guess—grandfather cropping out. This time he wore no cap. His thick light hair, not brushed back like the London shop-boys, but parted on the side, yet untidy for all that, suited him exactly and gave him a touch of wildness.

"Well," he asked, "what would you like to do, Uncle Jim? I'm at your service, and I've got the whole afternoon till supper at seven-thirty." I told him I'd like to go through that wood. "All right," he said, "come along. I'll show you." He gave me one quick glance, but said no more. "I'd like to see if I feel anything this time," I explained. "We'll locate the very spot, maybe." He nodded.

"You know where I mean, don't you?" I asked, "because you saw me there?" He just said yes, and then we started.

It was hot, and air was scarce. I remember that we went uphill, and that I realised there was considerable difference in our ages. We crossed some fields first—smothered in flowers so thick that I wondered how much grass the cows got out of it!—and then came to a sprinkling of fine young larches that looked as soft as velvet. There was no path, just a wild mountain side. I had very little breath on the steep zigzags, but Arthur talked easily—and talked mighty well, too: the light and shade, the colouring, and the effect of all this wilderness of lonely beauty on the mind.

He kept all this suppressed at home in business. It was safety valves. I twigged *that*. It was the artist in him talking. He seemed to think there was nothing in the world but Beauty—with a big B all the time. And the odd thing was he took for granted that I felt the same. It was cute of him to flatter me that way. "Daulis and the lone Cephissian vale," I heard; and a few moments later—with a sort of reverence in his voice like worship—he called out a great singing name: "*Astarte!*"

"Day is her face, and midnight is her hair,
And morning hours are but the golden stair
By which she climbs to Night."

It was here first that a queer change began to grow upon me too.

"Steady on, boy! I've forgotten all my classics ages ago," I cried.

He turned and gazed down on me, his big eyes glowing, and not a sign of perspiration on his skin.

"That's nothing," he exclaimed in his musical, deep voice. "You know it, or you'd never have felt things in this wood last night; and you wouldn't have wanted to come out with me *now*!"

"How?" I gasped. "How's that?"

"You've come," he continued quietly, "to the only valley in this artificial country that has atmosphere. This valley is *alive*—especially this end of it. There's superstition here, thank God! Even the peasants know things."

I stared at him. "See here, Arthur," I objected. "I'm not a Cath. And I don't know a thing—at least it's all dead in me and forgotten—about poetry or classics or your gods and pan—pantheism—in spite of grandfather——"

His face turned like a dream face.

"Hush!" he said quickly. "Don't mention *him*. There's a bit of him in you as well as in me, and it was here, you know, he wrote——"

I didn't hear the rest of what he said. A creep came over me. I remembered that this ancestor of ours lived for years in the isolation of some Swiss forest where he claimed—he used that setting for his writing—he had found the exiled gods, their ghosts, their beauty, their eternal essences—or something astonishing of that sort. I had clean forgotten it till this moment. It all rushed back upon me, a memory of my boyhood.

And, as I say, a creep came over me—something as near to awe as ever could be. The sunshine on that field of yellow daisies and blue forget-me-nots turned pale. That warm valley wind had a touch of snow in it. And, ashamed and frightened of my baby mood, I looked at Arthur, meaning to choke him off with all this rubbish—and then saw something in his eyes that scared me stiff.

I admit it. What's the use? There was an expression on his fine big face that made my blood go curdled. I got cold feet right there. It mastered me. In him, behind him, near him—blest if I know which, *through* him probably—came an enormous thing that turned me insignificant. It downed me utterly.

It was over in a second, the flash of a wing. I recovered instantly. No mere boy should come these muzzy tricks on me, scholar or no scholar. For the change in me was on the increase, and I shrank.

"See here, Arthur," I said plainly once again, "I don't know what your game is, but—there's something queer up here I don't quite get at. I'm only a business man, with classics and poetry all gone dry in me twenty years ago and more——"

He looked at me so strangely that I stopped, confused.

"But, Uncle Jim," he said as quietly as though we talked tobacco brands, "you needn't be alarmed. It's natural you should feel the place. You and I belong to it. We've both got *him* in us. You're just as proud of him as I am, only in a different way." And then he added, with a touch of disappointment: "I thought you'd like it. You weren't afraid last night. You felt the beauty *then*."

Flattery is a darned subtle thing at any time. To see him standing over me in that superior way and talking down at my poor business mind—well, it just came over me that I was laying my cards on the table a bit too early. After so many years of city life——!

Anyway, I pulled myself together. "I was only kidding you, boy," I laughed. "I feel this beauty just as much as you do. Only, I guess, you're more accustomed to it than I am. Come on now," I added with energy, getting upon my feet, "let's push on and see the wood. I want to find that place again."

He pulled me with a hand of iron, laughing as he did so. Gee! I wished I had his teeth, as well as the muscles in his arm. Yet I felt younger, somehow, too—youth flowed more and more into my veins. I had forgotten how sweet the winds and woods and flowers could be. Something melted in me. For it was Spring, and the whole world was singing like a dream. Beauty was creeping over me. I don't know. I began to feel all big and tender and open to a thousand wonderful sensations. The thought of streets and houses seemed like death.. . .

We went on again, not talking much; my breath got shorter and shorter, and he kept looking about him as though he expected something. But we passed no living soul, not even a peasant; there were no chalets, no cattle, no cattle shelters even. And then I realised that the valley lay at our feet in haze and that we had been climbing at least a couple of hours.

"Why, last night I got home in twenty minutes at the outside," I said.

He shook his head, smiling. "It seemed like that," he replied, "but you really took much longer. It was long after ten when I found you in the hall."

I reflected a moment. "Now I come to think of it, you're right, Arthur. Seems curious, though, somehow."

He looked closely at me. "I followed you all the way," he said.

"You followed me!"

"And you went at a good pace too. It was your feelings that made it seem so short—you were singing to yourself and happy as a dancing faun. We kept close behind you for a long way."

I think it was "we" he said, but for some reason or other I didn't care to ask.

"Maybe," I answered shortly, trying uncomfortably to recall what particular capers I had cut. "I guess that's right." And then I added something about the loneliness, and how deserted all this slope of mountain was. And he explained that the peasants were afraid of it and called it No Man's Land. From one year's end to another no human foot went up or down it; the hay was never cut; no cattle grazed along the splendid pastures; no chalet had even been built within a mile of the wood we slowly made for.

"They're superstitious," he told me. "It was just the same a hundred years ago when *he* discovered it—there was a little natural cave on the edge of the forest where he used to sleep sometimes—I'll show it to you presently—but for generations this entire mountain-side has been undisturbed. You'll never meet a living soul in any part of it." He stopped and pointed above us to where the pine wood hung in mid-air, like a dim blue carpet. "It's just the place for Them, you see."

And a thrill of power went smashing through me. I can't describe it. It drenched me like a waterfall. I thought of Greece—Mount Ida and a thousand songs! Something in me—it was like the click of a shutter—announced that the "change" was suddenly complete. I was another man; or rather a deeper part of me took command. My very language showed it.

The calm of halcyon weather lay over all. Overhead the peaks rose clear as crystal; below us the village lay in a bluish smudge of smoke and haze, as though a great finger had rubbed them softly into the earth. Absolute loneliness fell upon me like a clap. From the world of human beings, we seemed quite shut off. And there began to steal over me again the strange elation of the night before.. . . We found ourselves almost at once against the edge of the wood.

It rose in front of us, a big wall of splendid trees, motionless as if cut out of dark green metal, the branches hanging stiff, and the crowd of trunks lost in the blue dimness underneath. I shaded my eyes with one hand, trying to peer into the solemn gloom. The contrast between the brilliant sunshine on the pastures and this region of heavy shadows blurred my sight.

"It's like the entrance to another world," I whispered.

"It is," said Arthur, watching me. "We will go in. You shall pluck asphodel.. . ."

And, before I knew it, he had me by the hand. We were advancing. We left the light behind us. The cool air dropped upon me like a sheet. There was a temple silence. The sun ran down behind the sky, leaving a marvellous blue radiance everywhere. Nothing stirred. But through the stillness there rose power, power that has no name, power that hides at the foundations somewhere—foundations that are changeless, invisible, everlasting. What do I mean? My mind grew to the dimensions of a planet. We were among the roots of life—whence issues that *one thing* in infinite guise that seeks so many temporary names from the protean minds of men.

"You shall pluck asphodel in the meadows this side of Erebus," Arthur was chanting. "Hermes himself, the Psychopomp, shall lead, and Malahide shall welcome us."

Malahide . . .!

To hear him use that name, the name of our scholar-ancestor, now dead and buried close upon a century—the way he half chanted it—gave me the goose-flesh. I stopped against a tree-stem, thinking of escape. No words came to me at the moment, for I didn't know what to say; but, on turning to find the bright green slopes just left behind, I saw only a crowd of trees and shadows hanging thick as a curtain—as though we had walked a mile. And it was a shock. The way out was lost. The trees closed up behind us like a tide.

"It's all right," said Arthur; "just keep an open mind and a heart alive with love. It has a shattering effect at first, but that will pass." He saw I was afraid, for I shrank visibly enough. He stood beside me in his grey flannel suit, with his brilliant eyes and his great shock of hair, looking more like a column of light than a human being. "It's all quite right and natural," he repeated; "we have passed the gateway, and Hecate, who presides over gateways, will let us out again. Do not make discord by feeling fear. This is a pine wood, and pines are the oldest, simplest trees; they are true primitives. They are an open channel; and in a pine wood where no human life has ever been you shall often find gateways where Hecate is kind to such as us."

He took my hand—he must have felt mine trembling, but his own was cool and strong and felt like silver—and led me forward into the depths of a wood that seemed to me quite endless. It felt endless, that is to say. I don't know what came over me. Fear slipped away, and elation took its place. . ... As we advanced over ground that seemed level, or slightly undulating, I saw bright pools of sunshine here and there upon the forest floor. Great shafts of light dropped in slantingly between the trunks. There was movement everywhere, though I never could see what moved. A delicious, scented air stirred through the lower branches. Running water sang not very far away. Figures I did not actually see; yet there were limbs and flowing draperies and flying hair from time to time, ever just beyond the pools of sunlight.. . . Surprise went from me too. I was on air.

The atmosphere of dream came round me, but a dream of something just hovering outside the world I knew—a dream wrought in gold and silver, with shining eyes, with graceful beckoning hands, and with voices that rang like bells of music.... And the pools of light grew larger, merging one into another, until a delicate soft light shone equably throughout the entire forest. Into this zone of light, we passed together. Then something fell abruptly at our feet, as though thrown down ... two marvellous, shining sprays of blossom such as I had never seen in all my days before!

"Asphodel!" cried my companion, stooping to pick them up and handing one to me. I took it from him with a delight I could not understand. "Keep it," he murmured; "it is the sign that we are welcome. For Malahide has dropped these on our path."

And at the use of that ancestral name, it seemed that a spirit passed before my face and the hair of my head stood up. There was a sense of violent, unhappy contrast. A composite picture presented itself, then rushed away. What was it? My youth in England, music and poetry at Cambridge and my passionate love of Greek that lasted two terms at most, when Malahide's great books formed part of the curriculum. Over against this, then, the drag and smother of solid worldly business, the sordid weight of modern ugliness, the bitterness of an ambitious, over-striving life.

And abruptly—beyond both pictures—a shining, marvellous

Beauty that scattered stars beneath my feet and scarved the universe with gold. All this flashed before me with the utterance of that old family name. An alternative sprang up. There seemed some radical, elemental choice presented to me—to what I used to call my soul. My soul could take or leave it as it pleased. . . .

I looked at Arthur moving beside me like a shaft of light. What had come over me? How had our walk and talk and mood, our quite recent everyday and ordinary view, our normal relationship with the things of the world—how had it all slipped into this? So insensibly, so easily, so naturally!

"Was it worthwhile?"

The question—*I* didn't ask it—jumped up in me of its own accord. Was "what" worthwhile? Why, my present life of commonplace and grubbing toil, of course; my city existence, with its meagre, unremunerative ambitions. Ah, it was this new Beauty calling me, this shining dream that lay beyond the two pictures I have mentioned. . . . I did not argue it, even to myself. But I understood. There was a radical change in me. The buried poet, too long hidden, rushed into the air like some great singing bird.

I glanced again at Arthur moving along lightly by my side, half dancing almost in his brimming happiness. "Wait till you see Them," I heard him singing. "Wait till you hear the call of Artemis and the footsteps of her flying nymphs. Wait till Orion thunders overhead and Selene, crowned with the crescent moon, drives up the zenith in her white-horsed chariot. The choice will be beyond all question then . . . !"

A great silent bird, with soft brown plumage, whirred across our path, pausing an instant as though to peep, then disappearing with a muted sound into an eddy of the wind it made. The big trees hid it. It was an owl. The same moment I heard a rush of liquid song come pouring through the forest with a gush of almost human notes, and a pair of glossy wings flashed past us, swerving upwards to find the open sky—blue-black, pointed wings.

"His favourites!" exclaimed my companion with clear joy in his voice. "They all are here! Athene's bird, Procne and Philomela too! The owl—the swallow—and the nightingale! Tereus and Itys are not far away." And the entire forest, as he said it, stirred with movement, as though that great bird's quiet wings had waked the sea of ancient shadows. There were voices too—ringing, laughing voices, as though his words woke echoes that had been listening for it. For I heard sweet singing in the distance. The names he had used perplexed me. Yet even

I, stranger as I was to such refined delights, could not mistake the passion of the nightingale and the dart of the eager swallow. That wild burst of music, that curve of swift escape, were unmistakable.

And I struck a stalwart tree-stem with my open hand, feeling the need of hearing, touching, sensing it. My link with known, remembered things was breaking. I craved the satisfaction of the commonplace. I got that satisfaction; but I got something more as well. For the trunk was round and smooth and comely. It was no dead thing I struck. Somehow it brushed me into intercourse with inanimate Nature. And next the desire came to hear my voice—my own familiar, high-pitched voice with the twang and accent the New World climate brings, so-called American:

"Exchange Place, Noo York City. I'm in that business, buying and selling of exchange between the banks of two civilised countries, one of them stoopid and old-fashioned, the other leading all creation . . .!"

It was an effort; but I made it firmly. It sounded odd, remote, unreal.

"Sunlit woods and a wind among the branches", followed close and sweet upon my words. But who, in the name of Wall Street, said it?

"England's buying gold," I tried again. "We've had a private wire. Cut in quick. First National is selling!"

Great-faced Hephæstus, how ridiculous! It was like saying, "I'll take your scalp unless you give me meat." It was barbaric, savage, centuries ago. Again, there came another voice that caught up my own and turned it into common syntax. Some heady beauty of the Earth rose about me like a cloud.

"Hark! Night comes, with the dusk upon her eyelids. She brings those dreams that every dew-drop holds at dawn. Daughter of Thanatos and Hypnos . . .!"

But again—who said the words? It surely was not Arthur, my nephew Arthur, of Today, learning French in a Swiss mountain village! I felt—well, what did I feel? In the name of the Stock Exchange and Wall Street, what was the cash surrender of amazing feelings?

3

And, turning to look at him, I made a discovery. I don't know how to tell it quite; such shadowy marvels have never been my line of goods. He looked several things at once—taller, slighter, sweeter, but chiefly—it sounds so crazy when I write it down—grander is the word, I think. And all spread out with some power that flowed like

Spring when it pours upon a landscape. Eternally young and glorious—young, I mean, in the sense of a field of flowers in the Spring looks young; and glorious in the sense the sky looks glorious at dawn or sunset. Something big shone through him like a storm, something that would go on for ever just as the Earth goes on, always renewing itself, something of gigantic life that in the human sense could never age at all—something the old gods had.

But the figure, so far as there was any figure at all, was that old family picture come to life. Our great ancestor and Arthur were one being, and that one being was vaster than a million people. Yet it was Malahide I saw. . . .

"They laid me in the earth I loved," he said in a strange, thrilling voice like running wind and water, "and I found eternal life. I live now for ever in Their divine existence. I share the life that changes yet can never pass away."

I felt myself rising like a cloud as he said it. A roaring beauty captured me completely. If I could tell it in honest newspaper language—the common language used in flats and offices—why, I guess I could patent a new meaning in ordinary words, a new power of expression, the thing that all the churches and poets and thinkers have been trying to say since the world began. I caught on to a fact so fine and simple that it knocked me silly to think I'd never realised it before.

I had read it, yes; but now I *knew* it. The Earth, the whole bustling universe, was nothing after all but a visible production of eternal, living Powers—spiritual powers, mind you—that just happened to include the particular little type of strutting creature we called mankind. And these Powers, as seen in Nature, were the gods. It was our refusal of their grand appeal, so wild and sweet and beautiful, that caused "evil." It was this barrier between ourselves and the rest of . . .

My thoughts and feelings swept away upon the rising flood as the "figure" came upon me like a shaft of moonlight, melting the last remnant of opposition that was in me. I took my brain, my reason, chucking them aside for the futile little mechanism I suddenly saw them to be. In place of them came—oh, God, I hate to say it, for only nursery talk can get within a mile of it, and yet what I need is something simpler even than the words that children use. Under one arm I carried a whole forest breathing in the wind, and beneath the other a hundred meadows full of singing streams with golden marigolds and blue forget-me-nots along their banks.

Upon my back and shoulders lay the clouded hills with dew and moonlight in their brimmed, capacious hollows. Thick in my hair hung the unaging powers that are stars and sunlight; though the sun was far away, it sweetened the currents of my blood with liquid gold. Breast and throat and face, as I advanced, met all the rivers of the world and all the winds of heaven, their strength and swiftness melting into me as light melts into everything it touches. And into my eyes passed all the radiant colours that weave the cloth of Nature as she takes the sun.

And this "figure," pouring upon me like a burst of moonlight, spoke:

"They all are in you—air, and fire, and water. . . ."

"And I—my feet stand—on the *Earth*," my own voice interrupted, deep power lifting through the sound of it.

"The Earth!" He laughed gigantically. He spread. He seemed everywhere about me. He seemed a race of men. My life swam forth in waves of some immense sensation that issued from the mountain and the forest, then returned to them again. I reeled. I clutched at something in me that was slipping beyond control, slipping down a bank towards a deep, dark river flowing at my feet. A shadowy boat appeared, a still more shadowy outline at the helm. I was in the act of stepping into it. For the tree I caught at was only air. I couldn't stop myself. I tried to scream.

"You have plucked asphodel," sang the voice beside me, "and you shall pluck more. . . ."

I slipped and slipped, the speed increasing horribly. Then something caught, as though a cog held fast and stopped me. I remembered my business in New York City.

"Arthur!" I yelled. "Arthur!" I shouted again as hard as I could shout. There was frantic terror in me. I felt as though I should never get back to myself again. Death!

The answer came in his normal voice: "Keep close to me. I know the way. . . ."

The scenery dwindled suddenly; the trees came back. I was walking in the forest beside my nephew, and the moonlight lay in patches and little shafts of silver. The crests of the pines just murmured in a wind that scarcely stirred, and through an opening on our right I saw the deep valley clasped about the twinkling village lights. Towering in splendour the spectral snowfields hung upon the sky, huge summits guarding them. And Arthur took my arm—oh, solidly enough this time. Thank heaven, he asked no questions of me.

"There's a smell of myrrh," he whispered, "and we are very near the undying, ancient things."

I said something about the resin from the trees, but he took no notice.

"It enclosed its body in an egg of myrrh," he went on, smiling down at me; "then, setting it on fire, rose from the ashes with its life renewed. Once every five hundred years, you see———"

"What did?" I cried, feeling that loss of self, stealing over me again. And his answer came like a blow between the eyes:

"The Phoenix. They called it a bird, but, of course, the true. . . ."

"But my life's insured in that," I cried, for he had named the company that took large yearly premiums from me; "and I pay. . . ."

"Your life's insured in *this*," he said quietly, waving his arms to indicate the Earth. "Your love of Nature and your sympathy with it make you safe." He gazed at me. There was a marvellous expression in his eyes. I understood why poets talked of stars and flowers in a human face. But behind the face crept back another look as well. There grew about his figure an indeterminate extension. The outline of Malahide again stirred through his own. A pale, delicate hand reached out to take my own. And something broke in me.

I was conscious of two things—a burst of joy that meant losing myself entirely, and a rush of terror that meant staying as I was, a small, painful, struggling item of individual life. Another spray of that awful asphodel fell fluttering through the air in front of my face. It rested on the earth against my feet. And Arthur—this weirdly changing Arthur—stooped to pick it for me. I kicked it with my foot beyond his reach. . . .then turned and ran as though the Furies of that ancient world were after me. I ran for my very life.

How I escaped from that thick wood without banging my body to bits against the trees I can't explain. I ran from something I desired and yet feared. I leaped along in a succession of flying bounds. Each tree I passed turned of its own accord and flung after me until the entire forest followed. But I got out. I reached the open. Upon the sloping field in the full, clear light of the moon I collapsed in a panting heap. The Earth drew back with a great shuddering sigh behind me. There was this strange, tumultuous sound upon the night. I lay beneath the open heavens that were full of moonlight. I was myself—but there were tears in me. Beauty too high for understanding had slipped between my fingers. I had lost Malahide. I had lost the gods of Earth. . . .Yet I had seen. . . .and felt. I had not lost all. Something remained that

255

I could never lose again. . . .

I don't know how it happened exactly, but presently I heard Arthur saying: "You'll catch your death of cold if you lie on that soaking grass," and felt his hand seize mine to pull me to my feet.

"I feel safer on earth," I believe I answered. And then he said: "Yes, but it's such a stupid way to die—a chill!"

4

I got up then, and we went downhill together towards the village lights. I danced—oh, I admit it—I sang as well. There was a flood of joy and power about me that beat anything I'd ever felt before. I didn't think or hesitate; there was no self-consciousness; I just let it rip for all there was, and if there had been ten thousand people there in front of me, I could have made them feel it too. That was the kind of feeling—power and confidence and a sort of raging happiness. I think I know what it was too. I say this soberly, with reverence. . . .all wool and no fading. There was a bit of God in me, God's power that drives the Earth and pours through Nature—the imperishable Beauty expressed in those old-world nature-deities!

And the fear I'd felt was nothing but the little tickling point of losing my ordinary two-cent self, the dread of letting go, the shrinking before the plunge—what a fellow feels when he's falling in love, and hesitates, and tries to think it out and hold back, and is afraid to let the enormous tide flow in and drown him.

Oh, yes, I began to think it over a bit as we raced down the mountain-side that glorious night. I've read some in my day; my brain's all right; I've heard of dual personality and subliminal uprush and conversion—no new line of goods, all that. But somehow these stunts of the psychologists and philosophers didn't cut any ice with me just then, because I'd *experienced* what they merely *explained*. And explanation was just a bargain sale. The best things can't be explained at all. There's no real value in a bargain sale.

Arthur had trouble to keep up with me. We were running due east, and the Earth was turning, therefore, with us. We all three ran together at *her* pace—terrific! The moonlight danced along the summits, and the snow-fields flew like spreading robes, and the forests everywhere, far and near, hung watching us and booming like a thousand organs. There were uncaged winds about; you could hear them whistling among the precipices. But the great thing that I knew was—Beauty, a beauty of the common old familiar Earth, and a beauty that's stayed with me ever since, and given me joy and strength and a source of power and delight I'd never guessed existed before.

★★★★★★★★★★

As we dropped lower into the thicker air of the valley I sobered down. Gradually the ecstasy passed from me. We slowed up a bit. The lights and the houses and the sight of the hotel where people were dancing in a stuffy ballroom, all this put blotting-paper on something that had been flowing.

Now you'll think this an odd thing too—but when we reached the village street, I just took Arthur's hand and shook it and said good-night and went up to bed and slept like a two-year-old till morning. And from that day to this I've never set eyes on the boy again.

Perhaps it's difficult to explain, and perhaps it isn't. I can explain it to myself in two lines—I was afraid to see him. I was afraid he might "explain." I was afraid he might explain "away." I just left a note—he never replied to it—and went off by a morning train. Can you understand that? Because if you can't you haven't understood this account I've tried to give, of the experience Arthur gave me. Well—anyway—I'll just let it go at that.

Arthur's a director now in his father's wholesale chemical business, and I—well, I'm doing better than ever in the buying and selling of exchange between banks in New York City as before.

But when I said I was still drawing dividends on my Swiss investment, I meant it. And it's not "scenery." Everybody gets a thrill from "scenery." It's a darned sight more than that. It's those little wayward patches of blue on a cloudy day; those blue pools in the sky just above Trinity Church steeple when I pass out of Wall Street into Lower Broadway; it's the rustle of the sea-wind among the Battery trees; the wash of the waves when the Ferry's starting for Staten Island, and the glint of the sun far down the Bay, or dropping a bit of pearl into the old East River. And sometimes it's the strip of cloud in the west above the Jersey shore of the Hudson, the first star, the sickle of the new moon behind the masts and shipping. But usually it's something nearer, bigger, simpler than all or any of these. It's just the certainty that, when I hurry along the hard stone pavements from bank to bank, I'm walking on the—Earth. It's just that—*the Earth!*

LEONAUR

ALSO FROM LEONAUR
AVAILABLE IN SOFTCOVER OR HARDCOVER WITH DUST JACKET

MR MUKERJI'S GHOSTS *by S. Mukerji*—Supernatural tales from the British Raj period by India's Ghost story collector.

KIPLINGS GHOSTS *by Rudyard Kipling*—Twelve stories of Ghosts, Hauntings, Curses, Werewolves & Magic.

THE COLLECTED SUPERNATURAL AND WEIRD FICTION OF WASHINGTON IRVING: VOLUME 1 *by Washington Irving*—Including one novel 'A History of New York', and nine short stories of the Strange and Unusual.

THE COLLECTED SUPERNATURAL AND WEIRD FICTION OF WASHINGTON IRVING: VOLUME 2 *by Washington Irving*—Including three novelettes 'The Legend of the Sleepy Hollow', 'Dolph Heyliger', 'The Adventure of the Black Fisherman' and thirty-two short stories of the Strange and Unusual.

THE COLLECTED SUPERNATURAL AND WEIRD FICTION OF JOHN KENDRICK BANGS: VOLUME 1 *by John Kendrick Bangs*—Including one novel 'Toppleton's Client or A Spirit in Exile', and ten short stories of the Strange and Unusual.

THE COLLECTED SUPERNATURAL AND WEIRD FICTION OF JOHN KENDRICK BANGS: VOLUME 2 *by John Kendrick Bangs*—Including four novellas 'A House-Boat on the Styx', 'The Pursuit of the House-Boat', 'The Enchanted Typewriter' and 'Mr. Munchausen' of the Strange and Unusual.

THE COLLECTED SUPERNATURAL AND WEIRD FICTION OF JOHN KENDRICK BANGS: VOLUME 3 *by John Kendrick Bangs*—Including twor novellas 'Olympian Nights', 'Roger Camerden: A Strange Story', and ten short stories of the Strange and Unusual.

THE COLLECTED SUPERNATURAL AND WEIRD FICTION OF MARY SHELLEY: VOLUME 1 *by Mary Shelley*—Including one novel 'Frankenstein or the Modern Prometheus', and fourteen short stories of the Strange and Unusual.

THE COLLECTED SUPERNATURAL AND WEIRD FICTION OF MARY SHELLEY: VOLUME 2 *by Mary Shelley*—Including one novel 'The Last Man', and three short stories of the Strange and Unusual.

THE COLLECTED SUPERNATURAL AND WEIRD FICTION OF AMELIA B. EDWARDS *by Amelia B. Edwards*—Contains two novelettes 'Monsieur Maurice', and 'The Discovery of the Treasure Isles', one ballad 'A Legend of Boisguilbert' and seventeen short stories to cill the blood.